C. C. Humphreys was born in Toronto, Canada, and grew up in London. An actor for twenty-five years, his leading roles have included Hamlet and the gladiator Caleb in the miniseries *Anno Domini*, as well as Jack Absolute in Sheridan's *The Rivals*. His plays have also been produced in the UK and Canada. A schoolboy fencing champion, and later a fight choreographer for the stage, Chris turned his love of swashbuckling towards historical fiction. His first novel, *The French Executioner*, was shortlisted for the CWA Steel Dagger. The sequel, *Blood Ties*, was published in 2003. His third novel, *Jack Absolute*, began the series about the master spy, followed by *The Blooding of Jack Absolute*. *Absolute Honour* is Jack's latest rousing adventure. Chris lives in Vancouver with his wife and son. Visit his website at www.cchumphreys.com.

By C. C. Humphreys

NOVELS

The Fetch
Absolute Honour
The Blooding of Jack Absolute
Jack Absolute
Blood Ties
The French Executioner

PLAYS

A Cage Without Bars
Glimpses of the Moon
Touching Wood

SCREENPLAY

The French Executioner

ABSOLUTE HONOUR

C. C. HUMPHREYS

First published in Canada in 2006 by
McArthur & Company
322 King Street West, Suite 402
Toronto, Ontario
M5V 1J2
www.mcarthur-co.com

This paperback edition first published in Canada in 2007 by
McArthur & Company

Library and Archives Canada Cataloguing in Publication

Humphreys, C. C. (Chris C.)
Absolute honour / C.C. Humphreys.

ISBN 978-1-55278-652-9

I. Title.

PS8565.U5576A62 2007   C813'.6   C2007-901717-7

The publisher would like to acknowledge the financial support of the
Government of Canada through the Book Publishing Industry Development
Program (BPIDP) and the Canada Council for our publishing activities. The
publisher further wishes to acknowledge the financial support of the Ontario
Arts Council for our publishing program.

10 9 8 7 6 5 4 3 2 1

To Jon Wood

Honour's a fine imaginary notion
That draws in raw and unexperienced men
To real mischiefs while they hunt a shadow
JOSEPH ADDISON – *Cato*

— PART ONE —

The Irish Grenadier

– ONE –

The Widow

Newport, Rhode Island, April 1761

A frigid wind blew off the shore, sending the waves that had crashed against the dock back across the harbour, bobbling the ships there like apples in a barrel of cider. Shrugging ever deeper into his coat, Jack Absolute watched two of the three vessels make ready to depart. Men scrambled along yards to unfurl the sails, others worked the capstan; an anchor broke surface and was laboriously hauled the last few feet. On the third ship, however, the one on which his passage was booked, there was no such activity, though he knew the master of the *Sweet Eliza* was as keen to put to sea as the others. The jolly boat had rowed out to it not ten minutes before with some last provisions, the boatswain's mate shouting that they would return for him shortly. Furthermore, it was added, if the last passenger was not dockside by then, they'd throw his goods into the harbour and sail without him.

Jack sighed. He should have gone with them. But his impatience to be aboard had little to do with the prospect of the voyage itself. He had vomited steadily for the first two weeks of the sailing to Canada eighteen months before and then, he'd been informed, the seas had been positively calm. No, he just hated farewells. All that could be said – and done – had been said and done at daybreak.

3

'Does such a sigh indicate, perhaps, a change of heart, Lieutenant Absolute?'

Jack took a moment to compose his face before he turned to her. She need not see how keen he was to be off at last. For all she had given him, he owed her a sadness equal to her own.

'It does not, Mrs Simkin. Alas, it cannot, as you know.'

'Despite all that is on offer here?' She raised her face, those astonishing azure eyes peering up at him from beneath the white bonnet's fringe. 'I speak of our successes in trade, of course.' Her gaze dropped again, fixing on the gloved hands resting demurely on her black cloak.

You speak of our bodies hotly pressed together, Jack thought. Not three hours previously, before her servants stirred at dawn and Jack had to creep back to his own bed, she had woken him as she always used to do, with busy fingers and lips under his nightgown. And this in spite of her recent tendency to awaken nauseous. Indeed, Jack had barely slept. If there had been something to sink onto dockside he would have done so, his knees felt so weak.

'Yet you know, madam,' he said, 'that once I have discharged my duty to the King . . .'

He trailed off, disturbed by the slight shake of her head. It had been a comforting myth, this idea that, his messages delivered, he would resign his commission and return to her bed and her business, both of which he'd immersed himself in during the months he'd been in Newport. General Murray's dispatches, given to Jack in Montreal the previous September when the French surrendered there, were old news now. King George would have been informed of his army's final victory by other means; while Jack, who was meant to bear the joyous news, had missed the last autumn sailings – first in Boston, then here – and had been forced to wait for the first of the spring.

They both knew the lie, even if neither of them stated it.

4

And yet, even though he was ready for the off, was this not as poignant as any farewell could be? For during those few months, what a partnership they had made, in and out of her bed. He looked at her now, saw her as the sailors must have seen her, glancing once, glancing away, just as he had first glanced and dismissed her – a Quaker woman, in her uniform of black dress and white bonnet, not a hair astray beneath it which could hint at anything other than purity, not a trace of paint upon the full lips, around those eyes. He too would never have looked again had not business forced him into her company for longer than that first glance.

He studied her now and blessed the Absolute fortune once again. Since Murray had assumed he would be homeward bound in weeks, he had provided Jack with a uniform, a berth requisition and a mere five pounds in coin – enough to see him aboard and little more. Jack, after a year's hard campaigning, had felt quite justified in drinking and gambling most of that away on his first three nights in Boston. When he'd been sent on to Newport and the hope of a ship, the last of the coins had been swiftly swallowed in inedible food and indifferent lodgings. There was no authority to issue him with more – Newport was a trading town, not a military garrison. A few grim nights followed, living on credit and lies. Yet there was little doubt that he would soon be evicted even from the poor boarding house, with winter and hunger biting hard. He'd survived the previous Canadian winter in a cave with his Iroquois blood brother, Até, and had considered those lodgings uncomfortable; but they were a vision of warmth and plenty compared to what a penniless soldier could expect in frigid Rhode Island.

Then that fortune had smiled. Loitering outside a store, wondering if he should go in and finally sell the skin of the bear he had killed that previous winter, he heard a familiar language being spoken: the Iroquois Até had taught him. A

5

storekeeper and an Indian were engaged in hot debate, each speaking their own tongue, each descending swiftly into insult and threat. Jack had intervened, ascertained that the two were actually close as to price, and helped them settle the deal. His cut had been a meal from the storekeeper and, after a few celebratory jugs of Newport's own fine Guinea rum, an offer from the Iroquois – a Seneca named Thayada – to accompany him and some of the local Indians on a hunting and trapping trip, and then to help them broker the best price for their goods when they returned. Jack, fed up both with poverty and the piety of the town – the churches outnumbered the taverns three to one – readily accepted.

When they came back two months later, however, with a hundred ermine skins and a welcome supply of deer meat, the storekeeper could only offer them credit. When Jack, on the natives' behalf, refused, he'd been sulkily directed elsewhere.

'You'm be best t' go see the Widow Simkin, then,' he spat. 'She's as rich as a whorehouse keeper and twice as holy as God.'

The Widow Simkin. She stood before him now as she had that first time, when he'd paid her so little attention: head downcast, hands clasped, unspeaking. He had soon learned from her that silence was like a sword, luring an opponent off true. She'd once taken him, in an effort to bring her lodger to God, to a Quaker service. They'd sat in complete silence for over two hours! And she had gotten the better of him in their first dealings by saying almost nothing. Thayada and the Nippising Indians he led had seemed content, however, and had departed to drink most of their profit. He would have joined them if the Widow Simkin had not finally asked a question. She'd looked up and Jack had noticed, for the first time, those eyes. 'I am about to break bread, Lieutenant Absolute. Perhaps you would care to join me?' Jack was thirsty after two months in the woods. But something in those eyes, beyond their colour, had made him accept.

God damn it, will that jolly boat never return? Jack thought now, but did not say. Not for the cruelty of his pressing desire to be away. Cursing was just not something you did before the Widow Simkin. She knew – and demanded – things that would have made a Covent Garden courtesan blush. Yet take the name of the Lord in vain in her house . . .

Some moisture had come into her downcast eyes. The bitter wind, he assumed, for he knew the Widow only cried in the night, when held in the aftermath of passion. Yet when she spoke again, there was a tremor in her voice. 'We have discussed how . . . beneficial it would be for us both for you to return. Your abilities . . .' she coloured slightly, '. . . your abilities with the savages have been of great use in my dealings with them. You have increased my profit and have, I believe, profited yourself.'

Indeed I have, Jack thought, with another hundred ermine skins aboard the ship and the name of a furrier in Whitechapel to visit who would pay full price. If he was returning to a Dragoon lieutenant's salary, he must find ways to supplement it, or London would be dull indeed.

'And you have but seen our little town in its winter coat. Believe me, it is quite a different place when warm. And when the summer comes and the real trade begins, a strong man such as yourself would be of—'

He interrupted her. 'It is not a trade I wish to be involved in, madam. As I have told you before.'

He hadn't thought much about slavery in his former life, despite his mother's occasional diatribe on the subject. His time as a slave of the Abenaki tribe the previous year had, however, revolutionized his attitude. And he still could scarce believe that the Widow was one of the foremost slave traders

7

in Newport, the main port for such activity in the Northern Colonies. She and her fellow Quakers were dominant in it.

'Well. Enough of that.' She reverted to the silence that ended arguments. But the colour on her cheeks and the moisture in her eyes lingered, and he remembered the first time he saw her flush, a week after he'd accepted her invitation of a room above her barn together with a salary for his interpreting skills and a share of profits. She was over twice his age, in her late thirties, and a good and God-fearing widow since the death of Mr Simkin ten years before. Then, one Sunday evening, she came to tell him that her bathing water was still warm in a barrel in the kitchen and his if he should desire it. He'd trodden the snowy path to the main house, found the kitchen empty of servants – they all had the Lord's day off to return to their families, it transpired – and lowered himself into water still gloriously hot, the first surprise. The second was when the Widow Simkin – not clothed in black, not clothed at all – lowered herself in beside him. The barrel was snug anyway and she was a large woman, yet of near perfect proportions. He'd nearly drowned twice; once in the water, once in her breasts.

The memory gave him a blush to match hers and he turned to the ocean, to see that the *Sweet Eliza*'s jolly boat had set off again for the shore. It would be dockside in moments. Time for a last farewell.

He'd left a little something in verse under her pillow but he also had a speech prepared. He was about to deliver it when, to his great surprise, she took his hands. 'Jack,' she whispered, another shock because she never used his name except when they were alone, 'I want you to know that I have never . . . never done before the things I have done with you . . .'

Well, Jack thought, you must have read some bloody good books! Though he had done some things in that line – a few anyway – he was about to echo her, for sentiment's sake, but she rushed on. 'I have never felt like this before. That is why I need to tell you . . . to tell you—'

'Lieutenant Absolute! Sir, sir!' One of the sailors was calling from the water. The jolly boat was nearly at the dock.

The Widow Simkin stepped back, leaving something in Jack's hands. Without looking at him, she said, 'Read it when you are at sea. Question your heart. Perhaps what is within will bring you back to me.'

He looked at the plain envelope, felt the sheet of paper inside. How sweet, he thought, she writes me a farewell as I have written her. (Though not in Alexandrine couplets, I suspect.) 'I will treasure it,' he declared.

'No,' she said, 'you—'

'Lieutenant Absolute!' The call followed the bang of wood on wood as the boat reached the jetty. A rope landed near Jack, followed by a sailor. 'If you please, sir,' the seaman said, 'the Captain says bugger the Irishman . . . er, beggin' yer pardon, ma'am. Wait any longer an' we'll miss the poxy tide. And if we dock again we'll lose half the crew, for they've already drunk their joining bounty.'

Whether it was the sailor's cursing or the emotion of the moment, the Widow had turned, was walking swiftly up the sloping wood to the shore. Jack called after, 'Thank you, Mrs Simkin. Thank you for your . . . kindnesses.'

But there was no acknowledgement in the black back, hunched against the wind. The wind that will blow me back to England, Jack thought, suddenly exultant. It had all ended rather well. A touch of sentiment, a few written words to supplement the memories across the Atlantic. He would miss the Widow and her ways. Yet . . .

One sailor helped him down into the prow of the jolly boat, the other cast off. Soon they were rowing fast through the choppy water toward the *Sweet Eliza*, his home for the next . . . weeks? months? With a good wind and a good navigator, ships could make the Atlantic crossing in five weeks. But bad luck with both, or either . . . he'd heard of vessels taking six months.

Perhaps the thought of discomfort ahead added to the poignancy of the parting, and he fixed his eyes upon that black cloak, fast receding up the slope that led from the harbour. He didn't hold her farewell missive to his heart – sailors had a way of talking and he was careful of her reputation – but he held it there in his mind as well as his hand while she was yet in his sight.

She was nearly at the top of the hill when he saw her jerk to a stop, step swiftly to the side. A moment later, what had been a faint noise beneath the sound of waves, wind and gulls became clearer: men shouting. But the first to appear over the crest was not one of the shouters. No doubt because he was engaged in running so very fast.

Jack couldn't at first make out what was wrong with the vision. A halloo was not uncommon in towns either side of the Atlantic. A cut-purse perhaps, caught in the act, making a break for it. But strangely it was the black figure of the Widow, turning away from the sprinting figure that made Jack see what previously he'd missed.

The runner was stark-bollock naked.

Jack clearly heard, 'Stop him', from the pack who had now crested the hill in pursuit, followed by a word that might be 'trader', which seemed, however, an odd thing to yell in a port.

The sailors had stopped rowing to stare, although shouts from the *Sweet Eliza* urged them on. Even Jack, no seafarer, could see that if the wind veered much more there'd be no putting to sea that day. Under orders, they began to row again.

On the shore, the naked figure had reached the dock, the pursuit about fifty yards behind. Jack could now see that the man was tall, his naked physique strong, and that he had bright red hair trailing out behind him like a flame. Arriving at the water's edge, the man skidded to a stop. Jack didn't blame him; it was a brisk day for a plunge. But he had mistook; for the man paused only to survey the water before him, note the one other rowboat pulled up to the jetty, pick up a small barrel that awaited collection and hurl it into the vessel, sinking it almost on the instant. Then, pausing only to raise two fingers to the pursuing men, he hurled himself into the Atlantic.

The sailors had stopped rowing again in shock, despite the continuous calls from their officers. Reluctantly, they hefted their oars once more. 'Hold there,' countermanded Jack. Since he was dressed in the uniform of the King, they obeyed. 'By God,' he said, rising a little on his bench, 'I think that fellow is making for us.'

It was true. With a scrambling motion that drove him powerfully through the water, the red-haired man moved towards them like a spaniel after a shot duck. Behind him, the men on the dock continued yelling, the wind still making their yells indistinct. Some gesticulated for the *Sweet Eliza*'s jolly boat to return, others ran further down the dock, seeking a vessel for pursuit.

Despite his obvious strength, the man was labouring, flailing. Then a combination of stroke and tide brought him close.

'Here, sir, here,' yelled Jack. 'Take hold.'

While the sailors shouted warnings and leaned away to counterbalance him, Jack reached out. The man's fingers brushed Jack's, a wave forced them apart, then together again. Jack grabbed, held a finger, a thumb. Bringing over his other arm, he grasped the hand of the swimmer. Another wave sucked at him again but the man reached his other hand and this time Jack had him. With an immense heave, he pulled him into the boat like a gaffed tuna.

It nearly spilled them. But, with the man lying in the scuppers, Jack sitting and the sailors back at their oars, the boat gradually steadied.

Jack looked at the newcomer. He was blue where he wasn't red with hair, which was in most places but especially thick at chest and groin, like the pelt of some huge scarlet sea otter. The only lightness came from scars, of which he had an inordinate supply, criss-crossing his body like worm casts. Instantly Jack had his cloak off, and thrown over the man, who clutched at it but remained unable to speak.

'Which way, sir?' said one sailor to Jack. 'Ship or shore?'

Having been a fugitive himself – on several occasions – Jack paused now to consider the plight of the quarry. The blue-tinged nakedness gave a sort of infant innocence to the fellow; and there was only one person in slaver's Newport he cared a fig about. 'Are you a cut-purse, sir? Should we be returning you to the authorities and a deserved noose?'

The head shook. Chattering lips tried to form words. 'Ne . . . Ne . . .'

'I fink 'e's the last passenger we was waitin' for,' the other sailor, a Cockney, said.

The man nodded and words came, the Irish accent unmistakeable. 'That I a- a- am! And if y- y- you take me back, oagh, boys . . . well,' he threw back the cloak, and gestured to his shrunken privates, 'the lady-in-question's hu-hu- husband will finish the job that the sea has st- started and render me truly the last King of Ireland!'

The sailors laughed and Jack joined them. 'Row,' he said, then reached down, grasped the hand before him. 'Jack Absolute, sir, at your service.'

'A service I will repay for plucking me from the waves like Anchises from the flames of Troy. For, faith, I forget neither slight nor favour. And that's as sure as my name is Red Hugh McClune.'

It was only when Jack drew back his hand that he realized that something had lately occupied it. When he remembered what, he looked again swiftly to the sea. But water had drowned the Widow's parting words.

Never mind, thought Jack, patting his chest. I have her here. And she will always have a little piece of me in her.

— TWO —

Stink, Drink and
Captain Link

'What the Honourable fails to realize,' Captain Link declared, 'is that when I impregnate one of these black heathen sluts, I serve God, my employers and the slut herself.'

'How so, Captain?' The purser, Durkin, ever the crony, fed him the question.

'Because the slut receives a Christian's blessing, her offspring the inheritance of England's blood – and my employers get half as much again for a proven brood mare!' He guffawed as he raised his mug of rum. 'To profit, gentlemen. Profit and fornication!'

'Fornication!' came the echo from the purser and the surgeon, the cry briefly rousing the slumbering First Lieutenant Engledue, who lifted his mug, sipped then slid his head back onto his hand.

Jack sighed and did not drink. He abhorred the toast, but he'd also had quite enough. This Guinea rum, Newport's finest export and the ship's main cargo for the run to Bristol – where it would be sold to traders who would eventually swap it for slaves – had the strength of a donkey's kick. He had vowed this night to be moderate, to dilute it half and half with rainwater. However, he was aware that he had promised himself the same every night from the end of the second week of the voyage when his nausea had passed. The only thing worse than being in Captain Link's company was being drunk in his company. Yet he had failed to keep his vow above a half dozen times, such failures resulting in outbursts that had given the Captain weapons to use against him. He never called Jack anything other than 'the Honourable' since he'd blurted out that he was the son of a baronet and would be treated with respect. He'd also reacted badly to the realization that the ship transporting him was a slaver, and had been foolish enough to voice his opposition to the trade. Since that night, Captain Link had not let an evening pass when he would not lecture Jack as to the Christian rightness of it and describe its every detail. And having once seen Jack's disgust when he'd volunteered how he always fucked at least a dozen of the slave women on the voyage, he returned again and again to the subject, like a dog to his own vomit.

Link slammed his empty mug down. Immediately, his body slave, Barabbas, limped up to refill it. Jack found himself staring yet again at the Negro's pouring hand. Three fingers and half a thumb, and not a knuckle on what remained unbroken. Link often boasted that Barabbas was the most spirited among a group of rebellious slaves he'd transported ten years before, and that he'd tamed him with whips and thumbscrews. He'd done Link's bidding ever since.

As the laughter continued and Barabbas slipped again into the shadows, Jack glanced away, to the man who shared his side of the table. The Irishman returned his gaze, a slight shake of the head indicating that Jack should leave this conversation well alone. But Jack had always found that hard to do.

'Perhaps, sir,' he said, 'if you had experienced the helplessness of a slave you would be less prepared to exploit it.'

Link leaned his jowly, purple-bruised face across at Jack. The man was scorbutic, his foul breath and decaying teeth additional indicators of the scurvy that had taken half the crew. 'Do you speak again of your *weeks* spent with the Abenaki savages?'

Jack nodded. He had told the story of his capture and escape after the Battle of Quebec in the early nights of the voyage when they had all still been polite strangers. Now, two months into the crossing, it was another source of mockery for Link. 'I do. And may I say—'

'*May I say,*' interrupted the Captain, his Bristol accent fashioning a mockery of Jack's Westminster School-ed one, 'that you were *never* a slave.'

'Are you calling a me a liar, sir?'

Jack's voice, instead of rising, had dropped to a whisper. Link recognized the danger. The challenge went, if the mockery did not. 'Not at all. But I do say you mistook your state. For you are both white, Christian and, above all, a Briton. And as you well know,' he opened his half-toothed jaw and sang, ' "Britons never never never will be slaves." '

The purser and the surgeon, when they recognized the tune, joined in, thumping their approval with pewter mugs.

The verse done, the Captain continued. 'Now, shall I tell you my favourites from among the tribes?' He licked his lips. 'The Yaruba, see, are tall and strong but have narry enough flesh on 'em, to my taste. The Mina are squat and too plump. No, sirs, for breasts and thighs, there's none that can compare with your Ibo.'

When Link's cronies had finished with their huzzahs, when silence was brought by the necessity of more guzzling, a quiet voice intruded. 'Now, Captain, I was wondering, so I was, about a little point you might clarify for me?'

Link wiped his mouth. Since the Irishman rarely spoke at his table the Captain had few weapons against him, apart from the more obvious jibes at his country. 'Well, sir?'

'I was wondering,' Red Hugh continued, 'how Mrs Link and all the little Links of Bristol – six of the small blessings, I believe you said – how they received the joyous news of so many African siblings?'

Jack only saw it because he happened to glance at Barabbas who was carrying the rum jug away. But that broken hand was raised, just failing to conceal the briefest of smiles.

The slave was swifter than the master. 'Mrs Link . . .' he gaped.

'And all the little Links,' Red Hugh repeated.

Comprehension came. 'You dare – dare! – to place my wife in the same breath as . . . as . . .'

'But, to be sure, as you were mentioning your progeny so fondly yourself, I thought your help-meet must share in your joy. Not to mention all the little Links.'

Something about the repetition seemed to cause a dangerous mottling and puffing of the already purple jowls, and almost made Jack laugh, for as the Captain began to push himself up from the table he looked like nothing so much as a deranged and dangerous turkey.

'Do . . . you know, sir, who you insult? I am God aboard my own ship. I could have you . . . make you . . . you would be stripped . . . whipped . . .'

Link had taken three steps forward, bringing his head level to the taller man's chest, for Red Hugh had also risen. They could not have been more opposite in shape – a bull terrier pressing into a heron. The Captain's hand was shoved into the Irishman's immaculate waistcoat – how the man remained so clean when the rest of them were so grubby mystified Jack – and he appeared to be engaged in wrenching off a pearl button. But as Jack watched, he saw the Irishman's hand – its knuckles as covered in red hair as the rest of him – drop onto the Captain's wrist.

'What do you—' Link began, then stopped, his eyes suddenly quizzical, the purple of his face whitening.

17

'Now, now,' said Red Hugh softly. 'Now, now.'

There was no sudden movement, nothing seemed to happen. But the Captain suddenly pulled away, backwards, sitting down hard into his chair. And as soon as he did, he vomited, spraying rum and salt cod across the table.

It was Red Hugh who reached him first, an arm around his back. 'Dear Captain, dear soul. Some water there, heh?'

Water was brought, drunk, spewed up. The surgeon came and felt the Captain's head. Link himself, gagging still, sat with filmy eyes.

'I think, my dears, that our leader requires his bed. A good signal to retire to ours, eh, young Jack?'

Jack, who had hardly left off staring at Link, enjoying what he was seeing, nodded. While Barabbas, the purser and the surgeon half-dragged Link across the room to his bunk, Jack and Red Hugh went to the cabin door accompanied by Lieutenant Engledue, who was awake at last. He yawned. 'I think I will seize the moment, too,' he murmured, holding the door open for them. 'Pity about our noble leader. This Guinea rum, eh? It's meant for the black traders, of course, who sell their kin to us. White folk can hardly handle it. Give me a smooth Madeira any day.'

With a knowing smile to Red Hugh and a bow to Jack, he headed to his own bunk.

The Irishman pulled Jack the other way, towards the quarterdeck. 'A breath, do you not think, lad?'

The air, as it had been for several days now, was heavy and hot. The south-westerlies that had at first driven them fast across the Atlantic, trailing a memory of icy New Found Land, had died on them two weeks before. Since then progress had been slow, every sail hoisted to catch what little breeze there was. Moreover, it was clear that no one was quite sure exactly where they were. Though he knew little of navigation, Jack was aware a midday sighting of the sun was required to gauge latitude. And the clouds that held the muggy heat upon them had prevented a view for several days now.

Still, after the stench of Link's cabin, even this air was an elixir. Down below, while the winds had driven them and it was too cold to stay on deck, they'd lived in a fug compounded of bodies that were never washed, of men succumbing to scurvy as their teeth rotted, of damp wool and canvas washed in urine and never given a chance to dry. They'd eaten weevil-filled biscuits and green meat, and belched out too much rum by the light and reek of whale-sperm candles. And beneath all this, the base note of all scents still survived, no matter how often vinegar was scrubbed across the decks and gunpowder flashed in the holds: the stink of a slave ship where Negroes had been chained together in their own shit and vomit and ceaseless terror. As soon as the weather improved a jot, both Red Hugh and Jack had slung their hammocks on the quarter-deck. Even if he'd shivered the first few nights, at least Jack still had his bearskin – and never did he think he'd say that its lingering smell was close to sweet. Yet, after eight weeks of imprisonment by the wind, it almost was.

'Onion?'

Jack shuddered. 'Must I?'

'You know you must. Unless you care for a touch of what's making our noble Captain's breath fouler than nature already did?'

'And why are you certain this has any effect on the condition?' grumbled Jack, taking the yellowing bulb and reaching for his paring knife.

'Sure, and did I not read James Lind's great treatise on the subject? Did not my company of Grenadiers survive the six-month siege of Kiskunhalas by eating almost nothing else?' Red Hugh had expertly peeled the skin in one piece and now dropped it onto the deck. 'We had the complexion of choirboys at the end of it,' he said, munching happily, 'and farts that could have floated a coach and four.'

Jack laughed and began peeling his onion, as the tinkle of a bell told him that a friend drew near. Jeremiah, sole survivor of the five goats taken on board at Newport, nipped at his trouser leg. The goat had already snaffled the Irishman's dropped onion skin, so, to a disapproving grunt from his companion – Jack was ever an easy mark for the goat – he sliced off a quarter of his onion and let it fall. The three chewed for a while in silence until Jeremiah, seeing that nothing else was forthcoming, went off to scrounge elsewhere.

Suddenly Jack remembered what had allowed them this escape to the deck. 'The Captain. What did you do to him?'

'Poor auld fella was taken ill suddenly, is all.'

'Tell me.'

Red Hugh considered, then swallowed the last of his onion. 'Finish that and give me your hand.' With a grimace, Jack duly did. The Irishman held him almost in a handshake but slightly higher, on the wrist, the grip light. 'Now now,' he said, as he had to the Captain, 'now, now.' Then he squeezed hard, the pad beneath his forefinger boring in under Jack's thumb.

The pain was sudden, intense and made Jack's knees give. Red Hugh prevented his fall. Taking his hand back, Jack rubbed it, inhaling deeply to clear the nausea. 'How . . . ?' he said after several moments.

Red Hugh shrugged. 'I had it from a man who had it from a man who had it from a man . . . from Transylvania.'

'Where?'

'It's up on the border with the Turks. Some of our lads fought there.' He smiled. 'And now you have it.'

Jack pushed himself off the rail, eager. 'You'll have to show me again.'

'I will. But later. You can only learn it by the receiving of the thing. And you'll be needing a little time to gather yesself.'

Jack looked at his companion, wondering yet again. What did he truly know of this Red Hugh McClune? The man had leaked out some information about his past, on certain subjects – women often, some cases he'd taken as a lawyer in Dublin, for example. Mostly, since his audience demanded it, he'd told of his time in the Austrian Army. He'd not been a mere soldier but a Grenze. All had heard of them, the finest light infantry in Europe it was said, drawn largely from the Balkan provinces to serve the Hapsburgs against the Turks. Why an Irishman had joined them was never explained, though apparently he was one of many. The man was a born storyteller, could entrance an audience with his tales of breaches stormed, ambuscades laid, hideous tortures undergone. Yet question him on his present, as Jack tried to do, and only vagueness came. A trader, he'd say, sometimes. An engineer, at others.

Jack rubbed his wrist. 'I think, sir, that you are a very dangerous man.'

His companion turned his face again to the sea. 'Oh no, lad. I used to be a dangerous man, when I was younger. Not any more.'

He had never stated his age. Jack took him to be near forty, a little grey in the beard he'd started growing the day he came aboard, which was full within a week – unlike Jack's black one, only now coming into its prime. If they were nearly of a height, the thick mat of curly hair – the colour nearly the scarlet of the Dragoon coat Jack had stowed below – made the Irishman seem much taller. And if they matched each other in a slim physique, Red Hugh's seemed to be constructed entirely from whipcord and scar.

Jack laughed. 'Not too old to be swimming in the Atlantic in April, though?'

'Ah, well!' Red Hugh laughed, too. 'That's different. If

21

danger goes, folly with the ladies is the one thing age does not seem to alter.' He turned to Jack, his blue eyes sparkling. 'As I am sure you will continue to discover.'

Jack, in an effort not to appear a completely dull dog, had told a few tales of his own; especially of Fanny Harper, the courtesan who'd undertaken aspects of his 'education' not covered by the curriculum at Westminster School. The Irishman's jest made him think on her, wonder again what had become of her.

The last time he'd seen Fanny she'd been standing near naked and shamed in the Rotunda Pleasure Gardens, at Vauxhall, moments before the man who'd kept her, Lord Melbury, was shot to death by Jack's father in a duel. The consequences of that night had led him . . . here, he supposed, to the deck of the *Sweet Eliza* by way of war, slavery and a Quaker widow's flannel sheets. He hoped that Fanny had survived her disgrace, her charms leading her to another rich man's bed. It was how she lived, after all.

This sudden memory – both of her and the mayhem caused by the discovery of their affair – now made him sigh. 'I regret to say you may be in the right.'

Red Hugh dropped a hand onto Jack's shoulder. '*Nunquam paenitet*, lad. Never regret. Isn't it the motto of the family McClune?' His fingers suddenly dug in. 'You know, I seem to recall there's another point somewhere . . . in here.'

Jack shrugged from the grip, catching the Irishman's hand, twisting it back. He knew a few tricks of his own from his upbringing in Cornwall. They wrestled, hands slipping and gripping, seeking dominance, both laughing, until they heard a footfall and pulled apart to see who came.

It was the boatswain, McRae. A Scot, Jack had parted with an outrageous two ermine skins to the fellow for a set of sailor's clothes when it became clear that the two changes he'd allowed for the voyage would be insufficient, especially in the storms when nothing dried. So, like Jack, he was

22

dressed in canvas trowsers – infinitely preferable with their drawstring to wool breeches, especially in the Heads when the ship was bucking and plunging and buttons annoyed – a bum-freezer jacket and check shirt. They were both London pigeons to Red Hugh's peacock. Somehow, the Irishman, even in the worst of the weather, always contrived to have dry, clean clothes which, moreover, would not have been unfashionable at St James's Palace. The dark-green waistcoat and burgundy coat he sported now caused Jack especial envy.

McRae put knuckles to forehead, a sailor's salute. 'Mr McClune, we've pipes lit and a jug in the fo'castle, if you care to join us.'

'Does Murphy play? Or is he too drunk?'

The sailor nodded. 'He's had just enough to make his bow fly, and not enough to bring it crashing to the earth. Yet.'

'Then I will join you with pleasure before it does. For he's a demon with the fiddle.' The sailor headed for'ard while Red Hugh turned to Jack. 'So, my lad, I'll to my countryman and you to your rest. Unless . . .' He called up the deck, 'McRae, can my young friend not join us this night?'

Jack saw the sailor's cheery face cloud, knew what that was. McRae, indeed all of the ship's company, had seen the Dragoon uniform he first wore aboard, knew him for an officer and a guest at the Captain's table. They could not see beyond the scarlet and braid, which Jack had only worn for less than two years, to the young man who'd drunk and sung in half the low taverns of London. They saw a baronet's son and a lieutenant. Aboard even a merchant ship that rank divided.

'It is fine, Hugh. I'll to my hammock.'

'Nonsense. The night is just beginning and you must hear Murphy play while he's still sober.' He took Jack's arm, led him to the waiting McRae. 'I'll vouch for him.'

The frown did not leave the face. 'Aye, sir.'

The whole larboard watch – Larbollians, as they were

known – were crammed into the hold and all cheered when Red Hugh stooped through the low doorway. The cheer faded when Jack followed. Most men looked down, some stared challengingly.

His guide did not hesitate. Seizing Jack's arm, he thrust the younger man forward. 'Now, lads. I know what you think you see here. An officer in King George's Army, a gentleman. And maybe he is, maybe he is. But I tell you, mere appearances can deceive.' He stooped and grabbed a bulky seaman from his squat, yanking him up as if he were gossamer. Each of his knuckles bore a letter, the left hand spelling 'Hold' the right 'Fast', a reminder when high up in the rigging. As Red Hugh rolled back the man's shirt sleeve, he revealed more black stains – a ship, a swallow, an anchor. They were all, Jack noticed, rather well done. 'You, Williams. You think you've a fine collection there, do you not?'

'I 'ave.' The Welshman thrust his chin out. 'Best on the ship.'

'Better than these?' Before he could stop him, Red Hugh had leaned forward and wrenched Jack's shirt open. Any protest he might have made was cut off by the approving gasp of the sailors as they saw the wolf's jaws on his chest, the wreath of oak leaves around his shoulder that Até had rendered so beautifully – and painfully! – in their cave the winter before.

'Executed by a painted savage, no less!' the Irishman declared. 'And without the benefit of your fine needles.'

Williams peered close. 'Not bad,' he grunted. 'Seen better.'

Red Hugh was not the only one who jeered. Pushing him back down, the Irishman pointed to another sailor. 'Ingvarsson, you lump of fjord filth. How many men is it you claim to have killed?'

The man had no eyebrows on a forehead that sloped into his eyes, and a scar that split his nose and ran to each ear.

'Claim? It is five, by God. Five! And I could do six with pleasure,' he growled.

The others hooted. Then Red Hugh spoke, quietly now. 'Well, 'tis obvious none of you have heard the tale – nay, the legend – of Black Jack, saviour of Canada.'

Jack looked about him, wondering of whom these words were spoken. When he realized, he flushed pink, but no one noticed for all eyes were on Red Hugh. It was obvious that here, as at the Captain's table, the Irishman could hold an audience.

'Yer man, the Viking here, claims five souls despatched, one for each decade of his life. But I have to tell you that Black Jack . . .' he paused and they waited, eager, 'has four more scalps to his name, so he has. That's nine for those who can't count – and him scarce eighteen years of age. Nine! Dead at his hand, and not stabbed with a shive down a back alley nor shot genteelly and safely with a pistol firing over the red ranks. Killed face to face, man to man, with tomahawk and sword and his own strong hands. Frenchies and wild savages in equal numbers.'

Jack was not sure whether to look modest or appalled at the revelation of what he'd told Red Hugh in private. He was not proud of the tally. In each case, they'd been necessary, that was all. And they were just the ones he could remember.

The men had no such doubts. A cheer came which Red Hugh rode, calling out over it, 'And to top it all, his mother was Jane Fitzsimmons, the nightingale of the Smock Alley Theatre, Dublin. By Christ, lads, he's halfway to being an Irishman!'

The cheering by now had become almost universal. Stooping again, Red Hugh grabbed the mug offered, Guinea rum spilling over its lip, then cried, 'I give you that scourge of French manhood, that bed-warmer for their ladies, the newest member of the Fo'castle Club of the *Sweet Eliza* – Black Jack Absolute!'

'Black Jack!' came the cry, followed immediately by shouts of, 'Pledge, pledge, pledge!' A mug was thrust at Jack, and he seized it, slopping some of its contents down his shirt, raising it before him. He was still feeling a little nauseous from Red Hugh's grip on deck but hesitation here would spell an end to a society he desperately wanted to enter. He knew what to do. 'My lords,' he cried, 'a pox on all Puritans and a rope for all politicians.'

'Huzzah!' was the response.

It seemed to take an inordinately long time to reach the bottom of the pewter but when he did he felt instantly better. Even more so when he'd sat rather suddenly down and Murphy began to play.

McRae had been right about the fiddler. There'd been a glorious hour when the balance between rum swallowed and fine notes produced had been just right; a further half-hour when voices drowned out the faulty notes. Then he'd attempted some sad lament that only he seemed to know. On one especially long and tortured note, with the man's nose almost touching his knee, another sailor stepped forward and grabbed bow and fiddle just before Murphy sank soundless to the deck.

The silence only lasted a moment. There were boys as well as men in the room and one of these youths now stood up. With hands behind his back, and in a sweet voice not yet broken, he began to sing, 'Lochaber, No More'.

Of those still awake, more than half joined in the chorus of the old Jacobite song and Jack, with his eyes tight closed, was one of them. For the time of the singing he was no longer aboard the *Sweet Eliza* but back with his friends at Westminster, in a private room at the Five Chimneys on Tothill Fields where, three June 10ths in a row, each scholar sported a white rose to show their allegiance on the Old Pretender's birthday:

I gae then, my lass, to win honour and fame
And if I should chance to come gloriously home
I'll bring a heart to thee with love running o'er
And then I'll leave thee and Lochaber no more.

The chorus ended and Jack opened his eyes to find Red Hugh staring at him. The Irishman's voice was soft, audible only to Jack, the song continuing beyond it.

'Are those tears, lad?'

Jack rubbed, laughed. 'Possibly. It's smoky down here, is it not?'

Red Hugh regarded him for a moment. 'Are you not, then, a follower of the Lost King?'

Jack thought for a moment then shook his head. Any following he'd done had been merely a schoolboy attraction to the romance of a doomed cause. 'In truth, I am not. Though I grew up in a house where my father is a Tory of the old school who damned the Hanoverians even while he fought for them in all their wars.'

'And your mother?'

'I think my mother saw Ireland's liberty in the Old King's cause, at least for a while. But her beliefs have become more . . . extreme of late.' He chuckled. 'Indeed, I think she has moved beyond all kings.'

The man before him nodded and gazed away to the singer, but not before Jack noticed something dark come into his regard.

'And you?' Jack asked. 'Have you worn the oak leaf of the Stuarts yourself?'

Red Hugh looked back. Whatever had fleeted in his eyes was gone. He smiled. 'Aye, lad. I was out in the forty-five.'

'You fought—'

'I did. Stood under English grapeshot on that damn moor. Shed my own blood and the blood of others. Many others, may God have mercy upon me.'

Jack thought back to the two battles he'd fought the previous year, both before the walls of Quebec. 'I knew a Scotsman who was also at Culloden. A fine man. Donald Macdonald of—'

'Of the Royal Ecossais! I know him well, heard he'd taken the Hanoverian shilling as I had taken the Austrian.' He paused. 'Knew, you said?'

Jack nodded. 'He died at the second battle of Quebec.'

The Irishman sighed. 'Another who'll come no more. Like the Bonnie Prince.'

'His cause is finished, then?'

'With Charles Stuart a drunk in Germany, a wife-beater, a madman taken to the Anglican communion to gain support?' He snorted his disgust. 'Aye, most think that cause is through, to be sure.'

'Do you?'

Red Hugh shook his head. 'I used to be a Jacobite, lad. Used to be. No more. And, sure, am I not about only me own business now?' He turned to the boy who had just finished his performance. 'But I do love the songs still. So sing, young Conor, sing us that one again.'

The boy, delighted to have an audience still awake, did as he was bid. Red Hugh reached for two rum mugs, handed one to Jack, then raised him up and led him by the arm across to a butt that held rainwater. 'The songs and the toasts. Shall we have an old one?' He turned back, kicked out at some dozers at his feet who grumbled awake. 'Here's one, lads: to the King across the water!'

As he spoke, he moved his mug over the bucket. Jack nearly did the same. In the shelter of certain Jacobite taverns in Whitechapel and Shadwell, sought out with his friends for the illicit thrill of them, he often *had* done the same. Yet that was before he'd joined the Army, before he'd sworn an officer's oath to King George, to England. So he just raised his mug straight up and, when the Irishman turned back to him, said, 'I'll drink to this, sir: to friendship and Red Hugh McClune.'

That something, that darkness was there again, there and gone. Light and good humour ruled his face once more. 'And I'll drink to you, Jack Absolute. To you!'

Privateer

He woke where he'd fallen asleep, alone in the forecastle hold, his arm around Jeremiah. The goat was chewing his shirt-tail. Yet it was not that movement but the ship's that caused him to jerk his head up. His yelp at the pain disturbed the ruminant, who bleated and shambled off. No, he realized, not movement. A lack of it.

The *Sweet Eliza* appeared to have come to a dead stop.

He stood and swayed, not only from the effects of motion on his head. The cabin's floor seemed to be angled more acutely than ever. He knew, because the Captain swore about it continuously, that the ship was more prone to heel than most. It seemed that the constant trimming required had been somewhat neglected. Unless . . .

Jack suddenly thought of the other reason they could have stopped. They'd made port. While he slept, the wind had freshened and driven them into some haven.

Two grazed shins and a banged head later – the gun deck through which he tripped had no guns but was stuffed with goods in barrels and bails – he climbed the steep stair eagerly toward the light. And such light! The sun sliced into him, heating what was already hot. He closed his eyes, using his hands to feel the last few steps up. When he reached the quarterdeck, the combined effects of motion, sudden light and vicious heat had their effect. He staggered right, even though it seemed uphill, and vomited over the rail. Only then did he see that they had reached no port, that the sea still stretched away to the horizon and that it was as flat as the duck ponds in Hyde Park. He looked up. Such sails as were on the yards hung limp. Finally, he looked across to the larboard rail where, it appeared, the entire ship's company stood, no doubt adding to the degree of heel. All had their backs to him, their attention, fortunately, on something else. Hoping perhaps that land lay thither, and recognizing the exquisite linen of one particular shirt, Jack made his way over.

'What is it?' he said, sliding between the Irishman and the purser. Both of them had telescopes raised, along with half a dozen others. 'What do you all—'

'Hush!' Red Hugh lifted a finger to his lips, then pointed.

At first Jack could see nothing, such was the glare of sun behind him on the water. Squinting, eventually he saw what everyone was staring at.

It was another ship. Having no clue as to its size, he was uncertain how far away it was. Far enough so he could distinguish no person upon its decks; not so far that he could not tell that its sails, like those above him, also hung slack on the yards.

Despite the heat, Jack suddenly flushed cool, the pain inside his head forgotten. 'Which colours does she fly?' he whispered.

'It is the question we'd all like answered,' came the soft reply.

Jack stared harder. There was a piece of cloth on the ship's stern that may have been a flag, but without wind to unfurl it, there was nothing to expel the sudden fear now knotting his stomach as the residue of rum had knotted it. All knew that French privateers cruised the sea lanes awaiting such lone vessels as the *Sweet Eliza*. There was a good chance, of course, that it was an English privateer or indeed a ship from a host of other neutral countries. There was a smaller chance that it owed allegiance to no country at all and flew under whatever colour it chose. Black, often, the universal sign of the pirate.

Jack swallowed, looked about him at the silent, staring men. 'Why is no one doing anything?'

'And what would you have them do?' There was irritation in Red Hugh's reply. 'You may have noticed that there's no wind.'

Jack looked again at the limp cloths above him. 'What happened to it?'

'It died, dear joy, it died.'

Jack rubbed his eyes, looked again. It had to be a trick of light on water. Or maybe his eyes were just getting more used to the glare. But the other ship's details appeared a touch clearer.

'They're not making way, are they?'

'They are.'

That cold flush came again. 'But how?' he said, suddenly annoyed. 'How can they be? If the wind's dead for us, it must be dead for them, too!'

For reply, Red Hugh handed over his telescope. Jack looked to the prow of the ship, searched, didn't see it to start with. Then he detected movement. Oars were moving in the flat water. Not from one boat either. There were three, pulling the ship ever so slowly towards them.

From the side of his mouth, Jack whispered, 'Why are we not doing the same?'

'For we have but the one jolly boat. It tells you something of the size of their crew,' Red Hugh replied, taking back his telescope.

'Have you made her yet, Engledue?' Link called down the line.

All looked to the oldest man there. Red Hugh had told Jack that the Lieutenant was the most experienced man on the ship, more so even than his Captain; had served thirty years, mainly in the Royal Navy, his hair turning white under shrouds across the world. Apparently, he'd long since quit the sea but penury and a taste for rum had driven him back upon it. He lowered his telescope now, pinched his nose between his closed eyes, sighed.

'Well, man?' snapped Link.

'She's a French frigate—'

'I can see her apple-cheeked bow for myself. Means nothing,' Link interrupted loudly to quell the muttering that arose. 'Half those who sail the Bristol Roads are French prizes. But do 'ee know her?'

Engledue thrust out a lower lip. 'She has the cut of the *Marquis de Tourney*. Captured by Chislet in the *Lion* in forty-seven.'

Those who had telescopes raised them. Jack whispered, hopefully, 'She's English, then?'

Red Hugh gave a faint smile. 'She might be. But I've heard of ships that have been fought, captured, fought again, captured back, and that have flown under five different flags just in this one war. Wait, lad.'

'So what will she carry?' Link's harsh voice came again.

Engledue turned to look at his master. 'Perhaps, sir, I should give you my thoughts in private—'

Link shook his head. 'The crew will see her sides for themselves soon enough. So tell us *all* your thoughts, if you please.'

'I think she's a cruiser of twenty-four guns.' Engledue said quietly. 'Nine- and six-pounders probably, for if she is the *Tourney* or her near sister, she's not big enough for more.'

'Big enough e'en so,' muttered Red Hugh. Jack looked down the line of men. All seemed to share the Irishman's opinion in their dropped eyes, their sudden frowns. He knew that they only carried eighteen guns and those mere four-pounders. He could see them now for they were all lashed alongside their ports on the quarterdeck, forecastle and poop. Though the *Sweet Eliza* was also born a frigate, she'd been converted to bear slaves, and the gun deck below that had served as their prison now contained only the trade goods being transported, its ports *en flute*, caulked shut against heavy seas. As a cavalryman, he knew little more about gunnery than he did about the ocean, but even he could tell that they were seriously outgunned.

'What now?' he whispered, a question apparent in the eyes of all who looked to the Captain and Lieutenant.

Aware of their attention, Link handed his eyeglass to his slave, Barabbas, who stood, as ever, a pace behind him. 'Let us run out our guns anyway and not sit here like a mouse before a cat. Show 'em we mean to fight 'em.'

'Even if we do not, Cap'n?' It was Williams, the tattooed Welshman, who called down from the con, though his hands barely rested on the wheel.

Link glowered but held his temper. 'Let's see his colours before we decide that, man.'

The crew moved reluctantly to their guns, confusing Jack. 'Why do they move so slowly? Surely Link will order them to fight?'

Red Hugh shook his head. 'On a King's ship he could command. But I've even heard of captains in the Royal Navy striking their colours without a shot, if the odds were impossible and the crew unwilling.' He tipped his chin to the other ship, creeping slowly nearer. 'And these odds do not look good.'

Jack had considered this possibility; anyone journeying the dangerous sea lanes of the Atlantic had to. He had no especial desire to be shot at by superior guns at a distance. He had seen men before the walls of Quebec stand in their red lines and receive shot, witnessed limbs shorn and heads lopped. Yet the idea of surrendering to a Frenchman without a fight . . .

The Irishman noticed the struggle on his face. A hand came onto his shoulder. 'Still and all, lad, yon fellow might well hail from half a dozen other nations, including the English. As Link says, let's wait till we see his colours.'

The man turned to observe the crew about the lashings on the gun carriages. Jack looked back over the rail, to the approaching ship. Perhaps he was thus the only man aboard who was not occupied with other tasks, the only man to see something stir the limp cloth at the stern of the ship. It was indeed a flag. It unfurled, and the instant it did he knew it. The same flag had preceded the regiments which had marched down upon him on the Plains of Abraham last year.

'It's white! White, by God. The Flag of the Bourbon, the flag of France!'

All turned at his cry. All saw. And several noticed what Jack had not – the wind that had stirred the flag now stirred the sails. A few moments later that same wind reached them, bringing to their nostrils heat and a strange, rich scent.

'The wind, by Christ. Let's get before it and outrun this poxy Frenchman,' yelled Link.

'But it's a full quartering breeze, Captain,' said his conman, Williams, 'and he'll be sailing large upon't. While we're in irons.'

Jack looked up. He may not have understood the jargon but he could see that they were heading prow first into the eye of the wind, the fore and aft sails barely drawing.

'We'll box-haul her, then,' cried Link. 'Pipe me "all hands".' While his boatswain, McRae, plied his pipe – though Jack was sure no one could be below deck – Link yelled, 'Hold a larboard rudder. Get aloft and brace the foresails to larboard.'

Men ran for the foremast. The first had barely set his foot on the rigging when Engledue called out, 'Sir, I submit it will take too long. We're close-hauled on the larboard tack. And look!'

All followed his pointing hand. The Frenchman's sails were full, though Jack thought it odd that only a few were flying.

The Captain explained it. 'He'll not fill his yards till he lays his boats alongside.'

'Aye, Cap'n,' replied Engledue, 'but with respect, it will not take him long and he'll be upon us when we're halfway round.'

Link's mottled face darkened at this opposition. But he knew his Lieutenant's experience as well as any man there. And like any man there, he had no desire to spend time under shot or in a Bourbon prison. 'What alternative do you suggest, man?'

'Club-haul her, sir.'

The face darkened further. 'What, and lose my main anchor?'

'It will save us a glass, Cap'n. And a glass may get us to the Azores and a Portuguese harbour.'

A glass of sand ran for half an hour, Jack knew. Engledue was seeking to buy them the tiniest of leads.

All eyes looked to the Captain. The men on the foremast rigging had their feet suspended between rungs. Finally Link shrugged, then bellowed, 'We'll club-haul her. McRae, take the starboard watch to their anchor. Ingvarsson, get the men into the yards. Prepare to brace on the starboard tack.'

Red Hugh had moved over to Jack. 'Do you have any idea what yer men are talking about?'

'You know,' replied Jack, 'I speak French, Iroquois, Latin and Greek – and I haven't a bloody clue!'

They may not have understood the words but actions and orders soon made this 'club-hauling' clear enough. Some men made ready the starboard anchor for its drop. Others tied line to the anchor ring, then hauled the rope the length of the ship to a hole just before the stern. The ship was now pointed directly into the wind and, as soon as it was in the eye of it, the fore and aft sails went limp, while the mainsails filled the wrong way. The *Sweet Eliza* began to drift slowly to stern.

Link called along the quarterdeck, with a touch of bitterness. 'Since this is your idea, Engledue, perhaps you'd give the orders. And, by God, I'll have your hide if you founder my ship.'

'Aye, Captain.' Engledue looked swiftly afore. 'Now, men, now,' he cried, and immediately the crew about the anchor began to let it out swiftly. 'And the spring,' he turned and shouted aft. 'Lively now.'

The aft line, also attached to the anchor, was run out as fast. The ship continued to make sternway. Engledue was standing still, slap in the middle of the quarterdeck. His face was into the wind, his eyes shut.

'Now, Lieutenant?' Link queried testily.

'A moment. A moment,' came the murmur. The *Sweet Eliza* continued its drift to stern. Jack, even if he did not understand exactly what was happening, held his breath. He only expelled it when the Lieutenant suddenly opened his eyes and yelled, 'Now!'

The Captain's 'Now!' came hard upon it, and the aft crew immediately wound the spring line round a capstan, halting its tumble into the sea with the groan of rope suddenly tethered to wood, while the anchor continued to be paid out.

'Brace the yards. Starboard tack,' cried Link, and the crew aloft did just that, the yards and their burden of sail swinging into the wind, held there. At either rope, a man raised an axe high into the air.

'Steady, lads. Steady,' Engledue called softly, and Jack remembered how that same word was as calmly repeated by the officers of the 78th when he'd stood with them on the

Plains of Abraham eighteen months before, holding their soldiers' fingers light on their triggers until the French were nearly at their muskets' mouths. He'd understood what he was waiting for then. He didn't now. Yet he knew that it was every bit as important to his survival. He looked up and saw the sails were full of wind.

'Now,' said Engledue, softly, but loud enough for the axe-men at the ropes to hear, to bring their weapons crashing down. Up they rose, to fall again and then again. The ropes sheered, parted and ran into the sea, while the ship seemed to buck and plunge forward with the wind full in the sails.

Jack's and Red Hugh's cheers were lost in those of the crew. Engledue took off his hat, dipped it in acknowledgement. Glancing at the Captain, Jack saw relief and jealousy war briefly on the florid face. 'I want every man aloft and every sail hoisted from the spirit to the mizzen,' he bellowed, his men scrambling to obey.

'And if you have a handkerchief would you be kind enough to wave it now,' said Red Hugh. Engledue was just passing them and the Irishman halted him. 'That was finely done, sir, will it be enough?'

Engledue glanced in the direction of the nod. Jack, too. The French ship did not appear any closer. But its boats had been gathered and it was making way. 'We've a glass's lead and however long he'll take to come up with us.' He paused. 'By my noon sighting, the island of Flores should lie afore. I think we passed her a couple of nights ago.'

'Think?'

'One can never be certain. I've got the latitude and the bearing and . . . this.' He tapped his nose. 'And prayer, sir. Prayer!'

'Amen,' said the Irishman, as the Lieutenant moved on. 'Are you a praying man, Absolute?'

'No. Never got the knack of it.'

'Then I'll say some for the pair of us.' Red Hugh was

looking past Jack's shoulder. 'But first I think the Captain wants a little word.'

Jack turned. Link was indeed beckoning them. 'What does he want, do you think?'

'I've a fairly good idea.' As they moved forward, he leaned down and said softly, 'Now, did I ever tell you, dear Jack, how I had the honour of practising the law for a short while in Dublin?'

Jack smiled. There was nothing, it seemed, that the man had not done. 'You did. Why do you raise the subject now?'

'Because, if the conversation we are about to have goes the way I think it will, you may want to allow me to act on your behalf.'

'I don't quite under—'

Red Hugh gripped his upper arm and squeezed. 'As I am interceding for the pair of us in heaven, I may as well do the same here on earth. Agreed?'

Jack was still puzzled but nodded anyway. 'So long as there is no slight to my honour.'

'Ah no, dear soul. I would never dream of compromising that.'

— FOUR —

Honour, Part One

Link stood at his table, sea charts held down by instruments before him.

'Come, gentlemen, come,' he said, beckoning them in. 'You'll take rum?'

Jack and Red Hugh both had to stoop beneath the ceiling. But they slowed their progress further, instantly suspicious of the politeness in the Captain's voice.

'Sit, dear sirs, please do.' He gestured them down and Barabbas forward. Rum was poured carefully into mugs. 'The King's health!' he said, raising his and gulping. Jack took a sip for the toast's sake, grimacing as the taste reminded him of his waking. Red Hugh let his mug lie.

'Now, sirs,' Link continued briskly, 'despite the Lieutenant's skill in turning us about,' Jack could hear the envy in the voice, 'my calculations do not agree with his. We are nowhere near the Azores, no haven awaits. Our ship's crank and a frigate will easily forereach us ee'n to leeward.'

There was a pause. 'Any idea, Jack?'

'None.'

Link glowered. 'The Frenchman will catch us within the span of four glasses.'

Two hours, Jack thought, and contemplated another sip of rum. Christ!

'So we must prepare to fight him. Do you not agree?'

Red Hugh tipped his head. 'But was not the Lieutenant's estimate of our pursuer as skilled as his seamanship? Are we not seriously outgunned?'

A scowl and a brisk nod. 'We are. But the Frenchman will not fire on us, sir. Not above a broadside, perhaps, to awe us.'

'Oh, just the one?' Red Hugh smiled. 'And why will he not do more?'

'He wants us undamaged, of course. The ship and all its goods.'

Jack interjected. 'So he'll board us?'

A nod. 'He will. And that's where we will have him. As a privateer, he may have three times our numbers—'

'Will have,' Red Hugh commented.

'Aye, will have. But three to one are English odds, by God. Our history is full of fighting at such odds and triumphing.'

As I am sure French history is full of the reverse, Jack thought.

'So we'll let them come aboard and drive them back with our ferocity,' Link concluded. 'What do you say?'

Jack looked at Red Hugh. The Irishman was finding some detail on his forefinger fascinating. 'And why should we fight?' he said softly.

'Wh- why?' The word obviously stuck in the Captain's throat. 'The men look up to you, sir. You are both soldiers. They would . . .' Their silence provoked him. 'You would be prisoners of the French?'

'I have been before. Charming people. We'll drink far better on their ship than we do on ours, Jack.' He leaned forward to push the rum mug away from him. 'And, with a cartel, we'll be free within months of reaching a port.'

Of course! Relief filled Jack with the thought. Prisoners

were exchanged on cartel all the time. Suddenly French wine and a swift release seemed preferable to even one broadside and hot work on a sloping deck.

Link was still finding the Irishman's reluctance astonishing. 'But, sir! Sir! What about your honour?'

'Ah, honour. Weren't we just discussing that, Jack? Now, I've always thought that honour was a somewhat flexible thing. One man's conceit of it is very different to another's.'

The Captain gave up any pretence of politeness. 'An Englishman's may be very different to an *Irishman's*,' he exploded.

Red Hugh's voice was a soft contrast. 'Now, you see, there we have an example of that very flexibility. You may call me a coward and I may choose to see that as an insult to my honour or as a compliment to my good sense. I may then choose to fight you for it or no. But to impugn my honour due to the country of my birth is, well,' he rose slowly, 'quite another matter.'

Link instinctively began to rub his wrist. 'I . . . I . . . meant no disrespect,' he muttered, looking hastily at Jack. 'But you, sir. You are an officer in the King's army. Surely it is your duty to fight?'

Jack was about to speak when Red Hugh sat again, laying a hand on his forearm. 'It is his duty not to. On two counts.' Jack listened as a lawyer's tones filled the Irish voice. '*Primus*, he is a messenger of that King, his duty thus to bear the dispatches back, not stop to get involved in every local quarrel. *Secundus*,' he raised his voice and hand to override Link's protest, 'he has stated time and again that you are about a trade he abhors. *Ergo*, honour demands that he does not help you conserve the goods that will pay for further slave trading voyages. *Quod est demonstrandum*.'

'*Erat*,' whispered Jack. 'You've already demonstrated it.'

'Damn! Age has rotted my declensions.'

Link's mouth was wide, his eyes confused. Finally, he spluttered at Jack, 'Well, sir?'

Jack looked between the two, shrugged. 'What he said.'

Before another squawk could come, Red Hugh went on, 'Now, personally, I've never been adverse to a little scrap. And it's true my . . . business would prefer that I made for Bristol directly and not via a French prison. Since we have discounted honour and duty as reasons to fight, may I suggest another thing that might – just might, mark – persuade the lad and myself.'

Link looked cowed by the verbal assault. 'What?' he sighed.

Red Hugh smiled. 'Money.'

'Money?'

'Aye. I've always found it an excellent recruiter in the past. When honour's honoured and valour is cooled, money's still there, keeping one warm.'

A short time later, pausing only for a brief conversation with Engledue, Jack followed Red Hugh as he wove through the stacked goods on the gundeck. Each was clutching a piece of paper, intent on stowing it safely in their chests.

'Now, lad, did I not say leave it to me? I've taken a great care of your future.' He tapped the paper in Jack's hand with his own.

Jack looked down at the contract Link had been forced to sign. He'd tried to fob them off with a cockswain's one and a half share but Red Hugh had insisted on a lieutenant's six or they'd sit out the fight.

'What could this mean?'

'Why, Jack, six shares of a rich prize?' The Irishman's eyes glowed even in the dim light of the deck. 'Did you never hear of the *Nuestra Señora de Cabodonga*? Taken by Captain Anson in forty-three?' Jack shook his head. 'It was a treasure ship, lad, on the return from New Spain. Loaded with gold and silver. The common sailors took close to two hundred pounds apiece. That's nine years pay for 'em. But the officers got not much short of five thousand.'

Jack whistled. Five thousand pounds would set a man up for life. Then he shrugged. 'But a treasure ship does not pursue us. It's a French privateer, which probably has empty holds and hungry men.' They'd stopped by his sea chest and Jack pulled the key from his pocket.

'Depends. Perhaps she is returning to port, bulging with loot; and us the transport she requires to help carry it. If we take her, she could still make us rich men.'

'Perhaps.' Jack dropped the paper in, re-locked the chest, stood. 'But I have fought the French, as I know you have. They are not such sorry dogs as Link would have us believe. And with so many more men . . .'

Red Hugh nodded. 'It's true. Except I have ways of evening the numbers.'

'What ways?'

The Irishman smiled, crooked a finger. 'Let me show you.'

His goods were stowed further forward. When he had locked his own paper away, in a chest considerably more ancient and battered than Jack's, he turned to a large square crate beside it. 'Pass me that jemmy, will you, dear soul?' he murmured.

The carpenter's tool was handed across, its flat end pressed under the lid. The top was carefully prised up. Then each side was also pulled away, the back laid down. What looked like a mound of straw lay exposed.

Jack sneezed three times. 'What will this do?' he asked. 'Make them too busy wiping their noses to fight?'

'It's in the nature of a Trojan horse. For what's within . . .' Red Hugh said, adding, 'Oi! Get out of it, you beast.' Jeremiah the goat had appeared at the scent of this new provender and received a kick in its haunches for its pains. It retired a few feet, regarding them balefully as it munched the strands it had seized. Meanwhile, Red Hugh was carefully pulling the straw aside. Soon a stack of wooden racks, three levels deep, was revealed. On each rack, spherical objects the size of small footballs were wrapped in sacking.

'What are they?' asked Jack stretching out his hand to the nearest one.

'Grenades,' said the Irishman, laughing as Jack snatched his hand back and took a step away. 'Phish, Jack, never fear. These boys are only dangerous when they are introduced to the fuses.' He kicked another smaller box to the side. 'Bit like the Presbyterians and my boys back home. Only make trouble when we meet.' He reached forward, slipping the sack off one and picking it up. The dark iron globe sat in his hand, just overlapping the palm. He mimed a lob. 'Play any cricket, have you?'

'I was in the team at Westminster. A batsman though.'

'A pity. For the pitching's much the same. Sure, I've taken a few wickets myself in my time.'

Jack was not sure if he was speaking in metaphors. 'You carry grenades with you.'

It was not a question. 'Oagh,' came the reply. 'You never know when you'll have need of a good grenade.' He noticed Jack's look. 'I told you I was an engineer. These are the best things for blasting through rock.'

'Of course they are. And these are good grenades?'

'The best. Made them up myself.' He spun one up in the air, caught it behind his back. 'These on the top rack are pure powder with a heavy case. Good for blowing things up. These,' he picked one off the second level, 'are full of shot.' He shook one. 'Plays havoc with tight bunches of men.'

'Or rocks?'

The Irishman was not discountenanced. 'Or rocks, indeed.'

'And these?' Jack pointed to the bottom layer.

'*Pot à feu*. Have a sniff.'

Jack did and made a face.

'That's right. Mainly sulphur and stuff. Makes a right old whiff. Did you never make stink bombs at that fancy school of yours?'

'We made do with the latrines.' Jack shook his head. 'And are these ready for use?'

'The powder will have settled. Tends to go into its separate ingredients then it doesn't go off. So I'll give each one a shake in a bit, then add these fuses.' He opened the box, and showed Jack what looked like a pipe bowl with a straight wooden stem below it. 'When we're up top, I'll tell you how long to wait before you throw 'em.'

'You mean, once they're lit, you wait?' said Jack, appalled.

'Oh, aye, unless you want 'em thrown back at ye. Remember, I made each of these fuses myself. It's a science. The right mix gives you the exact time and I've set each rack to go off differently. These beauties, for example,' he waved to the ball-filled bombs on the second racks, 'have ten-second fuses. So you hold them till the count of eight then let fly.'

'Eight?'

'Haven't I held it till eight and a half if I wanted to explode it over the head of an enemy platoon. And didn't One-Handed Tom often hold it till nine?'

'One-Handed Tom?'

'Well,' the Irishman grinned, 'he got careless.' He mimed another lob.

'Does one have to throw with one's left hand?'

'No, no. 'Tis only myself that's shaped that way, despite the priests who tied my arm to my side to try to cure me of Satan's sign.' He grinned. 'Old Nick doesn't affect the grenade throwing. But when I get a sword in my hand, the devil's in the blade, certain.'

Jack nodded. He had fought left-handers at Angelo's school in the Haymarket. They were indeed devilishly tricky.

They heard a soft footfall. McRae appeared. 'Cap'n says

he's calling us together shortly. Going to ask us if we wants to fight, I 'spect.' He had tobacco in his mouth, gathered phlegm then leaned to the gun-port to spit, stopping when he remembered that these were caulked up. Swallowing, he continued, 'You'll tell him to fuck hisself, won't you, McClune?'

'Maybe not, boyo.' He stepped closer to the man. 'For hasn't the Lieutenant recognized yon ship. Says it's the *Robuste*, out of Nantes this whole year. It'll have holds crammed with goods.' He stepped away and Jack could see the sudden gleam in the sailor's eyes. 'Tell the Captain we'll be up presently.'

'Right then.'

As the sailor moved away to the stair, Red Hugh sighed. 'Most lads will fight the Frogs if they think they have even a little chance. But I wish I had something other than greed with which to inspire them.'

'Like what?'

'Ah, lad. You should have seen me in the uniform of a Grenz Grenadier. With my Khobuk hat, my dolman, pantaloons and sash, my long moustaches and my hair done just so . . .' He corkscrewed a twist of his red hair up beside his face. 'The French usually ran the moment they looked upon us.'

Jack smiled, then remembered: he had seen the French run, at Quebec, from the impoverished line of red-clad men who had waited till they were impossibly close before they fired.

'Red-clad,' he murmured.

'Aye, Jack?' came the reply, mistaking him.

He looked at the Irishman. 'You may not have your uniform. But I have mine.'

He turned, walked back to his own trunk. He had it open by the time Red Hugh joined him. He lifted the jacket. It was more bright scarlet than russet red, having never been exposed to weather. Jack had found a wonderful tailor in Newport and, since his old Dragoon uniform had been stripped off him by the Abenaki, he had commissioned this one. He wasn't going to present himself to the King in the dead Lobster-back's castaways he'd been issued with in Quebec. He'd traded the tailor ten ermine skins, a fortune, but he'd got what he paid for. The cloth could not have been bettered, nor better cut, in Jermyn Street. The silver buttons needed a polish, as did the front plate on the cavalryman's cap, so they'd provide a brighter contrast to the black facings at lapel and cuff, the black of his regiment, the 16th Light Dragoons.

Red Hugh was peering over his shoulder. 'You are not thinking of wearing that, are you, son?'

'Why not? Were you not just wishing for your old uniform?'

'But mine was green and I was dressed like hundreds of my fellows when I wore it. You will stand out, and draw bullets as fast as shit draws flies.' He tried to pull the material from Jack's hand. 'No, lad. Keep to your sailor's gear and look like everyone else.'

Jack rubbed the material for a long moment. 'You wish me to skulk.'

'Blend in—'

Jack raised a hand. 'Forgive me, sir. I will, of course, take your advice in all matters pertaining to grenades. But I have a uniform here, the uniform of my regiment. To have it and not fight in it would be a dishonour to it. To my regiment. To the name of Absolute.' He rose and looked straight into the Irishman's eyes. 'This is *my* point of honour, sir. And I will not budge from it.'

'By God.' Red Hugh's eyes filled with light and moisture. Then, to Jack's great surprise, he leaned forward, grabbed Jack by the back of his head and kissed him smack on the mouth. 'By God, this *is* indeed the spirit that conquered

Canada. And I can see the half Irishman in you, plain as day. 'Twill be an honour to fight beside you – even if you'll be drawing half their cannon and all their sharpshooters.'

He laughed and, after a moment of reconsideration, Jack did, too. 'I'll see you aloft, Red Hugh.'

'Aloft, Black Jack.'

The Irishman made for the stairs and Jack began to dress, slowly, enjoying the quality of silk and serge as he pulled each item on. If the cavalry sabre he'd acquired in Newport was not of the first order, it had an edge that was keen enough and nicks that attested to its experience. And he had other weapons, too. Reaching again into the trunk, he pulled out his tomahawk, thrust it beside the sword into his belt. Then, as he heard the pipes call 'All hands', the cries of 'Bundle up' urging all men below to the deck, he stretched behind the sea chest and brought out the rifle for which he'd traded five flagons of rum with the Niantic Indians of Newport.

Not *all* the sharpshooters will be on their decks, he thought.

— FIVE —

The Sea Fight

A detour to the galley kept Jack from the deck. With the hot water and some rough soap he found there, he plied his straight razor, taking off his beard, as voices rose and fell above him, words indistinct, disagreement clear. He took his time, for he wanted no nicks and, as with his dressing, there was something soothing in this attention to ritual. Finally, he pulled a stock from his waistcoat pocket, the material cut from the same dark cloth as his regimental facings, and bound his long black hair into a cue.

On his way up to the deck, he spared a moment to duck into the Captain's cabin, to the only mirror on the ship. It showed him an officer who would disgrace neither name nor regiment. Sticking out his tongue at this other self, cap tucked under his arm, he climbed the steep stair.

He emerged onto the quarterdeck, but the officers were gathered on the poop, facing that majority of the crew who were not aloft in the rigging. His movement through them brought silence, many regarding him as if they had never seen him before. He ascended to the poop deck and stood behind Link's left shoulder, just as Red Hugh flanked him on the right.

The Captain gestured to him immediately. 'You talk of the

fiercesome French, Williams. But we have bold warriors ourselves, do we not?'

'Not doubting their courage, Cap'n,' the tattooed Welshman replied from the wheel, 'but courage itself fires no shots. And the Frenchie will fire plenty.' He looked to starboard. Jack could see how much the French ship had closed. Half the distance at least. Two glasses gone, no more than two remained. One hour.

'He won't, as I have told you,' Link said, his voice strained. 'He'll want us fresh and unhurt. He'll come for the grapple, sure. And that's how we'll beat him.'

'With him double or triple our men?' It was the Scandinavian, Ingvarsson, who spoke.

'You know the way of it. Christ, most of you have served under a letter of marque or for the King yourselves.' Link leaned over the rail. 'He'll board with half, leave half on his ship. So we'll kill the half that comes, and then go get t'other over there.'

'And that's where the gold will be,' said Engledue. 'Remember, lads, she's the *Robuste*, sure, and heavily laden with booty. Look how she lies down in the water.'

All looked again. She didn't seem to move so sluggishly to Jack. But various of the seamen nodded.

'So how will we kill the half that comes?' McRae had stepped forward. 'Most of us have fought before, right enough, but we had less grey in our pigtails then. And if their ship is ever so full of gold, they got it by fighting. The odds are still long against us.'

A murmur echoed agreement to this. It was an Irish voice that cut through it. 'Well then,' Red Hugh said, 'won't we just have to shorten them?'

He stepped around Link, bent at the knees, drew his hand back. Something black flew over the rail, landing with a distinct thud on the deck.

'Grenade!'

Men yelped, scattered. As they did, Red Hugh turned to Jack. 'Did you see the bend at the knee, the gentleness of the lob. All in ease, Jack, all in ease. Your first lesson.' He winked, then, turning back, he shouted, 'What do you think of those odds now, fellows, with an Irish Grenadier and an English Dragoon to back ye?'

Heads lifted. Link recognized the moment. 'And I've an issue of rum now and fifty pounds later, aside from your shares, for each man who plants his feet on the enemy deck. What say ye?'

It was handsome enough. With a cheer, the men crowded around the cockswain who stood before a rum barrel awaiting this moment. Mugs were filled, drained, lifted hopefully again. The slave, Barabbas, appeared with a tray for the poop deck. Jack did not hesitate. He remembered how, before Quebec, he had turned down a tot. He wasn't going to make that mistake again.

Red Hugh nodded approvingly. 'That's it. 'Tis a fine balance, much like the mix of gunpowder in a fuse. Too much rum and one's abilities are hampered. Too little and one's courage is restrained.' He held out his palm, refusing a second mug. 'I think I've got the mix just about right.'

Jack felt he could have had a little more. But seeing Link slurp at a second overfilled mug like a hound at a bucket, he too declined.

Red Hugh came over, placed an arm around Jack's shoulder. 'Now,' he said, 'to make sure you don't end up like One-Handed Tom, let me apprise you of a few other things you'll need to know about grenades.'

Engledue had been wrong or perhaps over-hopeful. The second glass had barely begun to decant its sand into the lower chamber and the enemy was already not more than two hundred yards astern. Indeed, Jack had watched the sailors there reef some sails, obviously slowing the vessel to the *Sweet Eliza*'s pace.

'Why don't she fire?' whispered Jack from his place on the poop.

Engledue heard him. 'French frigates don't have a chase gun,' he said. 'And we have none astern to trouble him. Since he has the weather gauge he's content to hang back and awe us with his numbers. He thinks we'll strike before we fight.'

The Captain of the *Robuste* – for so she was, the name now clear in gold letters on the prow, a cloth ostentatiously removed to reveal it – had obviously ordered all hands to the rails where they jeered and shook weapons. Music blared, too, and Jack could make out several fiddles, drums and horns. Indeed, the numbers told him that the original estimate had been more likely: they were closer to triple the *Sweet Eliza*'s strength of forty-six men than double.

Jack licked dry lips. Wonder if it's too late for another rum? he thought. Then he saw it probably was, for the sails that had been reefed were hoisted again and the enemy began to overhaul them.

'Raise the portholes. To the guns!'

Men ran to their stations. The nine four-pounders on the starboard station were rolled out. Immediately the jeering redoubled on the French ship and, a moment later, their portholes were raised. But their guns rolled out not only on their quarterdeck, for their gundeck was not *en flute*. Double the number of barrels pointed to larboard and Jack remembered Engledue saying these were likely to be nine-pounders. Double the weight of ball, too, then.

'Steady, lads. On my command!'

Jack felt bound by the order, even though the French ship was now coming into good range of his rifle. There was also a peculiar feeling that, if neither of them started the fight, it would not happen. Besides, as the ship got closer, Jack could see the enemy wasn't quite ready to commence.

'*Messieurs! Messieurs!*'

A Frenchman, dressed as if for breakfast with a napkin shoved into his silk shirt, was balanced on the bowsprit like a tumbler at the Vauxhall Pleasure Gardens. He leaned far out over the water, waving his tricorn hat with one hand casually threaded round the stay that ran to the foremast; his other hand pressed a bullhorn to his mouth.

'Does anyone here speak French?' called Link.

Jack looked to Red Hugh. The Irishman tutted. 'No, no, Jack, I defer to you. Mine's rusted and largely conned for use in taverns and brothels. I'd only offend the fellow and provoke his fire. You have a chat. I'll just back you up.'

'I'll speak to him, Captain, if you like.'

'Do so,' said Link. 'Damn his eyes and tell him we've only salt cod aboard.'

Jack nodded. He was handed a bullhorn and stepped up to the rail, Red Hugh a pace behind him. The *Robuste*'s prow was now nearly level with the *Eliza*'s stern.

'*Monsieur!*' The man shouted. '*Parlez-vous français, monsieur?*'

'*Oui. Et vous anglais?*'

'Ah yes, a little little.' He seemed to be attempting some sort of bow then, suddenly, he sneezed very loudly. '*Merde*,' he said.

'*Santé*,' called Jack.

'*Merci.*' Pausing only to wipe his nose on his sleeve, the man continued. 'You are army officer, yes?'

'*Oui. Avec tout mon régiment au-dessous.*' Jack gestured below decks, to where the rest of the 16th Light Dragoons obviously lurked.

The Frenchman laughed. 'Ah. I think you make a *pleasanterie* with me, *hein*? I think you have . . . *les Nègres* there.'

'*Non. Pas des Nègres. Seulement . . . le salt cod*,' said Jack. At the man's blankness he called out, '*Les poissons au sel.*'

'*Pas seulement, je crois.*' The Frenchman gave a big smile.

'But if you have this only, then you let us look? *Si seulement les poissons,*' he shrugged, 'we let you go, *hein?*'

'Tell him to bugger himself, Absolute,' Link called.

Though Jack knew many degrading words in French, that term wasn't one. '*Non, monsieur. Ce n'est pas possible.*'

There came another shrug. '*Quel dommage. Eh bien,* I see you momently.' He sneezed again.

'*Santé,*' said Jack but the Frenchman didn't thank him this time. He'd turned and lightly run down the bowsprit to his forecastle.

'I've a bullet that will cure that cold, Froggie,' Jack muttered, turning quickly yet obviously not quickly enough, for Red Hugh seized his arm and yanked him down behind the elm boards that had been brought from the hold and lined the railings. These were better able to withstand the bullet that smashed into them than Jack's Dragoon coat would have been.

'I suppose that means the *parlez* is over,' said Jack with a shaky grin, but the Irishman's reply was lost in the roar of French shot that followed the musket's fire. Jack had always assumed that a broadside would be just that, a single thing. But what came from the enemy was not one explosion but a short, irregularly staggered series of them, blasts of cannon interspersed with the results of the shot; again, not the thudding of ball against timber he'd expected but the whistle and shriek of many objects flying through the air.

He looked up. Rents and gashes had appeared in several of the *Eliza*'s sails, stays and shrouds had been severed, rigging flapped or fell. 'What's that?' he shouted, as items began to fall onto the deck, then had his answer in the two balls joined by a length of chain that landed not three foot from him. Elsewhere, iron bars dropped, metal tumbled from the sky.

'They try to cripple us but look how she still flies,' Engledue cried. 'Let's give 'em three huzzahs, boys, and their scrap back with interest.'

Jack had heard how the British were tighter at their guns than the French, and here it was proved. Peering through the gap between two elm boards, he saw that the crews had waited till the ship was rolling down the wave, their muzzles thus pointing slightly down. The explosions began with the first of the three cheers and ended not much beyond the last, and in those brief seconds he saw most of the British ball strike between wind and water. Several stove in at the gundeck, cannon ports torn wider. He could hear the yelps of fear and agony.

'Load with langrage,' he heard Link cry, and knew they were thus close enough for the ball and metal fragments, similar to what the army called grapeshot. As the crews tended their guns, as they heard the French doing the same, each preparing a last surprise before collision. Red Hugh, head low, began scuttling down to the quarterdeck. 'Will you join me, Jack? I've me own little gift for our guests.'

'A moment.' Cannon may have been halted but muskets kept up a steady smash into board, deck and railing. Jack had noted the marksman who first shot at him perched in the top of the foremast. It was time he became more than a target.

He had already loaded his rifle before laying it carefully down. The priming was in the pan. Lifting it carefully, he raised himself above the boards. The sharpshooter who had aimed at him before was pointing towards him again. Grinding butt into shoulder, Jack swiftly cocked, aimed and shot. His opponent reeled back and then tumbled, screaming, to the deck.

'Will you come, Jack?'

Jack laid his rifle back down. His one glimpse had told him that the *Robuste* was gliding into them fast. Single bullets were not going to make much difference now. It was time to try and remember exactly what Red Hugh had said about grenades.

As he slid down the stairs and ducked inside the door, Jack saw that not all his ship's company were engaged in fighting – at least, not directly. Despite the fire being poured onto them, men were swarming in the foremast's rigging, some already splicing together what had been torn. Engledue was standing at the base of the foremast. 'Now, Captain,' he called to Link, who stood beside his conman, his great meaty hands paralleling Williams' on the wheel.

'Now!' Link screamed.

'Now!' echoed Engledue up the mast. 'Brace abox!' His crew braced the three yards there, the foremast sails all suddenly backed against the wind, slowing the ship on the instant. A moment later, Link gave a roar and both he and McRae began to pull hard on the helm to larboard. The ship slewed sharp across, denying the enemy the advantage of laying her whole length alongside. Instead, their prow drove straight at the *Eliza*'s quarterdeck.

'Fire!' The gun captains' cries came, and the cannons blasted their langrage shot just before the *Robuste*'s bowsprit, a good ten foot above the quarterdeck, came over, followed by the prow smashing into the bulwarks.

'Good sailing, by God,' cried Red Hugh. 'He'll only be able to board us forward and his numbers will count for less.' He bent to the rack they'd positioned earlier beneath the poop deck and lifted two balls from the rack. 'There's these for you, Jack,' he said, handing them over. 'This,' he dropped two extra fuses into Jack's bullet satchel, 'in case one splutters out. Unlikely, but if it does just twist the auld one out, shove this one in, forget the count and hurl the thing.' He smiled. 'And this,' he added as he shoved a glowing cord into Jack's cross belt, 'will set 'em off nicely, so it will. Just remember, once it's sparking, to point it downwards. Nothing annoys a Grenadier more than being burnt by the fella next to him.'

'Remind me again,' said Jack, weighing the balls as if

measuring two bags of manure, 'what's the bloody animal I count to? Is it a hippopotamus?'

The Irishman laughed, 'You'd lose more than One-Handed Tom did with two extra syllables. It's elephant, nice and steady, like the beast itself. One elephant, two elephant . . .' He nodded towards the deck. 'And aren't you going to start moving through the herd any minute?'

Jack looked. After the smash of ships, their own crew had scattered, partly to avoid the swivel guns the French would direct at them, partly because Red Hugh had advised them to keep well clear. Half were still aloft, scrambling like Barbary apes on the rigging, moving marks for muskets. The rest were crouched back beneath the forecastle, forming a shelter with boards dragged across the doorway, clutching an assortment of spears, axes, swords and pistols. Ducking under the lintel, Jack took a swift glimpse up to the *Robuste*. Similar weapons were brandished there. He saw ropes swinging, heard the whirr of grappling hooks, the thud as they reached the quarterdeck.

'Ready, lad?'

What could he do save nod?

'Match.' Red Hugh lifted the fuse, Jack did the same, and both pressed the glowing cord to the small tuft of quick match that stood proud of the powder.

'One hippopot—'

'ELEPHANT!' yelled the Irishman.

'Two elephant,' they said together.

A great cheer rose from the French ship. In a rush they came, bare feet sliding down ropes, thumping onto the quarterdeck. Directly above, Jack heard the cock of muskets, the command of 'Fire!' from Captain Link, the cry of victims.

'Four elephant, five—'

'*Now* elephant!' Red Hugh led the way out of the door, Jack at his shoulder. He'd lost the count but it didn't matter;

he just paralleled the Irishman's movements, bent at the knee, brought the sputtering ball back, lobbed it forward. It shot from his sweaty hand, flew high where Red Hugh's went low. Both arrived at the same time, Jack saw in the swiftest of glances before he was hurling himself the other way, sliding to the bulwark, his head buried under his arms.

The explosions came hard upon each other, like a heart-beat, preceded by a cry, followed by many. Jack had twisted as soon as he heard them, was already making to rise. But the sight through the clearing smoke stopped him.

Red Hugh had told him they would begin with hard shot grenades, not ball and scrap. Stun them, he'd said. It had done much more than that. Of the dozen or so men who had landed on the deck, only one was standing, and that only because he'd been flung against the rail and somehow twisted an arm around a shroud there. The rest were thrown, separately and in piles, limbs bent grotesquely – if they were still joined to the body at all.

'By God!' murmured Jack. 'By God!'

They were beaten already, he thought. And even as he thought it, he looked up and saw another group of French-men massing at the *Robuste*'s prow. Immediately he touched the fuse of his second grenade to the cord. 'One elephant,' he yelled.

'Not yet, Jack! Not—'

He was moving forward, muttering the count. He had to get closer, despite the shot now pinging around him. Plant a grenade on top of that mass of men and the fight would be over, surely.

'Jack!'

He ignored the call. He knew what he had to do. Wasn't he an Irish Grenadier now, to be sure, to be sure? Laughing, he lobbed on the fourth elephant, judging the ball had further to go. He laughed again as he heard the thud of it landing on the enemy's forecastle.

'Have that, bastards!' he shouted.

He only realized what he'd done when the first Frenchman landed beside him. They were close enough to shake hands, if the Frenchman's hadn't been occupied by a sword.

He didn't even have time to curse. He'd been quite alone, now there were twenty men beside him, and more were sliding down ropes to join them. The explosion came, some men shrieked above – the few of the enemy who hadn't vacated their forecastle in time. Only a few though as the majority had undoubtedly saved themselves by joining Jack on the quarterdeck of the *Sweet Eliza*. For a moment they all seemed as stunned as he was. Then that first Frenchman yelled, *'Con!'*, raising a wide-bladed cutlass high above his head.

There could be no hesitation. Jack stepped close, caught the man's wrist in both hands before the weapon could descend, then dropped, using his weight to pull man and weapon to the side and down. His back met another, hard, while the man he gripped yelled more obscenities and tried to jerk his arm free. The one behind was turning, undoubtedly also with steel in his hand, so Jack spun out, twirling his mercifully lighter opponent, smashing the two of them together. As they met, he released his grip, rolled away on his haunches. The cutlass banged into the deck where he'd been but now he was to the edge of the enemy group, with two other men turning to him. His hand reached for his sabre . . .

'Now!' came the cry. 'For England and the *Eliza*.'

The crew ran from the forecastle led by Engledue, Link bringing his men down from the poop. As Jack's opponents turned to face the threat, he scrambled away, reached the railing, at last had time to draw his sword there. The deck filled with swirling, yelling men. Pistols flashed, blades clashed and spears were thrust, some driving into flesh, some turned aside by axe or sword. He had no time to watch the scene, though, for the man whose blow he'd dodged before came for him again, the cutlass raised high; yet it was the other hand that concerned Jack first. It held a pistol and at five paces the Frenchman screamed, raised and fired. Jack could do no more than duck, felt heat and a sting in his left ear. There was no time to check any injury, not with the man running at him, and Jack's attention switched to the sword, his own rising before him. Strangely, it was the pistol that was thrust at him first and Jack, swinging his right leg back, his sword paralleling it, brought his left hand across to push the now harmless pistol aside.

Except it wasn't harmless, Jack realized as the bayonet blade on the pistol's muzzle sliced across the palm of his thrusting hand. 'Ayee,' he yelled, agonized, his opponent now bringing the cutlass over in a sweep to finish what his boarding pistol had started. But thrusting with such a short weapon had brought him close to Jack, closer than he should have been. Despite the sudden pain, he smashed the guard of his sword into the Frenchman's mouth.

The man staggered back, into the heart of the fray, stumbling, falling, causing one of his comrades to trip, and allowing McRae to finish him with a cutlass. Jack looked down at his palm. It was gouting blood, the cut deep and wide. Cursing, checking that no one was leaving the mêlée to seek him out, he whipped off the stock that tamed his hair, wrapped it around the hand and drew his tomahawk to hold it in place. With both weapons before him, he turned back to battle.

'Come on, then!' he screamed, charging in.

No doubt it was the number of French bodies upon the deck, and the relatively few British among them, but no sooner had he re-joined the fight than it suddenly ceased, the enemy seeming to give up as one, those who could running for their own ship's prow where it overhung the *Sweet Eliza*.

'They flee!' cried Captain Link. 'By God, we've won, boys.'

As the cheer faded, an Irish voice rose above it. 'They flee to fight again. We must follow or they'll stand off and blow us from the water. Look, lads!' Red Hugh was waving at the deck of the *Robuste*. All could see that those few who were helping their comrades back aboard were outnumbered by those backing their sails, trying to catch the wind and haul their ship clear while others were hacking at the grapplings that bound the two vessels together. More had picked up muskets, gone to the swivel guns that had yet to come into play. Instantly, Jack could see what was going to happen. Greed had lured the Frenchmen in, but once clear they would be able to do what they should have done in the beginning: reduce the ship and its crew to skeletons before boarding again to pick clean the bones.

Looking down, Jack saw that the *Eliza*'s first broadside had blasted a hole in the *Robuste*'s gundeck two portholes wide, and that some of the fleeing Frenchmen were scrambling through it three abreast.

'There, Red Hugh,' Jack yelled, seizing the man's arm, turning him. 'There lies our way.'

'You are in the right, lad. Are you sure you've not fought on a ship before?' A brief smile then the Irishman turned. 'Can you keep us snug to her, Captain?'

'I can.' Link's florid face was further coloured with powder and blood. 'I will.'

'Then,' he turned to the crew, 'Larbollians! You've fought for the *Sweet Eliza*, now fight for the prize. With me!' And thus leaving the starboard watch aboard to shoot and handle the ship, Red Hugh led twenty drinking companions and one Jack Absolute to board the enemy frigate.

The coat-tail of the last of the enemy had only just vanished but already someone had noticed the pursuit. Pistols cracked as Red Hugh stepped onto the *Robuste*. He drew back, turned to Jack. 'Lieutenant Absolute, would you be so good as to fetch us two grenades?'

'Certainly, Captain McClune. Which rack?'

'The bottom. Now it's us that don't want to damage our profits. So let's stink these Frenchies out.'

Jack crossed to the poop between shot being given by both sides. He returned in moments, an iron globe in each hand. 'Wrap your scarf around your mouth.' Red Hugh's voice was muffled beneath his own. Each man there wore one, Jack making do with the black stock from his neck. The Irishman, who'd taken the bombs while Jack masked himself, now handed one back. 'And will you wait till I throw this time?'

'I will.'

Fuses were lit, elephants counted and, on eight, grenades lobbed into the splintered hole. Shrieks came from within, sounds of men scattering. Then two dull crumps were heard and the world instantly filled with yellow, reeking smoke.

'We'll wait just a moment, lads,' announced Red Hugh, as two Frenchmen fell out of the hole, cursing, one slipping between the ships with a wail, the other dragged onboard the British ship and cudgelled into quietness.

'Now, I think,' came the soft voice, drowned by the yell as the crew of the *Sweet Eliza* stormed into the enemy's vessel.

At first, Jack could see nothing, partly due to the foul-smelling cloud that lingered, partly because his eyes were clogged with tears. Wiping them at least cleared the latter and he could see such Frenchmen that had survived the blast now running between the guns for the front and rear stairs.

'Stick close to them, lads,' cried Red Hugh, leading as he spoke.

The enemy were choking more than their masked pursuit, and blocked the stairs in blinded panic. Several were easily cut down and the rest chased up and onto the quarterdeck.

Jack, who'd engaged swords with one of the few

Frenchmen fighting until he too took to the stairs, paused to cough and catch breath. Most of the Larbollians had surged upwards and, for a moment, he was alone; yet not, it seemed, entirely so.

'Sir! Sir! For God's sake, help us.'

Jack couldn't for the life of him find where the voice was coming from. He looked up to the deck where the action sounded fierce, then along the gundeck to where he'd been. Nothing. Then he glanced down and stepped back, startled.

A grating covered the stairs that led from the gundeck to the main deck below. And there were at least half a dozen faces pressed to it.

'Sir!' That same voice came from a face in the middle of the grating. The one word led to a series of coughs before the gentleman – his accent showed him to be one – spoke again. 'Are you English, sir?'

'I am,' said Jack, crouching.

'Thank God. And you wear a uniform. So it is a ship of His Majesty's Navy that attacks?'

'Alas, no. We are a merchantman alone. But we are doing well enough.' He tipped his head to the sounds from above. 'And if you'll excuse me . . . I will return when the ship is ours.'

'Sir!' The coughs came again, then the voice, holding him. 'We are Englishmen here, too. Free us from this hell-hole and we will help you take the ship.'

'How many of you are there?'

'Forty. From the *Constantine* out of Liverpool, taken a month ago.'

His inclination was to rush up and continue the fight. But forty! Forty could swing it. He looked at the grating. A giant padlock held it.

'Is there a key?'

'They bring it when they feed us.'

Damn! Jack looked around the deck. There were a few gun

tools lying around, a hammer. But the lock and its mounting were undoubtedly strong; it would take too long and even his absence could cost the fight. He was about to abandon them when he remembered something. Bending to the lock, he scrabbled in his bullet pouch. 'Have you room to retire there, sir?'

'We have.'

'Then do so, if you please.'

Jack laid both fuses atop the lock. To his left was a metal plate. He held this in one hand, shoved the glowing cord into the fuses, placed the plate onto them and retired sharpish.

He didn't count elephants. The fuses exploded smartly enough. Stepping up, Jack peered through the smoke. The grating had been lifted by the explosion. Of the padlock there was no remnant. He called down, 'Bring your men up, sir.'

Those who emerged from below did so shakily, as if long deprived of the use of their legs. He could see that each had the paleness of confinement and several coughed; hardly surprising, for sulphurous smoke from McClune's grenades yet lingered.

'Briskly now,' said Jack, his hand on arms pulling them up, 'there's weapons a-plenty lying about.'

The assembly and arming took too long for Jack's liking. He could hear the fight was still furious above but he knew it could end in a moment, as it had on the *Eliza*'s deck. Yet he had to wait despite his desire to rush up. One man appearing would not alter the odds. Forty could win the ship.

At last they were ready. 'Gentlemen, I am an officer of the King. Will you follow me?'

'Huzzah,' came the cry, strong enough despite their gaol pallor.

Jack took the stairs two at a time and, as he emerged into the light, he bellowed, 'For England!'

At first all he saw was chaos. Men fought everywhere, in every way; some locked together like old comrades well met, beating at backs with pommels; others stood far apart, sword tips circling like flies in a sunbeam.

And then, drawn by the roars, the bodies, the red hair and blood, Jack saw his friend. He'd been isolated just before the *Robuste*'s poop deck, the numbers fighting there testifying it was the heart of the French defence. Three men dodged before him and there must have been more, for bodies lay at his feet. In that brief moment, he could see the Irishman's left-handed skill with his sabre. The enemy were finding it hard to attack. He was steering one opponent into another, always to his own right, guarded side, making their blows awkward. And yet, as he watched, he saw what Red Hugh, preoccupied, could not: a fourth man, emerging from the aft cabin, a belaying pin raised above that wild red hair.

Jack's attack had emerged onto the quarterdeck at the forecastle stair; he knew he was too far away to get there in time. Unless . . .

The fight before him suddenly parted, like the sea before Moses. In a moment, there was passage forward. Half running, half sliding – for the deck was slick with blood – he got as far as he could before the club reached the height from which Jack knew it would descend. His sword went into his left hand, his right pulling the tomahawk from his belt. There was no time to think. He could only do what Até had taught him to do during the long winter in the forest: brace, breathe, look and throw.

The blade took the man on the shoulder. He reeled away, lost again to the swirl of battle.

Jack noted then what his Irish comrade must already have seen: the *Robuste*'s resistance centred on that poop deck, where the white flag of the Bourbon flew. It was where the French had gathered in numbers – and where those numbers were telling against what remained of the *Sweet Eliza*'s boarding party. 'With me,' called Jack, his sword lifted high. The *Constantine*'s crew followed him with a shout.

By the time Jack had cut his way there, Red Hugh's opponents were down to two. 'Heh,' yelled Jack, stepping in, his own blade circling to lift one of theirs. The man was surprised, stepping back to trip over the body of another with a tomahawk stuck in his shoulder. Taking advantage, Red Hugh feinted high, cut low and slid the sabre blade across his man's chest. With a shriek he too fell backwards, joined the one who'd fallen before Jack, both kicking frantically to drive themselves into the shelter of the poop cabin.

'Jack!' The Irishman's smile was wide and wild, his beard redder for the blood that had streamed down his face from a cut to his crown. 'And where did you find these boyos?'

Suddenly, the numbers were even and the French were giving way under the onslaught.

'Recruited 'em down below,' gasped Jack. 'Can you use 'em?'

'I can, lad, and that now. For if we take this,' he tapped his bloodied sabre on the poop deck, 'we take the ship.'

Jack looked. Twin stairs led to the deck above. 'Shall we?' He gestured with his sword to the left.

Red Hugh waved to the right. 'Last to their colour buys the first beer in Bristol?'

'Agreed.'

Each turned. But Jack's delay in bending to retrieve his tomahawk meant that men from the *Constantine*, their blood up, preceded him. Two died attempting the stair but two more forced their way up and Jack followed. He saw the flagpole immediately through a swirl of bodies, the colour flapping. A glance right told him that the Irishman had chosen the more congested route. There was a way open to Jack, carved by the men before him. He would be first to the pole! If he could just get past the man who guarded it.

That man was dressed more gaudily than his crew, in a bright blue coat studded with silver decorations, a red silk neckerchief at his throat and a tricorn upon his head. As he moved closer, Jack recognized him. It was the man he'd talked with before the battle – and he had since donned the uniform of a captain.

Jack brought his sabre guard up to his lips in a swift salute. '*Bonjour, mon capitaine.*'

The man's eyes fixed on Jack. '*Ah, le soldat! Que désirez-vous?*'

It didn't seem right to be speaking the enemy's language. 'Your ship, if you wouldn't mind. I'll trade you a piece of salt cod for it.'

The Frenchman's English obviously wasn't too impoverished. '*Merde*,' he said, reaching into his belt. He was cocking the pistol when Jack attacked, striking down hard, hitting the weapon's barrel, knocking the gun from his hand. The Frenchman's sabre then struck at Jack's left side. Parrying hard as he moved right, he drove the captain's blade against the bulwark, pinned it there, his other hand raising the retrieved tomahawk. The moment he did, he felt the man's grip on his sword slacken.

He could speak French again now. '*C'est finis, monsieur.*'

The Frenchman sighed. '*Oui, c'est finis.*' He pulled his sword slowly back, threat no longer in it or in him. Reversing it, he held the grip out. '*C'est finis*,' he said again, mournfully.

Jack pushed the tomahawk into his belt, took the proffered sword. Then he used it to slash at the ropes of the white flag of France. It plunged down, to the cries of those still defending the deck, to the joy of those who had stormed it. The fighting carried on in pockets for a moment, then even that, too, died. Men who had lately been trying to kill each other were suddenly standing still, weapons lowering to the floor.

Jack reversed the sword again, offered it back. '*Monsieur?*'

The Captain reached forward, stumbling slightly. Grasping the hilt brought their faces close together. 'Atchoo,' he sneezed, as he had during their earlier conversation.

'*Santé*,' said Jack, wiping the droplets from his face.

– SIX –
Fever

Hands were on him and cloth was being pulled over him. What kind? Of his many nightmares, the worst was of being sewn into a canvas coffin.

He tried to lift his hands to hold it off, but they would not move. Then something hard was pressed to his mouth; liquid spilled out. Beer, he thought, joyfully – until he tasted it. Water! Foul stuff! He never drank water. Fish fucked in it. *He* fucked in it, or had anyway, in Newport. He let it dribble out of his mouth.

'You see, sir, he rejects it. Another sign that I am correct.'

Whose voice was that? Who was he addressing? Who else was there?

'Let me up!' Jack demanded, flapping at the hands on the cloth.

'He stirs.' A different voice came, one he recognized. It belonged to a friend.

Jack's eyelids fluttered open. Men peered down at him. He knew them all. But the only one he could name was Red Hugh McClune.

'And you'll observe, there's no yellow in his eyes. So it's never Yellow Jack.'

'And since when did you qualify as a surgeon, sir?'

That was it. The first man who'd spoken was the ship's surgeon.

'I am not one,' Red Hugh smiled. 'But did my father not die before I was born? In my country, any so orphaned are compensated with a special gift for the cure of all fevers. Means I can recognize the grippe when I see it.'

Jack wasn't certain he'd heard correctly. He'd been slightly deaf in his left ear ever since a French bullet had grazed it. But the third man looking down had heard well enough.

'Superstition!' roared Captain Link. 'You ask us to be ruled by . . . peasant fancies?'

The Irishman spoke softly. 'Sir, you put an insult upon my country once before. I only let it pass because our needs pressed. Now I warn you—'

'And I warn you!' Link's jowls shaded a deeper purple as his voice rose. 'I command here. I will not be threatened. And the crew will not support you in this. They fear the contagion as much as we do. They held their meeting and agreed: all sick from the *Eliza* and the prize to be put ashore in the Azores. There's a hospital on Corvo.'

'A plague pit, you mean, where every illness flourishes. Of a hundred men who enter those places with one disease, ninety die of something else entirely.'

The surgeon waved at the bunk. 'If this is not Yellow Jack, sir, then it is camp or gaol fever and we must be rid of him.'

Camp fever! Though he had only partially followed the conversation so far, this was a term Jack understood. He had seen camp fever at Quebec – hundreds of men in their tents, sweating, crying out, talking to the ghosts they were soon to join. Jack shivered, suddenly as cold as he'd been over-heated before. 'Bla . . . bla . . . blanket,' he stuttered.

Red Hugh tucked one to his chin. 'I tell you, yer man has the grippe, serious enough but never typhus. I've been in both camps and gaols and know *that* contagion when I see it.

71

Those who have passed their crisis on the *Robuste*, and from the *Constantine*, are all recovering well.'

'Aye, with over a third of both crews dead. I will not let it spread to mine.'

'Your men are sick, Captain, whether they are showing it yet or no. Jack here is just the first of many.'

Of course. Jack remembered now, before the illness struck him, the skeletal English prisoners he'd led up from the hold, near half of them now on the ocean floor, alongside the Captain of the *Robuste* and a good measure of his crew. It had transpired that they'd only tried to capture the *Sweet Eliza* to offload their dying. But even had they won, death would not be so cozened, it seemed.

'And that's why we will put him ashore.'

'Will you not consider an alternative?' the Irishman said.

'Which is?'

'Sail for Lisbon. 'Tis a fair city, not a plague island, where proper treatment can be had. Offload your sick into quarantine and let the prize agents there handle the *Robuste*.'

Link growled. 'I told you, McClune, I am taking my prize to Bristol.'

'Do not the regulations state that prizes should be dealt with at the nearest port?'

'Damn your regulations, sir!' Link glared. 'The *Robuste*'s too valuable. I've been cheated by those jackals in Lisbon once before and will not be again.'

That's right, Jack thought. They had a prize that had taken at least three other ships. Its holds were crammed. If it was not a treasure ship, it was laden and rich enough.

Link continued, 'So to Bristol we will return. The sick who recover will follow on as best they may – from Corvo.'

Red Hugh sighed, shaking his head. 'I can see, Captain, that you are trying to claim back that Lieutenant's share you so grudgingly gave my young friend here. But as his representative, I cannot allow that to happen. And since I rather thought this might be the way of it I have taken precautions. These are only the first of them.'

The Irishman had stepped away from the table. Jack had to look hard and then again to be sure. But it was true – pistols had appeared in the man's hands. He waved them. 'You will be good enough to vacate this cabin.'

No sound came for a long moment, Link's colour darkening still further. 'You mutiny, sir?'

'I do not. This is not your ship but the *Robuste*, which you would not have taken without yer man lying there. So I think he is entitled to rest in the Captain's cabin.'

Link was apoplectic. 'But I am the law aboard either ship.'

'*Silent enim leges inter arma.* I think that's it. Cannot recall who that is. If our young friend here wasn't delirious, he'd be able to tell us, being the more recent classical scholar.' He waved a muzzle to the door. 'Now, gentlemen, if you please.'

The surgeon retreated smartly, Link slower and snarling. 'By God, I'll muster the men and have you out of here in moments.'

'You are at liberty to try. But you might want to point something out to them.' Jack watched Red Hugh lean away, heard a muzzle clink on other metal. 'As I said, pistols are just the first of my precautions. And since your men have seen the effect of my little friends here,' the tapping came again, 'you could find them a wee bit reluctant to back ye.'

Any rejoinder Link might have made was cut off by the slamming of the door. Jack could hear his now muffled threats, his heavy tread on the stair, his shouted orders. 'Beer,' he whispered.

'Sorry, lad, it's water for you and plenty of it.' He lifted a ladle and Jack's head; reluctantly, he drank. 'We had a rainfall last night so at least this is fresh.'

'Will he . . .' Jack muttered. 'Are we . . .'

'Safe? Hardly. But I think my dissuaders here might have their effect. And Link's not loved. He'll fume and rage and attempt to starve us out – then he'll sail both ships for Bristol and try to have me hanged when we arrive.'

Hotter than he'd ever been, the sweat gushing from him, Jack yet shook with cold. 'Am I going to die?' he whispered.

The Irishman smiled. 'Did you not hear me say how I have the power of the Cure?' He reached for his hat and waved it above Jack. 'Did you never notice the mistletoe? It's not mere decoration. Makes a fine tea. And then . . . let me see.' He searched in the hat band then produced what looked like a hazelnut. 'Now, we'll just have to see if we can find a spider for this.'

'A spider?' Jack shook his head. 'Of course – spider needs a house.' He giggled as his eyelids slowly closed, the Latin Red Hugh had quoted accompanying his drift back into the fog. The Irishman had been right – Jack did indeed know it.

'Cicero,' he muttered. 'Laws are silent in time of war.'

'How fare ye, Lieutenant Absolute?'

'Well, sir,' Jack replied. 'Well, indeed.'

It was an exaggeration. Since that day the week before – eight days into his fever – when what Red Hugh had termed his 'crisis' had passed, Jack had felt a little better with each dawn. Full health was yet some weeks off, but the fever had finally broken, even if he could do little more than sit in a chair and watch the *Robuste* power through the seas. It was a fine sight, all sails that flew filled with the wind that had driven them up from Portugal and which showed no sign of abating.

'Glad to hear it.' Engledue turned, calling out, 'Let's take in the forestay, Lavalier. Then braille up the main course and spanker, if you please.' He turned back to Jack. 'We'll find ourselves broaching-to, if we don't hearken to that wind.'

He tipped his hat, walked off. Jack may not have understood ships or the terms by which they were sailed, but he understood two things clearly: Engledue, with his boots on his own quarterdeck, had shed years to become the sailor he'd obviously once been, and he was using those skills to slow the French privateer so he could keep the *Sweet Eliza* astern to larboard and in range of a telescope.

Jack glanced back. It was a speck in the distance to his naked eye. He understood why Engledue was keeping them apart. Link would have been furious to see Jack Absolute or Red Hugh McClune upon the deck when he'd ordered Engledue to storm the cabin and take them.

But Engledue had needed the Irishman's physician skills to help with the crew that had been cobbled together from the *Sweet Eliza* the *Robuste* and the *Constantine.* Near half of them had died. All said it would have been many more without Red Hugh's insistence on rest and rainwater.

The Irishman had administered as well as he could while reserving special treatments for his special patient: mistletoe tea, sulphurous poultices made up from his stock of gunpowder, and most especially the nut that he'd tied to Jack's neck with a blue woollen thread and insisted was never taken off.

'It has the power, lad, trust me,' he said. 'Sure, hasn't the same thing saved the McClunes three times in the last hundred years?'

Jack hadn't been hallucinating. The nut did indeed serve as house to a spider. He sometimes thought he could hear the creature scratching at its prison walls but his weakened fingers had failed to prise open the caulking with which it had been sealed. Now he held it, looked at the water and thought of Até, his blood brother. The Mohawk would have liked the nut because it would have given him the chance to quote from his infernal *Hamlet,* the only entertainment they'd had during that winter in the cave: but since he wasn't there, and Jack found himself missing the savage, he stared at the horizon and quoted for him: 'Oh I could be

75

bounded in a nutshell, and count myself the King of infinite space, were it not that I have bad dreams.'

'I thought you weren't a praying man, lad.' Red Hugh had approached quietly as Jack stared at the waves.

'I'm not. Just talking to myself.'

He offered a bowl which Jack accepted, though he sighed at the savoury smell. It seemed heartless to be supping upon his old comrade Jeremiah the goat, even if it did aid his recovery. He sipped. 'How fare the rest of your patients?'

The Irishman rolled his shoulders. 'Two more dead in the night. But at least the last five have had their crisis and survived it. So we're not doing too badly. Unlike them.' He nodded back to the *Sweet Eliza*.

'What do you mean? How can you know?' Jack feared the Irishman was going to start talking about the senses he'd acquired as the seventh son of a seventh son or some such bollocks but the answer was more prosaic.

'Why do you think Engledue keeps holding us back?'

'The *Eliza*'s a slower ship.'

'Aye. But the crew are telling me she's sailing even slower because she's being sailed poorly. Now, Link is every kind of poltroon but he's canny of sea, wind and sail. Something's up. Engledue's slowing us so we can find out what.' He nodded to starboard. 'See that cloud? That's the coast of France, at the tip of Normandy. Pass that, and it's a clear run to Bristol. A few days, I'm told, if this wind keeps up.'

'England. Home,' said Jack, feeling his chest flutter as he said the words.

'England, anyway.' That darkness that could sometimes eclipse the light even in Red Hugh's eyes came.

'Do you go on to Ireland straightaway?'

'Ireland?' The darkness faded. 'Sure, did I not leave my poor country twenty years ago to make my fortune and vow not to go back until it was made?'

'But the prize money. You said—'

'Unhappily, the *Robuste* has not proved a treasure ship, though I've no doubt she'll pay handsomely enough. Still and all, it'll be a teardrop in yon ocean. McClune Hall is mortgaged nine times over. And I've other owings.' He slapped Jack's shoulder. 'What do you say, lad? Shall we post an advertisement in the *Bristol Record*, gather a crew of cut-throats and turn privateer? Three more voyages like this one might make a dint in the auld debt.' He laughed. 'Once this story gets turned to a song, won't they flock to the brave Grenadiers of the *Sweet Eliza*?' He began to whistle.

'I'm sorry, but if I ever set foot on a deck again it will be too soon. And as for elephants . . .' Jack shuddered.

'Now, lad, and after all the fun we've had?' Red Hugh smiled.

Jack looked past his friend's shoulder. The slowing of the *Robuste* had brought the *Sweet Eliza* and Link a little closer. 'Fun that will be leading us to the yardarm perhaps. Isn't that the punishment for mutiny?'

Red Hugh looked where Jack did. 'Now now. The good Captain will listen to reason. I have no doubt upon it.'

Captain Link would not listen to reason. For the very good reason that he was dead.

'Three days,' said the Scot, McRae, when he arrived in the Eliza's jolly boat. He had taken on the running of the ship. 'The grippe got him and didnae let him go. Despite *his* caring.' He nodded down to the boat, where Barabbas, the Negro, rested on an oar.

Jack tipped his head. 'Link's slave had the tending of him?'

'Aye. Never left his side. Despite the screams and curses and the last two days of whimpering. I took the Cap'n for a man of stronger will. He made more noise than any of the other sick.'

They all looked at each other, then looked away. Jack glanced down, into the boat. Barabbas held his gaze. Jack shivered, took a breath. 'What will happen to him? Will he still be a slave to the Links?'

'Now there's a strange thing,' replied McRae, 'for didn't the Cap'n give the Darkie his manumission before he died? We thought he was too delirious to write but there was his signature, clear as day. And witnessed by the surgeon.' He paused, sucked at his teeth. 'Which was a wee bit strange, ken. Seeing as he'd been dead himself near a week.' He shook his head. 'So, like the Bible story, our Lord dies and Barabbas goes free – and immediately expressed a desire to serve with this crew.'

Each was still finding something else to study. Finally, Red Hugh spoke. 'So, does Link feed the fishes now?'

'He doesnae. He was a shareholder in the company and an alderman of the city.' McRae smiled. 'So we've given him one last taste of the grog he so loved. He's pickled and waits in a barrel below.'

Jack tried to find anything sad in the situation. He failed. 'Well,' he said, 'at least with his last act Link has made some reparation for his evil trade.'

'What, man? Freeing Barabbas?'

Jack smiled. 'Spoiling the liquor. No man will be turned into a slave for *that* cask of Guinea rum.'

— SEVEN —

Ghosts

He lay there, back pressed into wood, bayonet already in his hand. He didn't remember drawing it nor descending the path to reach this log barrier. Night and mist obscured his sight and his fingers were numb with cold. All that *was* clear was the sound that must have halted him there – footsteps on shale, coming ever closer, up from the beach below. Instinct had prompted him to unsheathe his weapon. Instinct would tell him what to do next.

And yet, when he heard the voices, recognized the enemy tongues – French, Abenaki – instinct failed. He could not move. Even when a leg came over the log, when both his duty and his need urged him to the attack, he couldn't. All he could do was drop the bayonet, press himself back into the rough wood. Perhaps they might not notice him if he made himself very small.

Another leg followed, a body, a face. And though he'd only seen this face so briefly on this same path up the cliffs of Quebec, on another night long ago, he recognized it. He'd never forget the face of the young Frenchman he'd killed. The first man he'd ever killed.

And yet here he was, walking past, without a glance down. Other men came over, other victims. He'd killed them all, these shadows flowing over the log. Here were the two cavalrymen he'd stabbed on the Plains of Abraham. Three Abenaki followed, slain on the same field, then and later. Then three more came, French again but not regular soldiers, *coureurs de bois*, in their furs and tasselled caps, the last one still clutching the arrow in his chest that Jack had shot into him. Yet he was laughing with his companions, following them up the slope. Finally, men he could not recognize but wearing the varied garb of privateers came, marching on into the dark.

Jack breathed, a long exhalation of relief. Though they each bore terrible wounds, which he had inflicted, it didn't seem to inconvenience any of them. They were alive, all these men he thought he'd killed. And even though their deaths had been necessary, in battle and fair fight and for survival – his own, and that of his comrades – he thought it was better that they were still alive. And so, presumably, did they.

The idea made him chuckle. He had better be moving on, away from his dead. He was just beginning to rise when he heard another slip of shale from below him. He sank back just as a body swathed in red serge straddled the log, dropped his side of it.

This was wrong. This man wore the King's uniform. Jack hadn't killed anyone on his own side. And then he remembered and, just as he did, the man turned and looked at him.

'How do, Jack?'

'Craster.'

The sight of him brought all kinds of memories. Cousins, both Absolutes, Jack and Craster had grown up together and loathed each other from the very beginning. Yet loathing had turned to something far worse; for when this brute ravished the girl Jack had adored, Jack had tried to kill Craster at the Vauxhall Pleasure Gardens in revenge. They had even fought a duel, of sorts, their schoolboy efforts dwarfed by the larger event, when Jack's father had killed His Majesty's Minister, Lord Melbury. What the actions of that night had set in motion! At the least, all the men who had preceded his cousin up the slope would still be alive – if only Craster Absolute had not raped Clothilde Guen.

He studied his cousin now. Thinner than he remembered him. Haggard. A winter in a cave will do that, Jack knew by experience. Then he remembered what he had done to this man. He had not killed him, merely marooned him in the middle of the Canadian wilderness with his wits, a knife, enough food to last only a week, and something else. He'd left him there with some . . . one else.

'Fancy some breakfast, Jack?' His cousin spoke in the accent they'd both largely shed, that of their shared Cornish boyhood. And he had something in his hand, hidden behind his body. A pasty?

'That'd be proper,' Jack said, and watched as the hand began to emerge from behind his cousin's back. It came slowly, as did Jack's scream, when he saw that what Craster Absolute was offering him was a human head; an Abenaki head, grasped by the warrior's top-knot above another face Jack recognized . . .

He thought it was his scream that woke him, no longer bounded by his dream. Or perhaps it was the hardness of wood, because he'd forced the thin mattress off the frame and splintering slats dug into him. Or it may have been the cold, the blankets were all thrown about. Whatever it was, it took a while to halt the scream, until the thin window coverings could be ripped aside and dawn's wretched light reveal to him a room cleared of ghosts.

Footsteps came – up stairs, not shale. He crossed to the bed, managed to get the mattress centred on the frame and a blanket half across him before the door opened.

'Awright, my lover?' Clary stood there, a gated lantern in her hand. She was across to him swiftly, the lantern put

81

down, her hand reaching to caress his forehead. 'So hot, Master Jack,' she said. 'Shall I fetch 'ee some water?'

'Ale,' Jack replied. It was early but he only needed to quench his thirst. Small beer would do him no harm. And the water in this inn had a curious taint.

'I'll fetch it right away,' Clary said, but did not move, her hand still to his head, the other moving to the opening of his shirt. 'So hot,' she said again, in a different way, as her hand slipped inside.

His own came up to meet and hold it. 'Ale, Clary.' He let go her hand and she withdrew it reluctantly.

'Are ye sure, Master Jack?' She was twisting a curl back under her Abigail's bonnet. 'S' just everyone's still abed, like, and . . .'

He had made a mistake the week before. A relapse in his fever had forced Red Hugh to leave him at the Llandoger Trow tavern on Bristol Docks and journey only he knew where, vowing to return soon. He'd taken a kiss and, this first course accepted, the main meal was immediately proposed. He blamed his weakness for the result, unable to resist or, indeed, to take much of an active part. He was determined not to fall even thus far again. It was not that Clary was unattractive. She was slim at hip, small but well formed at bosom, with lascivious lips and a low gurgle of a laugh that lured. If she was none too clean, well, neither was he. As his recovery progressed, he'd been ever more tempted . . . and then he'd hear that same low gurgle, counterpointed by many groans, somewhere in the attic rooms above him. And some mornings Clary would appear with a new bonnet or bracelet, a new tortoiseshell comb for her hair. He didn't blame her at all, a maid's wages would be poor. Yet to succumb again did not seem quite . . . honourable.

However, Clary took his musing silence as a signal. Her hand returned, lower, and he groaned. Thus encouraged, she lifted the blanket, her hand sliding down still further,

'Course, if you are still feeling weak, sir, your Clary could be as . . . obliging as she was afore, if'n . . . oh, Master Jack!' Her fingers had slipped all the way down and a big smile came, before head followed hand under the blanket.

'Clary . . .' he said, trying to sound firm. Then both reacted to the cry from the corridor, a heavier tread that made the floorboards creak. Clary emerged, but was still bent over the bed, when the door opened.

'What are you about there, girl?'

Mrs Hardcastle, the tavern's landlady, stood in the door-way, making it seem small. When Jack saw who it was, he sighed. Temptation came in various forms.

'Lieutenant Absolute, dear sir! Say the fever has not returned.' She marched in, elbowing Clary aside. 'A jug of water, quick there!'

The maid hovered, reluctant to cede the ground. 'The master's asked for ale.'

'Then why are you still here? Be fast about it, you lazy slut.' She turned back, did not see the tongue stuck out at her before Clary left. 'I heard your cry, dear man, and hastened even thus from my bed.'

Mrs Hardcastle gestured to the loose gown that just contained her. She was built along similar lines to the Widow Simkin, with a bosom Jack could have rested his pint pot upon. Perhaps it was the way this was so often thrust at him, or the resemblance to his recent Quaker lover, but Jack had, with more firmness, already declined what was only slightly more subtly on offer. To begin with, there was a Mr Hardcastle somewhere about, the innkeeper. Yet even if the husband was drunk and unconscious by supper, it was not that which finally deterred Jack.

With little to do but lie and think, he'd mused on his recent history of both death and love. In a little less than two years, he'd killed perhaps a dozen men and made love to just two women, a disparity in numbers he dreamed of correcting. And yet . . . Those two had both been older than him by many years. Their experience had taught him well and he had been a diligent, delighted student. But he had loved neither Fanny Harper nor the Widow Simkin. The only girl he had loved, and in anything like an honourable fashion, had been Clothilde Guen, the goldsmith's daughter of Thrift Street, Soho. Her innocence and stirring sensuality were a vivid contrast to the voracious widow and the skilled courtesan. What was she doing now? he wondered with a sigh. Absolute gold had expiated Craster's crime, enabled her to marry a man she did not love for the sake of respectability. She had probably borne him two children by now.

Mrs Hardcastle, with a deep bend to gather the bed clothes, offered further glimpses of what could be his. The maid returned, set down the beer and began a tussle over a blanket. For a long moment they had it stretched out above him, obscuring his view of the door, but he had no need to see to recognize the speaker.

'The divil! Sure and that's not a shroud you're laying over my poor friend?'

'About bloody time,' said Jack.

'Am I in the nick, dear heart?' Red Hugh strode into the room. 'Shoo, you vultures, and leave my comrade to recover his strength.'

'I can assure you, sir,' Mrs Hardcastle had drawn herself up, more like an enraged goose than a vulture, 'that we—'

'Be calm, pray,' interrupted the Irishman, 'for if my friend has been too sick or too particular to take advantage of what you would tender him, I'd be delighted to hold up the honour of the Lords of McClune with each of you, one after the other, or both at once, as you may choose.'

'You . . . you damn'd potato face!' Mrs Hardcastle, firmly putting away what had been on offer, swept furiously from the room.

Clary, however, lingered. 'Shall I prepare a room for your honour?' she said, with the smallest of curtsys.

'It would have to be a very *large* room, to be sure,' he guffawed while Jack groaned. 'But alas, my jewel, I am come to collect and not to stay. So if you'd just bring the twin to that,' he pointed at the jug of beer, '– for what's my poor comrade to drink? – then we'll trouble you no more.'

'Oh, I'm sure *you'd* give me no trouble at all, sir.' She stared quite brazenly at the Irishman's groin, then swept out with that familiar gurgling laugh.

Red Hugh gazed after her. 'The trollop! Sure, I'm tempted to take that room. I am certain they rent by the hour here.' He turned to Jack. 'As I am also certain, my lad, that you've been having a fine auld time.'

'Actually, I have not.'

'Too sick?'

'No, I am quite recovered.' Jack sighed. 'Too . . .' he waved a hand. 'I have been musing on honour.'

'Ah, honour!' With a leap, Red Hugh was instantly lying beside Jack on the bed, snapping at least two struts in the process. With his hands behind his head he continued, 'Did I never tell you my favourite poem?' He coughed:

> *'She offered her honour*
> *He honoured her offer*
> *And for the rest of the night*
> *It was honour and offer.'*

He roared and, after a moment, Jack laughed too. 'And is that how you honour *all* ladies?'

'Indeed not. There was one . . .' That darkness came into his eyes again. 'But another hour for sorry tales, eh?' He swung off the bed. 'Where's that damn'd beer? We must toast my endeavours. Ah, there you are, you minx.'

Clary returned, placing a jug beside the other on the small

table. She looked as though she would speak but a shriek from Mrs Hardcastle summoned her. With a distinct sway of her hips, she left.

Red Hugh watched her go again. 'I'm certain I would not have lasted a week of that temptation. Probably not much over the hour.' He made for the jugs, handed one to Jack, the pewter pots disdained. 'I never took you for a puritan, Jack. Your own tales of actresses and Quakers hardly indicated it.'

'I am not one. But . . .' He stopped. He had his own sorry tale. He had never mentioned Clothilde to his companion.

Red Hugh was studying him. 'Well then,' he said eventually, 'your health! Now tell me, lad, before I give you all my news, what are your plans?'

Jack had thought of several. He had his duty to his King, even if the dispatches he bore were half a year beyond their expectation. His regiment? He had no thought as to where the 16th Light Dragoons and its commander, John Burgoyne, might be. He'd left them training in London in the summer of 1759 when he'd been sent as King's Messenger to Wolfe at Quebec. That was over eighteen months before. His father? Well, Sir James would probably still be at war in Germany, waiting out the repercussions of his slaying of Lord Melbury in the duel at Vauxhall, the duel Jack had provoked by daring to woo Melbury's mistress, Fanny Harper. While his mother . . .

The thought of her uplifted him. 'I suppose I go to London.'

'How?'

'How?' It was a strange question. 'By horse, naturally. I am a cavalryman not a bloody Grenadier.'

'Jack, you're swaying on the edge of that bed. I think anything livelier is beyond you. And why do you go?'

'To deliver—'

'Out of date messages.'

'And to report—'

'To a regiment that is probably at war somewhere else.'

Jack was starting to be annoyed with the badgering. 'And what would you have me do, sir?'

'Come to Bath.'

'Bath?'

'It's where I've been this last week.'

Jack laughed. It was such an absurd idea. 'And what would I do in Bath? Take the waters?'

'Exactly. It's what invalids do. And as your physician, I advise you that galloping to London and then, no doubt, throwing yourself onto the delights of the town will undo all my good work and the work of our little friend here.' He tapped the nutshell still on Jack's neck. 'You can send the dispatches on with an officer fit to bear them, and word to family and regiment, who will summon you if duty calls and your health permits. Meanwhile, you can recover properly from an illness that has nearly killed you.'

The man had a point. And Jack had always wanted to visit a city so dedicated to pleasure. 'But what of you? I thought business and family were both drawing you away.'

'Now isn't that the most marvellous thing? For haven't I discovered that the two of them are also met? And are they not the both of them in Bath?'

Jack was finding the Irish-isms a little hard to follow. 'Does that mean they are or they aren't?'

'They are.' The Irishman beamed. 'I've a deal to clinch in the city that might go halfway to undoing my family's entire woe. And now my cousin has just arrived there to seal my happiness.'

'Your cousin?'

'Laetitia Fitzpatrick, the most beautiful girl in all Ireland.'

'*Is* she?'

'She is.' The jug was halted halfway to the lips. 'But you can take that gleam from your eye, Absolute. For you'll be getting nowhere near her, sure.'

Jack frowned. 'Why not, pray?'

Red Hugh laid a hand on Jack's shoulder. 'Lad, you have told me your history of courtesans and widow women and the like. And did I not discover you just now with two tavern hellions fighting over your favours? I've told you, my boy, you remind me strangely of myself when I was your age,' he smiled, 'which is the main reason I'll be keeping you far away from my lovely cousin.'

Jack laid down his beer. 'Sir, I agree that some of my actions may not always have been entirely honourable. But I would remind you that, youth aside, I am also the son of a baronet and raised a gentleman.' He flushed. 'And as such, I know how to behave with a lady.'

Red Hugh regarded him thoughtfully. 'Well, Jack, I shall weigh your future conduct against your past misdeameanours.' He smiled. 'Still, seeing as we'll all be neighbours I suppose there's every chance that you may meet her anyway.'

'Neighbours?'

'Aye, lad. My cousin and her guardian – Mrs O'Farrell, another cousin of mine and her aunt – as befits relatives of the Earl of Clare, have taken a house in a new construction called the Circus. It's in the Upper Town, where everything is sparkling and bright. They're even offering one of the houses to King George when he visits in a fortnight. And haven't I found rooms for us in the very same circle?'

'Such rooms cannot have come cheap. How have we paid for them?'

'And why do you think you rest at the Llandoger Trow? This is where all the prize agents gather. They have assessed a lieutenant's share of the *Robuste* at near two hundred pounds, not the five thousand of a treasure ship but handsome enough. They have advanced each of us forty. Which reminds me.' From a pocket came a sack of coin. 'There's over twenty guineas there, after our Bath accommodation expenses.'

Jack weighed the bag in his hand. Twenty guineas to add to the thirty he'd got for the ermine, which he'd sold to a Bristol furrier. It was a lot of money, over a year of lieutenant's pay. And he had dreamed of all the things on which to spend his share of the prize. Why not begin with a little luxury in the pleasure capital of England?

He raised his jug and toasted. 'Well, then, sir – to Bath!'

'Bath!'

Now he was committed, all his concerns dropped away. Messages would be sent, regiment and family placated for a time. But the best thing, he realized, looking around the room lately haunted by his ghosts, was that in whatever adventure lay ahead, no dead man would plague his dreams at the end of it.

— EIGHT —

All the World's a Stage

Rain on the road and a horse's thrown shoe delayed them. By the time they reached Bath, Red Hugh insisted they proceed direct to the theatre. They were dropped a few streets away, the carriage sent on to their lodgings with their sea chests.

'But why the hurry?' Jack grumbled, as the Irishman dragged him through the crowd.

'I hate to miss the beginning of a play,' came the reply. 'And besides, I told my cousins I'd accompany them to their box.'

Jack stopped and two men bumped into him, before cursing and passing around. 'I can't meet your cousin like this.' He gestured to his uniform, the ghastly one he'd worn since Quebec and during his illness, ill-fitting and stained. 'My good one's in my trunk.'

Red Hugh had barely turned. 'It makes no nevermind. I have no intention of introducing you to Laetitia tonight – if at all.'

'Nevertheless, one can't appear at the theatre dressed in rags.'

'I wouldn't worry too much, you Macaroni. For I doubt we'll get a ticket we're so late. Now come!'

They did get tickets but only in the sixpenny gallery,

among those whose clothes aped Jack's in poverty. Red Hugh, as ever, stood out in the quality of his attire, Jack feeling like a shabby servant beside him. Once they had forced themselves onto the benches – and Jack was sure he would not last an act if the fat woman next to him did not remove her elbow from his ribs – the Irishman leaned forward to view the crowd below.

'Is she there?' Jack said, trying not to sound too curious.

Red Hugh leaned back. 'Their box is unoccupied at present.' He shrugged. 'Perhaps Mrs O'Farrell has been unable to lure Laetitia away from her books.'

'She's studious, is she?'

A snort came. 'I use the term books loosely. Laetitia's only flaw is that she is obsessed with *novels*.'

'A flaw I share. I am myself fond of Richardson, Gaunt—'

'No, no, Jack. Not those kind. *Romantic* novels! *The Tarnished Heart. Sundered by the Moor. By Bower and Byre.*' He shuddered. 'These tales all seem to concern a wealthy heiress, forced to marry aged and ugly Lord How-Do-Ye-Do. So she elopes with impoverished Ensign Who's-Me-Father instead. Lives in a byre, starves prettily to death in a bower, no doubt. Or t'other way round.' He shook his head in disgust. 'You know, I've heard the maid declare that, whatever our uncle, the Earl's, plans for a noble alliance, she will choose for herself and let rank and money go hang. Why, no doubt she would even consider you, a mere baronet's son, too elevated by far. She will marry for love, she says, and the poorer the suitor the better! Imagine such a thing. This, sir, is what comes of reading.'

Before Jack could counter that the words 'mere' and 'baronet' should not be placed in conjunction, the small orchestra, which had been playing various country airs, now struck up something more martial. The audience sighed and settled. 'Did I never tell you, lad,' said Red Hugh excitedly, 'that I played upon the Dublin stage myself in my youth?

Minor roles,' he circled a wrist, 'tragic parts. At Smock Alley, where your own mother so shone.' His own eyes gleamed as he leaned forward. 'Ah, the play's the thing.'

Some plays might be. This one was not, Jack thought, after a bare few scenes. He had never seen *Henry IV Part I* before but he did not think it the greatest of Shakespeare's works, alternating uneasily between the blown rhetoric of the court and the farce of the tavern. The playing, too, was highly variable. Perhaps he was spoiled by Drury Lane and Covent Garden where his mother had taken him regularly, but the innovations of Garrick in the style of acting, where declamation had given way to a more intimate, natural manner, seemed not yet to have reached the Provinces. The younger performers were the worst. They essentially faced front and shouted. It was all noise. Only a couple of the more experienced players engaged. Falstaff had a generous stomach to suit the knight and a way with his words both amusing and melancholy; while in the small part of Mistress Quickly, one Miss Scudder gave a fine impersonation of a bustling, drunk and forward landlady. Jack could almost have sworn that Mrs Hardcastle had followed him from Bristol.

Or perhaps he was too distracted to enjoy any play. Red Hugh's obvious reluctance to talk of his cousin, and then just to mock her reading tastes, had intrigued Jack further. He found that if his companion's eyes were fixed upon the stage, his own kept shifting to the box she was meant to occupy.

Trumpets blared, Hotspur shouted and Jack squirmed. The bench was damnably uncomfortable! This, no doubt, was another source of his discontent. He was used to the best view in the house, in the pit, with a hired cushion to soothe his arse. The pain only grew as the play proceeded, so when the fiddle, fife and French horn that composed the playhouse orchestra signalled the end of Act Three, he rose quickly.

'Coming, Hugh?' A stretch and an ale were what he sought during this middle, long interval. The pantomimes and country dances that would fill the gap he could do without.

'Nay, lad, you carry on. I'll just sit here and linger with the Bard's words.' Shaking his head – the man's eyes were actually full of tears! – Jack began to squeeze past legs. The stairs led down via the side of the pit and took far longer than it should have, largely due to the two huge men who stood either side of the staircase, forcing people to pass between them in single file while they stared rudely into each face. Jack returned glare for glare as he pushed through. By the time he reached the pit, the crowd was thick before the vendors of nuts, fruit and juices, blocking progress to the street and the adjacent tavern. Frustrated, Jack waited while a mob cleared before him, glancing up to the stage where some of the players had returned to give the entr'acte – in this case an episode from mythology with a maiden Cupid in a toga. He was immediately held, less by the fine legs displayed under Cupid's miniscule dress, than by her face. For he knew it.

'Fanny Harper!' he whispered. 'By God, Fanny!'

Immediately, and to the disapproval of those behind him, he began to push the other way. The usher was distracted by a drunk and Jack managed to slip unnoticed beneath the rope that was meant to keep the gallery's peasants from the pit. Beyond it, the crowd was thinner. Jack made for the stairs that led up beside the forestage. By the time he reached them, Cupid had shot love's arrow and was already exiting.

'Fanny! Fanny!'

Her kohl-lined eyes looked blankly at him then suddenly widened in shock.

'Jack? I don't believe . . . Jack Absolute?'

She'd halted and another actor bumped into her. 'Jesus, Fanny, move yer fat arse.' He darted round her, as she tapped the usher on the shoulder, pointed at Jack and said, 'Let him up.' Then, with a quick and still amazed glance back, she disappeared stage right.

Jack found her in a canvas-enclosed space in the wings. Two other actresses shared the cramped area, each engaged, as Fanny was, in changing costume.

'Eh, Lobster Back,' snapped one of them, 'you're not allowed in 'ere.'

'Leave 'im be,' the younger one cooed. ''E's my admirer, aintcha, love?'

'Mine, actually,' said Fanny. 'And aren't you ladies on?'

Sticks were being thumped on stage, whistles blown. The two pushed past him, the older one grumpily, the younger with a wink and blown kiss. Through a gap in the curtains, he glimpsed them joining the others on stage. A wild chase began.

He turned back. 'Fanny, what . . . what are you doing here?'

'Playing, obviously. I returned to my trade. No, was forced to return to my trade. You may remember why.'

The words were spoken with a degree of frost that made Jack flush. He also looked away, for Fanny had pulled Cupid's short toga over her head. She had nothing on beneath, recalling for Jack the last time he'd seen her, before he left for Canada. She'd been similarly unclad, shamed in the middle of the Pleasure Gardens' Rotunda by Lord Melbury.

'Why turn away, Jack? You have seen my charms before.'

The anger was still there. Justified, Jack knew. Her disgrace had been largely his fault. 'Fanny, I am so sorry. I—'

'Too late for that.' He looked again, as she dropped a shift over her head.

'Is it so bad? All this?'

'It is not my house in Golden Square, my servants, my little luxuries. It is the life of a player and I thought I'd left that behind.' Reaching behind him for a brush, she began to stroke it through her long, brown hair.

He watched her, embarrassed. 'Look, you are busy. Can we meet later, tomorrow perhaps?'

She flicked her hair to the other side, ran the brush through it vigorously. 'I don't think so. Harper wouldn't like it.'

'Harper?'

'My former husband. He took me back, got me into this company. But he won't marry me again. So I play under my maiden name of Scudder.' The brush was thrown down, pins picked up, the hair gathered. With her hand folding it on top of her head, she looked at him properly for the first time. 'My,' she said softly after a long moment, 'but haven't you changed?'

'I've had a fever.'

'It's not that. You're thinner, yes, but there's more.' She stepped closer. 'Yes,' she said softly, 'I see what it is. You've become a man, Jack Absolute.'

He turned away, uncomfortable under that appraising gaze. 'I've . . . I've had some experiences.'

She stepped away. 'Haven't we all, dear?' She began to put up her hair. With pins in the mouth she mumbled, 'Though I am most surprised by the clothes, Jack. You were always such a peacock. And I'd heard you'd enlisted in the Queen's, not some troop of the Cumberland yeomanry.'

'This?' Jack tried to smooth down a crease. Embarrassment made him seek an excuse. 'This is more in the nature of,' he looked about him for inspiration, 'a costume.'

'Well, then, you will certainly be at home in Bath.' Hair up, she took his arm, pulled aside a curtain to reveal the crowd milling in the pit. 'The town is a giant theatre, Jack, and everyone here is a player. We are merely the professional ones, and not necessarily the best, either. For all here is

95

artifice, a glittering façade. And beneath that glitter, Bath hides every human frailty, all its vices.'

Jack glanced up, to the gallery. Red Hugh, dressed in purple, should have stood clear among all the brown and grey up there. But strangely, all Jack saw were the two huge men who'd blocked his progress down the stairs, and who now seemed to be searching for something.

Fanny's words drew him back. 'Ah,' she said, 'and here one of our newest players makes her entrance. In Bath but two days and regard the legion of her admirers.'

Jack looked where Fanny did. Indeed, it was hard to look anywhere else. For a body of men were pushing down the pit's side aisle, moving forward while simultaneously looking back. Many stumbled but the progress was not halted. What was driving it was clear. Or rather whom.

She moved slowly, steadily, not so much walking as gliding, so that her hooped dress appeared to float before her, rolling her admirers on like jetsam before a tide. The theatre was not large and Jack's eyes were good. Yet he felt like rubbing them, because they had to be deceiving him. He could not believe that anyone – anything – on the whole planet could be so beautiful.

Of what did beauty consist? A fortunate combination of eye, nose and lip? These could be altered, with colour and shading, yet he knew the face he beheld betrayed the merest breath of paint. Was beauty in that sweep of an eyebrow, the fall of curl upon the forehead, the magenta-redness of both a contrast to the churned cream of the skin? Or did beauty rest finally in the eyes themselves that, even at a distance, fast diminishing due to her approach and the intensity of his regard, seemed to be all the greens of the world? Her beauty was all these things and more that he could not comprehend, swept into a whole that had him actually gasping as he looked. In that instant, all thoughts of McClune and his bookish cousin were swept away. For he had seen the lady he would pursue in Bath.

'What . . . what is her name?'

'Laetitia Fitzpatrick.'

Jack gasped again. He had dismissed her the moment before and now he had to take her up again. How easy that was!

Fanny continued, 'Niece of the Earl of Clare, it is reported, which seems unfair for it makes her rich as well as . . . well, as you see.' She snorted. 'Perhaps not so unfair. For even this beauty will fade while her gold will ever glister. They say she's come to Bath to marry and is destined for nothing less than a duke.' She had finished dressing; now she reached forward and turned to Jack. 'God spare me, not another recruit!'

He could not reply. Could not talk about new love before an old, even if he'd been able to find words. Instead he looked at her, at her transformation, for her legs were now swathed in a bulky skirt, her bosom lost within the folds of a dull grey blouse. There was an Abigail's cap on her head. 'You are Mistress Quickly,' he said.

'I am. And I am soon on again. The play begins anew. So . . . shoo!' She took his arm, began leading him towards the stage, where the interval pantomime was just concluding.

'You are the best thing in the piece.'

'I know.' she said. 'Me and Harper.' She gestured to the wings opposite where Falstaff was mustering his girth. Halting, she then pursed her lips and whistled. A boy occupying the end of one of the onstage benches looked up. She beckoned him over and reluctantly he ceded his perch. 'There, you goose,' she shoved Jack toward the vacant seat. 'Now you can sit and gaze upon your love.'

'Fanny, I—'

'Tut! 'Tis all done, Jack. In the past. And yet,' a little smile came, 'perhaps you can look at this as my revenge upon you.'

'How so?' He paused, looked back, just as the orchestra struck up and the audience scrambled for their seats.

'Remember what I told you of Bath. Of what lies beneath. For I have met the fair Lady of Clare. Only for a moment, but I could see that she too has her secret. And it is something dark.'

On that word she was gone. Jack forced his way onto the bench. He looked into the box. Her face was in profile, for she had turned to talk to the older woman – her aunt, no doubt – who had accompanied her progress through the theatre.

A dark secret, Jack thought as the actors returned to the stage. How much would I give to find it out?

— NINE —

Footpads

After the play had ended it was hard to note anyone in the frenzy of Orchard Street. The majority of the audience showed no desire to be swiftly away on this warm, still bright June evening. Indeed, Fanny's words on the nature of Bath as its own theatre were proven as its occupants strutted and fretted before the playhouse doors. All conversations were carried on in tones designed to carry to the Upper Town, and all had to shout to be heard above the braying of French horns. Bath seemed full of them, both day or night, and they were usually sported by Negro musicians whose skills varied enormously. Chairs stood everywhere, their chairmen either in fine livery, awaiting their masters, or in drabber clothes, seeking fares. When one was filled, the men, clutching the poles, would bellow for their way to be cleared, words generally having slight effect unless accompanied by a pole end up the arse. Jack gained a slight elevation on a doorstep opposite the theatre entrance to wait for Red Hugh – and his cousin – to appear.

The door behind him creaked open. He was about to vacate his vantage point when there was a hiss. 'Don't move, Jack. And don't turn around.'

He obeyed, froze. 'Hugh?' he whispered.

'Aye.'

'What do you—'

'Shh!' The caution was harsh and brought a pause. 'Do you see two men? Large brutes, looking for something? Someone?'

Jack had again met the two he'd encountered on the stairs when he'd left the theatre, once more slowing progress with their bulk. 'Yes, they're inside. Who are they?'

A sigh came. 'Creditors; or their lackeys anyway. That business deal I was telling you of in Bristol? To effect it I had to raise certain sums and gave a guarantor who was ficticious. I did not think they would find out but it appears to the contrary. These men have been sent to take back what I no longer possess.'

'Oh, Hugh!'

'Yes, lad, it is unfortunate; especially as it seems we will not be sharing that fine house after all. I'll have to find meaner lodgings and lie low.'

Jack felt something prod him in the spine. He reached back and grasped a large key. 'It's number twenty-two, the Circus. A servant comes with the place. He'll see to your needs. And I'll be by, if my dealings allow.'

Jack's attention was suddenly drawn by a bulge of men forcing their way out of the theatre's main doors, revealing the sight he most wanted to see – Laetitia Fitzpatrick. She did not walk with eyes demurely downcast now but boldly and face up, with a smile to mock the compliments un- doubtedly being poured upon her. As she had been a tide driving men into the playhouse, here she was pushing them out. She was aided by her guardian Mrs O'Farrell, a lady of some girth, who used that to keep the young men moving, flapping at them with her fan as if they were bothersome insects.

He had the advantage of sight over the man behind the door. Casually, he asked, 'But what of your cousin, Hugh?'

The reply was cool. 'What's my cousin to you, may I ask?'

'Weren't you going to chaperone her about the town?'

'I was.'

'Well, given your present inconvenience, I thought that perhaps I could oblige tonight?'

A silence, followed by a sigh. 'Well, I suppose I have little choice. But if you plan on wooing her, Absolute, I'll remind you to consider this honour you were so lately dwelling upon.'

'Of course.'

'She's not some tavern slattern or actress. And be advised—'

'Shh! Those men are back.'

Indeed, the two brutes – obviously bailiffs now the Irishman had announced their role – had emerged from the theatre again, scanned the crowd then strode off up the street. They brushed past Laetitia and her guardian, who were just entering into a chair, unusual in that it was for two persons, and secured by one of her many hovering suitors.

'They've gone.'

'But I'll remain here, just to be sure. You go.'

Still looking where his hidden friend could not – the hinged flap in the roof was being raised to accommodate the older woman's enormously tall hair – Jack said, 'I'll await your relations and see them home. Good luck, Hugh.'

'And you, lad. I'll be about.'

The two chairmen, nearly as large as the bailiffs, bent to their poles, lifted and began to clear the way with curses and indelicate prods. Preceded by a link boy, whose torch was barely required – it was, Jack noted by a clock on the face of the building, past nine o'clock – and pursued by a pack of at least five admirers, the party finally gained the main thoroughfare, turning left before the West Parade.

He followed, his mind churning. The sudden departure forced on Red Hugh was disappointing; Jack had looked forward to a carouse about the town in his fine company. And yet the fellow had been reluctant even to introduce Jack to his divine cousin. All that talk of eligibility. Well, he may be a 'mere baronet's' son, but fellows like himself made elevated marriages all the time. His own commander in the 16th, John Burgoyne, had eloped with the daughter of the Earl of Derby, and he'd eventually been forgiven and embraced, winning woman and fortune, too.

He smiled. He'd miss Red Hugh's company, of course. But the sudden appearance of these creditors did give Jack a certain freedom now. He must make sure to take advantage of it.

To start with, the slow pace of the chair suited Jack and he only had to use his stick a few times to carve a way through loiterers. The chairmen threaded through the crowds emerging from Simpson's Assembly Rooms and the Orange Grove before it took to the narrow lanes of the Abbey Churchyard. Beyond them, however, Cheap Street widened into Westgate Street, the crowds diminished and the chairmen eased into their natural gait, the same in Bath as in London – a trot. If this proved taxing for Jack, it quickly dissuaded the last two pursuing bucks. With a few final compliments, verses shouted, fingers kissed, they turned back to the town.

'They say she could pay off half the National Debt,' one said, as they passed Jack.

'Hang the money. I'll just take those devilish eyes,' his companion replied.

'Share her, then? Like we did that trollop in Gloucester?'

'Why not?'

'Agreed. But this time I have her first!'

With hooting laughs and fists raised to be pushed together, the two veered to the doors of a tavern. Jack swallowed down an instant anger, smiling as he realized – he hadn't even met the girl and already he was jealous! – then turned back to the road. The chair was by now fifty paces ahead. He could not force himself into her company now, he decided, it would not be seemly. No, he would wait till the morrow, be up to watch her door and follow her to the Pump Rooms where she would undoubtedly take the waters. Then he would contrive a meeting.

Though he was following a little more slowly now, the link boy's torch was still a beacon in the twilight. Thus he was a little surprised not to see it vanish round the corner into Union Street. Surely the most direct route to the Circus, he thought. Although he did not know Bath, he had spent most of the journey from Bristol – when the surface of the highway allowed it – studying a guidebook with map that Red Hugh had provided. Ever since that winter spent hunting with Até in the wilderness of Quebec and the subsequent final campaign against the French, he had enjoyed calculating the most direct routes. Their lives had often depended on such knowledge.

He reached into his coat pocket for the guide. The map was small but the summer sun still gave just enough light and confirmed what he suspected: the women were being taken out of their way.

Perhaps this slight diversion was to avoid a blocked road or follow a better lit one, he reasoned. He was not too concerned, therefore, when thin Parsonage Lane was not taken, nor Bridewell Lane. Though when the torch failed to disappear round the Upper Westgate Buildings but proceeded instead through the West Gate itself and out beyond the ruined Roman walls of Old Bath, Jack dropped the book back into his pocket and increased his pace. This was more than a diversion, a longer route to demand more coin. Something was up.

As the larger townhouses gave way to impoverished cottages and patches of scrub land, Jack slipped into another way of being, that of the Mohawk warrior he'd become after the year spent with Até. Moving in shadows, nothing sounded beneath his feet.

The last of the shacks were passed and meadows began. Jack remembered from the map that this area was called Kingsmead. He could scent the Avon, while the air sounded with waterfowl. A duck plunged toward the distant river. Three geese rose from reeds, honking their way toward the sunset.

He wondered why these were the only sounds, save for the slap of the chairmen's shoes upon the earth, their occasional grunt; why no cry or question had come from behind the leather blinds. Then one did, just as the chairmen stepped away from the last recognizable piece of roadway into the trees.

'You there! Why have we not yet arrived?'

A blind rose. A gasp came. The same voice – the older woman's – spoke again.

'By heaven! Where are we? You! Stop this instant!'

The men did the reverse, breaking into a run that carried the chair deeper into the meadows. The path dropped into a dell that the last of the day's sun had forsaken.

'Set us down,' came the cry, and this time the men obeyed. With a thump the chair was dropped; the leather straps slipped from their shoulders, the men stepped away. The link boy thrust the butt of the reed torch into the ground and it flared there, casting their malformed shadows into the canopy.

'Get out,' one man said. 'Now!'

The reply was a high contrast, panicked. 'We shan't. What do you want? Oh, help!'

The cry is Mrs O'Farrell's, Jack thought, as he slipped closer behind a tree. Laetitia is silent, held in terror, no doubt.

The door of the chair was wrenched open. 'Out, you bitches. Out!' said the second man. Irish beyond a doubt, but without the cultured tones of Red Hugh.

'Shall I spark 'em out?' The link boy was English and eager, reaching back to his torch.

'No need.' A purple-gloved hand emerged. It belonged to Laetitia Fitzpatrick. And it had a gun in it.

'Shite!' said the English footpad.

But the Irish one laughed, a nasty sound. 'Sure and 'tis only a lady's piece. Like their lapdogs and with as dangerous a bite.'

'Possibly. Though even a lapdog's teeth will hurt if they attach somewhere painful.'

No matter that Jack was fully engaged in getting quietly closer, the voice affected him, the soft Irish lilt containing steel in it, even within fear.

He was fifteen paces away now – still too far – and the footpads had moved, spread wide. The tiny barrel jerked between them, following now one, now the other.

'D'ye think you can plug all three of us?' the Englishman jeered as the muzzle wavered between them. Then he yelled, 'Boo!' The link boy darted forward and the Irishman stepped swiftly in, grabbing and twisting the wrist in one hand, dropping the pistol into his other hand, chucking it over his shoulder. Laetitia was wrenched out.

'Leave her, you brute. Oh!' The elder woman gave a wail, as the second footpad reached in and jerked her from the chair.

'Rest easy, you old cow,' he said. It was hard for her to do, with his hands roving over her. After a moment, he shook his head.

The Irish one nodded to the chair. 'Must have it stashed. Search it,' he ordered the boy, who dived in. The other two men leaned in to watch, the women before them, their arms pinned.

Now or never, thought Jack. He walked forward quickly. He'd sent his sword along with his other belongings, more was the pity; but swords, anyway, had long been banned in every part of genteel Bath. His stick, though, wasn't one of the new fancy canes from India but was hewn from good English blackthorn, with a silver pommel and an iron ferrule at the tip.

Lifting it, he poked the English footpad lightly in the shoulder. 'Good evening,' he said, cheerily.

'Shite,' bellowed the man again, doing what Jack was hoping he would do, releasing the old lady's arms, stepping to one side. Raising the stick swiftly, Jack lunged and struck down, using it like a cavalry sabre. It was almost as heavy, and the metal tip caught the man hard on the top of his head. He fell, blood cascading between his fingers on the instant.

Jack stepped away immediately, paralleling the Irishman who used Laetitia as a shield until he'd gained some distance. Then he threw her towards Jack. She fell on her knees with a cry. Hands now free, the man drew a huge cudgel from within his coat and ran forward with a shout. Jack moved sharply sideways, the wind of the heavy club passing uncomfortably close; fever-racked, he was not as agile as he'd been in Quebec or aboard the *Sweet Eliza*.

But I am still a soldier, he thought, and I've faced better men than you.

'Have this!' He lunged, using the stick like a small sword now, the tip aimed at the Irishman's face. It forced the man to stagger back to save his eye, but even as Jack straightened up again, looked for another opening, he was aware of movement beside him.

The link boy was coming out of the chair. And he had a knife.

Shite, thought Jack, in an echo.

The blade flicked at him and he spun away from it, his left hand spread wide. When it wrapped around the stump of the torch, he jerked it from the ground and thrust forward, the flare halting the boy's next lunge.

The older woman was making a terrible noise, incomprehensible words in a steady shriek. The younger, in Jack's quick glance, was kneeling by her, staring up at him. The other man was still *hors de combat*, clutching his head and groaning. The three fighters breathed, weapons raised. 'You'd best be off,' Jack said, waving his stick towards the screaming woman, 'we're not that far out of Bath.'

Instead of retreating, the Irishman gave a bellow and ran at him. Jack couldn't get his stick across in time. Even if he had, the cudgel would have smashed it. Instead, he jerked up the torch. It saved his head but it exploded, flaming reeds scattered everywhere.

Tossing the wreckage at the boy, who'd lunged at his exposed left side, Jack moved fast to the right, jabbing as he went. The Irishman came for him again, swung and missed, the cudgel thudding into the soft earth. Jack leapt again to strike, but his foot caught something. He fell.

With a shout, the footpad advanced, swinging. Down came the club and Jack rolled, rolled again, thrusting the stick to try to thwart each attack, aware that it was not a defence that could last long.

And then he rolled over something. As his body cleared it, even as he thrust up again, his trailing hand reached back, grabbed, lifted. And as the Irishman raised the cudgel for a finishing blow, Jack rolled to his knees and levelled Laetitia's pistol at him.

'Enough,' he said, breathing heavily. Laetitia had some-how only pulled the trigger halfway back. But Jack wasn't going to go off half-cock.

The Irishman flinched as the trigger clicked. The cudgel was still held high. The boy joined him, the dagger thrust out, his eyes twitching at the barrel. The old lady had stopped her screaming to stare, the second man had raised his bloody face. Strangely, and but for a moment, Jack could only think of the extraordinary green of Laetitia's eyes, now fixed firmly upon him.

'Sure now,' said the man at last, 'the powder will all have been knocked from the pan.'

'It's quite possible,' replied Jack from his crouch, the pistol still aimed straight into the man's face.

'And anyway, it's a tiny ball.'

'You are right. 'Twould hardly trouble a fly.'

'And there's still the two of us,' bellowed the footpad, getting angrier. 'You'll not be getting us both.'

'I don't intend it,' said Jack mockingly, adopting the accent as he rose slowly to his feet, 'for isn't it my plan to shoot only you?'

Silence, bar breathing and groans, held for just a moment. And then the Irishman, muttering curses, was moving toward his bleeding companion, who was already using the chair door to pull himself up, his other hand still clutched to his head. With a backward glance, a last curse, the three stumbled from the dell towards the river.

'You forgot your chair,' called Jack, then noticed that the pistol, hitherto quite steady, had begun to shake. Uncocking it, he slipped it into his waistcoat pocket, moved towards the women. The younger had helped the elder to rise only for her to sit again on the sill of the chair, her fan vibrating wildly before her.

'Oh sir! Sir!' she exclaimed as Jack approached. 'Are they gone? Quite gone?'

'Certain they are,' replied Jack. 'Your sister's pistol has put them to flight.'

There was a pause in the fan's vibration. 'My . . . sister? Oh, do you mean Miss Fitzpatrick?' A small smile came. 'Indeed we have oft been mistaken for siblings.' The fan started up again. 'Though I am, in fact, her aunt. Mrs O'Farrell.'

'The resemblance is startling.' In fact, there was none at all. The word was entirely reserved for the eyes Jack had glanced into again.

'Startling, 'tis certain.'

It was only the second time he had heard her speak; the first when she did not have a gun in her hand. And Jack was delighted to note that it was not merely the sight of the weapon that had so thrilled him. Red Hugh had said that his cousin was seventeen, but even those few words showed a voice with a maturity beyond her years. It also had a little catch, something lurking in the depths.

Jack had to clear his own throat. 'Uh-hum. Now, we must get you both aid. Shall I go to the road and summon it?'

'You would not leave us, sir?' Mrs O'Farrell grabbed Jack's arm. 'You could not be so unkind?'

'I could never be unkind to you,' Jack said, his words for the aunt, his eyes on the niece, 'but are you able to walk?'

'We can, sir. We will.' Laetitia was gently pulling her aunt to her feet. 'And if the gentleman would lend an arm?'

The gentleman did. It was slow progress out of the dell and back to the roadway, a little swifter upon it. Jack was happy with the pace, hardly surprised, now the crisis was passed, that his own legs were weakened, too.

With the ruined walls of Bath in sight, Laetitia said, 'A moment, pray, for us to compose ourselves before we enter?'

There was a wall before a cottage and the elder lady lowered herself onto it.

Jack, who'd spent much of the last minutes gazing on Laetitia's profile, now found his scrutiny returned. She spoke. 'May we enquire, sir, the name of our rescuer? And his rank? You are obviously in the Army?'

He was about to declare himself, attempt the formalities that the violence of their introduction had superceded – his connection to their family, his delight in making their acquaintance – when he saw that this last question had directed the green gaze upon his uniform. At first, he sought disgust there, the same he felt when he saw the dreadful, stained and patched hand-me-down he'd reluctantly worn since Quebec. But then he noticed the quality of the look. Not disgust, not at all. Fascination. And the words Red Hugh had spoken earlier that night came suddenly back to him: *She will marry for love and the poorer the suitor, the better!*

'My rank? Well, I am a Cornet, miss – with hopes of one day being made up to lieutenant.'

'I am sure that day will be soon, if courage speeds promotion,' the older lady smiled.

'Alas, gold is more likely to. Of which, as you can most certainly tell, I have but little. Or rather none.' He laughed, gesturing to his ill-fitting apparel.

'And your name, sir?' The eyes had risen, from this badge of his poverty, to his own.

'My name?' Jack thought, but only for a moment. He had never read any of these 'romances' Red Hugh had so disparaged. But he had seen inumerable plays which had similar themes. And playwrights, like novelists, always called their heroes similar things. Something like . . . '*Beverley* is my name, Miss Fitzpatrick. Cornet Beverley. And your servant.'

'Debtors have no servants. Rather the reverse. However shall we repay you?'

They smiled at each other. The gaze held and Mrs O'Farrell, perceiving it, suddenly rose. 'I believe I am rested enough to proceed.'

They passed through the West Gate. 'Shall I secure you a chair?' He saw the fear return to the aunt's face. 'If I urge them to go slow and ward you all the way to the Circus?'

Surprise replaced the fear. 'And how do you know where we live, sir?'

Damn! 'I, um, was standing close when you entered the chair. Heard you give the destination.' It sounded reasonable. Emboldened, he went on, 'Didn't like the look of those fellows who took you off. So I decided to follow.'

'Thank the Lord you did, sir.'

'I will. I do.'

A chair was secured and Jack handed the aunt in.

'I will walk,' Laetitia said, 'if you will accompany us, sir.'

'I shall be delighted.'

'But will we not take you far from your way, sir?' Mrs O'Farrell had leaned from the window to enquire.

'No, no. I am bound for the Circus also.'

'You are?' That gaze was again considering the poverty of his clothes.

Damn, again! He really needed to sit down and concoct a proper story. 'I have . . . an aunt too, ha-ha. Lives on the Circus. I haven't visited her yet today.'

'And you will do so at this hour?'

Jack smiled, at least with his mouth. 'Insomniac. Insists I drop by to tell her of the play. Though truly, I think she just wants to be certain I eat.'

'How kind she is.'

To end this examination, Jack tapped the chair with his stick and told the men to go steady. He and Laetitia followed a few paces behind. Picking up their conversation, Jack said,

'I can think of one repayment for my services, if you still consider it necessary to make one.'

'Which is?'

'Let me see you tomorrow?'

'A small price for such a large obligation.'

''Tis all I require – for now.'

Laetitia tipped her head to the side, looked at him with a faint smile. 'For now?' When he said nothing further, she added, in a lower tone, 'My aunt is vigilant. And however much she is obliged to you, she is obliged to our family name the more. She will countenance no cornet attentions.' She sighed. 'It appears that I am to be wooed by nothing less than a duke. So *they* say. But we shall see about that.'

The voice had settled even lower as she spoke her defiance, hovering in that catch he was already half-besotted by. 'Well, miss, I can only assure you that I am somewhat skilled in subterfuge.'

She smiled back, then looked away. 'Tomorrow, you say? Well, I shall, as usual, take the waters. And it is a public bath. They will admit *anybody*.' She looked up. 'Perhaps I shall see you there?'

They walked on, Jack's heart beating nearly as fast as it had at Kingsmead Fields. They were on Gay Street before she spoke again.

'You must not stare so, Cornet Beverley.'

Jack shook his head. 'I am helpless to do other, Miss Fitzpatrick.'

They had fallen behind the chair by twenty paces. Jack looked away from Laetitia to see it turn left down Queen's Parade Place. The Circus was straight on.

He caught up quickly. 'What do you do, fellow? Your destination is ahead.'

The aunt leaned out of the window. ''Twas my orders, Cornet Beverley. The front of our house is being reconstructed. We are forced to use the rear entrance for now.'

The chair was carried up a gravelled path that ran parallel to Gay Street and, Jack presumed, on behind the Circus. Indeed, after five or six rear gates were passed, a tap halted the chairmen.

'This is ours,' said Laetitia. The chair was set down and Jack beat one of the men to the door, offering his hand. Mrs O'Farrell stepped out, smiling her thanks. As she reached for a large purse, he resisted the urge to pay. Receiving their fare, the chairmen lurched off. A yawning servant had appeared at the gate, a lantern in his hand. Mrs O'Farrell stepped towards him. 'There are not words to express our gratitude, dear Cornet. We hope to see you about the town.'

'Indeed, ma'am, I often visit my aunt on the other side of the Circus here. We are sure to run into each other.'

'This aunt who lives on the Circus – perhaps you are not from quite so impoverished a family?'

With one eye on Laetitia, he replied, 'A distant aunt, alas. A Methodist. Does not believe in the Army as a suitable career.'

'Ah well.' Mrs O'Farrell moved towards the still yawning servant.

'Till tomorrow,' whispered Laetitia. There was a touch on his arm, and she was gone.

Jack stayed staring at the gate for some time, until the servant returned and glared at him, forcing him to move on. He could have finally visited his lodgings, but he knew he would be unable to sleep just yet. Instead he walked into the parkland that backed the buildings, musing on the night and its beauty. From this high elevation, the lights of the town gleamed through the trees below him. To his left, lanterns shone in the windows of what had to be the Circus. No doubt by the light of one of them she was beginning to undress.

'Laetitia,' he murmured, running his hands down his chest. His left reached something hard. He pulled out the pistol.

He cocked the piece, raised it into the air and pulled the trigger. *Click.* No shot, not even the puff of a misfire. The gun had indeed disgorged all its powder.

Replacing the gun in the pocket, he smiled. It was just as well that the Irishman had chosen flight over valour. Just as well.

— TEN —

The Pleasures of the Town

It was a scream that woke him, jerking him from pleasant dream to a startled, instant wakefulness, his hand reaching to the bedside table, to the pocket pistol there. He had never returned it to her, keeping it as a first token of love. He was glad of that now, glad that powder was in the pan and the flint renewed. But the room, daylight etching the shutters, presented no target. When the scream came again – a long drawn-out wail ending in a series of barks – Jack shook his head, uncocked the pistol and set it down.

'Damn'd seagulls!' he muttered. The birds, so common in Bath despite the city's distance from the sea, continued their Bedlam cries.

He lay back. Beside the gun was his pocket watch, the time displayed close to eight in the morning. The bird had fulfilled the duty that his servant had not. He was meant to arise at seven, to follow her chair to the town. He would just have to catch up with her at the Pump Rooms.

And what did today hold? he wondered, hands behind his head. Much the same as the ten days that had preceded it since the night of the footpads, no doubt. The social round of Bath.

Hang the place! It was too tame by half for a lad of any

spirit. The regular hours stupefied. Balls ended at eleven sharp, taverns closed their doors soon after and Jack had yet to discover the equivalent of a Derry's Cider House from Covent Garden where the more restless souls could carouse till dawn. He doubted there was one – mere awareness of its existence would have jangled the nerves of the invalids, drawn in their thousands to the town for its healing waters; though they were equally drawn by the peculiar mix of the society. No one was refused a place so long as they could afford the subscriptions to the baths, booksellers and balls, the private walks and assembly rooms; and behaved at them in a dully prescribed manner. The Wapping landlady could make a fourth in a quadrille with a duchess if she wore the correct dress, trod the formal steps and didn't spit. Indeed, it was the nobility, used to a laxer mode of being, that more often were the ones ejected for some offence. Really, the standards of etiquette would have disgraced no court in Europe. Might have bored the Kings to death but . . .

Jack was glad his role as Beverley required him to appear poor. The ghastly uniform he resented wearing at least denied him entrance to most events. He was able to be the observer, amused by the pretensions and follies displayed, when he was not focused on the main reason for his observations.

Letty. She'd let him call her that after their fourth meeting – though he was always and simply 'Beverley', his invention failing when attempting to find a first name that matched the romance of this second one. He'd taken her hand while Mrs O'Farrell dozed beside her on the garden bench; at their Circus house he'd climbed the wall as soon as he'd heard her snore.

'Letty.' He breathed it out, stretched his arms and legs, laughed. Her name, simply uttered, had an effect on him that none had ever had before. Neither the gifted courtesan Fanny nor the lusty Widow Simkin, and not even Clothilde Guen, idol of his youth. She had been his first infatuation and he had wooed her with all a schoolboy's ardour including poems, sweetmeats, and touches escalating from fingertips to lips. He had loved Clothilde as a boy loves and, as Fanny had observed his first night in Bath, he was now a man. And if that man was known as Beverley or Absolute, did it matter? His love was not a lie, and his goal was honourable. You did not seduce a woman such as Laetitia then depart. You married her. And did not all lovers don masks, selecting aspects of themselves to reveal? Did not all lovers use subterfuge and invention to conquer?

Ten days in Bath and he had turned into Love's Philosopher! But surely the characteristics of the lover Letty desired were as much a part of him as his black hair; this mask merely allowed him to bring them more quickly to the fore. There could be no dilatoriness, no hints over a hand of whist, no whispers as couples met and parted in the dance. In fact, he'd become convinced that the pretence actually heightened truth. Feelings had to be gauged more swiftly, expressed sooner, then acted upon. Ten days in Bath and they had already reached the point that ten weeks of society could not have gained them. She had got to know the real Jack – yes, by another name but still the man who had fought Frenchmen and privateers, endured slavery, killed a bear, been tattooed. And he had got to know the real Letty, beyond the entrancing green eyes and that voice caught somewhere between velvet and the grindstone. For it was what the voice spoke, what the eyes conveyed that truly entranced. Indeed, her desire to spite her family and fall in love with someone poor was her only sign of silliness, instantly forgiven when set against her virtues. Her wit amused, especially when, in his stalking of her, he observed how she dealt with her suitors. She was cruel only to boorishness and would act for him her merciless put-downs of the Norwich wool merchant or the Harrovian marquis with a skill in mimicry that could have earned her a living upon the stage.

Jack sniffed. He had caught a slight chill – not a relapse of his fever, fortunately – standing in the rain under her window, though she had never appeared. And he still had a mark from a stone on one knee where he'd kneeled too long on the hoggin outside her back door, hoping he'd be noticed. Each pain was worth it, as he got ever closer to his goal. If he could persuade her to an elopement – the ultimate aim of all those novels – he was then certain that the 'divine poverty' she intended to be their life together would be swiftly curtailed by its direct experience. A week of squalor, a few weeks of penitence and they could approach her family. His rank, his own person, would win them over. A large fortune would be his – and a wife as beautiful as she was rich. She would eventually forgive him his deception, married bliss would soothe her – along with a little touch of Absolute in the night!

A knocking coincided with his contented sigh. 'Come,' he shouted.

The servants' door, recessed into the wall so as to be almost invisible and not spoil the symmetry of the room, swung in and Fagg entered. In Bath, servants often came with the house and Jack had been happy he needn't search one out, though the man was next to useless, cross-eyed, mono-syllabic and surly with it. He now set down a bowl of chocolate and what was sure to be a stale bun.

'Breakfast,' the fellow muttered, moving slowly to open the shutters.

'Oh, *thank* you,' replied Jack, propping himself higher up on the bolster, 'and at such a fine hour.'

The rebuke was ignored. Light filled the room. It was going to be another glorious day. At the sight, Jack began to whistle, getting louder when he saw the man wince. Fagg was un-doubtedly sick from the night before. Jack had learned he could rely on this servant for no late-night cheese toast in the chafing dish. He would be drunk and snoring in his attic by ten.

At the door, Fagg stopped, turned. 'Forgot,' he said, and shuffled back. 'Post.'

Two letters were dropped on the bed. Jack's whistling ceased. He'd sent letters to London only ten days before. That replies had come so swiftly was amazing. Some Bath fellow called Allen ran the best service in the country, apparently.

Fagg stood looking down at him. 'News, sir?' he said, as if the idea was the dullest imaginable.

Jack looked at the envelopes. One was from Mayfair and Absolute House, the other from Hertford, though Jack knew no one there. Turning it over, he saw that the wax seal bore the regimental insignia of the 16th Light Dragoons. 'I'll let you know, Fagg.'

'Oh, good.' The fellow limped out, forgetting to close the door.

Jack studied the envelopes again. Putting off the news from his regiment, he opened the one from home. The envelope did not bear his mother's elegant copperplate, however, and he was surprised to discover it was from Nancy, the Absolute housekeeper. He hadn't known she could write.

'Dear Jack,' it read. 'Lawks we woz glad to here from you tho only me and Timothy woz ere to tost the news. First they says you woz missin praps dead then alive. You cawzed your mother sum grief sartain.'

Jack looked up, thought. Because of his capture by the Abenaki on the Plains of Abraham in the autumn of 1759, report had been returned that he was probably dead. When he'd shown up alive in the spring, he'd written to his mother then and eventually received a reply. However, she could not yet know that he had missed his ship and sat out another winter in America.

He returned to the page. 'She's gawn, joined your father in Germoney where ee fights the war. She was too flestered ere with scummy loyers talking confiscashun and such . . .'

That would be because of the duel his father had fought on Jack's behalf, killing Lord Melbury. Both Absolutes had gone to war to avoid the consequences and perhaps win glory enough to mitigate the law's harshness. Duelling was illegal anyway but Melbury had also been a King's Minister.

'. . . but so far tis only talk. I ave sent your letter on to Hangover. Timothy and I keep the house and awate the safe return of all Absolutes. God bless and keep ye Jack, Your Nance.'

So his parents were still in Hanover. He would have been glad to see them, with so much to tell. But perhaps it was for the best. They would have something to say about his plans no doubt. He hadn't yet heard of a parent who did not want to interfere in their offspring's romances. Far better to have it done and introduce them to their rich and beautiful daughter-in-law anon.

He picked up the second letter with reluctance. He'd only written to his regiment because not doing so would be the first step to desertion. The writing was as neat as Nance's had been wild, the contents confined to three terse sentences: 'You will report to the regiment's surgeon immediately. Colonel Burgoyne in command of two troops in attack on Belleisle. Needs replacement officers.' It was signed by the quartermaster at what had to be the regiment's new head-quarters in Hertford.

Jack sighed. They'd want to take a look at him and, if he could walk, ship him off to fight. He did not want to go. This war was over, near enough, the newspapers testifying to the fact that the French were beaten nearly everywhere. This attack on Belleisle, an island just off their Atlantic coast, was a mere diversion, drawing resources away from the war in

Germany. It would just be his luck, having survived all he had, to be killed on the last day of the war.

Still, he would have to report. But they could not know how quickly the letter had reached him, nor the affairs he must settle before he went. And if one particularly ended the way he hoped . . . well, he'd been a reluctant soldier anyway, circumstance forcing him in. And he'd done enough. If the war *was* nearly over, he saw no future in a peace-time career. The uniform was pretty but there were many colours he preferred over scarlet. And more comfortable places to spend winters than a barracks.

Energized, he arose, made a quick toilet and dressed. The tattered uniform was smelling worse by the day, Fagg's cleaning being as slack as his other labours. He hoped she wouldn't notice it when he proposed. It would detract somewhat from the romantic image she so desired.

He left, as ever, via the back door. He doubted she or Mrs O'Farrell watched the front but he needed to maintain the illusion of the aunt whom he visited occasionally. Leaving by the front door just after eight in the morning would not serve that.

Jack proceeded by a side path to the Circus. Once reached, he looked first to the house on the other side, number six, where his love resided. The front door was still shrouded in scaffolding. Indeed, it seemed to Jack that nothing had been done to it in the time he'd been there. Certainly he'd never seen a workman upon it. It must have annoyed Mrs O'Farrell especially, always having to use the garden entrance.

He looked behind him, to the magnificent doorway of his own number twenty-two. He'd been little concerned with architecture though knew this style was called Palladian; also knew enough to recognize these Woods – father and son – had built well, although a little extravagantly for his taste. A frieze of figures derived from antiquity, children's toys and,

Jack noted, Masonic ritual ran through each house on its architrave, linking each to its neighbour. The whole gave the impression of some Roman Coliseum, and though many opposed this constant harping on the Classical, Jack found it reassuring. It reminded him of London and especially his own Mayfair.

It will be good when they finish it, he thought. Letty's was only one of about ten still being worked upon, though near all labour was concentrated at number twenty-one. Red Hugh had mentioned that the activity was to do with the visit of no one less than the King of England. George, third of that name and succeeding to the throne the year before, was making his first progress through his realm. And the Corporation of Bath thought they might draw an even wealthier crowd to their town if they bribed the King to stay by gifting him one of John Wood's superb new houses in this, the most fashionable new development in the town.

A group was attempting to insert a chandelier through the front door, the glass structure wider than the frame. Jack smiled at some of the language, in a variety of provincial tongues, thought he could hear some good Cornish curses among them. He'd met a countryman of his on the works, one Dirk Trewennan, who was convinced Jack left by the back door each morning because he was tupping some rich married woman inside. He'd also told Jack to prevail upon her to let him stay the next day, when the house was to be presented to 'Georgie'. 'From that house you'll have the best view in all of Bath, young squire,' he'd declared.

Jack truly didn't care. If there must be kings – and his mother kept assuring him that there did not have to be – he preferred the late one to his grandson. At least the old George was a cavalryman. In fact, he'd knighted Jack's father on the field at Dettingen. Not to mention sending Jack as his messenger to Canada. Besides, Jack Absolute had far more important affairs to deal with.

He found her at the King's Bath. There was a bit of a struggle to gain a viewing step – the town urchins would cling to the rail and bawl, 'Murder!' if he didn't buy one off – but a groat secured him the place.

He didn't see her at first, such was the crowd, all dressed in the uniform of the bather, the plain linen smock that covered everyone ankle to chin. Half crowded the edge, half were in the water looking, from his elevation, like so many spaniels aimlessly seeking duck. The women wore loose bonnets, the men went barehead, both sexes pushing little floating trays that held their snuff, nosegays, cloths and other trinkets. It was early enough for the surface of the water not to be too thick with scum. Later bathers, Jack knew, would be cutting courses like ploughs through a manure-rich field.

He shuddered as he kept up the search. Give him a clear Canadian river for his bathing any day! Despite the quacks' opinions, such immersion could not be good for one. He knew that the water flowed direct from the ground but once in the pool, what horrors of the human body did it mix with? The same revulsion made him avoid drinking the waters. It may have been pumped straight into his glass from volcanic depths but it tasted as if it had run over a few scrofulous bodies first, all sulphur and iron. He'd never liked to drink water, even when he knew he had to aboard the *Robuste*. Fortunately the beer in Bath was excellent. From small beer in the morning that would not affect his motion, through pints of porter in the afternoon that made him smile, ending with a few strong ales in the evening to hasten sleep, he had renewed his love for all things brewed. Give him beer and he was happy. It delighted the senses, ruddied the complexion and had already begun to put back the weight the fever had taken away. He was halfway to health with his self-prescribed treatments. The quacks could go hang!

Then he saw her, and all thought of beer, of illnesses, of

anything else, vanished. She rose from the water almost directly beneath him, with the linen sack that was meant to obliterate all distinctions of the body spectacularly failing to do so. He assumed it was the same as everyone else wore there, a shapeless sack. But whereas everyone else's clung to them in a unifyingly dull manner, hers was pushed out by what could only be a pair of the most divinely shaped breasts, then fell to splay over gently rounded hips. Even the plain bonnet seemed to enhance rather than obscure the natural magenta of her hair.

She climbed the stone steps slowly, carefully. At the top she paused, a naked ankle glimpsed as her foot sought a drier piece of stone from which to advance. And as she paused she looked up, straight at him. She knew he'd be there. He knew she knew. But the surprise that widened those extraordinary green eyes was so genuine, so delighted, he couldn't help a thrilled laugh. He winked, she winked back. Then he saw a bonnet following Letty. He stepped away. Mrs O'Farrell must not catch him there; indeed anywhere. Her guardian had grown careful ever since she'd discovered some trifle of a poem he'd sent. Though he'd signed it 'your Anonymous Amour', she had guessed at its provenance, and Letty had been ordered to spurn all future contact and return, un-opened, any correspondence. If he encountered them in the street, he was allowed polite formalities for the sake of his gallantry ten nights before; but he was allowed no private audience – that she knew of! Jack didn't mind. It heightened Letty's sense of persecution. When that became unbearable . . .

He ran a hand through his straggling black hair. As always, the force of his desire took him by surprise. Sometimes when he was plotting, he thought that was all this was – a plot, an escapade to be carried out with daring and pluck – and then he'd see her.

She emerged in a speedy half-hour, that magnificence now

held within a fetching gown of lavender silk, her arm through Mrs O'Farrell's. Jack ducked behind a column, watched them cross from the baths towards the south side of the Abbey. He knew where they were bound; their daily activities followed a fixed pattern. After their ablutions they would take refreshments, either at a coffee-house reserved for ladies or at a subscription library. One of each faced the Orange Grove at the far side of the church.

Jack watched them disappear round the corner. Normally he would leave them to it. But with the sun now warm on his face and the memory of clinging linen so fresh in his mind, he decided to follow. Perhaps she would look back and he could kiss his fingers to her?

They passed the ladies' coffee-house, walked into the doorway of Frederick's bookshop and library. Even though he knew he shouldn't, Jack followed.

He had been there once before, when he'd sought inspiration for his romantic gestures, and had stood between the stacks of books skimming through one entitled *The Vanquish'd Heart*. He had learned much of what behaviour was expected in the five minutes before Frederick himself discovered he had no subscription and no desire to take one out. Fortunately this day the owner was not stood sentinel at the table by the entrance.

It was a long room, from the far end of which came the thrum of low-voiced conversation, the clink of spoon in cup. Two rows of bookcases of about shoulder height stood between the volume-lined walls, making three passages. In the central one, he could make out Mrs O'Farrell's towering hair. 'I'll order us a bowl and buns, my dear. You may browse,' he heard her say. Immediately there came a loud 'Shhh!' and the hair nodded its way to the far end of the room, where talk was allowed and gossip encouraged.

Crouching, Jack slid along the first bookcase till he could see. He stepped immediately back. Two dresses occupied the middle passage; the lavender was the second. He tip-toed up the side of the room and, when he was opposite where he calculated she would be, he popped up.

'Good day,' he said brightly.

'Shh!' came the harsh reply from a mottled, puffy face opposite him of a woman some way beyond sixty.

'So sorry.' Jack glanced left, as Letty rose from inspecting a lower shelf. Her eyes widened when she saw him. He smiled at the fury in front of him, turned and gestured with his head to the right, then sank down again to disappear behind the bookcase. He heard her follow, her heels loud upon the wooden floor. He went the opposite way to the one he'd indicated and, when he sensed she was about to turn the corner, he turned his. He was now in the central passage; the she-dragon glared at him. He moved on to the opposite wall, listening for those footsteps again. When they stopped near him, he rose.

She was a foot away, facing him across the stack. She had covered the last few feet silently. And he was meant to be the forest stalker!

'Ahem!' he said.

'Shh!' came the admonition again, this time from two mouths. Letty put a finger to her lips then used it to point out a sign hung on the wall: 'Silence amidst the stacks.' Then she mouthed a word at him, indicating with her head the end of the room and her clearly visible guardian. He shrugged in incomprehension.

She took her lower lip between her teeth, looked down to the shelves before her. Her eyes suddenly narrowed and she bent, snatched up a book. She fiddled for a moment, then raised its spine to him. Her fingers obscured two parts of the title, highlighting a single word.

Fool, he read.

He shook his head, feigning hurt, and reached for the volume. She withdrew it, replaced it, crossed her arms, raised one exquisite eyebrow.

A-ha, a challenge! He looked down, at the spines and their gold writing. He appeared to be before some works of fact and he did not think *Horse-hoeing* would serve his purpose. Then he glanced left, saw it and snatched it out, needing to block out no words. He tried to look abashed as he raised it but could not help the grin.

The Mistakes of the Heart.

She crossed her eyes at him, then lifted *Journal of a Bedlamite.* She indicated, with a look of pity, that he was certainly the author.

Mad, was he? He took up another volume, placed his fingers, leaving only *Cruel* exposed.

Truth was ventured.

Chains of love, he gave her as an excuse.

She sought a little longer, then offered him *Desire,* the question in the tilt of her head. Then she shifted fingers, revealing a second word, another question.

Freedom?

By now, silent though they were among the stacks, their suppressed giggles were attracting attention. The older lady had turned a more dangerous red, trying to figure out what they were doing and how to object to it; while a swift glance right showed him that Mrs O'Farrell, drawn by noise or some sense of danger, had risen from her table and was coming to look for her ward.

Letty noted the approach, too, looked back. For a moment their eyes met, then both looked down, racing the other for the deciding volume. Bollocks, he thought, why the hell do they mix up manuals and novels? In desperation he reached, grabbed.

'Laetitia?' came the call.

'Shh!' went the she-dragon.

He placed his fingers, lifted. She read and looked puzzled. He turned the book and saw what he had done. In his haste he had obscured the name of the author, not the words in the title. She had read *Observations in Husbandry* instead of what he had meant to say: *Husband.*

She waited till he was looking into her eyes before she slowly lifted the volume she held. She didn't need any fingers. The title was plain.

'*The Triumph of Woman?*' he bellowed, aloud. 'That was in your pocket!'

Her eyes widened again. Innocent as the dawn. Guilty as hell.

'Laetitia!'

He crouched, turned, scuttled along the stack. He may have lost the fight, but at least he knew how to flee a battlefield undetected.

In excellent spirits, he went to a coffee-house to breakfast. He had taken a subscription of a crown and quarter under yet another false name. He needed somewhere to rest while he waited for Letty's next event – the Abbey at noon. He'd follow her there, let her see him, but he would not enter. He had managed to excuse himself the service, telling her that he could not afford the plate. In reality, he'd detested church from school. And this Abbey was worse than most, for in addition to the turgid sermons, it was noisesome – too many bodies buried too shallow within the walls and under flagstones, giving off a decided whiff of putrefaction.

With a bowl of coffee and a fresh Bath bun, he settled down for the wait. The latest *Public Advertiser* told of the resignation of Pitt, the King's First Minister. Apparently he was the one man in the country who thought the war would continue because the Spanish would ally with the French and prolong it. Jack thought it unlikely as well as undesirable. However, it reminded him of the summons from his regiment, of time marching to its own steady drum. The thought took away his appetite.

'I must bring this matter to a crisis,' he muttered,

throwing the half-eaten bun down. A servant thought he was asking for more coffee and topped up his bowl.

He must talk with her tonight, when the she-dragon slept. He'd kneel on that damn hoggin in her garden, plead for her to make him the happiest fellow in the realm by fleeing with him to Scotland where English law did not run and an obliging Presbyterian could be found to marry them forthwith. Elopement would serve them both – her sense of adventure and his of honour for, with a marriage at the end of it, her reputation would not suffer while his would be enhanced!

Excited now, Jack could no longer read. He left, waited opposite Frederick's. He saw her see him as he dogged their steps to the Abbey. But he couldn't wait for the service to end; she could take a chair back to her house without his vigilance for once. He needed to think, to plan the fine details of elopement as well as how best to delay his return to the Army. And the best way to do that was to use a pint of beer and a game of billiards to free his mind.

The Three Tuns in Stall Street had been recommended to him by his fellow Cornishman, Trewennan. It was Jack's favourite kind of inn – strong ale, fresh turtle soup and one of the few public billiard tables in the back. This room was deserted – it was still a little early for the gentlemen of the baize to be abroad, which suited Jack's purpose. He could practise a trick shot he'd seen one of the fellows execute the day before – taking Jack's wagered crown with a double baulked cannon – and use the activity to clear his mind and plot his future.

He'd planned some of the elopement, but the shot still eluded him more than twice in five attempts. Certain that both matters could be settled by a second mug of ale, he had duly ordered it. Crouching, his cue tip high on the ball to give it the requisite spin, he heard the door open. 'Just set it down on the table,' he said, not taking his eyes from the target. It wasn't just the spin but the angle the spinning ball made, plus the force of the shot. It needed a short, punchy motion. He drew back the cue . . .

'Is this what you call military service, sirrah?'

The words came on a roar that could have drowned out the bells of the Abbey. Shocked, Jack's hand shot the cue forward and hit, not the top of the target but its bottom, the force lifting the ball from the baize and launching it off the table – where it was caught.

Jack stepped swiftly back, cue raised before him, pointing like a sword at the man now tossing the ivory sphere into the air, catching it, tossing it again.

His father.

— ELEVEN —

Fatherly Love

Jack was so shocked he couldn't even stutter, just stood there hissing like a snake, stuck on the first sound of 'sir'.

'Well, boy?' Sir James Absolute leaned forward and rolled the ball down the table. It sank into a pocket. 'Nothing to say? Lost your capacity for speech?'

'Uh . . .' offered Jack. He could not have been more surprised. Having only that morning consigned his father to the safety of a war a thousand miles away, it was almost impossible to accept his appearance before him now.

'No doubt you were going to offer me this beer,' said Sir James, pointing to the one the tavern servant was just carrying in. 'Don't mind if I do.'

The short time it took for his father to drain the pot restored Jack's speech. At least to the servant. 'T-two more of those, if you please.'

'Ah,' said his father with a smack of lips. 'Thirsty work on the roads. And good English ale will wash away the dust swifter than any of those Hanoverian laagers I've been drinking of late.' He tilted the mug, searching for a last drop.

'When . . . how . . .'

'How did I find you?' Sir James grunted. 'Your letter to Absolute House gave your address in Bath. I went there and a countryman of ours who was working next door said that in the afternoon you always could be found here.' He glared. '*Always* was the word used, ye dog. I spent all that money on a Westminster education and bought you a commission in one of the fanciest of regiments for you to become a frequenter of *billiard halls.*'

This last was said with such a distasteful glance around the room that Jack could only smile. He hadn't seen his father for nearly two years. In that time he had fought battles – two by land and one by sea – spent a winter in a cave eating bear meat, endured slavery, killed men, loved women . . . and here he was being chastized for a schoolboy's profligacy!

'If you would rather go somewhere else, sir?'

'No. Ordered the ale now. Might as well drink it.'

His father sat – heavily, Jack noticed. Now that he studied him he was surprised to note his apparel. Sir James loved clothes even more than his son, and had a purse to indulge his appetite. Yet here he was dressed in a leather frock coat such as a coachman might wear, patched shirt poking up from beneath a threadbare vest. Grey flannel breeches were tucked into riding boots that yawned between upper and sole. The whole was covered in the mud and dust that the indifferent roadways of England always conjured. It lay like lady's powder on his father's face, dulling the bushy black eyebrows, lining the large Absolute nose, but not obscuring the purplish bags under his eyes.

He is tired, Jack thought, more tired than I've ever seen him.

The ales came and his father drank full half of the pint. Jack sipped and waited. His father had not come all this way – and at some speed – to drink beer or chastize his son. A sudden fear came. 'My mother? She is—'

'Well, boy. Waiting for me in Hanover. I have a letter, somewhere,' he patted his coat, raising a cloud, 'though we did not know for certain you had crossed back over the ocean. She would not stay in London alone, once you and I were both gone. She never was one to obey orders.' He smiled faintly. 'But even she accepted that I could travel faster on my own.'

'You go back to the war? Is it not soon over?'

'Tell that to the Frogs. Seem unwilling to acknowledge that they are beat.' The smile vanished. 'Meantime, I had to take some measures, see some people at court and in the government in secret. My enemies are determined, it seems, to proceed with their act of attainder against our family. I have forestalled them, but only for a while, perhaps.'

'This secrecy accounts for your clothes. I suppose?'

'My clothes?' His father looked down, then slapped at his coat in disgust, raising more dust. 'Indeed. I am still, technically, a criminal and liable for the taking. So these rags are a concealment.' He looked his son up and down. 'What's your excuse?'

'These?' Jack said, pulling at the soiled serge of his short coat. 'These are also in the nature of a disguise.'

For a moment, both Absolutes looked at each other, a slight smile in their eyes. Then Sir James shook his head and continued. 'In the wars, I am, once more, building up a reputation as a cavalry commander that might wipe away the memory of my killing of Lord Melbury.' He nodded at Jack. 'A killing undertaken on your behalf, I will have you remember.'

'I remember it well, sir. And I have been doing my best to add honour to the name of Absolute. I have . . . done some things, by way of atonement.'

'I am sure you have, boy. Sure of it. And will continue to do so, I know. Absolute blood, eh?' He raised his mug, as did Jack, and they both drank long till his father belched. 'Which is why, when Nancy informed me that you had indeed made landfall and where you were, I came straight here rather than returning to Germany. Your timely return means you can make further atonement immediately.'

'Immediately, sir?' His voice could not conceal his concern. Sir James would have him back to the Dragoons or transferred to a regiment under his own command – in either case off to war again – in a trice. He was far keener on his son's military career than Jack had ever been.

'More or less.' Sir James set his mug down. 'These things take a little organizing, of course.'

'What things?' said Jack nervously.

Sir James leaned forward. 'I have told you that friends of mine – of ours – are engaged in a campaign to protect us against the repercussions caused by the death of Melbury. They may not be able to do so for long. Especially since certain individuals require suborning with gold which our friends cannot spare and I would find hard to raise from my exile.'

Jack coughed. 'I am expecting near two hundred pounds, sir, and would of course make it available—'

His father snorted. 'A piss drop in a chamber pot! Melbury had many allies while I have always made enemies. If they are not bought off, if they make common cause, well, their squadrons may overwhelm us. We need reinforcements. We need an alliance of both wealth and power.' He raised a hand triumphantly. 'What we need, sir, is a wife!'

Jack blinked. 'But, um, Father, you are already married. At least, I had always assumed so. To my mother?'

His father blinked back, then bellowed, 'The wife is not for me, you simpleton. The wife is for you.'

He had been so certain his father was going to march him off to war again that this news appeared to him as a kind of joke. He even laughed. 'That's impossible.'

'I can assure you it is not. It is not only possible, it will happen.'

Jack flushed cold. 'You would force me to marry?'

'I would expect you to obey. Why, only now you sought further atonement.' He glared. 'This is it!'

Suddenly, war seemed preferable. 'There are limits to atonement, sir. This is surely one. I cannot love just anyone.'

'Love my arse! What has love got to do with the price of cod? The girl herself is immaterial. It's the alliance that matters.' Sir James drank again, smacked his lips. 'We must ally with a powerful, rich and well-connected family who will help us to fight off those who would strip us of our title, our lands. Who will secure our lines of retreat with gold should my other stratagems fail.'

'But who . . . who is this girl? I assume you have someone in mind. It *is* a girl?'

'Girl. Woman. Aged spinster,' Sir James grunted. 'It matters not.'

'It matters to me. Surely you see it must matter to me.'

'Why?'

'Why?' He was going mad! 'What if she is hideous? Twice my weight? A crone with a temper?'

'You would still marry her and write poems to her slender beauty and her equanimity,' Sir James sneered. 'Wasn't it a poem that led you into this mess with Melbury? Now's your chance to write a better one!'

Hitherto, shock had kept Jack's voice low. Now his volume grew to match his father's. 'I can assure you, sir, that I will not marry this . . . whomever it is you have chosen. I will not. I cannot! Because I have already chosen for myself. And she is—'

'I care not who she is. She is your past. Your future is to marry as I tell you.'

'And I tell you, sir, that I will not.'

The door of the room opened. A servant stepped in. 'Can I get you gentlemen—'

'Get OUT!' bellowed both Absolutes, and the man staggered from the blast, slamming the door in his panic. But the intrusion had broken the flow of anger – at least on Sir

James' part. His voice, when it came, was almost quiet, twice as frightening.

'I have restrained myself. I have been patience itself. Your mother would have been proud. She said you might dare to object.' He tugged the collar away from a neck fast turning purple under the dust. 'But I will not expose myself to any more of your insolence. Tonight I will wait in the front porch of the Abbey during the twelve strokes of midnight. If, by the twelfth, you have not appeared and agreed to submit entirely to my will,' he walked to the door, opened it, 'well then, you are no longer a son of mine. I will find the gold I require even if I have to sell all our tin mines, for you will no longer require an inheritance. And I will fight the battle for the family honour alone.'

He left. Jack watched the open doorway for several moments, then walked to it. 'You there,' he called, leaning through. The servant appeared, somewhat nervously. 'Another pint of ale, if you please.'

Jack returned slowly to the billiards table. There he set up two balls, one red, one white. The cue wobbled as he bent and he had to take several deep breaths to steady it. When he was quite ready, he sighted and shot.

As he squatted in a bush outside the servants' entrance to Simpson's Assembly Rooms, there was only one thing of which Jack was certain – he was not going to marry some raddled old harridan just to please his father. Blood or no blood, there were other ways for him to atone for his youthful errors. Besides, if it was a wealthy and powerful alliance Sir James sought, surely a niece of the Earl of Clare would be as useful as any? All he had to do – to use his father's terminology – was to make a final assault upon the fortress, storm the breech, pour in his Grenadiers, pull down the enemy's shift – uh, colours . . .

Bollocks to the language of war, Jack thought. I am a

soldier of love now. I need to secure the girl. I need to do that tonight.

As what he was hoping for happened – a servant struggling with too big a load, grateful for Jack's assistance on the other side of the tray – a final thought came as he stepped inside the building: the threat of disinheritance meant he could act the role of the impoverished suitor for real. A little truth in his performance tonight would not hurt.

Depositing the tray, receiving thanks – and a curious look – from the servant, Jack pushed his way through the jostle. It was chaotic in the kitchen, for the music had just stopped and refreshments were required after the dance. Pausing by the entrance to the main room, Jack scoured the scene, glad that he was once again the observer not the observed. That would have been the problem with paying for a ticket and trying to enter in the customary manner.

Whereas at the baths it was the universal plainness of linen shifts that had hidden his quarry, here the opposite led to as great a concealment, for there now swirled before Jack a *mélange* of colours, almost nauseating in their variety. Everything was for display, and the wearers strutted; here a lime-green chest speckled with cornflowers, there an orange and pink confection of drape and frill – and that was just the men! The women were twice as colourful, twice as laden with material. The style, since Jack had been away, seemed to have turned largely in favour of the silk apron, thus allowing each of them to wear not one dress but, essentially, two. These did not always combine well; as was the case of a very small woman with no neck who looked like a yellow macaroon, her heated face the cherry atop it. There were also trollopes in every shade of God's creation and none, whose two-yard trains when stood on caused a constant tripping, making the whole assembly appear as if it partially consisted of bobbing ducks.

Fortunately, the swirl was separating, as the assembly

137

made for the side rooms for refreshment or cards. And it was into one of those rooms that he saw her go, the naturalness of her hair colour, the simplicity of its styling a decided contrast to the artificiality around her.

He was about to cross towards her when he became aware of attention focused upon him. He looked to his left and saw two Macaronies, a type of youth that seemed to have quadrupled in number since Jack left for war. These, somewhat older than the norm, had hair teased into columns above their heads, their faces powdered, lips shaded in crimson, eyebrows plucked to a line. One wore a pink coat and yellow vest, the other reversed the colours on his apparel, though both sported identical satin slippers of luminous green. They each supported one elbow on a hand, their other hand pressing a glass on a wand to the eye. They gazed at Jack through them, looking like nothing so much as Chelsea porcelain bookends.

'Rough,' said one, shivering with disgust, his eyes on Jack's red jacket.

'Rough,' agreed the other, but in an entirely different tone, looking Jack straight in the face.

Both their gazes travelled slowly south. 'Boots!' they both exclaimed, and the first speaker went on, 'Really, young gent, you cannot wear such things in company. Have you come straight from the farmyard? Take them off, sirrah! Take them off!'

'Take it all off,' said his companion, in the same tone he'd used before.

'Gladly, sirs,' said Jack, somewhat flustered. 'Just as soon as I've . . . you know . . . important message to deliver . . .'

He was gone, moving across to where he'd last seen her. But the voices pursued him. 'Send for Derrick! It will not do. Shameful! Eject him.'

A dart to the left, a jig right and he thought he'd lost the Fashion Watch in the crowd. Yet he knew there'd be a further hue and cry. He must succeed with his mission and leave before he was, indeed, ejected.

He saw her immediately, just settling into a chair at a card table. A swift glance around revealed no guardian; Mrs O'Farrell was tucking into the sweetmeats next door, no doubt. The chairs to either side of Letty were already occupied by two older ladies while a young man was just enquiring as to the empty seat opposite her.

Jack was across in three strides. 'So sorry I am late,' he gasped, flinging himself into the chair. 'Thank you,' he said, to the shocked young man whose hands were still on it. With a finger to his lips, the briefest of silencing gestures to the wide-eyed beauty opposite him, he snatched up a deck of cards, turned to the woman on his left and said, 'My deal, is it not?'

The young man harumphed and walked away. The woman – closer to fifty than the thirty her face paint aspired to – picked up a fan, flapped it and said, 'We 'ave not cut the deck yet, sir. But hif'n the geneelman wants t' go first, is it for the ladies to disoblige 'im?' The words, delivered in tones that were purest Thames at Puddle Dock, made Jack smile and begin. He assumed the game was whist, it nearly always was. So he dealt thirteen cards to each of them and, once he had fanned his, finally looked over them at Letty.

The shock had not left her face entirely. It showed most in those wondrous green eyes. He had never been with her in a public arena before – Mrs O'Farrell would not have countenanced it. Fortunately for the lovers, the guardian was most fond of a concoction called Hungary-water, a mix of lavender and rosemary in spirits of wine which some people used as perfume or to rub on minor wounds while others saw it as an aid to digestion. Jack was grateful that Mrs O'Farrell seemed so troubled in the guts; she drank a lot of it and it made her soporific, allowing Jack his visits to the Circus house garden.

I'll recommend a double dose the night we flee, he thought. His plan was made. He just had to find a way of conveying it to Letty.

He looked at his cards. Though he preferred more active games he had always done well with whist. But there was little to be gained with these cards. Not a royal among 'em and only one middling trump. He'd take one trick at the most.

The cockney pigeon – richly feathered, there was certainly money in fish – laid down the first card. The rounds proceeded and Letty took nine, her ten of spades trumping Jack's eight. Her cards were not all winners, she had just played them well. As the lady to his left gathered the cards to shuffle, Letty spoke.

'What makes a soldier among us, sir? Are we so short on wars?'

'Alas, I have taken a wound, miss, and needs must seek remedy.'

'A wound?' the lady on his other side asked. She was less richly dressed than the Londoner, better spoken. 'Nothing too threatening, I hope?'

'It is around the heart, so dangerous enough, I fear. Though perhaps here I will find the cure,' he replied, his eyes on Letty.

'Perhaps you will, sir,' she said, and he thrilled, as ever, to that low voice. 'I do hope so.'

'Lawks, don' concern yesself there, lovey,' squawked the fishwife, 'they've cures for all sorts 'ere. Deal again, shall I?'

Some agitation at the door made him turn to see his twin admirers from before, manicured fingers pointing at Jack, shooing a small neat man ahead of them. A whispering crowd followed.

The man marched up to the table. 'And who, sir, are you?'

'Who is it that enquires?' Jack said softly, folding his hand, laying it down. A good one too, eminently winnable. He was a little disappointed when he realized he was not going to get the chance. You didn't want the girl you loved to beat you at cards without a response.

His reply caused several to gasp. ''Ee's the Mistress of Ceremony,' whispered the lady from London, helpfully.

'I am Samuel Derrick, sir,' the man said with an icy look at Jack's abettor, who lowered her gaze with a nervous giggle, 'the *Master* of the Ceremonies. And you?'

'I am Cornet—'

He never finished his title. 'Interloper!' hissed the more aggressive of the Macaronies. 'Cornet Interloper . . . with his boots!' Jack was rising so the squeal went up a tone. 'See, Derrick, see how hideous they are! They reek of the farmyard.'

Jack turned slowly. 'If they reek, sir, 'tis of horse sweat, gunpowder and Frenchman's blood. Perhaps you should come nearer so as to be able to note the difference.'

The crowd was getting larger, louder. And all Jack wanted was an audience of one. So he turned back to Derrick, whose head only just reached Jack's chin and was puffing out his embroidered chest in compensation. 'Yet since you object to them, sir, I will remove them forthwith.' Another gasp came and he smiled. 'And myself in them, have no fear. But first there is a matter of honour I must deal with.' He looked for a moment at the Macaroni who shrank back against his companion. Then he turned back to the table, to his new friend. 'What was the stake, madam, for which we were playing?'

It was Letty who answered, not the Londoner. 'A trifle, sir. One hand dealt and no opportunity for the luck to swing your way. Please do not think on it.'

Jack looked at her, keeping his voice level. 'Even a trifle leaves me still in your debt.' He searched in his pockets, sighed. 'But it seems I have not even a single coin to recompense you.'

'I'll pay your debts, luvvie. And you can recompense me all night – and most of the mornin'.'

Half the throng laughed, half tutted. Jack bowed. 'I thank you, madam, for the kindness of your offer. But a gentleman must settle his own accounts.' He bent, seized the pencil used for marking scores, disdained the paper beside it. Instead, he reached into his own hand, the one he'd been unable to play. Swiftly, he wrote upon the back of a card. 'My address here in Bath. Please send a servant in the morning and I will pay both him for his trouble and you for your trifle.'

He flicked the card across. It landed face up, the writing pressed to the baize.

The card was the Jack of Clubs. She picked it up, read. nodded. 'I will do exactly as you desire, sir,' she replied.

I pray you will, tonight and for ever, he thought as he bowed to her, and both the other players at the table. Then he moved through the crowd, the Macaronies parting with a show of mock fearfulness before him. Two liveried flunkeys accompanied him to the main door and some way beyond it.

A little bold, he thought, once he was back on the street, looking back. Too showy perhaps? Yet it was certainly what a hero in one of her romantic novels would have done. The sudden appearance. The flick of the card. The etched lines:

'Spring Gardens stairs. Eleven o'clock. Come alone.'

— TWELVE —

Three Encounters

He had chosen the river stairs because, although they were busy by day for ferries to the Spring Gardens on the opposite bank of the Avon, by night they were deserted, Letty would know them and they were but a three-minute walk from Simpson's through a stretch of parkland. When the sounds of departing revellers, coach horses and chairmen had announced the end of the gathering, he had eagerly expected her almost immediately – and she did not come. By a quarter past the hour, he was biting his nails. At the half he was pacing back and forth along the dock. A dozen times he had started back toward the tumult, but there were several paths through the park and he could not be certain which one she would take. He had to wait, though his whole being strained to be away.

The Abbey bell was tolling quarter to midnight when he first heard her, in the swish of satin upon gravel, then saw her, running down the moonlit path. 'Letty,' he called, and in a moment she was in his arms.

'Oh, Beverley! My Beverley!'

Previously, he had only gone so far as pressing his lips to the inside of her wrist. Now, she was close enough for him to feel the speed of her heartbeat. He bent, sought, found lips, kissed. A moment of resistance, a longer one of giving, and then she pulled away, looking back the way she had come.

'Are you pursued?' he said.

'I am not certain.'

There was an alcove in the stonework of the dock. Jack pulled her into it, a space so small that he had to keep her pressed to him. 'Why were you so long? I thought you weren't coming.'

'My aunt was hard to elude. Especially when she heard the gossip.'

'What gossip?'

His eyes had adjusted to the night. He could see the smile. 'About you, sir. Our whist partner suspected something. I had to spill tea over the cards to get a new deck and prevent her looking at the Jack of Clubs. This increased her suspicions. "Lawks, 'ee was ever so 'andsome, weren't 'ee, sugar? Did you not fink so?"'

They both laughed. The accent was, as ever, finely done. 'She was seeking to know if I had any prior claim. Otherwise I believe I could have sold her the "address to your lodgings" for ten guineas.' She reached into her purse, produced the card. In a softer voice, she said, 'But I would not part with it for a thousand, nay, at any price.'

The look she gave him then, the memory of her lips upon his, made him pull her closer again. Then from the park came the sound of voices, calling her name.

He moved away. 'We must be swift, my love. Your aunt's vigilance will be all the more severe now. We may not get the chance to meet and talk again. We must make our plans now.'

'Plans?'

'For our elopement.' She gasped and he bent again, till he could see into her eyes. 'You will marry me, won't you, Letty?'

'Well . . .' Her eyes had flicked downwards and he realized

what she wanted. Instantly, he kneeled. 'Laetitia Fitzpatrick,' he said softly, 'will you make me the happiest man on the planet? Will you consent to be my wife?'

'I will,' she replied, and raised him once again to her lips, to a kiss that left them both breathless and his mind adrift.

Those voices, calling again, brought it back. 'We must fly, as soon as I can organize everything. A week, at most—'

'It must be tomorrow, Beverley,' she interrupted, her voice urgent, 'because something has happened. Something terrible.'

'What?'

'My aunt met a man in the street yesterday. He'd been seeking her out apparently. They conferred for some time in a coffee-house while I was taking communion. I emerged to discover . . .' She paused, looked up at him and tears had come to her eyes, 'that she had betrothed me to this man's son.' It was Jack's turn to gasp and she went on, 'So you have a rival, sir, and one they will try to force me to marry. They want me to meet him at breakfast and accept him before lunch.'

Jack was surprised at the intensity of his jealousy. Here he had won the girl and she was being promised to someone else. 'Who is this rival?' he said.

'They only told me his name at the very end, as if it did not matter, as if it was of no concern.' She had grown angry now. 'And as soon as I heard it I thought: how poorly that name contrasts with my dear Beverley's.'

'Yes,' said Jack, his jaw tight, 'but who is he?'

'His name's Absolute,' she said. 'Jack Absolute.'

For the briefest moment, his anger held him, as if he hadn't really heard the name but was prepared to hate the man regardless. When realization came, he could only stutter, 'J- J- Jack . . .'

'Absolute. Do you know him?'

145

Too many answers came all at once. 'Do you know, I think . . . I may have met him once—'

'If he is anything like his father he is a rough, big-nosed, black-browed Cornishman. Does that sound like the man?'

'Um, possibly. I scarcely remember the fellow. Not *too* big a nose, as I recall.'

His mind was swamped. Should he reveal himself to her, now that all – save she – were in favour of the union? He was tempted instantly to resolve matters that had become so complicated. But he'd wooed and won her as Beverley. It was a stratagem whose . . . subtlety she might not yet appreciate. And since she seemed so set against all things Absolute, that revelation should probably await another time. Perhaps when they were standing before an altar.

Once more, voices, much closer now, brought him back to present concerns. Seizing her hands, he whispered, 'You are right. Tomorrow it must be. Make sure your aunt has more than her usual dose of Hungary-water. I will be behind your house at midnight with a coach.'

'A coach? How can my poor Beverley's purse run to that?'

He must be careful! 'Egad, you are right. It will have to be horses. I'll steal them. Can you ride?'

She gave him a contemptuous look. 'I am from the County of Clare, sir, where the best horses in the world are raised and raced and—'

'Yes, well, I doubt I'll find you one of those,' Jack said, 'but I'll . . .' Another noise distracted him. Not voices this time. 'What is that?'

She tipped her head. 'The Abbey bells. It must be midnight.'

Midnight, Jack thought, his much-confused brain seeking something. Twelve bells . . .

Then he was gone, out of the alcove, sprinting flat out.

'Beverley,' she cried.

'Tomorrow,' he called back. 'Midnight.'

He was aware of others in the park, quite close by. A woman's voice came. 'You! Whoever you are! Stop!'

He couldn't stop. He had nothing to say to Mrs O'Farrell. Especially when the fourth bell of midnight had just sounded.

He'd always been fast. But his fever had perhaps sapped a little speed and his boots were meant for a stirrup, not gravel and grass. Still he was convinced he'd have made a run he estimated at about two hundred yards before the twelfth bell sounded if he hadn't been laughing so hard.

His father was going to disinherit him unless he married the girl he wanted to marry! It was almost too perfect.

The final bell's echo was still in the air when Jack slid along the cobbles into the Abbey churchyard. Bath, as usual, was cleared of inhabitants, all gone to rest up for their invalid exertions the next day. So the figure just about to disappear up an alley opposite the church's portico had to be . . .

'Sir! Sir!' Jack called.

The figure took a few more steps, then halted, did not turn. Jack ran across.

'Father?'

The coat was the same rough garment Sir James had worn earlier, the voice when it came, undoubtedly his. 'Well, puppy?'

Relief warred with breathlessness. Jack put his hands on his knees, breathed deep. 'A moment . . . sir . . . if you please . . .'

'Quickly, ye poltroon. For whom has the bell tolled? For thee, boy. For thee!'

Jack was unaware that his father was conversant with John Donne, his reading being mainly confined to the broad-sheets, so he could damn the government, and military manuals so he could fight the French. Lady Jane's influence, certainly. 'I noted it, sir, and thank you for your indulgence. Might we extend it further and go to a tavern—'

'I go nowhere with a disobedient dog,' Sir James growled, 'and I desire to spend no time with someone who is no longer my son.'

'But I hope to own that title again, sir,' Jack breathed deep, 'by submitting entirely to your will.'

'What's that?' Shock turned his father. 'What do you say?'

Jack straightened. 'I have reflected on your words, your urgings to honour and the family. I have decided that you are, as usual, entirely in the right.' He wondered if he'd gone too far. Suspicion was still clear in his father's eyes. He hurried on. 'This is too dangerous a time for Absolutes to do anything other than their duty.'

'So you'll marry the girl?'

'Girl. Widow. Aged spinster. Whomsoever you choose.'

'Why, Jack! Jack!' His father had stepped back, arms wide, and before he knew it he was crushed in his father's embrace. 'Then let us to this tavern of yours and drink to sense and reconciliation, eh? But I thought there was nowhere in this plague house of a town where a man could quench his thirst after midnight.'

'Not usually, sir, indeed. But the innkeeper of the Three Tuns has profited much of me of late and might remember it.'

'I'll wager he has, ye dog.' Sir James slapped him hard upon the back. 'Let's to him, then, and on the way, I shall tell you what your insolence and passion prevented me from doing before. Of the beauty that is to be yours.'

'She's not a crone, then, sir? Twice my weight with a temper to go with her size?'

'I know naught of her temper. She's Irish and red-haired so likely to have one. I am acquainted with the type, since I am married to your mother.' His father shook his head ruefully. 'But as to beauty, she has that beyond anything a scoundrel like you deserves.'

As they walked, Sir James told him more of his good fortune. How the idea of an alliance with a powerful house had been sown into his mind by his friends in London and in his ride to Bath, the seed had taken root. 'And when, on arrival, I chanced to read that one Laetitia Fitzpatrick, niece to the Earl of Clare, was the toast of Bath society, well . . .' Again he clapped his son upon the back. 'As you know, I am not a religious man. But it appeared to me to be a sign as bright as any burning bush. For Clare is cousin to the Duke of Newcastle who, now Pitt has resigned, is the First Minister of the land.'

Jack shook his head. His father had planned to marry him off on the strength of a report in a tattle column! From anyone else such peremptory action would have seemed incredible. But this was 'Mad Jamie' Absolute after all, the man who'd charged all alone into a troop of French Dragoons at Dettingen and driven them from the field. Still, Jack knew he might not have been so sanguine about the tyranny had the object settled upon not been the woman he happened to love.

He halted and his father looked up. 'Isn't this the place we were at before?'

'It is, sir.'

They entered, and the sleepy landlord was coerced into bringing ale. Once tankards were before them, Sir James recommended expressing his self-satisfaction.

'I chanced to hear the girl's name called upon the West Parade. I advanced and victory was nigh certain. The only setback was your damned insolence.'

'For which I again apologize, sir,' Jack said dutifully, 'though I confess I am a little confused as to how you obtained her guardian's consent?'

'Ah. Well there, I admit, I was forced to employ a little

149

dissimulation.' His father grinned, leaned in. 'For Mrs O'Farrell had not heard of our family's temporary inconvenience. Since I did not mention it, she readily agreed to a union she was sure would meet the approval of her cousin, the Earl. Indeed, she informed me that their purpose in Bath was to find just such a suitable match and that her cousin had expressed such confidence in her judgement the banns could be read tomorrow and the girl married next Thursday.' He beamed. 'The business was concluded over a bowl of chocolate and only your assent required. Now we have that . . .' Sir James smacked his lips.

'And the girl's?'

'The girl's? Humph! What signifies that?' He waved a finger. 'Daughters know their places better than sons do, never fear. We will go and see her tomorrow to hear her joyful acceptance. Though I risk encountering someone I know – half the judiciary seem to be taking the waters here presently – it is a risk I will gladly take to see my son happy.' He drank and belched contentedly.

Jack traced a puddle of beer with his finger. 'Sir, may I suggest two things?'

'You may try.' Ale and acquiescence had mellowed the older man.

Jack attempted an earnest expression. 'I do worry for your safety. What would happen if you were taken and charged for Melbury's death before the business is complete?'

Sir James contemplated this. Encouraged, Jack continued. 'And I have heard of this girl. Indeed she is quite the topic in the coffee-houses. Gossip tells how she is whimsical. She is renowned for her passion for romance.'

'Romance?' His father snorted. 'What's that to duty?'

'Nothing to me, of course, sir. But apparently it is to her. If I could only get her to love me for myself as well as for the alliance . . .' He frowned earnestly. 'I believe, sir, that things would proceed so much more smoothly.'

Sir James drank, considered. 'You may be right. Young people today seem not to have the same respect as we did in my youth. And these matters take a little arranging anyway. So long as we announce the engagement, we bring the forces of the Earl of Clare into our army straightaway.'

'And if we announce it in two weeks?'

'Two weeks, eh? Hmm.' He finished the mug and Jack immediately signalled to the landlord for replenishment. 'I suppose a fortnight is not far off. It may take me that long to get back to your mother in Germany. And if I make the announcement from there, as soon as I arrive . . .' The beers came and Sir James raised his. 'Very well, boy, I'll indulge this romance you all seem so obsessed by. To love, you puppy. To love.'

The love I have, thought Jack. And two weeks on the highways, two weeks of unromantic poverty, should lessen my Letty's desire for it considerably. By the time all is revealed, I'll have my beautiful girl and her beautiful fortune. And I'll have done my Absolute duty.

Raising his tankard, he glimpsed the landlord staring at them from the corner and wondered which Absolute the fellow thought wore the more satisfied smile.

They drank deep into the night, the yawning publican contented by a gold crown to leave them to his barrels – though Jack was not sure he got a bargain. His father's good humour entirely restored, it was time to swap stories of their recent escapades. Sir James was a suitably impressed audience, loudly applauding all tales of combat, happily appalled by the tattoos Jack showed him on chest and forearm.

Light was in the sky when they staggered out. Sir James seemed to have drunk himself sober and would not hear of staying at Jack's house. 'I will away,' he said. 'It's a long ride to Harwich and a hazardous crossing to Hamburg. Your mother awaits.'

Jack knew there was no arguing with him. And to be

truthful, it was better he was gone. Sir James's moods were notoriously changeable. He'd wake with a sore head and haul Jack and Letty before a priest on a whim. 'Kiss her for me.'

'I will, lad. And you shall see us both soon – at your wedding.'

Not unless you ride via Scotland, Jack thought. He walked his father to his inn, saw his horse saddled. In his stirrups, Sir James leaned down.

'Godspeed, boy. If the girl is imbecilic enough to fall for your romance, I shall just have to accept that I will get idiots for grandchildren.' The smile belied the words. 'Love and duty,' Sir James cried, swinging the horse's head, digging in his heels.

Jack watched his father till a corner took him, then he began a slightly meandering ascent to the Upper Town. He was ready for his bed now, for the few hours sleep he could allow. He must be up early – an elopement took organizing and he only had one day to do it.

He thought of going in the front door. Surely the girl would not be watching from her house opposite at this hour? Yet caution, this close to the prize, made him tread the gravel behind the Circus. Next door, all remnants of building work had been cleared away. The house was almost ready for the royal visit.

He smiled, hiccoughed. King George arrives and Jack Absolute leaves. Quite a day for the Corporation of Bath!

He spent nearly half a minute trying to understand why his key didn't work. Then he realized the back door had been open and he had just locked it again.

'Bloody Fagg,' he muttered, pushing in. 'Lazy in everything.'

Tiredness was a strange thing. So complete the one moment when he thought he might not even make his bed. Completely gone the next, when a hand reached out from the dark and seized his arm.

Drunk he may still have been. Incapacitated he was not. And he had done a lot of wrestling in his Cornish youth.

The hand that gripped him was gripped in its turn, twisted against its inclination. At the same time Jack stepped away and back towards the door. Through it there was space for flight or further fight; above all, there was light.

His left hand had gone straight to the shoulder above the twisted arm, pushing the man's face towards the floor, turning his body away from him. If he had a knife or a cudgel in his other hand he should not be able to use it. If he had a pistol, mind . . .

'Faith, man, is this how you greet your friends?'

The voice was pained – and recognizable. 'Red Hugh?'

'The same. And if you're quite done with it, could I be after having me own arm back?'

Jack released his grip but, just in case his brain was playing him tricks, he also stepped the other way, to the door, throwing it open. A rectangle of pale light came through. In the centre of it squatted the Irish Grenadier.

'Christ, man, you've broken me bloody arm.'

'I don't think so,' said Jack, leaning against the doorframe, his legs suddenly weak. 'We'd have heard the crack.'

Suddenly, both men were laughing. Red Hugh rose, and they each extended a hand. 'Easy now, me lad. It might yet fall off.'

They shook and Jack saw the man wince. Looking down, even in the faint light, he could see a stain on both their palms, feel the stickiness of blood. 'I did not do that, did I?'

The Irishman shook his head. 'An earlier misfortune.'

'And this?' Now he was closer and his eyes adjusted to the light, he could see that his hand was not the only hurt sustained. There was bruising on his cheeks, one eye was nearly closed, and there was blood running from his nose.

'I know. I know.' Red Hugh saw the concern in Jack's eyes. ''Tis superficial only. Sure and you should see the other fella.' The laugh that came pained him and a hand went to his side.

'We should get you upstairs to a bed,' Jack said.

'That would be fine indeed. But I came in the dark and I must leave the same way, observed by no one.' He tipped his head to the ceiling. 'Will your servant not be about your business?'

'Fagg?' Jack snorted. 'He'll only be about the business of sleeping for a good two hours yet. You will not be seen.'

'Then I'll take that offer of a lie-down and perhaps some brandy if you've any about.'

Though he moved slowly, he did not need Jack's arm. And once he was sitting in a drawing-room armchair, brandy in hand, a pipe lit and the worst of the blood and dirt washed away, he seemed already revived.

'I thought there was a rib stoved but now I think 'tis only bruised. Other than that, just a few cuts and scrapes. This one,' he held up his right hand, wrapped in a handkerchief that Jack had supplied, 'might need some stitching, if you've needle and cat gut.'

'I can get some.' Jack shook his head, wonderingly. 'You've got another story to tell and no mistake.'

Red Hugh blew a smoke ring toward the ceiling. 'A dull one, my boy. Tawdry, to be truthful. Not the storming of a breech under a Turkish cannonade, or a night attack across an ice floe.' He sighed. 'I told you I had creditors in this town.'

'You did. Those men at the theatre were their represent-atives. You never told me what you owed or why.'

'Another piece of dullness. But these fellows decided that my bond was not good enough. They decided they wanted flesh as well. Or instead.' He smiled. 'Shylock, isn't it? Anyway, those big boys you saw came for me in an alley and,' he gestured to himself, 'well, I got away but I'm half sure I killed one of them before I did.'

Jack went across, filled the empty glass. 'And will they seek you again?'

'Undoubtedly. My time in Bath is over, methinks. If you wouldn't mind my sleeping here for the day, I'll slip out with the night.'

'You are most welcome. Though since it is our joint prize money that has paid for this abode, it's as much yours as mine. And didn't you stow some stuff in the cellar?' He received a nod. 'I don't know how much rest you'll get, though. They are presenting the house next door to the King today. There's bound to be a marching band, fanfares and other hot air.'

'The King? I had forgot. And next door, is it?' Red Hugh had put down the glass and was peeking under the handkerchief at his cut. 'Well, he'll not disturb me. Caesar entering Rome atop an elephant having triumphed over Vercingetorix would not wake a McClune when he has a mind to sleep. As he does.' He gave a huge yawn.

Jack poured the man another tot of brandy. 'Have you, uh, seen your cousin at all?'

'Laetitia? I have not. My troubles, alas, have kept me from her lovely company.' The glass was halted halfway to the mouth. 'You've met my cousin, then, Mr Absolute?'

'Ah,' said Jack, and proceeded, awkwardly, to tell his tale. It was received in silence and a cold stare, which began, gradually, to thaw. At its conclusion, a long silence held before the Irishman spoke again.

'And you say her guardian approves the match?'

'To Jack Absolute? She does,' replied Jack eagerly. 'Indeed, all parties do.'

'Well, I am not as close a relation as Mrs O'Farrell. But close enough to demand the family's honour is upheld.' He studied Jack closely. 'Will it be?'

Jack nodded. 'I swear to you, sir. The former self you disapproved of is no more. We love each other and she has consented to be my wife.'

Red Hugh smiled then frowned. 'Beverley's wife.'

'Ah, you have hit it, sir. There lies my problem.' Jack rose, began to walk up and down the room. 'The guise that enabled me to woo her now stands between us. I can't marry her as Beverley. I must own myself again. Yet if I do, will her cursed romantic nature not rebel at a marriage everyone approves of? Will she not resent the subterfuge I used to win her?' He sighed. 'I am at a loss, sir, I confess.'

Red Hugh came and placed a hand on Jack's shoulder. 'You said it yourself: two weeks of low inns on the road to Scotland will surely cure the romance of poverty. While two weeks of your company will win her for yourself, certain. Do not doubt your own power to attract, dear soul. I've told you, haven't I, how you remind me of me in my youth? And was there a lady of Clare that did not desire a better acquaintance with both my face and my mind? None, I say!'

'Then you think—'

'Give her the elopement she craves, lad. Then marry her as yourself.'

Jack flushed with excitement. 'By God, I will. I'll be about the preparations instantly. Midnight cannot come fast enough.'

He turned, as if to begin. But the Irishman's hand turned him back. 'Now there's the only point of disagreement between us. And it's the usual quarrel of age with youth. Do not attempt the elopement at midnight.'

'But I thought—'

'D'ye hear that rain?' They both listened. 'It's the type that will come and go all day and on through the night. The roads will be awash, the carriage ruts concealing holes to trap a horse's hoof. Six gets you three, you'll lose your way, circle about and, by dawn's light, be drenched and exhausted scarce five miles from Bath.' He raised a hand to forestall Jack's protest. 'I acknowledge romance almost demands the midnight escape. And I know you wish Laetitia to tire of poverty sooner rather than later. But not at five tomorrow morning.'

Jack was disappointed. Midnight was indeed the time prescribed for elopements in all those ghastly novels. However, he could also see the sense. 'What hour would you suggest?'

'Tomorrow still but early in the afternoon. People always think the night best for mischief but daylight is when no one's expecting it. I'll get a message to Mrs O'Farrell, luring her away from noon till three. And another, advising Letty. How's that for friendship?'

'I would not want you to risk encountering enemies on the street again.'

'Rest easy, I'll take care of that at no exposure to myself, I assure you. It's the least I can do – and probably the only wedding present I can afford.' He gripped Jack's shoulder, looked deep within his eyes. 'Sure, don't I already consider you a relation? I cannot tell you my delight in knowing that the relationship will soon be made official in a church – cousin!'

'Cousin!' echoed Jack with a grin. Preoccupied elsewhere, he had forgotten just how much he liked this man.

Another yawn came, larger than all the rest. 'But if I'm to accomplish anything today, I must get some sleep. Was there not an offer of a bed?'

Jack led the way from the parlour and up the stairs. 'I'll make sure I forestall the servant from entering. You will not be disturbed.'

'I am beyond gratitude.' He looked into the bedroom. 'A snug billet, sure. What's through there?' He pointed to the door on the other side of the landing.

'Another bedroom,' replied Jack, 'but empty of all furniture.'

Red Hugh had already gone and sat on the bed. He was pulling at his boots, and it obviously pained him, so Jack helped him off with them. Then he went to close the shutters and shut out the creeping daylight. Glancing into the street, he saw that some workmen were already before the house next door, about final preparations. Flowers were being arranged in pots, bunting threaded through the railings that fronted the building. What had his Cornish friend called his bedroom? 'The best view in Bath.'

'You know,' he murmured. 'I would not have minded seeing the King receive his house.'

A voice came from the bed, muggy with sleep. 'Don't worry, dear honey. I'll tell you how it all turns out.'

— THIRTEEN —

Hail to the King

It was hard labour, leading three horses through the streets of Bath. Two were sullen and venerable nags, typical of what could be hired at coaching inns across the land. The third, a bay gelding that Jack had mounted, was younger and at least had some spirit but showed it mainly by nipping at the others and, when they were unavailable, at passers-by. This latter activity increased as the crowds thickened at the top of Stall Street, causing him to be cursed frequently and, on two occasions, struck with sticks. There was a wall of backs ahead of him, heads reared to catch sight of the day's great attraction: the King, having bathed and taken the waters, progressing up the town toward the Circus and the presentation of number twenty-one.

The noise was horrendous, for not only did the crowds shout and huzzah at each glimpse of royalty, but the royal progress had attracted every brass player in Bath. There seemed to be a formal orchestra giving a bottom line to the music, a selection of popular favourites like Arthur o'Bradley or Black Eye'd Susan. But over it was a cacophony of mainly French horn, played by men with some talent, little or none.

The horses, already twitchy, did not react well. When he was jabbed a third time by an irate victim's stick, Jack turned and forced his horses back the way he'd come. The nags, sensing their home at the Three Tuns, sped up and Jack had to ply his own stick quite viciously to force them past the inn and finally onto the Lower Borough Walls. It was a round-about route to his goal. But since his was the same as the King's, there was no chance of getting there this side of Christmas if he followed the crowds.

Outside St Mary's Chapel he was blocked again by the surge of people pouring into Queen Square. He forced the horses left, glancing back once to glimpse a rotund man mounting a platform to general acclaim, a tricorn hat lifted from a bewigged head and waved. He had, at least, seen the King. As he led his horses on a further detour, he prayed that he would not see him again.

The chapel's bell had sounded one, an hour later than he had planned and Red Hugh had warned Letty of. It was yet another twenty minutes before Jack was tying the horses to railings behind her house. He sighed and tipped his head to the rain that had begun to fall again. It wasn't a warm day but his labours had soaked his uniform in sweat, great patches appearing at the armpit. Rain cooled him a little and, replacing his hat, he made a final check of the horses' cinches, bridles and stirrups, for though he was in a hurry, he feared that Mrs O'Farrell might have been distracted only so long, that he would have to snatch his prize, mount and ride fast. He had calculated Letty's height for her side-saddle, thought he had it right. One nag had Jack's – Beverley's – paltry possessions attached to it, with straps uncinched to take what Letty must bring. He hoped Red Hugh had passed on his advice to travel unencumbered.

At the back gate he paused, drew a deep breath, looked once more to the skies. 'Why are you doing this, boy?' he murmured. 'Why?'

Then he pushed the gate in and had his answer. She was pacing close to the house, her riding boots crunching on the

160

wet hoggin. She was dressed in the simplest of dark brown gowns, the apron atop it made of linen, not impractical silk. On her head she wore a man's tricorn, uncocked, so that the brim sloped down over the face that turned at his whispered, 'Letty!' The plainness of her dress only heightened the effect of her beauty, and Jack had to take another breath before she ran into his embrace.

'Your aunt?'

'Gone to see the King.'

'I think you and I must be the only people in Bath who have not.'

'I have my own king here.'

Jack laughed. It was a speech that could have come from any of those novels that she so loved, or most of the comedies in the playhouse. He had to keep remembering that she was only seventeen, a full year younger than him, with not one-tenth of his experience in the world. It was one of her delights, this naivety. So what if it was wrapped up in all this fol-de-rol? A man dallied with the Fannys and Clarys of the world; even the Widow Simkins. But the same man married a Letty.

He'd pulled her tight. Now he could feel her shaking. Disengaging slightly, he said, 'Are you cold, dearest? I have kept you waiting in this garden too long.'

'A little cold, yes. And I have not slept, for nights now, it seems.' Her lower lip was trembling and, as he looked, her eyes welled. 'But it is also . . . also . . .'

'What, my dearest? Come here.' He led her to the white garden bench. It was sheltered beneath a Judas tree and thus not too wet with rain, his cloak used to sweep aside some drops and the tree's few fallen seed pods, its purple flowers. 'Tell me,' he said.

She twisted her hands within his. 'Should we not be riding?'

'Presently. But if Mrs O'Farrell has gone to view the King

she surely will not leave until he has received his house. That will not be for a while because I suspect young Georgie is only now leaving Queen Square.'

Indeed a marching song had begun to play within the din. They had time. 'Tell me,' he said again.

'It's just . . . just.' The tears spilled out.

'Have you had second thoughts,' he said, 'about me?'

She clutched him tighter. 'Of you, never! Never! But it seems a low trick,' her lips trembled, 'to practise on the people who love me.'

Jack was suddenly stricken. It had all seemed such a game up to now. A play, one of a thousand enacted each day in Bath, just as Fanny Harper had said. There hadn't seemed any true harm in being a player in one of them. Yet now, as he touched a tear upon her face, it came to him that what he was about was not entirely honourable. Not honourable at all. He'd always planned on telling her, was certainly not going to let her marry 'Beverley', but he'd hoped to leave the revelation till they were away from Bath, from her inevitable instinct to run in anger back to her guardian. To tell her in a quiet of village in Scotland, after two weeks' travelling, of truly getting to know each other, knowledge deepening their love. Now her tears rebuked him.

'Letty,' he said, 'there's something—'

A finger came onto her lips. 'Hush! Hush now! Never mind me. Just a young girl's foolishness. Come!' She was rising, pulling Jack by the cuff of his jacket. 'We will talk more when we are certain we are safe.'

'No. You must hear me. I . . .' He was resisting her impulse and the rest of the words he would utter were taken away by a loud rip. Suddenly she was standing there looking down at him, with one of his red sleeves in her hand.

'Oh, Gemini,' she said and giggled, and so did he, and then they were both laughing so hard she had to sit down again. When she got her breath, she added, 'So sorry, sir.'

The play had suddenly turned farce! 'Pray, madam, give it no mind.' He took the sleeve back, held it to the dangling threads. 'Could only be an improvement to this damned coat.' The tailoring was poor, it had obviously been repaired before and the sweat of his labours had rotted the few threads that somehow had held it together. He hated the bloody thing! He loved his clothes and here he was disguised as a man with no purse and lamentable taste. What must she think of him? What would she think of him, when all was finally revealed, when she'd forgiven him the follies love had driven him to, when she stood before the Scotch parson and looked at him, stinking, rotten, sleeveless Scarecrow Beverley! No, he would be marrying her as Jack Absolute. And, dammit, he would be wearing Jack Absolute's uniform!

'Excuse me,' he said, rising. 'I will be but a moment.'

She rose in her turn, alarmed. 'Where are you going?'

'My lodgings.' She gasped. 'Do not fear. We still have time. If you will wait by the horses—'

'You cannot go!' she cried with a force that startled him. 'Hearken to the band, sir. They are getting closer. The crowds may prevent your swift return. There can be nothing of such importance—'

It was his turn to interrupt. 'Forgive me, but there is. I have another uniform there. Still poor,' he added hastily, 'but better than this horror. And now I remember, my sword is with it, necessary for the dangerous road.' He pulled away, began to move towards the gate. 'Do not fear. I will not go through the crowds. The park takes me around the back of the Circus.'

She seized his hand. 'I beg you. Do not leave me. I feel sure all will go amiss if we do not leave now!' The force of her declaration, the tears again in her eyes, made him hesitate. She saw, drew close to him again. 'Please, Beverley,' she said her tones softer, that husk coming into them. 'Please.'

She had pressed herself into him. Her dress was not the

163

swathes of cloth she wore to the Assemblies. It was more like the linen shift he'd watched her emerge from the water in, clinging to her shape. That shape pressed against him now, into him, at distinct points.

'My love,' he murmured, his timbre matching hers.

She raised her face to him. He looked into those eyes, thought, as ever, how he wanted to drown himself five fathoms deep in their greenness. He bent, kissed the lids that closed, and when his lips moved downwards, there was no holding back as there had been even in the kiss at the Spring Gardens. Her lips parted. He was lost.

Somehow they walked backwards, his hands up and cupping her face, hers reaching back. Her knees collided with the bench and she guided him down, the kissing frantic now, a jumble of give and take. When he ran the tip of his tongue along the roof of her mouth, she gave a cry that turned swiftly to a laugh. He threw her hat to the side, thrust his fingers into her piled-up hair.

Her mouth was close to his ear. 'Yes,' she whispered. 'Yes.'

'Yes?' Confirmation came in her sigh, in the way she suddenly pushed herself up off the bench and into him as she had before. His hands moved down slowly, fingers stroking from her neck, running around and then over each breast, pressing through the material, circling, feeling a firming there. 'Yes?' he asked again, the last question he thought he'd ever ask. For she didn't reply in words, just took one of his hands, kissed it and pushed it lower.

There was a moment perhaps when he still could have stopped, before the world became blurred by linen rising, flung aside, by cotton shifts furled like sails, by scent and sight and the sudden surprise of her thigh against his cheek. He rose up and her hands were steady at his breeches' buttons, where his fumbled. A slight pain came as his knees ground once more into the gravel of the garden; pain swiftly supplanted by sensations of a better kind, as he ripped the last of his buttons away, moved clear, moved inside her. A moan, but not of pain, swept the last cautions from his mind, as did her movements beneath him, not holding him off, guiding him, her legs so wrapped around him that he could not move if he'd wanted to, which he didn't; content to stay like that until . . . until that band, getting ever closer, played in tune at last. Which would be never.

He lifted and turned her so he was sat upon the bench and she upon him. The rain rolled off the bare shoulder thrust from her shift, fell onto him, cooling him but only a little as breaths came shorter, his matching hers, faster now, faster. Groans replaced breath, somehow they'd moved again and he was on top of her on the bench and the moment came when he could hold off no longer and she managed the impossible, pulling him even deeper inside, holding him there while all their moans passed, all their shudders subsided.

'Stay,' came the whispered order, and he obeyed, shifting only enough to take his weight off her, and to reach for his crumpled cloak to cover them both. They lay there, her eyes closed, his open so he could study a little pulse in her neck, fluttering like a moth trapped behind glass.

'Letty,' he whispered, and she wriggled into his chest. He stared up into the Judas tree that part-sheltered them, amazed that he'd never noticed before just how intense was the purple of its flowers . . .

He woke with a start, arm pressed between her body and the bench. He thought it was the pain that woke him, not the tuneless band that was now considerably nearer, was probably close to entering the Circus itself. When he moved his arm, she gave a little whimper but slept on. He watched her for a moment, then shivered. The rain was still falling lightly and if he was cold, he was sure she must be, too. For a moment he thought of waking her; but she looked so beautiful he didn't want to disturb her. She hadn't slept in a week, she'd said. Mrs O'Farrell would, surely, be gawking at the King. He could allow her a few minutes more. He just needed something to keep her warm. Another blanket would be useful for the journey too.

The rear door of the house was locked, her bags for the elopement outside it; mercifully few, he noted approvingly. She may have been a romantic but she was no fool. He stepped back, looked up to the first level, where the drawing rooms would be. A window was open a half inch. Between the pediment of the rear door and the window sill there was a six-foot gap.

The sill was a little slick with rain. But the exterior covering of the joist, a small metal shield, was not quite flush to the wall, giving him enough of a foothold to perch on, reach a hand, grip the underside of the window itself. With a heave he was balanced on the sill, then shoved the window up and was through it.

He was at the rear window of a drawing room, the one where Letty said Mrs O'Farrell would obligingly doze while her niece walked alone in the garden. Thus Jack expected a chair to be placed there, was surprised when there was not one; a surprise swiftly surpassed when he realized that not only was there no chair, there was no furniture in the room of any kind whatsoever.

He moved into the hallway, as cheers exploded below, and the band increased the discordance of their playing. The King was entering the square just as Jack entered the second drawing room to find it as barren as the first. As with the other room, it was clear that it had not been recently emptied of furniture. There had simply never been any furniture in it.

'No,' he said aloud, not believing. 'Oh no.'

A sprint to the top floor, to bedrooms devoid of beds. As he stood there gaping, even above the music from the street, he heard her cry.

'Beverley! Beverley! Where are you?'

He was down to the drawing room in a moment. 'Here,' he called, appearing at the window before thrusting himself through it, lowering himself to the hand- and footholds, reaching the ground, turning to her. She was standing by the bench, still beneath the Judas tree.

'What were you doing?' she asked as he moved to her.

'Looking for something to cover you up. I didn't find anything.'

Now he was close, he could see fear in her eyes. Not in her voice though. 'I've a cloak in my bags.'

'No,' he said, just holding back the anger. 'I didn't find *anything*. The house has not been lived in.' Suddenly he shouted, 'What is happening here?'

She flinched but did not recoil. 'I was going to tell you. My aunt decided to leave Bath. That is why we had to flee today. We . . .'

She stopped. Something in his face made her stop.

'You kept me here,' he said, gesturing to the bench. 'Isn't that what you did? Seduced me to keep me here.' He moved close, grabbed her arm roughly. 'Didn't you?'

'No, I didn't,' she cried, 'I swear it, Jack, I . . .' He let go of her arm. 'What?' she said. 'Why do you look at me like that?'

'Because you called me Jack.'

It was all he could do not to vomit. He felt as he had aboard the ships he'd voyaged in, sick in his stomach, the ground shifting beneath him. 'You called me Jack,' he repeated softly.

'Yes,' she shrugged, her eyes downcast. 'Jack.'

And suddenly it came, in recent voices, echoing.

You've the finest view in Bath.

I'll tell you how it all turns out.

And further back . . .

I used to be a dangerous man. Not any more.

And even longer ago . . . Men chasing a naked Irishman down to the dock at Newport, yelling a word after him, a word Jack hadn't quite been able to hear because the wind had changed suddenly. He'd thought they shouted, 'Trader!' and considered it odd at the time. *Traitor* – not trader.

'Your cousin, Red Hugh McClune,' he said softly. 'The traitor.'

'No, Bev . . . Jack, no, you must—'

He brushed her hand aside, turned and sprinted for the gate. Her cries after him blended with the shouts from the Circus and the tuneless French horns. Surprisingly, though, at last he could detect a rhythm.

'One elephant,' he muttered. 'Two elephants.'

The long way would be the quickest. The short route across the Circus would be blocked by people hailing the King.

A rough path paralleled the circle within. Part gravel, it often gave way to stretches of mud, sticky and thick after the day's downpours. He crossed two stable lanes that serviced the buildings, storage for carriages, stalls for horses. At the end of the second row of these structures, he glanced into the Circus itself. The platform in the very middle now swarmed with people. The bands had ceased and he could hear someone speaking poetry. As at Queen Square, there was another glimpse of that wig.

Three horses were tied up behind his lodgings, like the three he'd left at Letty's, equally laden. The door to the kitchen was open, and renewed cheering from the street covered his climb past the parlours and on up to the bedrooms. He stopped, listened. Under the noise from outside he could detect sounds in his bedroom, something heavy being dragged across the floor. Quietly, he slipped into the other room, the one he'd used for storage. The uniform he'd forgotten still hung from one bedpost. Ignoring it, he reached under the bed for the second thing he'd forgotten in his haste. Drawing his small sword, he moved again onto

168

the landing and across to his bedroom door, put a hand on the doorknob, took a breath . . .

He'd expected Red Hugh to be by the window, grenade in hand. In fact, the Irishman was stretched upon the bed, hands behind his head, though he moved fairly quickly when Jack came through the door; off the bed, into the corner with an indistinguishable yell.

'Jack,' he cried, clutching at his ribs. 'You near made me shit my breeches! I thought you were the Watch, so I did.'

Jack moved into the room, sword raised before him, his arm straight. Behind its guard he looked around swiftly, saw the things he expected – a chair by the window, a Dragoon pistol hanging in a holster from it, three grenades bunched on it, a fuse cord draped over it, glowing.

'You bloody traitor,' Jack whispered as he looked back.

Red Hugh shook his head. 'To whom? I serve the true King, that's all.'

'Actually, McClune, I meant a traitor to me.'

'No, lad, I—'

Red Hugh had come forward and Jack flicked the sword point at him, making him halt. 'All your reluctance to introduce me to Letty? A stratagem. You baited a hook for me, your friend . . .' He was finding words hard to come by, till his fury made him shout it out. 'You used your cousin like a whore, to seduce me.'

Hands came up in protest. 'What are you saying? I did no such thing, I swear it. Was I not wanting a good match for my lovely Laetitia? And did I not know of your dealings with women so far? Sure, I caught two hussies fighting over you like cats in the Llandoger Trow. You'd left that widow in Newport, an actress in London—'

Jack, staring over his blade, couldn't understand how, at this moment, they were discussing his liaisons. 'My ambitions for your cousin were always honourable while you . . .'

Another huzzah came from the Circus and both men glanced, glanced back swiftly. Red Hugh spoke again. 'Jack, I just assumed that what you came by too easily you would esteem too lightly. You'd have been off and straying in a year, with my cousin walled up in Absolute House or some such.'

'Can you think so little of me?'

'I think so little of all young men. I was one myself.' He lowered his hands, stretching them out towards Jack in appeal. 'So I made you take a little test.'

It was almost plausible. But the grenades did not allow Jack to believe even for a moment. 'You used me,' he swallowed, trying to contain his anger, 'to keep these rooms for you. And you couldn't afford two houses on the Circus, as you'd spent all your prize money on Letty's three dresses. Hence the nightly charade over there; courting her in the garden, never seeing her enter the house.' He waved beyond the music. That brought it back to him. 'By God,' he murmured. 'You have used me as a cover so you can blow up the King.'

'Now that's an entirely separate matter,' the Irishman said. 'I don't interfere in your politics and you should have the courtesy not to bedevil mine.'

Jack gaped. 'Separate? You have dragged me into your conspiracy, linked the name of Absolute with your treason, compromised my honour with your cousin, and her honour – if she has any – with me!' The sword point, still thrust forward, was beginning to waver with his rage. 'The lengths you were prepared to let her go to . . .' He choked on the memory. 'Well, I realized in the nick, did I not?'

'Did you, lad? Did you now?'

They had circled as they spoke, Jack moving past the window, the Irishman climbing over the bed. It was the suddenness of the music – the brass refrain loud, its contrast to the gentle Irish voice – that made Jack's eyes jerk to it and back only in time to see the other man reach into the corner there and produce a sword of his own, swiftly cleared from its scabbard. 'Now, lad,' Red Hugh went on again in the same quiet tone, 'let's be having no more nonsense, shall we?' His sword made a pass at the window. 'For haven't I got things to be getting on with?'

'Not while I stand here, you haven't,' Jack replied.

'Ah, it would hurt me to hurt you, boy. Put up. You know you cannot beat me.'

'Now why would I be knowing such a thing?' Jack said, mocking the accent, coming forward.

They fought in the narrow space between the bedposts and the window, as wide as the usual space between fighters in a salle, not as long. Red Hugh's sword was in his left hand as always, thus coming at Jack from the brightness of the window.

Jack had attended the fencing school in the Haymarket since the age of eleven. Lately, he'd been using other weapons – the heavier cavalry sabre, the Iroquois tomahawk – but the small sword was what he was trained in, the combination of wit, suppleness and strength of wrist what he loved.

He attacked, a feint to the open chest, the blade removed as the parry came across seeking metal, meeting air because Jack had flicked it under again, a slight withdrawal, a hard jab at the parrying hand. He missed, but only just, Red Hugh dropping hand and blade away, stepping back as he did. He brought his own weapon up and across to halt Jack's next lunge, a lunge he was not going to make. He merely took the space gained with a step forward and waited.

'Now, aren't you the prize cockerel?' Red Hugh smiled. 'I always knew I was fond of you, lad. I didn't know how much till I just saw you crow.' He gave a swift salute with his sword. 'Though I must ask you one thing before we recommence: the missing sleeve? Is it an English swordsman's thing?'

Jack grunted, came again, taking a high guard, his left hand reaching out far before him. Red Hugh stepped away, keeping the distance but leaning far forward, his long arm reaching so his own blade was advanced enough to take Jack's, lift it, keeping it there as each watched the other's eyes for the shift that would betray the next move. His blade holding Jack's up, the man could strike down – if he had the speed. But Jack would bet he didn't, not any more, and with a circle of the wrist to direct the weapon away, his own riposte would have his opponent too spread to protect himself. The fight would be over.

Red Hugh's eyes shifted, Jack dropped his blade, circled, missed metal, circled quicker, still missed it, stepping back. Something dazzled from the light of the window and he thought he caught it. He didn't. It caught him. The Irishman did have the speed after all.

Red Hugh had followed close, brought the thicker end of his weapon, the *forte*, tight into Jack's, forcing the younger man's blade down, pulling it slightly off the wrist. Then, with a sudden hard flick, it was gone, sailing across the bed, flopping into the pillow. And the point of the Irishman's weapon was pressed, lightly but distinctly, into Jack's throat.

'Now, now,' he said softly, just as he'd said to Captain Link before he rendered him nauseous aboard the *Sweet Eliza*. 'Now, now.'

Jack swallowed, the motion of his Adam's apple pressing the point a little harder into his skin, nicking him there. 'Are you going to kill me?'

'Kill my friend? How could you think me so uncivil? I am only here to kill a king.'

Jack, still looking in the Irishman's eyes, saw them move

on something behind him. He turned just enough to see a man with a cudgel coming up behind him, just quickly enough to recognize him as the footpad who had attacked Letty and Mrs O'Farrell, not quickly enough to prevent the cudgel falling.

— FOURTEEN —

Percussion and Repercussion

Jack knew a little about clubs. He had knocked out his cousin Craster with one in Montreal and the brute had not woken for six hours. He had himself taken a blow from an Abenaki war hammer that had him unconscious for near a day; nauseous and half-blind for three more. There were those who knew how to strike but not kill, and those who didn't.

The footpad didn't. There was pain and a little blood, but the unconsciousness must only have lasted a short while. The increasingly discordant music from the street that had merely annoyed before now physically hurt. The various musicians were now attempting 'Rule Britannia'. Once he realized he was awake to be pained by it, he knew he was awake.

He lay there, mastering himself. The footpad – it was obvious he was Red Hugh's cohort, the attack on Letty's chair merely another piece of theatre – must have crept up the servants' stair from the floor below, come through that recessed door. Where was Fagg, then? Unconscious or dead in his quarters, no doubt. There'd be no help there, no moment's distraction as he stumbled in.

He listened, below the music. Harsh words were being

spoken. Jack thought it must be the blow rendering them unintelligible until he realized it was another language, one he recognized from his childhood though he could not speak it. Anyway, Irish Gaelic was probably different from Cornish; that he knew neither did not matter. It was clear what was being planned. They would wait till the King stood below. And then they would drop a grenade on him.

To his ear, Gaelic was harsh anyway, but he was sure they were arguing in it. Then he heard the softer tones of Red Hugh, giving instructions, in words perhaps impossible to find in that more ancient tongue: 'One elephant, two elephants.'

He opened one eye. The men were crouched by the window, Red Hugh clutching a grenade, pointing at it, jabbering, the other man shaking his head. Two more of the metal balls were on the chair. From the street, the town-waits, obviously thrilled to have found notes and rhythm in common, gone back to the beginning of 'Rule Britannia'. The crowd was singing along.

> 'When Britain fir . . . ir . . . ir . . . ir . . . irst
> At Heaven's command
> Aro . . . o . . . o . . . o . . . o . . . o . . . ose
> From out the a . . . a . . . a . . . azure main
> Arose, Arose, Aro . . . o . . . o . . . ose
> From the az . . . ure main.'

'Arise,' thought Jack. But first he reached into his waist-coat pocket.

'You'll both step away from the window . . . now!'

The men did not move, Red Hugh's forefinger still pointing to the metal ball, the footpad's head arrested in mid-shake. But their eyes went to the pocket pistol in Jack's hand.

There was a silence. Only the singing went on, a popular

line increasing in volume: 'Britons never never never will be slaves.'

After a moment, both men stood, Red Hugh carefully laying the grenade down on the chair. 'Now, Jack,' he said calmly, 'it's only a lady's toy.'

'Yes,' Jack replied, 'but *this* time it's loaded. Go!' He shouted the last word, marched forward as he did, the pistol thrust before him, switching the muzzle between their two faces. The suddenness of the movement, his volume, had the false footpad stumbling back, Red Hugh trailing him. Jack kept coming, they kept retiring, until they stood by the half-open servants' door with Jack six feet away between bedpost and window.

Red Hugh took a step, until the pistol stopped him. He opened his hands towards it. 'Lad,' he said, 'you'll only shoot the one of us. And the other would then have to kill you. Give me the gun.'

'You know, you're right,' said Jack, 'I need to even the odds.'

He stepped back suddenly. It was awkward, keeping the gun up for the second it took to bend, scoop up a grenade with his other hand, snatch the glowing cord with a trailing finger. Somehow he managed it. When he looked again, they had only taken a pace forward, the footpad now slightly ahead, his leader's steering hand upon his shoulder.

'Jack, put it down. Put it down *now*!' On the shout, Red Hugh shoved the footpad forward. Jack fired. He had reloaded the gun with two balls and as much powder as he could cram in. It even gave a little kick and the discharge took the man in the chest, knocking him back, screaming in agony, into Red Hugh, who was trying to get past him. Jack ran towards the open bedroom door and, as he did, touched the cord end to the fuse.

Red Hugh, caught in the other man's agonized fall, was

half crouched on the ground, trying to extricate himself. He looked up, just as the grenade was lit.

'How many elephants?' Jack shouted.

'You crazy bastard!'

'How many?'

'Chuck it! Chuck it now!'

The man was too panicked to be lying. Jack turned and tossed the grenade out of the door and into the other bedroom, diving into the corner as he threw. He doubted the bomb had even hit the ground, so fast did the explosion come. It ripped the other room's door off, sent it smashing into their room, an end catching Jack's trailing foot with a blow that hurt. Chunks fell from the ceiling, a rain of plaster and horsehair. Simultaneously, there came the sound of windows exploding outwards, of glass panes shattering and showering debris onto the street below. Down there, most musicians had stopped playing. A few, drunker than the rest perhaps, went on a few bars more.

Red Hugh had caught some of the door as well. He lay crumbled against the wall, his fall snapping the legs of an armoire that he now appeared to be cradling. Through the dust, Jack could see his nose was splayed at a strange angle to his face.

'Shite, Jack.' He stared through the dust. 'You crazy bastard.'

Dazed, his ears filled with high-pitched whining, Jack sat up. The door had bounced, knocked the chair with the grenades onto the floor where one rolled. Red Hugh's pistol was still in the holster, its butt towards him. Jack reached forward, drew it out, cocked it.

Through the buzz, from the street, at first all he heard was screaming. Then there came the distinct sound of the front door being pounded. He could feel the vibration of the blows through the floor.

Red Hugh could feel it, too. Wiping blood from beneath his nose, he said. 'They'll be coming for me.'

Jack shook his head, trying to clear it. 'Good.'

'It will mean the Tyburn jig. After they've finished with me.'

Jack nodded. 'You deserve it.'

'Maybe so, lad. There's many who've predicted my last caress would be from a noose.' He peered through the falling plaster dust. 'But is that the fate you'd wish for a friend?' He nodded at the gun in Jack's hand, now levelled at him.

Jack snorted. 'A friend who has betrayed me? Allied me with his treachery, sullying the name of Absolute, possibly for ever? Pandered his cousin to me, made me fall in love . . .' Jack choked as he thought on Letty, knew it was not the dust that made him do so. The muzzle wavered. 'You tell me if a friend does that.'

The Irishman's voice came soft. 'Perhaps not, lad. But a friend does save another's life.'

The hammering below had changed. Someone had brought up something more solid, was using it to bludgeon the door. Jack looked at the Irishman, with his red hair, his red blood and remembered. Hauling him naked from the sea off Newport. Grenade lessons. The fight on the *Sweet Eliza*. The spider crawling around and around inside the nutshell as Red Hugh barricaded himself inside a cabin and refused to let them off-load Jack to die on a fever island. There was no question. He owed this man a life.

He lay the pistol down on the floor. 'Go, then.'

'Truly?' Red Hugh was up fast, throwing aside the shattered armoire. He bent to his fallen comrade, touched him at the neck. 'Dead. Who'd have thought it?' He straightened. 'I'll be off, then,' he said casually, turning toward the servants' staircase as if he had all the time in the world, as if the King's Guards were not nearly through the front door.

'Wait!' Jack took a step toward him. 'You have to knock me out. And do it better than your late friend did.'

Red Hugh came back. 'Are you sure? I could . . .' He lifted Jack's wrist, pressed the ball of his finger into the flesh. There was a flash of pain.

'No,' said Jack, 'they'd never believe it. I still don't believe it.'

'Very well.' The Irishman looked deep into Jack's eyes for a moment. 'You have to believe this, Jack. Yes, Letty was also working for the Jacobite cause. But she did love you. Does love you.'

The man picked the strangest times to discuss Jack's amours. But he couldn't help himself. 'How do you know?'

'Did she not tell me so herself?' Red Hugh smiled. 'Of course, the relation to the Earl of Clare is largely fictitious. But perhaps that won't bother you?'

'It will bother my father. As to me, we shall see.' It was too much to consider now, with the explosion still filling his ears, with men about to run up the stairs with weapons. He braced himself. 'Now, for Christ's sake, stop talking and hit me, man, will you?'

The Irishman smiled. 'You'll not regret this, my boy.'

'I already do.'

'And we will meet again.'

Jack sighed. 'I hope not. But if we do, McClune, remember this: you and I are quits.'

'I will remember.'

The noise from below doubled in volume; a door coming off its hinges, smashing down, a hallway suddenly filled with men, shouting. Then all went instantly quiet, from the sudden pain, within the sudden darkness.

Red Hugh *did* know how to hit a man. Jack wasn't sure how long he'd been unconscious but, when he woke up in an entirely different place, he had no memory of the journey there, so assumed he had been out for some time. He'd been carried, undoubtedly, but how long ago, by whom and for what reason he knew not.

The 'where' concerned him initially. The room was dark, but not completely so, some light slipping in from under what turned out, on a groping exploration, to be a thick oaken door, studded and banded with metal. His feeling around it was movement enough to make him nauseous, for his head pounded horribly from where he'd been struck by the footpad's blow to the back of the head and Red Hugh's cleaner punch to his jaw that seemed at first to have broken it but hadn't, as Jack discovered when he stretched it wide to vomit. Cautiously, he gauged the limits of the stone-lined room, discovered the only objects within it were a metal bedstead covered with a stinking straw paliasse, and a bucket, presumably for voiding, which he'd missed. The space was square, only a little over his height across and the same above, discovered when he stubbed his finger in reaching up.

He sat down heavily upon the bed. A stone box, he thought. Or a sarcophagus? The image made him jump up again, stagger to the faint light of the door. 'Hallo? Is there someone out there? Hallo-oh?'

He called and pounded till his head swam and his hand hurt, almost sobbing out the words. Then he heard something outside. Footsteps. 'You there! Open this door!'

The footsteps had stopped. He could feel someone on the other side. 'Hello?' he said, more quietly.

Then the sound of footsteps again, but slowly receding. 'Come back,' he called again, slapping the wood with the palm of one hand.

But no one came. He knew not how long he stood there hoping that they would. At last he lay down, still listening. Nothing. He took some breaths and gradually his heart calmed. There was nothing he could do but wait.

Maybe it was an hour, maybe more. He had not slept, had

not moved except to vomit once again, this time into the bucket. His mouth was a sand dune, dry and barren, but he'd checked the room again and there was nothing to relieve him. Then he heard footsteps again, not the stealthy approach of before but a rush of them, preceding a crash of bolts, inarticulate shouting, sudden light, a man storming in, grabbing Jack by the throat, running him into the wall . . .

'You fuckin' bastard! You fuckin' bogtrotting fuck.'

A monster had Jack, huge fingers gouging his Adam's apple, enormous face thrust at him, mouth yelling obscenities. Jack tried to push the monster away, to get a breath. But he was pulled forward, slammed back, driving out what little air remained. He was beginning to faint, he could feel it. And beyond fainting lay death if this man did not let him go. Over his shoulder, he noticed someone else standing in the doorway, an indistinct shape lined in red mist.

The shape spoke, one quiet word: 'Enough.'

Instantly, the hand left his throat, the monster stepped back, and Jack crumpled onto the stone floor. He lay there choking, dimly aware that other men had come quietly into the room, that one had set up a small writing table, and another had placed a lamp upon it and a chair behind it. Then the door closed again and the three of them were left together – Jack, the monster and the shape, still blurred to Jack's water-filled eyes.

The shape leaned forward. 'Well, Mr Monaghan. You have given us a little fright, have you not?'

— FIFTEEN —

The Offer

It was a struggle to get words formed in his battered head, then out through his bruised larynx. After several attempts, Jack managed. 'Not . . . Monaghan.'

The reaction was instantaneous. The monster – who Jack now perceived to be merely a man but at least six and a half foot of him – ran forward, hand raised.

'Don't you fuckin' lie to the Colonel, you fuckin' Irish . . .'

Jack leaned away, hands up helplessly, knowing that a slap from this man would be like a punch from most others, even Red Hugh. But the blow didn't fall.

'Enough, I said.' The voice was as quiet as before, and the man reacted to it as instantly, moving back behind the chair where he stood, glowering down like a dog denied meat. Jack would swear that he was panting.

The shape had finally resolved itself into a body, small and dressed in a simple dark-blue coat with a vest of slightly lighter hue. A short, grey horsehair wig sat upon his head. He reached up and began scratching underneath it, then, with a sigh, lifted it off and laid it down beside the papers before him. 'Dawkins doesn't like men of your land, I'm afraid.

Especially after what your colleague did to his colleague. You don't like Irishmen, do you, Dawkins?'

'Fucks,' growled the man behind.

'And he has a limited vocabulary. Still,' he leaned forward, 'we don't employ him for conversation. His talents lie elsewhere.' The man's huge hands moved in front of him, as if aching to be filled.

Jack mustered thought and voice. 'But I'm not Irish, sir.'

'Not Irish?' A grey eyebrow rose quizzically. 'But Monaghan is an Irish name.' He riffled the papers, lifted one. 'You rented this house, Mr Monaghan. I have your signature here.'

'It cannot be mine. I never saw the lease. It was rented for me.'

'By?'

Jack tried to swallow. 'By a friend.'

'Ah. A friend.' The man carefully slipped the paper back into place, picked out another, studied it. 'A friend named William Leadbetter? Or is it Thomas Lawson? Or . . . and this is my particular favourite, Josiah Tumbril.' Though the words came out as if he were amused there was not a trace of a smile. 'But perhaps you always knew the man as Red Hugh McClune.'

'I know a man by that name, yes. But he knows me as—'

'Monaghan?'

'Absolute. Jack Absolute.'

The man sucked in his lower lip as he again scanned the sheet before him. 'No, that's not one of the ones we have down here. But I shall add it.' He picked up a quill, dipped it in the ink well. 'New aliases always interest. Even if Absolute is as unlikely a name as Tumbril.' He began to scratch.

'Nevertheless, sir, it is my true and given name.'

'I fuckin' warned you . . .'

This time no command halted him. The slap came, mainly on Jack's ear, doubling the whining and the pain.

'Dear, dear,' said the other man softly, though he seemed to be referring to a paper. 'How would you confirm this absurd name? It would surprise me greatly if there was anyone in Bath who knew you as,' he squinted at the page, 'Absolute. Can you think of someone who will give me a reason not to let my man here have you for a while?'

Dawkins's huge hands twitched. Jack looked at them, swallowed and thought. Who? Who? Letty knew him as such, as she had mistakenly revealed. But he could not mention her. If this man and his mastiff did not know of her already, then Jack had no intention of leading them to her. Everywhere else he had introduced himself as Beverley to maintain his role. Fagg – if he were still alive – knew him so. The Cornish labourer, Trewennan, the same. Even the landlord at the Three Tuns and the billiard sharpers he'd played there, all thought of him as the impoverished Cornet. There was no one . . .

And then he remembered. 'Fanny Harper,' he blurted. 'She's at the theatre in Orchard Street. An actress.'

'An *actress*?' The word could not have come with any more contempt.

'She . . . knew me. sir, in London. Before I joined the army. I was in Canada, with Wolfe, you see, I . . .'

Jack's faltering words had threatened to become a torrent. The hand that had halted a further assault tapped the table, commanding silence. 'I will give you a moment to write down a few things only this woman would know of you as Jack Absolute. I will then visit the playhouse. And we shall see.' He leaned forward. 'But if this is just a delaying lie . . .'

The monster growled again. Jack crawled forward, reaching for the quill, but the man held it away for a moment. 'No lie, sir. I am a true-born Englishman, I swear it. And Fanny will inform you of others who can also vouch for me.'

'I think we'll just start with the player, shall we? Write.' The quill was at last offered. 'At the least, I shall learn what stories our enemies invent these days for their spies.' That no-smile came again. 'We have plenty of time. And the only space we could require.'

Jack dipped, thought, wrote. He'd covered half a side when the paper was snatched away. 'That will do,' said the man. 'If it is the truth it is enough, if lies then too much.' He stood. 'My name is Colonel Turnville, as I am sure you already know. And I will be back eventually.'

He left the cell, reading as he went. Other men came in, collected the chair and papers. The last to leave was Dawkins. 'You'll be mine, shit-sack,' he hissed. Jack was almost ready for the blow that came, taking it at least part on his shoulder. It still hurt. Growling, the man departed, leaving Jack to a rare prayer. Not to God, but to Fanny.

The little light faded, indicating night, yet no one came. Jack's thirst went from craving to torment; he was certain that if he did not drink soon, he would die. He disdained the bed – the lamplight before had shown stains Jack did not want to get near – and folded himself into a slightly less noxious corner. There, an approximation of sleep came, filled with brief dreams of snow, of water bubbling under ice, of Até offering him a drinking skin filled from a cool forest stream. He'd jerk awake, always just the moment before he drank. Once, he ran to the door, beat upon it till his palm was raw. There was a little barred window, a wood panel beyond it, and he put his lips to it, shouting for water. No one came. He'd sunk into the corner again, vowing to own the name of Monaghan next time. It might get him a drink.

He awoke to a little light and footsteps. His throat by now would not allow him to make words. But he began to crawl toward the door, just as the inset window opened and a face appeared for a brief moment. Then the panel was slammed shut, but not before he heard a woman's sob.

'Fanny?' he tried to croak.

Footsteps faded again and he fell back into his corner. If he'd had any moisture in his body he was sure he would have wept.

How long it was before someone approached again he did not know. Nor did he move, not even when the bolts were thrown, a key turned and the door swung open. A man he'd never seen before came in carrying a bucket and a plate. Another stood behind him in the doorway, holding keys and a cudgel. The bucket and plate were put down on the floor and Jack saw liquid slop over the lip. Then the men left. Jack crawled slowly forward. The bucket was filled with . . . well, he supposed it was water. It did not occupy its receptacle alone. But if it had been taken direct from the King's Bath after a full day of scrofulous bathers, Jack would still have drunk it dry.

He'd gulped about a quarter before he was sick. After that, he took it more slowly, sipping little and often. Gradually the terrible throbbing that had held his head for an eternity began to decline. He couldn't remember the last time he'd eaten, and though he had no appetite, he consumed the slab of dark bread down to the last crumb. With his immediate physical problems fading, his mind began again to function. He almost preferred the nothingness.

What kind of a stew am I in now? he wondered.

He had been in some before – too many! It seemed to be his nature, frig the thing. But this was serious. The man questioning him obviously believed Jack to be part of the conspiracy to kill the King. Looking at it from their side, they might assume that the grenade had gone off prematurely and Jack and McClune's cohort were victims of their own weapon. And yet, surely they'd have seen that the fellow was shot? They would not be able to explain that. Jack could explain it for them. After all, hadn't he spoilt the plot? Saved

186

the King? He was the hero, damn their eyes! How dare they treat him like this?

His anger lasted mere moments. He was no hero but a fool, blinded by love, charmed by friendship. He'd known Red Hugh was a Grenadier. Known he'd chosen the house next to the one to be presented to the King, shown up the day before the event, battered, bleeding . . . what had Turnville said? Something about Dawkins hating the Irish even more because of what one of them had done to his comrade? Of course, Red Hugh had no creditors. He'd fallen in with these men and killed one of them.

Jack had ignored everything obvious, so focused was he on the game of love. Still, they couldn't hang him for a being a fool, could they?

A little laugh came, as bitter as the taste lingering in his mouth. Half the men who danced the Tyburn jig were just and only that. It would appear that his Absolute luck, which had carried him through slavery, war and a dozen close rendezvous with death, had finally run out.

The footsteps came again.

A key turned, the bolts were shot. The two men who had brought him sustenance now brought in that same table, chair and lamp. Only when these were arranged did Turnville appear, Dawkins a step behind. He sat, shuffled a thicker sheaf of papers before him. The other men left, the door closed. For a long while there was silence, as Turnville read documents and Dawkins just stared. Jack's earlier panic had not allowed him really to study his interrogator. He saw him now, a man he suspected was in his fifties, though the face seemed younger, the skin pale, as if the Colonel did not spend much time in the field. Yet there was nothing soft in the grey eyes, split by a line that ran between the brows, straight down like a knife cut.

The eyes came up. 'Jack Absolute.'

He felt a little of his rigidity slip. It was a start. 'Mrs Harper told you?'

'She did. Though we nearly didn't find her since she now lives under the name of Scudder. Fortunately for you we are diligent.' He reached into his sheaf, pulled out a page. 'Jack Absolute,' he said again, reading it. 'You have had quite the life, have you not?'

'It has been . . . eventful.'

A snort came, humourless. 'An understatement. We have here a copy of a letter sent by General Murray in Quebec to the Secretary, William Pitt.' He scanned it. 'It seems you have a talent for disguise which proved useful to the General.'

'I made some contribution, yes, I—'

'He also says that you are ill-disciplined, insubordinate and prone to violence. True?'

'I do not consider myself especially . . . violent. I—'

Another page was pulled out. 'This report comes from London. It tells how you were involved in the assassination of Lord Melbury.'

Jack gasped. 'The report is wrong, sir! It was not political. Lord Melbury died in an honest duel with . . .' He hesitated.

'With your father. A fugitive now, gone to fight in Germany, though . . .' a scrap of paper was raised, 'we have a sighting of him at a tavern here in Bath a few days ago.' The note was laid down. 'So we have the King's minister killed, an attempt made on the King's life and Absolutes everywhere we look.'

'It is not what it appears to be, sir.'

'No?' Turnville leaned forward. 'Perhaps you would be so kind as to tell me, then, what it *is*.'

Jack frowned. 'It is a, uh, complicated story, sir. It will take some time.'

Turnville sat back. 'We have that. Years in your case,

perhaps. Wait!' He leaned back, called out, 'Holla!' The door opened. 'Send in Tully.'

Another man, smaller even than Turnville, bespectacled and hitherto unseen, entered. 'Sir?'

'A confession, Tully. Be so good as to bring your pencil.'

The man left, returned with a lap desk and his own chair to set up just behind the other. When he was ready Turnville waved at Jack. 'You may begin.'

Jack did, as near to the beginning as he could manage, from his father's duel with Lord Melbury. Occasionally, the Colonel displayed impatience with too much detail – he seemed distinctly uninterested in the various uses of a bear to survive a colonial winter, for example. Mostly he just sat and stared and, for a good hour, the only sound, other than Jack's voice, was the scrape of pencil on paper.

Jack told the whole truth – nearly. He didn't see that Letty's being Red Hugh's cousin was relevant, so he tried to reduce her to an anonymous woman the Irishman had encouraged him to pursue. He hoped it might shelter her from enquiry. But it provoked the only interruption to the flow of narrative.

'If you are referring to Laetitia Fitzpatrick,' Turnville said, 'she is not the innocent you claim her to be. Just seventeen and already a veteran traitor. Quite the player herself. Seems she was claiming an affiliation to the Earl of Clare, drawing half the eligible young men in Bath to seek her hand and bring their fortunes to the Jacobite cause. When in fact her only known relative is that impoverished rogue McClune.' He lifted a quill, tapped the feather against his teeth. 'We found her nest, a lodging house in the Lower Town. Long since deserted. It seems her cousin went and fetched her before he fled.'

This was a blow Jack tried to keep from his face. There was the slimmest hope that, if he could talk his way out of this, he could find Letty to confirm Red Hugh's words: that she loved

Jack, beyond the conspiracy. He'd been sure the Irishman would have no choice but to flee, unencumbered by women. He'd underestimated him again.

'On,' Turnville said, rapping a knuckle upon the desk.

The rest took little longer. Though Dawkins shook his head in obvious disbelief at the tale of Jack's thwarting of the assassination – and the clerk seemed to catch something in his throat when Jack mentioned elephants and had to scratch it out three times – the Colonel merely stared on impassively.

Finally, Jack's tale petered out. He had told them what had happened, why he had been so gulled. He realized how ridiculous it made him look. But ridiculous men could hope to leave a gaol. The guilty could not.

Turnville continued to study a point on the wall above Jack for some time. 'Quite the story. But I have a different version for you. Simpler. Far shorter.' He held up his fist and began to tell out his fingers. 'You are lying. You are guilty. You were turned. You are a Jacobite. You are no longer loyal to King George.'

'I am not a Jacobite. I have not been turned. I am guilty of nothing but stupidity. And,' he rose from the bedstead and Dawkins instantly stepped toward him; Jack looked at him – he would not let this man hit him again without a response. Then he looked down at the Colonel. 'And I assure you, sir, I am no liar.'

Turnville studied him for a long moment. Then, waving his man back, he stood, nodded. 'Well, that we shall soon verify. And God have mercy on you if you are proved false, because Dawkins won't.'

Then he was gone, the clerk following, the other men coming in to clear the room. When the last had left, Dawkins turned again. He stopped when he saw Jack had placed his back against the wall. And that he had the empty bucket in his hand.

'Yes?' asked Jack, and the man looked as if he was going to

come. Then Turnville called from the hall and, with a last growl, he too was gone.

Jack sat, his legs suddenly unsteady. He could not remember all he had said. He just knew it was the truth, most of it. His only hope now was that it would be enough.

When the door opened on what Jack thought was the fifth day of his captivity – time was hard to track in that near lightless world – he assumed it would be as every previous visit had been: a man bringing in water and some unidentifiable food once a day, another man warding him with cudgel or gun. But this time was different.

One of them stood in the doorway. He crooked a finger. 'You. Now.'

Jack, who had been standing on his hands against the wall in an effort to alleviate the boredom, dropped onto his feet. 'Where?' he asked apprehensively. He wasn't sure he would get a trial. He suspected that many who came into Turnville's orbit didn't.

The man just crooked the finger again. Another man, the one with the cudgel, stood behind him. Jack had no choice. 'Delighted,' he said.

The room three floors above was hardly ornate, simply an ordinary drawing room fitted out as a study. Yet the green of the patterned wallpaper was almost sickeningly vibrant after the cell. And though he could see rain falling through the tall windows, the day still appeared brighter than any summer he could remember. He stood there blinking, first at that light, then at the man behind the huge oaken desk.

Dawkins was also there, and he and the cudgel man stood behind Jack at the door. Turnville was writing. 'Get him a chair,' he said quietly, not ceasing his scratching, not looking up. One was brought, and Jack was forced roughly onto it. The men returned to their post. Silence, save for rain and the moving nib, lasted minutes. At last, Turnville looked up.

'I have your confession here,' he said, spinning a paper around, dipping and then holding out the quill to Jack. 'I have most of the details, I believe. Treason, murder, conspiracy. Usual stuff. Just sign at the bottom.'

Jack made no move forward. 'Why would I do that?'

'Because it will save your life, boy.' The goose feather was still held out. 'His Majesty has decided, based on your military service, your youth and your family's formerly good name, to spare you the noose. You will be transported, of course. To the Indies probably, where, if the fever doesn't get you and you live ten years, they may make you a free man again.'

Jack had experienced slavery with the Abenaki and fever aboard the *Robuste*. He wanted neither experience again. But the noose? In life, at least there was hope. He leaned forward, read: 'I, Jack Rombaud Absolute, do hereby confess to be a foul traitor to England and her glorious King George . . .'

He shook his head. 'It's a lie. I cannot sign it. Hang me for a fool, if you must. But I will not live as a slave and a traitor.'

The Colonel sighed. 'Are you quite sure?'

Jack felt his throat tighten – perhaps in anticipation. While he could still speak, he said, 'Quite.'

'Good lad,' said Turnville. Lifting the paper, he ripped it swiftly from end to end. 'Would have been very disappointed if you had.'

A signal was given, a man approached from the back. A crystal glass was held out, the scent of sherry rising from it. He quickly gripped it with two hands, did not lift it so they would not see his shakes. 'What . . . what is happening?'

Turnville sipped from his own glass, put it down. 'I'd like to offer you employment.'

Jack was not certain he'd heard correctly. He lifted the liquid to his lips, took half at a gulp. 'I beg your pardon?'

'Employment. In the service of His Majesty. Though since

you are already a soldier, perhaps you should consider it a transfer.'

Jack swallowed the rest of the sherry. 'May I have another?' Turnville nodded. The glass was filled and Jack now held it in one hand. 'You do not believe me to be a traitor?'

'I believe you to be what you just called yourself – a fool. Not a hanging offence and almost obligatory in one so young. Besides, you have other qualities attested to by,' he waved his hand over the desk, 'General Murray, Colonel Burgoyne, one Captain Engledue of the *Robuste*. Bravery, verging on the foolhardy. A taste for disguise. An ability with languages and weapons. All very useful to us.'

'Indeed?' Jack was content to sip this second sherry.

'But even more useful – no one knows you, at least in the spheres we move in. We could introduce you into a certain arena, give you another disguise, another name. A more likely one than Absolute, eh?' The man actually smiled.

'What arena?'

Instead of answering, the Colonel reversed a clump of paper, tied together with a thick bootlace. The top page had names on it. The first was the name he'd known him by, the rest were the aliases he'd heard at their first meeting in the cell below.

'Red Hugh McClune,' Jack read aloud. 'May I?'

'Later, perhaps. But allow me to *précis* a little.' Turnville rose, went to look out at the rain. 'The Irishman and I have had a long relationship. I faced him at Culloden, though I did not know it then. I nearly caught him in London in fifty-two when he planned to be one of four hundred men who would storm St James's Palace and seize the King. It was called the Elibank Plot. Heard of it?'

'I don't believe—'

'Not surprised. Most haven't. We try not to let these things come out. But he was there, as he has been at the bottom of most conspiracies against our State. We heard he was in America, seeking arms, fomenting discontent. And then we found him, quite by chance, in Bath!' Turnville turned. 'I was so pleased to meet him at last. Alas, we had only the one, brief conversation. I was to return in the morning – one week ago – to continue our talk.' He sighed. 'But by the morning he was gone. And Mr Dawkins's brother was dead.' He gestured to the man still standing behind Jack. 'And this Mr Dawkins was the smaller of the siblings.'

Turnville came round the desk, perched on its edge. 'Red Hugh McClune is a very dangerous man and our most capable opponent. He is always about something big. The Elibank Plot. Killing the King here in Bath. Now he's escaped he'll be planning something equally spectacular.' That half-smile returned. 'We had him. We lost him. We would like to have him back.'

'And you think—'

'You know him. I mean, you can actually recognize his face. Few alive can. I am amazed he let you live, as your story goes. He must be fond of you, which, again, may be useful. It is a weakness he has not yet displayed.' He reached for his own glass. 'We want you to find him, point him out to us. Then we can do the rest.'

Jack sipped the sherry. 'But how will I find him?'

Turnville came off the desk, moved back to his chair. Another paper was produced. 'We suspect he was the Methodist reverend seen taking an Antwerp-bound vessel with wife and daughter from Southampton. Yet even if he goes via the Low Countries he will still end up in France. He is employed and paid by the French equivalent of my own department – Le Secret du Roi, the Bourbon's intelligence. He will go to them for instructions and gold. He'll take the latter and largely ignore the former, unless they also suit the cause of the Lost King. And then we think he'll make for the centre of the Jacobite world.'

'Charles Edward?' Jack had heard that the Bonnie Prince was in Germany.

Turnville snorted. 'That drunkard? No, *Bliadnha Thearlaich*,' he mangled the Gaelic, 'was his chance and he lost. Charles's year was seventeen forty-five. As they sing in their taverns: "He'll come no more." '

'Then where?'

'The court of the exiled King, James the Third as he calls himself. The Pope still shelters him and the Jacobite diaspora gathers around him, a broken, dispirited crew in the main, living on cold soup and former glories. But that's where they still plot the Old Pretender's return. In Rome.'

'You wish me to go to Rome?'

'Yes. Infiltrate the Jacobite exiles. We'll give you a good story. Report all you can, who's in, who's out. You'll be doing useful work. And then when our quarry finally appears, you point him out and we take him. You will have time, for our fox will go to ground in France a while, 'tis certain. He'll also travel slower than a youth such as yourself, for I doubt he'll abandon his women. Did you know that the so-called Mrs O'Farrell is actually Bridget O'Doherty, his wife? No matter. His cousin will also undoubtedly go with them.'

Turnville was staring at Jack rather directly now. So he took a sip. 'My concern, sir, is that this latest outrage in Bath will have been reported in all the newspapers. My name might have been unearthed – you know how these scribblers desire all the story. Even if I was to travel incognito, might I not be exposed?'

The Colonel was looking at him quizzically. 'To what outrage do you refer?'

'The assassination attempt?'

'There wasn't one.'

'But—'

'There was an explosion of a gaseous substance at a house

on the Circus. Unfortunately it coincided with the King's visit. Some old scientist was experimenting, apparently. The landlord was shocked – it was quite against the terms of the tenancy.'

Jack shook his head. 'People will not believe that, surely?'

'They will believe what we wish them to believe.' Turnville nodded emphatically. 'They are not at liberty, sir, to publish what they wish.'

'Oh,' said Jack, somewhat sadly. 'I thought in England that they were.'

'Ah, youth,' said Turnville. Then he leaned forward and tapped the folder marked with aliases. 'Well? Do you read this or no?'

Jack stared at the inked names, the desk they sat on, Turnville and then beyond him, to the rain outside. Could he do this? Yes. Did he wish to do this? That required more thought. He hated the way he'd been deceived, used. It *was* treason of a sort, as he'd said to Red Hugh over his sword point, a betrayal of friendship. Above all, a violation of honour. He had made it clear to the Irishman when they were about to fight against the privateer and he donned the uniform of his regiment, that honour had clear lines for him, ones that must not be crossed. Red Hugh had trampled over his as if they did not exist. Now that they were 'quits', as he had said, it demanded redress. And he was being offered that chance. A chance also to fight for England, in a different way than he had previously.

Still, there were two things he had to clear first. 'Sir,' he said, 'I am ordered to report to my regiment.'

'They will be informed, to your credit, trust me. And the second?'

Jack hesitated. But he had to say it. 'I am not sure that, if I went, all my motives would be entirely pure. If I am honest, sir, Miss Fitzpatrick, uh, still . . . holds . . .'

He trailed off. Turnville had got up again, moved to stare

out at the rain. 'Hearken, Lieutenant Absolute, to the first law of espionage: No one engages in it for a single, pure reason. If they do, we waste no time on them for they are quickly dead. Some rejoice in the game of it, the codes, the disguises, the sudden betrayals, the unexpected triumphs. Some want power or gold, which are often linked.' He picked a small thread off what, Jack now noticed, was a beautifully tailored jacket of rich brocade, and let it float away. 'And if another is motivated by love, well – God help that man, I say. God help *you*.' He turned. 'And he will, just so long as, this time, you put loyalty first, eh?'

To whom? Jack thought, but he said, 'I am still unclear, sir, why you want me to do this? Surely there are more experienced men who also have seen the Irishman.'

'Such as?' Jack pointed a forefinger over his shoulder. Turnville snorted. 'Dawkins? Hardly. Not very bright, you see.' He looked past Jack. 'You're none too bright, are you, Dawkins?'

'No, sir,' came the grunted reply.

'And my other men? Too obvious or too old. Would find it hard to infiltrate, even if they were not personally known. Whereas you, with your youth and your background . . . I believe half of your generation find it to Rome on the so-called Grand Tour.' He shuddered. 'God knows why they should want to. Filthy inns, filthy food, filthy foreigners! I never desired to leave Britain, only did it with the regiment to kill Frogs. You shall fit easily into such a crowd. Many a youth visiting Rome is drawn to the supposed romance of the Stuart cause. Hmm?' He reached back, tapped the sheaf of papers. 'But it's up to you, *Lieutenant* Absolute. Choose to serve your country by helping to capture one of its most abhorrent enemies. Serve yourself as well,' a pitying smile came, 'or choose not to, and live with the consequences.'

Jack looked again into the appraising eyes, recognizing the threat of those final words. Did he have a choice? The taint of treachery would follow him throughout his life. And was not this a way to help redeem the threatened name of Absolute?

He reached forward and picked up the file. 'Red Hugh McClune,' he read aloud, 'William Leadbetter. Thomas Lawson. Josiah Tumbril . . .' He looked up, out of the window, to the rain. A thought came but this one he didn't speak.

I'll see you all in Rome.

— PART TWO —
Hunting the Shadow

— ONE —

Rome

'Huzzah! Huzzah!'

As he rose to the acclaim, the man took off his spectacles, his eyes receding to the size and shape of two currants on a frosted Chelsea bun. Where the frames had rested, bruises marked his cheeks in purple, stark against the sheen of the man's dripping face. Rome was an inferno, all sweated. Yet though Jack made sure he kept well to the leeward of some of the Jacobites – MacBrave, the lugubrious Hebridean, was especially fruity – somehow he could forgive this man anything, even his ripeness.

For Watkin Pounce had an extraordinary voice. Completely at variance with his bulk, it was a counter tenor, exquisitely modulated, and Jack settled back to enjoy it. The man always sang the final verse of this, his favourite Jacobite song, the sentiments heightened by the large tear that inevitably squeezed onto his cheek:

> *With heart and hand we'll join, boys,*
> *To set him on his throne;*
> *We'll all combine as one, boys,*
> *Till this great work be done.*
> *We'll pull down usurpation,*
> *And, spite of abjuration,*
> *And force of stubborn nation*
> *Great James's title own.*

Hard on the heels of the most raucous huzzahs yet, Watkin's voice dropped an octave and he bellowed, 'The King across the water!'

The King just round the corner, thought Jack, rising with the rest, his voice as loud as any. While the cheers echoed he turned, called to the two boys standing in the doorway of their snug: '*Raggazi, ancora vino, pronto.*' During his week in Rome it was most of the Italian he'd learned but he'd discovered he needed very little else. Those words and the wine they brought had won him the comradeship of the men in the room. It wasn't hard to buy a Jacobite a drink – quite the reverse – and finding them had been just as easy. Once he'd been told about the area surrounding King James's Palazzo Muti, he'd made for it directly – just another young Englishman come to gawk at the Old Pretender. His inform-ant, a clergyman in the English enclave of the Piazza di Spagna, had warned that youths such as himself were considered fine prey to the exiles there. The least that could be gotten from them was news of home, while others, if they displayed the smallest sympathy for the Lost King's cause, might be taken up and worked upon. Jack had made himself malleable.

Turnville had warned him against complacency. But truly, Jack thought, I am not complacent. I am just rather good at this.

He was especially pleased with his disguise. The story's facts may have been concocted by Turnville but the gilding came from Jack. He felt he had suffered quite enough as Beverley. The tailors of Rome were excellent and, after all, it was essential that 'Philip – Pip – Truman' moved easily through all ranks of Jacobite society. His silk shirt with its lutestring piping and his maroon breeches were quite ad-equate for the present company – the foot soldiers of the Cause – but their 'officers', the exiled nobility, had different ways of using their time and better filled purses. Jack was thrilled with the dove-grey suit and green waistcoat he'd commissioned for the opera that night. Just as well that Turnville's story had turned him into an earl's son, he thought, for it required him to provide a purse to match.

Pounce, who'd been relieving himself in the chamber pot in the corner, now returned. 'Are you well, Pip?' he said.

'Be better when this is filled,' replied Jack, lifting his glass and joining in the cheer as the wine was brought in. He seized the bottles and poured everyone there a tot. 'To your health, sirs,' he cried.

'To yours,' came the shout. There were ten men in the small room and, once the liquor was thrown down and more replaced it, the conversation became general.

'Allow me,' Jack said, leaning over to fill Pounce's already emptied bumper.

The faintest demur came. 'Ah, Pip! You gladden an old man's heart.'

Jack didn't know quite how it had happened. But from almost the moment Watkin had encountered him gazing up at the Palazzo Muti, they had begun a relationship reminiscent of the one in the play he'd seen in Bath. Somehow he'd become Prince Hal to Pounce's Falstaff, even if Mr Harper at Orchard Street could have fitted twice inside that threadbare black coat. Pounce was certainly as drunken as the stage knight, as prone to melancholy and bombast. Indeed he *was* a knight, but his estate in Norfolk was long forfeit, its recovery dependent on the Stuart restoration. Watkin, like Falstaff, was also quite content to spend Jack's gold, and Jack was quite happy to let him. Pounce had showed him the town and, most importantly, had connections at the Palazzo Muti.

It was about that very place that he now spoke. 'By the way, lad. The Anglican service at the Palazzo. I have obtained permission for you to attend.' He dug in a pocket of his waistcoat, produced a silver token, a cross wreathed in Stuart oak leaves upon it. 'So long as you do not disgrace yourself there . . .' Watkin let out a large belch. 'Oh, pardon me! You may use this to return again and again to your devotions.'

Jack, assuming what he hoped was a look both rapt and religious, took the token. To win over the Protestants – a large part of his following – the Catholic James had obtained permission from the Pope to have a Protestant chapel with a daily service – the only one in Rome. As soon as Jack heard of it, he knew he must have one of the precious tokens. It meant entry to the palace itself, surely the place that Red Hugh would come for his orders when he eventually reached Rome.

'Oh, too wonderful!' he exclaimed. 'Will you be able to accompany one, Watty?'

'As you know, my adorations are made elsewhere.' Pounce's sausage fingers made an elaborate crucifix in the air before they reached for his mug. Wine was again slurped noisily. 'And speaking of adorations,' he continued, a hand-kerchief dabbing at the flood on his face, 'tell me once more of the love that you were forced to leave behind. For in your sorrow I see the very portrait of mine own.'

On their first night together, even matching half glass to full bumper, Jack's tongue had run somewhat fast. He'd remembered to change Laetitia's name in the telling, as well as her country, the full complications of their wooing and the manner of their parting. But, fuelled by wine, he'd been unable to hide the extent of his hurt, and his passion had stirred up an equal one in Watkin, who, it transpired, had forsaken his own first love to serve his King.

'I'd rather hear again of yours,' said Jack. 'Her name, if I recall, was Rosamunde?'

'Rose of the world, she was indeed.' Pounce's lips shook, a ripple that went through all his flesh. 'I was but sixteen when we first met . . .' a thick wrist was waved, '. . . thirty years younger, ten stone lighter . . .'

Jack staggered down the Via Columbina, trying to stop twenty stone of slick Jacobite sliding into the street. Pounce had reached his height even later than was customary, the 8 a.m. bell just sounding as they emerged from the Angelo tavern. Fortunately, it was a short stagger to his lodgings and his one room was at street level. Jack knew he'd never get him up stairs.

There was another advantage to what had become a daily ritual, the guiding of the man home. The route took Jack past the one building Turnville had ordered him to look at every day for his signal. It was an ancient palazzo, long since deserted by its noble occupiers, now a tenement with a family in every room. Twice each day he would pass, between eight and nine, four and five, looking up to the right-side window just below the peak of the roof. So far it had always been open and empty. Today, however, a striped red sheet hung from it.

'At last,' he murmured.

Pounce, who had been leaning ever more heavily upon him, jerked his head up to stare blearily about. 'There already?'

'Nearly, sweet Knight. Just a little further.'

Glancing just once more at the striped sheet, Jack guided the man across a busy junction, between two carts, their drivers conducting a shouting argument over right of way.

'We are here, sir, and I must leave you.'

'Come in.' The little eyes barely opened in the large face. 'Think I have a bottle . . . somewhere. Yours!'

'Alas! I must sleep. I have to look my best for the Opera tonight.' Jack was trying to disengage the man's weighty arm, to lay it upon the stone railing.

'Opera! Ah, the divine Tenducci!' He bent to Jack to whisper. 'Thought I'd sing myself, once. But duty called!'

He tried to tap the side of his nose, succeeding on the third attempt.

'Music's loss, the Cause's gain.' Jack managed to lower Pounce upon the step. He'd make his own way in eventually.

He went the opposite way to the dangling sheet. It could have gone now anyway, as his contact might have noted him observing it. Turnville had told him he would be reached by this method. Now he had. Jack knew that he would not meet the fellow, his 'scoutmaster', but the signal meant that he had information for Jack. And he'd been told where he had to go to collect it.

Watkin Pounce's lodgings were quite close to the Piazza di Spagna and from that square there was an entrance to the gardens on Monte Pinchio, his destination. But after that first night in the Hotel de Londres, Jack had moved lodgings and strictly avoided that piazza. Though he was fairly certain he was not followed – the craft he'd learned in the forests of Quebec when fighting the French made him hard to stalk even on cobbles – where the English gathered in Rome was dangerous ground for 'Pip Truman'. Turnville had been right: the city was awash with young Englishmen on the Grand Tour. Jack had no doubt that many an Old Westminster was among them, schoolfellows all too delighted to bellow out, 'Jack Absolute!' He risked the sights because he always went between ten and noon, when no self-respecting Westminster would be up. Strangely, despite his alcoholic appetite, Pounce always was, and often accompanied him, an entertaining guide.

Jack made a wide circuit, cutting across the Piazza Barberini, ducking up a small pathway that ran alongside the palazzo of the same name. This cart track came to a fence, easily climbed, into the gardens on Monte Pinchio. These were open to the public, a kindness of the Borghese family who owned them. It was a favourite walk of Romans and their guests; for water flowed here, and trees gave a little shelter from the oppressive sun, though Jack, who had been there once before on Pounce's advice, again thought that the gardens themselves were poor compared to those of England. There were no rolling, lush lawns, only square rectangles of brownish, parched earth. Some of the walks were pleasant enough for their trees but people walked beneath them on sand, not gravel, while the occasional hedge was tall and poorly trimmed. Flowers grew not in the sweeping beds of the London parks, but in rows of earthen pots. It was all so regimented, with none of the artificial naturalness, the rustic simplicity, that so pleased the eye in England.

Still, Jack was not there for the views. He moved down the avenues a little quicker than most of the early strollers but not so fast as to draw attention. In his previous visit, he had traced at least half the route. So when he came to the plantation of pine trees – some four hundred, it was said – he began to move more slowly, to look for the signs.

A statue of a dryad, arms inevitably lopped, marked a side avenue to the right. He took it, looking for a dip after about a hundred yards, and noticed it by sound not sight. Voices came, laughter, hidden from his sight, as if they were beyond a ha-ha. He slowed, till he could peer over the slight crest. A couple were down there, a young fellow of dark complexion and in want of a shave, trying to put his arm about the waist of a buxom girl, dressed in the apron of a maid, she laughing and half-fighting him off. Then, as he watched, the youth grabbed at her wrist, pulled her up the slope and on down the avenue. A bend took them from sight, their laughter lingering.

Jack descended into the dip. Just at the point where it began to rise again, he looked left. The pines, perhaps six in each row and spaced about a dozen feet apart, descended to another parallel path below. He looked closer, to the nearer trees. There! A carving, two sets of initials within a laurel wreath. He passed the tree, scrunching over pine cones, counted four trees in, halted. He was quite well hidden in there, but he looked around to be sure. In the distance, he heard more laughter.

At head height, a bole had been hollowed out by some creature, then abandoned. He reached up, grabbed the paper lying there, then marched swiftly on, down to the next avenue, turning along it in the opposite direction to the way he'd come. He left by a different gate, mingling swiftly with the mob.

Jack had taken a small room in the eaves of the crumbling Palazzo Cesari, its principal advantages being the breeze that occasionally blew through his ever open shutters, and its proximity to the Palazzo Muti, the heart of Jacobitism. It also had an ancient caretaker whose gender Jack had never settled upon due to the swathes of cloth he/she sported day and night. He suspected that this personage was a member of the Cesari family itself, now impecunious. Families lived in the larger rooms below; only himself and one aged servant above. But the door had a stout lock, the window sills so decayed they would require an ape's skill to shimmy along, and the sexless caretaker, who lived directly below, possessed a dog of tiny size and loud yap. No one could approach Jack without his being forewarned.

As the dog's yelps began to subside, Jack sat on the bed and unfolded the piece of paper. A series of numbers, in groups of three, were scrawled upon it. Prising up a floorboard and pulling his copy of Herodotus from the hole, he began to decode them. It was the simplest of codes, but impossible to crack unless you had this particular edition of 'Lame' Littlebury's translation, which only he and his scoutmaster did. Then it was simple. The first line of numbers read: '323 122 896'.

Jack flicked to page 323, found line 22, and, ignoring the first two numbers of the last group, counted six words in.

The word he landed on was 'stag'. He wrote it down, then went on to decode the rest in the same fashion until he had the whole message: 'Stag leaves Paris twenty-seven.'

'Stag' was their quarry, Red Hugh McClune. So he'd left Paris on 27 June, three weeks ago. If he came directly through France, he would probably take a felucca from Nice to Genoa. But Turnville had said there were other courts he could visit en route, other people from whom to collect donations to bring to his King in Rome. If he was in Bavaria, he would come through the Tyrol and over the Brenner Pass. If via Vienna . . .

It doesn't matter, Jack thought suddenly. He couldn't guess which route the man had taken nor how soon he would be there. He'd been told that travel through Italy could be swift enough if you were lucky with postillions and horses. Many weren't. He couldn't know, as he'd taken the sea route via Gibraltar to Leghorn, his passage there, and on through Tuscany and into the Papal States, remarkably easy. But the journey wasn't the import of this message. Red Hugh was on the move, that was all that mattered. Besides, whoever had brought the news had reached the city in three weeks. And if they could . . .

Jack looked up, out of the window, into the sky. He *could* be here already. *She* could be here.

Taking his flint and strike light, he dropped sparks into a little copper bowl of dried leaves. The paper with the code caught fire easily and he held it, enjoying the flames, till a little pain came and he dropped it. The smoke rose before him but he did not notice it, looking once again into an orange Roman noon, wondering if she were looking at it as well.

'Letty!' He breathed her name out, as he'd done in Bath, as he continued to do every day. If it did not conjure the pleasure it had when first he'd uttered it, if it carried a weight now, compounded of the lies they'd both told each other, the shock of their revelation, the pain of her disappearance, what of it? Jack had had plenty of time on his journey to remember each touch, each word. He had been sent to Rome to identify Red Hugh, the enemy of England; but he had also come to discover if Laetitia Fitzpatrick still loved him as much as he still loved her.

Jack peered down from the uppermost gallery of the Teatro Argentina. He thought his nose might commence bleeding. Not even an amply provided spy could secure a ticket in the pit or boxes; they were the prime places in Rome to observe and be observed. The audience did not draw attention to themselves, as a London crowd would, by their wit; they relied solely on their person. Jack had been very pleased with his own ensemble of dove-grey suit and emerald waistcoat. The buckles on his gleaming shoes shone, the horsehair wig was exquisite. Yet he would have been drab down there, not only in cloth but because he sported no jewellery. The huge chandeliers, which made the ones in the Assembly Rooms in Bath seem like reed candles, reflected their thousand flames off a dazzling array of decorations and medals on the men, while the women glimmered in diamond tiaras, topaz rings, sapphire brooches. Their hair was piled up to extraordinary heights, which must have required the sacrifice of a horse apiece for their glue and the attentions of coiffeurs from dawn. They towered, and that was presumably why everyone sat so still. More than mild applause would have set up a vibration that may have brought an edifice crashing down; and if one fell, no doubt all would, one into the next, like a row of dominoes in an English county tavern.

The immobility was aped on the stage, where singers as well dressed as their audience faced front and warbled. Their voices were fine, undoubtedly; even Jack, who preferred songs in plain English and preferably accompanied by a dance, could tell that. But there was little drama. And as for anything alluring, well, female singers were not allowed in the Papal States and men dressed as women, howsoever fine their voices, did not stir him. He knew how those voices had been produced, and it gave him the wrong sort of feeling in his groin just watching them.

Two galleries of boxes were below him. Jack had squeezed onto a bench-end at the extreme left of the house and so was able, by craning around and over, to watch the three central boxes. These had been described for him by Watkin Pounce but there was no mistaking them anyway. The crest of the House of Stuart and the royal crest of Britain sat in two immense gilt shields.

'Alas for you, our King just yesterday removed himself to his villa at Albano to avoid the summer heat,' Pounce had said. 'But he leaves his boxes to those who, of necessity, must stay in the city. A reward for their services. You may see some of the most ardent defenders of the Cause there each night.' The fat man had sighed. 'I was invited once but alas . . .' He'd gestured down at his coat, so stained and patched, and sighed again.

Jack looked now. The Old Pretender's supporters, men and women, did not look any different from the rest of the gilded crowd. It vaguely disappointed Jack. He was no Jacobite but surely they could have maintained a more British decorum?

A drop of sweat ran from beneath his wig. Wiping it away, he tugged his lawn shirt from his neck. It was damned hot. In the boxes, the female peacocks fluttered their fans like feathers. And then, almost as one, they stopped. Jack looked to the stage, though he hadn't seen action there halt the constant flapping before. But no, the performers were still absent, the stage bare. Everyone had turned to something occurring in one of the boxes just out of Jack's vision. He leaned further out, inducing again that sense of vertigo. What were they looking at?

Not what, of course. Whom. And he understood why everyone had ceased to do anything but look. It was the contrast that held them at first perhaps, the simple elegance of her dress, the naturalness of her red, red hair, falling, not rising, falling in waves around her bare shoulders; the single ruby that hung just above her cleavage. Perhaps it was that – skin revealed in a place where nearly all was concealed, skin that spoke of coolness in the *bagnio*-like heat – that stopped the fans. And, looking at Laetitia make her entrance, Jack remembered that he had seen her first in just such a manner, walking into the Orchard Street playhouse in Bath. An English audience had paused just like this Roman one did, equally dumbstruck.

It could not last. A fan rose to shelter a cruel comment, others fluttered, heads turned away. Only those to whom Letty was introduced stayed facing her, men bending over her hand, lingering there in the most obvious manner. Beside her stood Mrs O'Farrell – Bridget O'Doherty, as Turnville had told him she was truly called, and McClune's wife – dressed more in the Roman manner, hair high, jewels prominent. A man made the introductions, but it was not Red Hugh, for this fellow was short and aged. Jack scoured the box on the off-chance that the Irishman would have felt safe enough to appear. But his tall frame was nowhere in sight. Jack was not surprised. Even in Rome, where the State openly supported the Pretender and his Cause, Red Hugh would not show himself – Hanoverian agents were nearly as present in the city as the men they watched. Jack had wondered if his own scoutmaster was in the audience. No, just as in Bath, Red Hugh would skulk under an assumed name in poorer quarters – assuming he had not sent his women ahead.

His women. As the performers took again to the stage, as chatter, even in the Jacobite box, diminished and the new-comers were shown to their seats, Jack leaned back. He brought out a handkerchief, wiped away what had become rivulets of sweat, not all of it caused by the Roman summer. Despite uttering her name each night like a prayer, he'd known he'd have no certainty about his feelings until he'd seen her again. Now he had – and he knew. Though everything had changed, nothing had changed. He still loved her, passionately, intensely, certainly. He just had to ascertain if she felt the same about him.

Shortly before the final act concluded, he took up a position opposite the front entrance to the theatre, behind a column of a *loggia*. When she appeared, shepherded by the small man and Bridget O'Doherty, he did not rush up to her, as an impulse dictated he should, and beg her to kill him or set him free. He waited, until the coach they all entered had fought clear of the mob; then he followed it, at the slow pace it was forced to take, through the streets of the city, back towards the area of the Palazzo Muti, aware of strange echoes, certain that there would be no false footpads this night. The carriage passed through the piazza that contained the Fontana di Trevi and stopped shortly afterwards before a grand-looking palazzo. When it did, Jack drew into the shadows, watched that same man hand the ladies down and follow them through the front door.

He waited, unsure what to do, unwilling to leave. Their appearance guaranteed nothing. The stag could be in the city or still on his way there, collecting favours and gold along the road. Turnville had been certain that Red Hugh would make for Rome, but surely someone so experienced would eschew the obvious? Perhaps he had sent the ladies ahead as distraction. Perhaps he had already returned to England for further plotting or to Ireland for recruits.

There was but one thing Jack could do for now.

Reluctantly, he turned his back to the building where Letty was preparing for sleep. There was little for him. Even though scouring Herodotus for the correct words to compose his message took but an hour, afterwards he could not shake the image of her. Dawn came before his eyes closed and he was awake again soon after. He had to be at the gardens on Monte Pinchio when they opened.

His message dropped in the tree trunk, he returned to some sleep at last, making sure he was called at three. At exactly four he passed beneath the window on the Via Columbina but no striped sheet hung. He contrived to pass again at the quarter and the half. Nothing. He waited at a nearby tavern. It was only when the bells sounded the hour that he turned the corner into the street in time to see the striped sheet drawn slowly into the attic room. He was tempted to stay, meet his contact. Prudence told him otherwise. There was good reason no one knew anyone in this game of spies. If one was caught, he could not betray another – whatever the methods of coercion. Suddenly, the singing castrati came to mind. Swallowing at this painful thought, Jack made, once more, for the park. No one walked the avenue, a relieving rain having driven most indoors. But a slightly damp paper met his fingers.

Back in the attic, the old Greek writer revealed only one word: 'Watch'.

— TWO —

The Watching

It was different from the scouting and spying he'd undertaken in Canada the previous year. Yet, despite the urban setting, it was almost the same. He stalked individuals, rather than bodies of troops, noting their movements, observing patterns. He casually conversed, not with Iroquois warriors or French farmers, but with servants and coachmen, though the currency of coercion was usually the same: liquor, liberally dispensed. He knew only that the plan was to take the Irishman when – if – he appeared. But the taking of such a dangerous man was always going to be a difficult thing. His role, as he saw it, was to gather information about the only weakness this enemy displayed: his love of his women. A truly careful man would have left the two of them in Bath and fled on his own. At considerable risk, McClune had not. It was a mistake, yet one he was likely to make again.

Jack watched. Laetitia and Bridget O'Doherty's movements were based on a triangle – from the Palazzo Cavalieri to the Palazzo Muti to the opera house and back. A coachman told Jack that '*la più bella*' was dutiful in her religious observations, attending, each day, the Protestant service in the King's palace. Jack, of course, had seen her do the same in Bath but he'd assumed that was because it was on 'the circuit', a place to see and be seen after the waters, before the ball. As a devout atheist, he found it hard to fathom true faith in anyone else and had also been surprised that someone aligned to the Jacobite cause was not a Catholic like their King. But Red Hugh had told him once that most supporters of the Cause were Protestant. Indeed, almost every Scottish clan that rose in '45 were Presbyterian of the most fanatical nature, and many in Ireland, too. Hence this chapel in Rome. James sent out a message of religious tolerance. On his restoration, all would be free to worship as they chose.

For two days, Jack watched all hours and barely slept. But exhaustion overcame both his excitement at being this close to her again and his desire to spot Red Hugh the moment he appeared. When he awoke, slumped in the doorway of the abandoned house opposite the Palazzo Cavalieri with a child going through his pockets, he knew he had to alter his habits. The Irishman was not someone to confront when tired. And Jack knew that the man, howsoever bold, was not going to appear in daylight. Not with all the spies in Rome. Night was his time, so Jack contrived to sleep at least some of the day, to be in position outside the opera when she attended and follow her carriage back, to maintain his vigil at the palazzo through the night and leave at dawn. He was awake again to walk by the house on the Via Columbina, but no striped sheet appeared and he left no messages himself at the tree on Monte Pinchio. He and his scoutmaster had nothing to say to each other until Red Hugh came to Rome.

And then he did.

On his fourth night of watching, Jack used a knife to push open the shutters of the abandoned house, force open a window and shimmy inside. The family who owned it, like so many Romans, must have fled the city heat for the hills. All their furniture was covered in sheets and on the first floor Jack found an armchair that he dragged to the window. His knife was put to use again, prising slats out of the shutters to create a narrow gap at the perfect height for his eyeline when his head rested against the chair back. On a table beside him he set up a flask of Orvieto wine – it was not as strong as the red Montepulciano and had a refreshing quality he much enjoyed – together with some bread, slices of *vitella mongana* – the best veal he'd ever tasted – and figs. Then he sat back and stared at the palazzo opposite.

He jerked awake, panicked at the sound of voices, until he realized they were not within the house but outside it, and that they were not speaking, but singing. Nearby was the Convent di Seruiti, and the nuns within were obviously about some observations. Cursing himself for his negligence – he noted that his resolution to only sip the wine had been ignored, for the flask was two-thirds gone – he rubbed his eyes, leaned forward . . .

Someone emerged directly below him; must, indeed, have been standing in the same doorway Jack had previously occupied. The figure was cloaked and hatted, an unusual sight in the summer heat. Indeed, as Jack watched, the figure removed the hat, a handkerchief rising to wipe his forehead and neck. Suddenly, there was movement opposite, a door opening in the palazzo. The hat was replaced. But there was near a full moon that night with no cloud, and the man had tilted his head for a brief moment before he disappeared from view again into Jack's doorway. There could be no doubt. Though his hair was cropped, though half his face was covered with a scarf and his clothes by the cloak, the man now sheltering a few feet below Jack was undoubtedly Red Hugh McClune.

Jack waited, almost not breathing, certainly not moving, the tip of his nose an inch from the slats. From the palazzo doorway opposite a squealing cat was hurled onto the cobblestones. Protesting, it slunk away, leaving the singing nuns as the only sound in the square.

He waited. Below him, nothing stirred. A minute, two,

five. The voices ceased. All was quiet. Then the figure stepped out again, moving swiftly to the door that had opened before. It must have been left unlocked deliberately, the disgruntled cat a pretext, for the Irishman was inside in a moment.

Jack sat again to his watch. Despite his thirst, he did not lift the wine flask. Thus he was awake when the first light was in the sky and the same cloaked figure emerged from the doorway. There was a pause, a woman's hand briefly kissed before it withdrew and the door was shut. Then the man crossed the street swiftly. McClune tipped his head again as he wrapped the scarf around his face, and Jack stepped away, but not before he'd taken note of a black beard, spectacles upon the nose, a white cravat at his neck. Turnville had said that their quarry had taken ship at Southampton posing as a Methodist minister. It appeared that he maintained that disguise still.

Jack heard footsteps recede. When they vanished, he finally reached for the wine flask. 'Welcome to Rome,' he said, and drained it.

His note, informing his scoutmaster of the stag's arrival, was answered the same day, with the same, frustrating word: 'Watch.' Now that the man was here, should not plans be made to take him? He had understood the need not to know anyone before, but surely he needed contacts now, a gathering of men in the Dawkins mould to whom he could point out the Irishman? What if the previous night was to be his only appearance? They could not rely on him lingering too long, however devoted. He would soon be about another mission, another assault upon Britain and the King. But there was little he, Jack, could do alone. Even if he could cudgel him in the dark, where would he imprison him, what would he do with him there? Cursing, Jack knew he could only obey the single word of his command.

That night, the nuns were again at their devotions when the Irishman appeared. No cat was thrown out, but otherwise the actions were just the same – the figure emerging from below him, the door briefly opened, then opened again to discharge him in the first of the dawn's light. He reported the pattern, but no striped sheet appeared to summon him. He returned again to the house, watched Letty in, waited, watched Red Hugh come and go, his frustration growing ever stronger. That morning he forsook sleep to wrestle longer with Herodotus, composing a message reporting the pattern but stating his fear: their quarry could leave at any time; why did they not act? But still no sheet hung.

It was the fifth day when, in longing rather than in any hope, he walked past the house again as the bell rang eight. And there it was. He kept straight on, disdaining the safer, circuitous route, even cutting through the Piazza di Spagna and straight past the Caffe degli Inglesi with his hat brim down. No countryman hailed him and he was soon in the park, swiftly at the tree. A paper was there, not the three sets of numbers he knew now would condemn him still to wait and watch, but a whole series that he did not recognize. Eagerly he rushed back to his lodgings, took the crib from its hiding place, translated the phrase. The first four words thrilled: 'We take them tonight.'

At last! It was going to happen. The waiting was ended. Almost too excited to try, he none the less decoded the last two words.

'Return home.'

Jack sat there, staring. Return home? He was not even to be there at the kill? That was beyond disappointment, it was an insult. Without him, they would not have Red Hugh McClune. And now they were dismissing him?

It did not take him long to realize that this was an order he would not, could not obey. They did not know how he watched from his eyrie in the closed-up house. The least he would do was see the man taken. And then he had business of his own to conclude. For if they thought he was leaving Rome without seeing her . . .

His hand shaking, Jack reached for his strike light and flint, his bowl of leaves. The dog on the floor below had begun its high-pitched yapping. As the paper caught alight, his eyes fixed on the insulting six words: 'We take them tonight . . .'

Them?

'Shite!' he muttered aloud, reaching burnt fingers to his mouth. He picked up the crib and, even though the letter was ash, turned to the page, tracked the line, found the word. There was no doubt. *Them.*

Turnville was not just taking Red Hugh. He was going to take the whole Jacobite brood. He was going to take . . . Letty!

Jack stared ahead, his mind swamped, the barking below filling it, shutting out all thought. He had previously summoned a host of huge rough men to guarantee the taking of the Irishman. Now he saw that same man seizing Letty, throwing her into some foul cell, a man like Turnville coming into the room, signalling his man to begin . . .

It could not be allowed to happen.

The sudden hammering on his door seemed monstrous, accompanied by an upsurge in yaps and what sounded like groans beyond the wood. Shocked, Jack seized the bowl, ran to the window, tipped the still-smouldering ashes out. The sounds at the door were loud enough to make him fear that it would soon be burst in so there was no time to replace the Herodotus in its hole. Flinging his coat over it, he unsheathed his sword, crossed to the door, turned the key and flung it open.

Watkin Pounce fell into the room. Hanging off him by its teeth was a small creature. 'Save me,' he gasped, 'Hotspur has me by the throat.'

The dog was, in fact, joined to the fat knight at the knee end of his breeches. Jack's shod toe caused it to release and run yelping out of the door.

Pounce had fallen onto the bed, which groaned but did not collapse. 'That cur! I did nothing but enquire of it the way to your room.' His breaths were coming in great heaves, pushing out the huge cheeks. He looked like a goldfish jerked rudely onto a riverbank. 'How do you live so high up? I do not think I have climbed so since . . . ever.' A fat wrist flapped. 'Have you no refreshment?'

Jack sheathed his sword with a grunt. 'Do you not think, Watkin, that this is an early hour, even for you?'

'I will alleviate your concern, sweet wag, by saying that I do not seek the first of the day but the last of the night.' He smiled. 'Is that an Orvieto I spy in the corner? Why, 'tis barely wine!'

Jack shook his head and went to the rope-wrapped bottle. He had two mugs and filled one. Then after only a moment's hesitation, he filled the second. 'Your health, sir,' he said, handing one across.

'And yours.' Pounce drank half the mug. 'You still look feverish, though, and have lost weight. Are you not recovered?'

Jack had sent word that a fever had taken him to excuse his absence from the Angelo and Pounce's company. 'Nearly. It was virulent, whatever took me.'

'The marshes of the *campagna* spread contagion into the city. Those who can, leave Rome for the summer months. Those who must, stay.' He sighed, drained his mug, held it out to Jack, who dutifully filled it. He sipped now, studying Jack as he did. 'But there's something else in your eyes, lad, beyond a sickness. Or is it another kind? The effects of Cupid's arrow?'

Jack looked at the man sprawled on his bed. In a strange way, he was the closest thing he had to a friend in Rome and though he had deceived him about who he was, and what he was about, he had largely confessed the truth about Letty. 'I am still hard struck, it is true,' he said, hesitantly, 'the worse because . . . because the lady in question has now appeared in Rome.'

'No!' Pounce raised himself on one elbow. 'Tell me all.'

Jack adapted the story to a circumstance that did not include Jacobites. He spoke of seeing her at the opera, of following her, of how his feelings were as strong as ever. The knight nodded and sighed. Finally, with a great effort, he sat up. 'You know what must be done.'

'What?'

'You must carry her away.'

It was Jack's turn to sigh. 'How?'

'How? What sort of word is that for a lover? The only words that need concern you are when and where! Establish those and how will resolve itself.'

'But to approach her will be nigh impossible.'

'Another craven word. Where does she stay?'

'In the Palazzo Cavalieri.'

Pounce whistled. 'I know it. Di Cavalieri's one of the richest families in Rome. The aged count himself lives there and if she is under his protection . . .' He shook his head. 'You must not attempt those walls. Is she never alone?'

'I do not think so. She goes from the house to the chapel then back to the house then to the opera, always accompanied, always—'

'Which chapel? Where does she worship?'

'She's Protestant, so—'

'So she goes to the Palazzo Muti. My boy!' Pounce actually levered himself up to sitting in his excitement. 'There is your opportunity. None of di Cavalieri's servants will accompany her into that chapel. Papists to a man!'

'But how do I get in there?'

'Why, Pip,' he replied, 'you have the token still, do you

not? The silver token that gains you admittance? Do you mean to say you have not used it?'

Jack thought. He had not followed Letty into the chapel for fear of being spotted by her. He got up now, searched through his various pockets. At last, in a waistcoat he had not worn in a week, he found it. 'Here it is,' he said.

'Will her aunt accompany her?'

Jack shook his head. 'She's always alone, except for servants, who wait at the gate.'

Pounce beamed. 'Then it should be easy enough for you to seize a moment with her. Enough to pass her a note at least, arrange a further rendezvous. And that's where you will carry her off.'

Jack thought about what the note had promised for the evening. *We take them tonight . . .*

'It would have to be today, this afternoon, and . . .' Then he remembered one of the few other places he knew well enough in Rome. 'I suppose I could get her to meet me at the gardens on Monte Pinchio.'

Pounce snapped his fingers. All effects of drunkenness seemed to have left him. 'Excellent! So many entrances. Do you know the cart track beside the Palazzo Barberini?'

'I do.'

'Good! I will rendezvous with you there at four in the afternoon, shall we say? With horses, laden with enough to get you to Civitavecchia. From there, a felucca to take you to Genoa. If Neptune favours lovers with a fair tide, you would be out of the Papal States in a day.' He frowned. 'Alas, though, I am afraid I will need, uh, a little gold to do this for you.'

Jack stared at him. This was madness! He had attempted exactly the same thing in Bath not two months previously and had failed. Yet, how could he not try? If she felt about him as he did about her, perhaps she *would* just come away with him. Especially as he would be saving her from Red

Hugh's capture and fate. As he would save her later from a charge of treason. For they would not condemn their own spy's wife, surely? 'By God, sir,' he said, thrusting a hand forward to be shaken, 'I will do as you advise.' He reached into the hole under the planks that usually contained the Herodotus, pulled out his purse. 'Would forty *scudi* be enough?' he said, counting coins.

Pounce dabbed sweat from his forehead. 'Fifty would secure it, and a dozen bottles of the Montepulciano to accompany you.'

Jack handed the coins over. 'What time is the service?'

'Eleven.'

Jack looked at his pocket watch. 'But that's less than an hour.'

Pounce rose, swayed, settled. 'Then I suggest we should be about our business. You to the chapel. Me to the farrier.' He reached forward, took Jack's hand. 'I will see you with the horses. And I will weep as I watch you ride off for I will then remember too clearly how I missed my chance to do the same. What might I have been if I had, eh? What might I have been?' A tear ran down his cheek, he waved a hand and was gone. His shouts and the dog's yaps faded, accompanying Jack's scribbling upon a scrap of paper.

It was only when he was on his way to the Palazzo Muti that Jack realized what this would mean if all his hopes were gratified, if Letty did indeed love as he loved and would give up everything, risk all these dangers, for that love. He would not be there at the taking of Red Hugh McClune. He would, with luck, be on a felucca bound for Genoa.

What is revenge, he thought, compared to love? With a chuckle he realized that he was obeying his orders, those of his scoutmaster to return home. Yet nowhere did those orders say he had to return home alone.

— THREE —

The Taking

Though he could have visited the Palazzo Muti before, Jack had shown little desire. As King James III had already left for his summer villa, those few who remained in Rome to endure the swelter were the obvious face of Jacobitism – courtiers and administrators, part of whose labour was to cultivate those who visited and try to turn them to the Cause. Jack had had enough of that at the Angelo.

Yet he cursed himself now for not taking the opportunity, because then he would not be lost! His token had gained him admittance at the main entrance where the porter had gestured vaguely through another and muttered, '*Cappella*.' But the door had led to a courtyard, a colonnade around it, doors leading off. The three he tried opened onto empty rooms, furniture shrouded and windows shuttered. At last he found a stair that took him up but the corridor there was equally deserted and the one serving girl he found had no English and his careful pronunciation of the word '*cappella*' produced no response. He strode along, barely glancing at the portraits that hung every few feet, Stuart kings, princes and their consorts gazing down upon lost kingdoms. A clock had struck eleven when he questioned the maid. He was, as ever, late.

Then he saw it, and only because it was just closing, the door no more distinctive than most of the others. Close to, he observed a small stone cross on the pediment, wreathed in Stuart oak leaves. The hand was still on the knob the other side as he jerked it open and a man stumbled out.

'*Scusi, signore,* is this . . . *cappella*?' And then he saw that it was, not needing the man's whispered Italian jabber to confirm it. The hand guided him inside, the door closed behind him.

It was dark in the royal chapel, and cool, for the interior seemed to be all marble, floor to ceiling, the light coming mainly from candelabra, though in the roof he could see two small windows that admitted a little sunshine and air. The casements were the plainest things on display for though he knew that the service to be held was Protestant, the chapel certainly wasn't, for it served the Catholic king as well. Statues of angels and the beatified gazed to heaven; the small choir was carved from mahogany, rococo angels clutching lyres over clouds and stars. Though incense did not burn now, its stale musk clung to the pews and the statuary. It was not a large space, no bigger than a small parish church in Cornwall, and thus overcrowded, claustrophobic. Jack stood for a moment to let his heart settle and his sight adjust.

It took him some moments to find her. When he did, he moved immediately to the right aisle. She sat on the extreme end of the pew, gazing up to the altar. The Rector was just commencing the service. There was hardly space in the pew behind her but Jack created some, forcing a large woman to gather her bulging dress and slide along. Movement rippled down, people adjusting with whispered protests.

Her head did not turn to the slight commotion, her gaze remaining fixed on the vicar. He could only see that small part of her but it was enough to make his breathing shallow, for he had not been this close to her since their parting in the garden in Bath. He saw the same neck he'd kissed, the wave of finest down rising up at the back to the hair; saw the edge of the ear he'd run his tongue along, making her laugh, then making her sigh. Saw the nose, one cheek, both powdered now, not then, for the rain had washed it off in the garden, leaving him to marvel at the tracery of freckles scattered on her skin like stars across the sky.

He couldn't help the moan that memory brought; and the vision before him instantly changed. A flush ran up the neck, into the hairline; the head began to turn. He leaned forward. 'Hush,' he whispered urgently. 'Do not cry out.'

A scolding 'Shh!' came from the woman beside him, a louder gasp from the one in front. Then both were fortuitously drowned by the first notes of the organ introducing the hymn. All rose, though Jack had to grab Letty's elbow to support her. She steadied, as the singing began.

The verse was not loudly sung, the largely English congregation displaying the usual national restraint. Only the woman beside him truly raised her voice. It was not tuneful, but it gave Jack the chance to lean in again.

'Do not turn around,' he said, 'but it *is* I, Jack. I have come for you.' Letty half-turned, her lips parted in shock, not song. 'Jack,' she mouthed. 'How . . . ? Oh, Jack.'

He found that he had no more words. The singing continued, a murmur further off, a roar nearby, yet even that dissonance seemed fitting somehow, a reminder of a world out of harmony. Something he was there to set right.

He found his voice again. 'You must come with me,' he said.

'What?' she replied, though he did not know whether she heard or she doubted. Perhaps both.

'Come with me,' he said, just as the hymn suddenly ceased. His words, spoken loudly, carried into the near silence.

The woman next to him was emboldened, since she was

not the only one now disturbed. 'This is the house of God, young man, not some drawing room! Worship ye and flirt ye no more.'

'I assure ye . . . you, madam, I—'

'Silence there! Silence.' The voice came from the vicar, peering down over his pince-nez. Others joined in a general mumble of condemnation.

'You must go.' Letty's voice was a gentle contrast. 'Please, Jack.'

He stepped from the pew, his back to the crowd, quickly taking her hymnal from her as he did so. The transfer of the paper he'd scribbled at his lodgings into it took just a moment and he laid the book on the shelf before her. 'Sing well,' he said and then he was moving, accompanied by a general clucking of disapproval, to the door.

As he found his way to the lower floor and the front door, he realized he would never be admitted back into the select congregation who attended the Chapel in the Palazzo Muti. He did not care. For if she sang lustily, read swiftly, came to their rendezvous promptly, the only church he ever wished to see after that would be the one in which he married her. Then, hang him if he was ever caught worshipping anything else again! Aside from her, of course.

He approached the gardens on the Monte Pinchio by his usual route, via the Piazza Barberini. No fat Jacobite with laden horses awaited him there, and he cursed the necessity of trusting a drunkard, until he remembered that he was early and that Watkin Pounce, even now, should be swaying to the rendezvous. And if he was not? Well, there were other stables nearby, and he had some *scudi* sewn into bits of apparel and fifty more in a purse in his satchel. The only matter of importance lay ahead of him, up the slope of Monte Pinchio, under the pine trees. Now he was there he was aware of the stupidity of arranging this meeting just where he collected his orders from his scoutmaster, but he had been in a hurry and it was, after all, one of the few places he knew well in Rome. There was a young cypress tree growing next to the fence. Kneeling, he wedged the satchel into a crook of branches. It could not be seen from the path. Buckling on his swordbelt, Jack strode up the hill.

Although he knew he was early it did not lessen the anxiety that grew as his pocket watch's hands crawled up the face to four. Had he been clear enough in the note? What if her guardian had detained her? What if Red Hugh had forsaken the night and swept them both out of Rome, the English trap betrayed by one of the myriad double agents who lurked in the city?

The appointed hour came, confirmed by a bell ringing in the villa that surmounted the hill, hidden from his view by the stand of pines. He stood square in the middle of the main avenue, just by the statue of the dryad who, if she had possessed arms, might have pointed the way to the oft-visited tree. The heat was near overpowering but at least it kept most Romans indoors, behind their shutters. No one disturbed the walk.

Where was she? Four o'clock he'd scrawled and it was now a quarter past. Suddenly, he was convinced that she could not come; or that she would not, her courage failing her; or, worse – far worse – that she had chosen not to because she did not love him enough. The thought made his gaze fall to the ground, to the prints made by his shuffling boots in the dust and sand.

And then she was there. He did not hear her for the dust swallowed the sound of her running feet and she was yet far enough off for her harsh breaths not to carry. But he looked along the avenue and there she was indeed, moving fast towards him. He closed the gap at an equal pace.

He couldn't believe she was in his arms again; the kiss

reassured him, so long was its duration. He had to break it. 'Come,' he said, making to drag her down the hill.

'No, Jack.' She was breathing heavily, from her running, from their reunion. A bench was close and she sank upon it.

'A friend has horses nearby,' he noticed her dress as he spoke, the beauty of the taffeta, the voluminous folds, 'and we will exchange them for a carriage. But we must go now, if we are to leave Rome before the gates are locked tonight.'

Still she did not move. 'Sit, please, but for a moment. There are things we must discuss.'

Discuss? A strange word, he thought, full of warnings. 'This is dangerous,' he said, taking her outstretched hand, 'I remember the last time you pulled me onto a bench.'

'*I* pulled you?' She struck his hand as he sat. 'A gentleman would remember it differently.'

'Perhaps I am none such.' A thought creased his brow. 'For I also remember that you pulled me down to distract me.'

'I didn't succeed.'

'Just as well. For if you had . . .' Jack shuddered. If he'd arrived a minute later, the King of England would have been dead and the Absolute name ruined for ever. But he had pondered long on this, recalling every detail; and each had told him that there had been no artifice in her loving. The fact that she was there now confirmed it.

He spoke on the thought. 'You love me.' Her nod was hesitant, but it was there. 'When did you know?'

'When?' A smile came, banishing the sadness in her eyes. 'I guessed at it when I first saw you, with your stick and your swagger, rescuing me.'

'But you knew it . . . ?'

She closed her eyes. 'In the library. Duelling with titles.'

'What? When you vanquished me?'

'Perhaps that's why. The hurt on your face!' She laughed.

For a moment, there was nothing else, just that memory and her hand in his, a drowsy afternoon that could have been Bath, or Rome or anywhere where time did not rule. And then she pulled free, leaned back. 'Jack, I do love you. But . . .'

He pressed a finger to her lips. 'That is not a word for us. "I do" will suffice, and we shall hear it again and soon. Yet only if we leave now.'

He rose. She did not. 'No, Jack, you must hear me. I *do* love you—'

'But?' He said it, the word he now hated.

'I cannot go with you. There was a moment when I could have. But that chance passed us by. Because of a torn sleeve.' The laugh that came now was mirthless.

'So you would have come with me, then? Despite all the lies?'

'Which we both told. Playing roles given to us by another.'

Jack knelt, just as he had in Bath, though there was no falsity now in the kneeling. 'I promise you, Letty, I was going to tell you the truth. Then, there, in that garden, I would have given you a choice.' He regarded her silence. 'You don't believe me?'

She leaned forward. 'I do. And you have to believe this. Yes, I would have come with you. Yes, I would have married you, lived with you, loved you.'

It was there, what he most wanted to hear. Except the sentence was in the past tense. To return them to the present, he seized her hand. 'Then nothing else matters. Come.'

Still she resisted him. 'I cannot. For . . . for, Jack!' She dragged her hand clear again. 'I am no longer free. I am betrothed.'

It had to be the heat. This word did not make sense. 'To whom?'

She sighed. 'I am betrothed to the Count di Cavalieri.'

In his mind he saw a small man in a black coat, handing her into an opera box, through a door, out of a carriage. 'He is ancient,' he said.

'He is fifty.'

'And a dwarf.'

'He is . . . very kind.'

'Kind?' It was another word that did not make sense.

She pressed on. 'And he is rich. Very rich. This is what poor girls do, Jack, if they have something to offer. They make a good match.'

He shook his head. It didn't clear it. 'Not in your novels.'

'I never read any novels,' she said firmly. 'I always knew what my life would be, where my duty lay.'

'Is that what you were serving on that other bench?'

She winced at his sudden anger. 'No,' she whispered. 'Then I truly believed it was a beginning, not an end. Then I thought that somehow duty and love had met and it seemed to me a sort of miracle. A story indeed for a novel.' She laughed again, a sad laugh, then stretched out a hand to him. 'But believe this, Jack, and know that I will always bless you for it: at least I tasted love once, before duty claimed me back.'

He did not take her hand. Instead he wiped his sleeve across his face. Insects hovered, their buzz in his ears. Shapes seemed to move in the trees off the path, shadows he could not focus on because he was searching for something in the cloudless sky. He found it, a word, the one she'd just spoken. 'Betrothed.'

'Pardon?'

There was her answer. 'You tasted more than love on that bench. That moment of . . . of joining, betrothed you – to me.' He took her hands now, tried to lift her up again from the bench. 'Don't you see? You cannot marry the Count. For his honour. For mine. Because you are prior contracted. You are *betrothed* to me.'

The drone of insects, the cracking of a stick between the trees, his heartbeat pulsing in his head. He studied her face, the bunched eyebrows, waited for her to deny the argument. She wouldn't be able to. She'd have to agree. Have to come away with him.

Her gaze had gone past him, into the tree-line. When it came back, he saw that her eyes had filled with tears. 'Oh, Jack,' she said softly, 'if that is what is binding you, then . . .'

'It is. It must.'

'. . . then let me relieve you on that point of honour.' A tear spilled out, ran down the cheek. 'For, you see, you were not the first.'

He almost laughed, such was the nonsense she spoke. The girl was barely seventeen. 'Then who was?'

Her gaze moved beyond him again. 'He was.'

Jack turned. Standing five paces away was Red Hugh McClune. Strangely, the first thought that came was not of the terrible betrayal, by his friend, by his lover. Instead, he remembered what Fanny Harper had said in the theatre that very first time he'd seen Letty. How she had a dark secret. He'd thought then that he would give anything to know it. He hadn't realized it would have to be his heart.

Jack looked up into the sky again, then around into the trees. He'd never have let these men creep up on him in the forests of Quebec. But he'd been distracted by what he'd thought was love. He'd not let that happen again.

He realized he knew them all. MacBrave from the Angelo. The young Roman lover who'd preceded him down the path the very first day he'd gone to the hollowed-out tree. Even the landlord of his lodgings, not that ancient or sexless it seemed, and the swathes of cloth he still wore were now parted to reveal a toothless smile, two pistols and a club.

And then there was the Irishman. He'd only seen him by moonlight, of course, hadn't realized just how cropped his hair was, how black he'd dyed it, the fullness of the beard. For just one moment, Jack regretted the passing of that red hair, those peacock clothes. Only one small moment though, that one before he drew his sword.

'Now don't be foolish . . .'

There were five paces between them. Jack covered them fast, so fast that Red Hugh made his first parry with his sword still half in its scabbard, twisting as he did, using the force of Jack's run to guide him past his right side. Halting, Jack slashed back, spinning around, knowing that the side of the small sword could not kill but could hurt the man badly, catch an eye perhaps, weaken him anyway, prepare him for Jack's point. But Red Hugh ducked swiftly, spun away, a gap created between them, his arms wide in an attitude of supplication. 'I pray you, Jack. You cannot win here. Put up.'

Jack couldn't, didn't. Again he came, flicking off his cloak, the gold coins in its hem bunching it into a length of heavy cloth that he flung at the Irishman, engulfing him in black. Red Hugh, briefly blinded, must nevertheless have felt the point driven at his belly; he cut down, deflected Jack's lunge just enough, though he sacrificed a button of his waistcoat.

'No!' the Irishman yelled, but not at Jack; at the men who had circled, whom Jack, with side vision, saw were brandishing cudgels. He didn't care, though. For now, the man he hated was still struggling to free himself from heavy black cloth.

'Yah!' yelled Jack, lunging again, straight at the exposed belly that was there and then was not because he'd forgotten again that the Irishman was a left-hander and hardly had to move to flick the blade in an outward circular parry, using Jack's momentum to bring him tight, so his right hand could drop and fasten on Jack's, his forefinger find that point under the thumb pad. With a yelp, Jack released his grip, his sword plunging to the dusty earth.

For a moment, Red Hugh held him there. Then the Irishman's eyes went beyond him and Jack waited for the blow that would tumble him into a familiar darkness, from which, perhaps, he would never emerge. Darkness came but no blow fell. Instead his own cloak was swirled around his head, pulled tight; men fell on him. His hands were swiftly bound and then he was half pushed, half dragged in a stumbling run down the hill. Sightless, all he had were the sounds. The worst of them, beyond Italian cursing and Irish cautions, were those that faded first – a woman's terrible sobs.

They left him bound and blind for several hours. Only when it was night did they remove the ropes, unwind the cloak, releasing him from one darkness to another. Light eventually came, showing him a long, high-ceilinged room. A gaol again, despite the bed, armoire, table and chairs; but in Bath he'd been held in a cellar while here muffled shouting from below indicated he was being restrained higher up. Bars prevented him reaching the shutters on the outside of the tall, deep-set windows, but he saw a catch, presumed they opened with the correct pole. The growing light also showed him a lantern, his strike light, flint and bowl beside it. Once lit, its glow also revealed the rest of his possessions that he'd abandoned in the attic. There was a basin and jug, both full of water. He drank the one, used the other to wash his face clear of the black dust of the path. A mirror in a large gilt frame hung on one wall above a fireplace, and Jack went close to behold a sorry version of himself.

His hair, hard to tame at the best of times, hung in knotted black shanks down his pale face, and there were purple bruises beneath his eyes. Sighing, he turned again to the water he had not yet drunk, washed again, found his comb and did what he could with his hair, tying it back. Then he sought out his best clothes, the ensemble he'd worn at the opera. There was no need to don the wig. But he would look as well as he could when he faced his inquisitors.

They came within the hour. Two remained outside the door.

'Good morrow to you, me boy,' Red Hugh said as he strode in. Jack saw that, like himself, the Irishman had been about his toilet. Gone was the beard, the black garb. Though his hair was not the red cascade it had been and he sported a wig, his clothes were once more the beautifully pressed display Jack had so envied aboard the *Sweet Eliza*. 'Are ye well there?'

'Well enough. And ready.'

'For what.'

'For whatever it is you intend to do to me.'

Red Hugh sat on one of the two chairs that faced each other, the table between. He produced a flask from one pocket, two small glasses from another. Extracting the cork with his teeth, he began to pour, speaking around the obstacle. 'And what is it you think I intend, dear heart? Come over, have a drink and tell me.'

Jack did not move. 'I am your enemy. I presume you want information from me.'

The cork was laid down. 'You are my friend, Jack, one who spared my life. Our differences in politics, well . . .' He shrugged. 'And there is nothing you have that I do not already know.'

'Nothing?'

'Well, let me see.' Red Hugh leaned back on the chair legs, still holding out one of the glasses. 'Come and sit; let us consider the matter.'

Jack came. He did not want to drink with this man. He wanted to kill him. But since that was plainly impossible for

236

the moment and since, despite the reassurance, Jack was convinced that torture was but a few moments away, he might as well take a drink. It might help dull the pain that was coming.

He sat. '*Slainte*,' said Red Hugh, knocking back the glass, immediately pouring another. 'I hate to tell you this – and I hope you won't feel too bad about it – but I already know it all.' He held up a fist, counted out the fingers. 'Your scout-master in England is Colonel Turnville. You do not know the one here, they would not have trusted you with that information. Am I not right?'

Jack shrugged.

'Ah, lad.' Eyes sparkled at him, a finger went up. 'He communicates via the tree on Monte Pinchio. We read the messages first, as we do your replies. Which reminds me . . .' He fished again into the seemingly bottomless pockets, extracted the copy of Herodotus and placed it on the table. 'It's always Herodotus or bloody Virgil. All you classical-inclined Englishmen! You should tell 'em to show a little more imagination. Sure, there are some fine Irish writers they could use. Still,' he patted the volume, 'they'll be bound to change their crib since your capture so you may have this. Should distract you in the time you have ahead.'

'My final hours?'

Red Hugh laughed. 'I know you have a low opinion of me, lad. But do you really think, after all we've been through, that I'd be so unfriendly as to torture and then kill you?'

Jack bit back the retort that came on a surge of anger. Anger was not what he needed here. 'So what is to become of me?' he said.

'I wish, me boy, that I could say you were free to go. We both know that is not going to happen. Nor can I tell you how long you must remain here. But I can tell you that your stay will not be too onerous, howsoever long. I could not, in all conscience, spend Jacobite gold on your hospitality. But it seems only right that what was extracted from the cloak you tried to snare me with should provide you with a little comfort to start you off. And for the rest of the time, if you would just sign this paper . . .' From within his jacket, a piece of parchment was pulled out, unfolded and set down alongside a quill and ink pot.

'What's this? My confession? I wouldn't sign one for Turnville and I'll be damned if I sign one for you!'

Red Hugh shook his head. 'Read.'

Jack read to himself.

I, Jack Absolute, do hereby relinquish all my shares and disbursements in the Robuste, *captured in the late action against the* Sweet Eliza *and give them, without let or hindrance, to Hugh Patrick Fergal McClune of Broad Street, Bristol. I state that there has been no coercion in this assignment and is in return only for services rendered by the aforementioned Hugh McClune, Esq.*

He looked up. 'No coercion?'

The Irishman shrugged. 'None. You must stay a prisoner, Jack. It's your choice if you do it at my expense, for which you will reimburse me, or . . . well, there are other places that are far less comfortable, I can assure you.'

'I'm sure you'd know,' muttered Jack, reaching for the quill, dipping it into the well, signing. He had no choice. He had been in an English cell and it was a hole. He suspected that an Italian one would be far worse.

Red Hugh leaned forward with an approving grin. 'Now date it, there's the thing. Marvellous! You won't regret it.' He blew on the ink, waved the parchment in the air. 'Not sure when I'll make it to Bristol but . . .'

Jack swirled the contents of his glass, then drained it. 'And you cannot tell me how long I am to be imprisoned?'

'Alas, I cannot. Who knows where the Cause will take me now?'

'Back to England to kill the King?'

'I think not. That was merely a piece of opportunism when I heard of his forthcoming visit to Bath. Besides, kill one Hanoverian, there's always another nearby to place his fat Teutonic arse on the throne.' His eyes focused above Jack. 'You know, I've always dreamed of doing something that would not just shake the throne but pull it down entirely. Something . . . spectacular.' His gaze returned. 'I've got a few thoughts on it, and must be about them now.' He smiled. 'But don't you fear, I'm always back in Rome every two or three years.'

Jack could not help the gasp that came. 'You would hold me for three years?'

'It's not so long, for a youth like yourself. Wasn't I prisoner to the Turks for as long? And in conditions far removed from these, I'll be telling you.' His hand came to rest on Jack's arm. 'For your gold will buy you wine and good food, and the guards have instructions to bring you whatever you like.' He winked. 'I've warned them of your appetites, my boy. Good clean girls will be provided and changed as often as your linen.'

Jack stared back, revolted. Coldly, he said, 'I think I have had enough dealings with whores, don't you?'

It was the first blow he'd landed on the Irishman and he saw him wince. 'Now, Jack, you wrong her. You—'

Jack shook his head. His anger, so banked down but always present, came out now. 'Your own cousin,' he spat. 'How could you? Did you give no thought at all to the honour of a man you said was your friend but that you could lead to a trough where you had guzzled?'

Red Hugh stared back. Jack could see he had hurt him again. Anger and sorrow duelled on the man's face. Both were mastered – slowly, painfully – before he spoke. 'I'll tell you something of my cousin, Absolute. She does what she does for greater reasons than you could ever comprehend.'

'For the Cause?' Jack's voice was sharp with mockery. 'What cause is it that can turn a girl into a whore and you into her pander?'

He thought the Irishman was going to go for him then, saw his colour change, his hand drop to the sword at his side, almost wished him to draw it. He knew he couldn't take this man, not yet, but a part of him wanted just one more try, and he pushed himself away from the table to give himself room.

Once more, Red Hugh controlled his temper. It took some deep breaths before the sword hilt was released and the Irishman rose to his feet. 'I know a little of what you are feeling,' he said. 'For I have felt such madness myself, born out of war and killing, jealousy and betrayals, as you see them.' He put a hand to the bridge of his nose, closed his eyes. For one insane moment Jack was tempted to leap at him. Then the eyes opened again. 'It was after one such time, only two years ago, that I returned to my country half-crazed and there I met a beauty and a kindness I had not encountered in years.' He shuddered. 'I abused that kindness, took what I had no right to take, a sin that has sent me to the priests in search of a forgiveness they can never grant, one that I can only strive to atone for in my own way.' He leaned down, his voice now a whisper. 'But I assure you, boy, if you are tormented, then welcome to my circle of hell.'

He turned to the door, and Jack thought he'd go through it and that would be that. Instead, he paused, turned back. 'Shall I tell you something else, Jack Absolute, before I go? About my cousin? And Bath?'

Jack nodded.

'The plot I laid against you there, with regard to her, I'd hoped to separate entirely from my political affairs. I simply wanted to make amends to one I love and had sinned

240

against; and to make you truly appreciate one worth the appraisal. I thought to help you both to marry for love *and* money. Oh aye, Honourable Jack, for money has always to be a part of it when you are as poor as she is.' He shook his head. 'But I did not order her to seduce you in Bath. And she did not tell me or anyone of your approach to her in the church here or of your rendezvous. Indeed, she slipped the guard I placed on her. For she needed you to know one thing at least – that if you were betrayed, she was not the betrayer.'

Then he was gone, his footsteps reverberating down the stairs before the door was closed and bolted again. Jack was left to his thoughts and, after only a short while, some tears.

It took three days to climb out of his despair, back to his anger. Three also to acquire the words he knew he'd need from his little-used Italian grammar. When he was ready and the least taciturn of the guards, a fellow of about his own years, came with his supper, he asked him. The man had a little English but he found Jack's request hard to understand, immediately presuming it was of the kind Red Hugh had said the young man would require.

'Woman,' he said, smiling lasciviously. '*Il signor* want woman, *si*?'

'Woman, no,' Jack replied. 'Man.'

The guard looked surprised, then shrugged. '*Uomo? Va bene.*'

'No, no! Signor, not . . . I need . . .' Jack stepped closer, searching for the newly acquired words. '*Il maestro . . . di spada.*' He made a gesture as if lunging with a sword. 'For exercise, yes?' He breathed deep, raised his arms beside him and shook them. '*Exercismo, si?*'

Understanding came. '*Ah, capito. Exercismo! Con il spaddacino. Si!*'

He turned to go but Jack halted him. '*Molto importante,*' he said. '*Il maestro sinistra. Capiche? Sinistra.*'

The man nodded, understanding the request if not its reason. '*Ah, si, si, capito!*'

Glad you do, thought Jack, as the door closed. For what I need most in the world is a left-handed fencing master.

— FOUR —

The Prisoner

Desperately Jack flung himself back, his feet pumping to drive him away, the speed of them the only thing keeping the sword point from his chest. His own blade – though he moved it frantically – was almost useless. He'd allowed the man to get close in again; once there, he was rarely dislodged without striking.

Sucking in his chest, he lunged back, bringing his blade up almost horizontal to his body and jerking his wrist hard right. The threatening point of his opponent went outwards, just enough. Coming *en garde* again in *sixte*, Jack maintained contact, held his opponent's weapon there. The man halted, and Jack's other hand reached back for balance – and encountered wallpaper.

Damn the fellow, Jack thought, breathing deep, watching the man's eyes. A flick of them, signalling renewal, and he'd have to find something else, though it was hard to think what. In the eternity of the previous ten seconds he'd driven all the way across the room, had the Italian almost as cramped as he was now . . . and then, somehow he'd given it all away, failed to make that final thrust, been driven all the way back.

'So,' the man said, slowly disengaging his blade. He walked back to the centre of the room. 'Again.'

Jack came forward, wiping the sweat onto his sleeve. It was hot work anyway, but early summer had brought back the intense Roman heat he'd almost forgotten through the long winter and chill spring.

He saluted, came *en garde*. Immediately the master took one step back. For months now Ubaldi had done thus, compelling Jack to attack. This was done at Jack's request, for he knew that if he ever again crossed swords with the man who'd incarcerated him there, he would have to be the one to take the initiative. But it was hard always to act first, not react. It was also the lesson he needed to learn. Twice now the Irishman had taken him, easily. It could not happen a third time.

The pace back signalled something else. Ever since Jack had told *il maestro* that the man he sought had trained in the French school, the Italian's national pride had been stirred. It was the only time Jack had seen him expressive about anything, explaining and demonstrating how the French liked to stay out of distance, picking off their opponents as they came in, or exploding in a sudden charge and lunge. The Italian way – the superior way, Jack was assured – was to get in close and let wrist, blade, speed and sudden changes of tempo do the work: stop him getting to you, close in and kill. With his step back, Ubaldi was once again assuming the French – the Irish – role.

Jack waited till his breath was close to normal. Then he stepped a pace right, assuming the position he must have if he was to take a man with a sword in his left hand – for that man, used to fighting right handers, delighted in keeping them square on and open. The right hander, to have any hope, had to deny him that advantage. He was ready to attack, yet he waited. In the first months of tutelage, with the impetuosity of his years, he'd gone at it hard and immediate.

And he'd been punished, not only in a swift riposte against him, but in the manner of it, the steel of even these blunted small swords whipped hard against the over-extended arm, the foolishly exposed shoulder or breast. In those months Jack's body had been a tapestry of blue and yellow bruises. Not so lately. *Il maestro* hit him, of course, but less often and only direct. The need to punish foolishness had passed with the snow.

He'd also learned to think, not one move ahead, nor three, but seven, at the least, yet always prepared to adapt, as an unexpected riposte changed his course. Yet thinking only got one so far. The real skill, he had discovered, was not to think at all.

He lunged, low, a reach for the groin, flicking around the blade that dropped to meet him and immediately launching for the face. The man gave ground, swinging his point out wide, offering his inner arm. Jack didn't fall for it. Instead he attacked, covered ground and got inside where the close work began. It looked like impetuosity, and it was meant to; it carried a risk and Jack took it.

Swords flashed through late-afternoon sunbeams, steel beat on steel. Ubaldi tried to regain his distance but Jack wouldn't let him, driving the man back till he was again almost touching the wall. The Italian's 'role' was swiftly dropped. He was fighting now for the hit, executing, with his immense skill, complex combinations of parry and riposte.

And then the hit came. A slipped parry, a turn of the wrist, a thrust from underneath. 'Hah,' cried Jack, as his sword tip touched flesh. Ubaldi was 'dead'.

A grunt came, an acknowledgement and the only praise Jack ever received. He had learned to distinguish between the man's grunts. This one was almost effusive.

Both men straightened.

'Again?' Ubaldi said.

'No, thank you,' he replied in Italian, the one other skill he'd part-developed over the months. 'It's late.'

Another grunt. 'We practise the move?'

Jack shook his head. Every master had his own, special moves. Tricks almost, deadly ones, that drew pupils once their effectiveness had been proven on the duelling grounds. Ubaldi's was indeed ingenious, and Jack had been made to practise it relentlessly, almost every day, for months now. It was awkward, so it had to become second nature. He was sure that if he didn't have it by now he never would.

'Tomorrow,' he replied, reaching out his hand, sad in the lie. This man was the closest thing in Rome to a friend Jack had, the only man, other than the uncommunicative guards, that he saw. But if all went well, this would be the last time that they met.

Ubaldi collected his weapons. Even blunted ones, tipped in cork, were forbidden by the Roman Inquisition whose prisoner Jack ultimately was, favouring the Jacobite Cause just as the Pope did, even down to holding the Old Pretender's enemies. 'Tomorrow,' he said, bowing, then went to the door and hammered upon it. It took only a few moments for the grille to be pulled back, the guard to see Jack standing, arms spread innocently wide, in the centre of the room. Bolts were shot, the door opened, *il maestro* left and Jack glimpsed the guard before the door slammed shut. It was Lorenzo, as he hoped it would be. Not because he was a pleasant man – the reverse, he was the surliest, the one most ready with petty cruelties – but because he was the only guard Jack had ever seen drunk and then, on those two occasions, the only one who had failed to check Jack every hour of his watch. The Roman Inquisition terrorized its servants to do their duty well. But a man's Saint's Day came, after all, but once a year, and tonight it was Lorenzo's.

Jack looked around him. As prisons went, this was sure to be one of the more comfortable, reserved for the elite of offenders against the Catholic Church and Papal States – or their favoured allies. He had a bed and changes of linen, adequate food, unlimited wine, even if he was abstemious with that on all but a few occasions. He could have had women, and some nights he'd been tempted. But a woman had brought him to Rome and, sullied though she was in his memory, he knew he would not forget her with drunkenness and whores. There was only one way to achieve such oblivion, and that was beyond this pretty cage, at a sword's point.

He ate, slept a little, awaking with each tolling of the bell of the nearby monastery. At two in the morning, with the grille bolt just slammed and the guard's slurred singing receding down the stairs, Jack rose and dressed swiftly. He'd accustomed his eyes to such light as there was but anyway had practised everything relentlessly in this darkness for weeks. He had only not filled his satchel before in fear of one of the frequent searches. Now he did, with a change of clothes and his eating knife. The Jacobites, despite their searching, had not found Jack's last reserve of *scudi*, three gold coins woven into the hair of his wig. These he transferred to a pocket. Then he pulled his chair over to the wardrobe and clambered on top of it.

His fingers found the slight ridge where his plasterwork joined the decoration of the ceiling. The whole piece gave. In truth, he'd always been somewhat amazed that his construction had never tumbled in, that no guard had spotted a trail of gouged plaster on the floor, a lick of glue around a rococo flower. His request to have a book of classical sculptures and the wherewithal to copy them had been at first refused, then, with persistence, granted, though the results were extensively mocked – he was no artist, the busts and heads around the room testimony to that. But this corner of moulding was a piece of art! Admiring it more than he had any work of Michelangelo, he lowered it carefully to the floor.

He thrust his head up into the attic space, breathing in the musty, dust-heavy air and listened. Nothing moved in the room below, the one next door to his that had been unoccupied now these two months. Heaving himself up, he edged along the beams, relying again on the experience of doing this again and again ever since he'd first broken through the ceiling. He came to the area near the far wall that he'd chosen as suitable and, taking out his knife, began to gouge out the plaster between the beams.

It took longer than he'd hoped and there was noise he could not help. Balanced on the two beams, sweat began to run from him, dripping from his nose and chin into the expanding hole. Whether it was the dry plaster's soaking, the hydration of the horsehair with which it was threaded, or Jack's increasing effort he could not know, but suddenly, a section the size of his fist gave way and fell, followed by one even larger. It reverberated in the room below, like a shout in a confessional. Panicked, Jack scrambled back across the beams, out of the hole and onto his wardrobe. He heard running footsteps in the corridor as he dropped to the ground, landing hard on his fake plaster moulding, shattering it. Covering himself with a sheet from the bed, he ripped the head off one of his latest efforts, a bust of Caesar, and laid it onto the floor, just as the grille in the door shot open.

Eyes reflected the light of a lantern held out there. 'Eh, what are you doing? What happened?' Lorenzo the guard said in Italian.

'I went for a piss,' Jack replied. 'I knocked this over.'

'What? Come over here. What you say?'

'Piss.' Jack approached slowly. 'Broke this.'

The guard eyed the shattered statue. 'This make noise?'

'Yes,' said Jack. 'See?' He dropped the head and it landed with a reasonable thud on the floor. 'Thus fell Caesar,' he smiled.

The man was obviously no classicist. 'Good. Ugly thing,' he said, his face relaxing.

Jack pressed his nose to the grille so the man wouldn't be able to see too much else. This close he could tell Lorenzo had definitely been celebrating his Saint's Day. 'Good wine?' he asked, but the guard merely grunted, stepped back and slammed the grille, nearly trapping Jack's nose. He waited till he heard feet descend the stairs before he pushed away from the door. He wanted to lie down but somehow he forced his legs to follow his previous route.

Holding himself between the wooden roof beams, he slowly lowered himself into the next door room, bending his legs to land on stockinged feet. Retrieving his boots and satchel, previously dropped, he tiptoed to the door of the empty room, paused and listened. Nothing! Putting on his boots, he reached for the door handle, then pulled.

The door did not give. He pulled harder. Still it did not budge. He jerked, tugged, all to no avail.

They had locked it! They had locked the door of an empty room and all Jack's plans were as shattered as the plaster on the floor around him. On the floor in his room, too, he suddenly remembered. He had a hole the size of a man in his ceiling and he'd crushed the thing that concealed it. Wherever he looked, discovery lay.

Glancing around the room, surprise replaced panic for a moment as he realized he could see. Moonlight was coming in through half-open shutters. It lit a room in disarray, not just from the shattered ceiling. This room was not occupied because it was being worked upon. Tools lay about. A large iron grille was on the floor . . .

He looked up. One of the windows was still barred but the other wasn't. In three strides he was across, edging onto the deep sill, pushing the shutters fully open. He looked down upon a courtyard and took his first breath of freedom.

Joy lasted a mere moment. He was still three storeys up. A swift, vertigo-inducing glance told him that, should he even have the courage, there was nothing to place his feet upon on the wall's smooth face, no way down . . . unless . . .

It took him but a moment. With the help of a workman's trestle, he was once more in the attic. For the fourth time he shimmied along the beams, slid through the hole and lowered himself into his own room. Rapidly gathering up all his sheets and blankets, he forced them ahead through both holes and returned, yet again, the way he'd come.

He thought the trestle, wedged under the window, would hold his weight. He was less sure of the knots. A sailor aboard the *Sweet Eliza* had tried to teach him knot-craft but he had obviously failed to pay sufficient attention for every hard pull seemed to separate the cloths. Finally he settled on the simplest knot and tugged and tugged to test it. It seemed well enough. Yet he knew the real test would only come when he was dangling from the ledge.

Shuddering, he threw the material out the window. It did not touch the ground, though from his height Jack could not see how large the gap was. As he tried to ascertain it, the monastery bell tolled again. Three o'clock. He hoped that Lorenzo was downstairs, comatose from honouring his namesake saint. But even if he wasn't, even if he was already approaching Jack's door, there was nothing to be done now. Try to escape, they'd told him, and your ease is over, perhaps even your life. The Roman Inquisition brooked no insurrection.

With the satchel flung over his shoulder, a last grimace and a determination only to look up, Jack lowered himself over the edge.

The sheet gave a lurch as his weight pulled the trestle snug to the window. One hand shot up, gripped the crumbling stone above him; one held to cloth. He clung for a minute, poised to scramble back up at the slightest ripping sound. But when none came, still reluctant, he put his second hand upon the sheet.

'Come on,' he muttered, 'the quicker, the better.'

Sweat poured down his face and he found it hard to ungrip his hand each time he had to reach. Then he placed his feet together, snagging cloth between them and the strain eased just slightly. He reached the next sill down, stood for too long breathing deeply, then began to lower himself again.

He was halfway to the next floor when he felt a slight giving; the next moment, shrieks came – his and the sheet's – as the material parted. He slipped, his feet encountering the stone of the sill below, and he flung himself forward, hands scrabbling at the shutter. One slid off, the other reached, while his kicking legs, seeking the stonework, caused the shutter to swing out from the window. Desperate, he grabbed the shutter, held on, and dangled there, looking between his feet at the sheet coiled into a spool far below him. The drop was twenty feet at the least.

He was not a praying man but he prayed then, even as he tried to swing his legs towards the sill. But as he did, the shutter lurched outwards and he looked up to see one of its hinges coming away from the wall. He stopped moving, kept praying, stared as if sight could force screws back into stone. For a moment, the shuddering of the shutter stopped. And then, beyond the rushing blood in his head, he heard another noise – someone was opening the outer door of the court-yard, coming in.

'Shite,' he muttered, looking again to the screws, then over the top of his shoulder to the sound of the door being opened, shut and relocked, and footsteps moving across the courtyard toward the main building – the man's route bound to take him directly under Jack.

There was a muttering, but the words were drawled; the man was obviously drunk. Jack reached out a toe to the sill, felt the shutter shudder again, saw another screw pop out. He froze, looked between his feet . . .

The man was just passing the fallen sheet. He even took a step beyond it. Then, with the slowness of the drunk, he looked at it, then away, then back again. His head began to tip up . . .

The screws came loose. The top half of the shutter ripped away from the wall, the bottom half following fast. Jack fell, heavier than the shutter so slightly faster. His feet struck the man as if he were trying to land on his shoulders, and he had the absurd impression of some Italian acrobatic act he'd seen in the theatre, one man leaping to stand upon another. But the man below him was no acrobat for he collapsed with a sharp cry, Jack smacking into the stone a moment after, the shutter striking both of them as it landed.

They lay there, the Italian groaning, the Englishman with not enough air to. When he could breathe, Jack lurched up, kneeling beside the man whose eyes popped wide, panicked. Reaching, Jack found the set of keys, just as he heard another one turning in the internal door of the courtyard. Up and staggering, he made for the outer door, praying again that he chose the correct key of the five on the link.

The door behind opened, a man stepped out, clutching a lantern. Lorenzo's slurred voice came. 'Who's there? What's happening?'

The first key was wrong! Jack fumbled out another, as the drunken guard moved into the yard, shouting at the figure he'd now seen upon the ground. Since both the man's collar bones were obviously snapped he couldn't point, but Jack saw him move his head towards the outer door just as the lock gave. He wrenched the door open, as Lorenzo ran at him, shouting. Jack was out in a moment, all his instincts urging him to flight; but his mind held him, because he knew he couldn't flee, not yet, not without more air and until the agony in his legs diminished. Between a drunk and him he'd favour the drunk in a foot race; a yelling drunk, too. Jack's plans for a quiet escape would be drowned in hue and cry. So he stepped straight into the shadow of the wall beside the door and, when Lorenzo rushed through, pausing to seek the fugitive, Jack hit him on the side of the head. It was not a strong punch, he had not the strength to deliver such a one, but it turned the man to the threat, his arms rising up to protect himself. Stepping between them, Jack used a different blow needing precision rather than strength, bringing his forehead hard down on the bridge of the man's nose in what, in his youth, he'd known as a Cornish kiss.

If the delivery smarted Jack, it poleaxed the guard, who collapsed back onto the cobbles with not even a groan. Bending swiftly, Jack saw that Lorenzo was indeed unconscious, blood gushing from a wound at least an inch wide. His breath was coming through liquid and Jack pushed him onto his side. It was barely a kindness. His own returning breath was bringing thought and he knew that if he were caught, as was still the most likely consequence, he was in enough trouble without having also drowned a man in his own blood.

Jack stepped back into the shadows of the wall, glancing up and down the street. Nothing stirred, but moans and shouts were coming from the courtyard behind him, the volume growing. He lurched from the shadows and ran.

Just before eight in the morning, from the shelter of a *loggia*, Jack watched the angry mob at the Porta del Popolo. Word of his escape had preceded him, for the number of guards had been tripled and everyone desiring entrance or egress was being thoroughly and slowly checked. Jack could see that not even the usual bribes were speeding things along. They would be taken, of course, but papers were still scrutinized, not usually a necessity after gold, so Jack's last *scudi* were now useless. Before he could probably have exited the city with coin, no papers and a wink. Not today.

Jack turned away with a sigh. The walls of Rome were crumbling, and he'd been told of places to scramble over for those without papers or bribes. Except Jack was fairly sure those obvious ones would be watched and he didn't know any others. But what was his choice? Every moment he remained in Rome was one of danger. He had to get to Florence, to the British Ambassador there, Tuscany having an embassy that the Papal States could not, due to their support of the Jacobite Cause. He'd thought of sending word via one of the many young Englishmen on their Grand Tour and had gone to the Piazza di Spagna to find one. But the square was full of watchful men in black cloaks and Jack had passed through without speaking to anyone.

His route now was purposeless, meandering. His mind turning, his eyes unfocused, he suddenly realized that somehow his feet had fallen into a familiar track. For he was on the corner where the Via Columbina began, with the house of the hanging sheet less than a hundred yards round the bend. Having nowhere else to go, he headed towards the familiar. There would be nothing there. Red Hugh had told him that the Jacobites had exposed all his connections in Rome. Indeed, he'd probably been watched from his very arrival. So much for Jack Absolute, master spy! he thought, slouching along.

And then he stopped dead. Hanging from the window in the attic of a house – *the* house – was a striped sheet.

Jack immediately stepped into a doorway, disturbing a scavenging cat, who snarled and sloped away. He looked up and down the street, saw nothing except Romans about their tasks; which did not mean there were not others about theirs, looking for him. Indeed, the hanging sheet seemed nothing more than a lure. Rush up to the house, to the only contact he had had in Rome. Be arrested immediately. And yet, who else did he know in Rome, aside from Jacobites, who would betray him instantly? Perhaps his scoutmaster did not know that his whole network had been destroyed. The sheet would seem to indicate that. Then was he perhaps still using the tree at Monte Pinchio? If so, Jack must disabuse him and get help at the same time. It was a chance, howsoever slim, as good and as risky as any he had that day in Rome.

Swiftly climbing through the plantation of pines in the gardens, he found a vantage point just three trees away. They were not the easiest things to climb, their branches too close, too thick with needle, but the one he chose was dying and he managed to force himself a little way up to concealment. He'd already noted that a letter did indeed await. Someone would be by to collect it.

Someone was. A young man, perhaps a little older than himself but not by much, slinking up to the hole, snatching what was there, replacing it with something of his own. He passed directly below Jack, muttering, 'Damn! About time!' Jack smiled at the phrase, the impatience displayed, smile turning to frown when he remembered that this circle of spies was compromised, that this young man would be betrayed, like Jack had been, as soon as his usefulness was past.

It could not have been more than an hour before he heard someone else approaching. This person – unlike the new agent, unlike Jack – made no attempt to tread softly, pine cones crunching underfoot, branches snapped. Above these sounds there was another, a hum Jack soon realized was a tune, notes turning to words as the man came off the main path and approached the tree.

> 'We'll pull down usurpation,
> And, spite of abjuration,
> And force of stubborn nation
> Great James' title own.'

Jack closed his eyes, had no need for sight. He knew both the voice and the song.

Watkin Pounce leaned against the pine, his head bent. Taking deep breaths, he mopped his face with a handkerchief. Then he reached up, took the letter, tapped it once against the trunk, tucked it inside that same ragged black suit he always wore, turned and retraced his steps. The humming recommenced as he came onto the central avenue and headed toward the main entrance of the park.

Watkin Pounce. As Jack scrambled down from his perch, he shook his head in bewilderment. Watkin was the scoutmaster, Turnville's man in Rome. And yet the man was also an acknowledged Jacobite. But of course that was his protection, allowing him access to those he spied upon. He laboured for both sides but owed his loyalty only to . . .

To whom? Jack stopped. For some reason, something Red Hugh had said all those months ago, almost the last thing he'd said, came to Jack. He'd disregarded it then, so great was his fury, his hurt. What was it? That Letty . . . Letty had not betrayed their rendezvous because she loved him, wanted to tell him that before she said goodbye.

Jack started forward again, slowly, Pounce still often enough in sight. This was what Até had taught him: how to pursue an enemy silently, unnoticed. And the reverse, being able always to spot any pursuit. So, even half blinded by love, would he not have known he was followed that day? And if he hadn't been and Red Hugh had spoken the truth – and why should he lie with his enemy now a prisoner – then it wasn't Letty who had told where Jack could be taken. Indeed, she'd begged him to fly without her. Only one other person knew of their rendezvous. The man who'd suggested it. Pounce.

Jack stopped. He knew where to find him. But how he dealt with him would depend on whether the man really was his betrayer, and there was one quick way to prove it.

Turning left, Jack cut down through the pine trees. The scent of the trees, the cones and browning needles underfoot reminded him of the previous year in Canada, a simpler time, with the enemy clear, and Até by his side. After all the lying, the betrayal of both his love and his friendship, how he now wished he'd accepted his blood brother's offer, resigned his commission and gone to live the life of an adopted Iroquois. They knew more about honesty than Jacobites or Hanoverians between them.

He came out close to the cart track that ran up beside the Palazzo Barberini. Vaulting the fence, he ran the few paces down to the cypress tree.

At first he didn't see it, so thick had the branches and needles grown during his incarceration. Then he did.

His satchel was still where he had wedged it. If he'd been followed that day, it would not have been.

He took out his knife, began cutting towards the bag. As he cut, he imagined each branch as one of Pounce's pudgy fingers and remembered how, in the play, John Falstaff owed God a death.

There was a small taverna almost opposite Pounce's lodgings. He had mentioned it as beneath contempt but another Jacobite had confided that the man was banished from the premises for various crimes, including the inevitable severe drunkenness and the less likely groping assault upon the innkeeper's daughter. When he went there at sunset, Jack found a pleasant enough place, with a room he was able to commandeer at the front, its snoring occupant ejected on the waving of one of Jack's gold *scudi*. This brought the best the house could offer, which was a serious improvement on prison fare.

Jack over-indulged in everything but the wine. The food he did not deny himself, reasoning that when he finally did escape the city he was likely to be travelling as a fugitive with little opportunity for feasting. So a spicy soup of livers and gizzards was followed by three pigeons, wrapped in tripe and dressed in oil, then some small toothsome squares, filled with cheese and herbs, called 'ravioli'. He declined the sheep brains on the grounds that they reeked of garlic. But figs and an excellent Parmesan cheese concluded the meal well. Then he settled himself in the window of his room, with a flask of the light vino bruscio, and waited.

Two hours later he saw the unmistakably portly figure shambling down the cobbles. Slipping quietly out of the tavern's door, Jack crossed the street swiftly, coming up as the man swayed before the door of his lodgings.

'Still have that bottle to share, Watkin?' Jack said softly.

Pounce turned, with the elaborate slowness of the drunk. Then his movements became suddenly very fast. He staggered back, flushing pale, nearly falling, hands flapping before him. 'P . . . P . . . Pip? But I thought you were . . .' He swallowed. 'By the stars, 'tis you? Faith, I was sure . . . sure that you'd . . . you'd . . . left Rome nine months ago!' He swayed backwards, looked as if he were going to fall, then leaned as far the other way, which seemed finally to unbalance him. He slipped backwards, sitting down suddenly upon the step. 'Come,' said Jack, reaching forward to grab an arm. 'Let us go inside.'

Pounce responded by heaving himself up and stumbling through the half-opened house door. 'Shh,' he said, to himself, since Jack was making no sound. His door creaked open and he largely fell through it, continuing his stumble toward a large, low chair beside a table on which glowed a lantern. He waved towards the armoire in the corner. 'That bottle, Pip. I've saved it for you. Hoping you might return. Fetch it here, sweet wag.'

Jack found a half-empty bottle of Montepulciano and two glasses. He extracted the cork with his teeth as he walked over. The wine did not smell of the freshest but he poured two tots anyway.

Pounce grasped one, raised it to eye level before him. 'To the Cause!' he cried.

'Which one?'

The question halted the movement of glass to lip. 'Eh? Why, the King across the water.'

Jack tipped his head to the side. 'Well enough – if the water's the Channel and the King's name is George.'

Pounce had the look of a frog unable to snag a mayfly. 'Eh?' he said again.

Jack pulled up a second chair. 'I know, Watkin.'

'Know what?'

'Know that you are my scoutmaster.'

The resemblance to an amphibian only increased as his mouth opened and closed repeatedly, the wobbly cheeks filling with and emptying air. The eyes dropped, noticed the glass, still suspended, and drained it in a shot. He held it out and Jack dutifully refilled it. The liquor brought a little steadiness to voice and hand.

'Well,' he said at last, 'shall we then toast Colonel Turnville?'

'Gladly.' Jack raised his glass but still did not drink. 'Once you have told me why you betrayed both him and me.' A sound came from the other man's throat – denial, protest. Wattles shook. Jack forestalled him. 'It could only have been you, Watkin. You sent me to that rendezvous. Which means that the Colonel is not your sole employer, is he? Perhaps not even your main one.'

Instead of replying, Pounce drained the glass, then reached forward for the bottle. Only a few dregs remained. 'Fetch another, Pip – *Jack* – there's a good lad. Over there.'

Jack went where he was directed. Amidst a heap of empty bottles he found one full. He turned – to Watkin sitting more upright, with a pistol in his hand. His voice, when it came, was still a little slurred yet not nearly so much as it had been before.

'How did you discover me?'

'I saw you on Monte Pinchio,' Jack replied quietly, not moving. 'Which told me something else as well.'

'What, pray?'

'You thought I was dead. Your reaction when you saw me outside confirmed it. Because you didn't bother to change your modus operandi. The same sheet, the same hollowed-out tree.'

Pounce grunted. 'Sheer laziness. I am getting too old for all this.' He glanced at the gun. 'Well, perhaps not *too* old. And yes, the Irishman told me you'd been dealt with. I thought he meant in the usual fashion.'

'He imprisoned me in the Palazzo Millini. I escaped last night.'

'From the Inquisition? So the hue and cry is for you? He shook his head. 'I am curious as to why the Irishman spared your life?'

Jack shrugged. 'I saved his, once.'

'Is that all?' Pounce snorted. 'Fellow's gone sentimental in his old age.'

He studied Jack, Jack studied the gun. A pocket pistol, a woman's toy really, similar to the one Letty had had in Bath. But as Red Hugh's confederate had discovered there, it was a toy that could still kill. He lifted the bottle. 'Do you not want this?'

'I do. But I want even more for you to put it down and place your back against the door,' he said, motioning slightly with the muzzle.

'Why, Watkin? Are you going to *deal* with me, as Red Hugh failed to do?'

'Do I have a choice?' He sighed. 'If I let you live, and if you, by some miracle, elude the Inquisition, who seem most anxious to have you back, you will eventually report to

Turnville. My livelihood would end and, I suspect, my life would soon follow.'

'Well.' As he leaned against the door, Jack reached behind him to the small of his back. The handle of his eating knife in one hand wasn't much, but it was something. 'I believe you do have a choice. Especially when killing me will achieve nothing.'

'It will achieve your silence. Unless . . .'

'Unless I have a letter written and in safe hands, only to be sent if I do not appear at a certain time and place.'

Pounce stared at him for a long moment. 'I wonder if I believe you.'

Jack smiled. 'I wonder if you dare not.'

A longer silence came then. Pounce moved only to rest his arm upon the chair, shifting the muzzle slightly off centre, Jack only to adjust his grip on the knife behind his back. At last he spoke again. 'I was curious as to when you first turned traitor.'

A shrug. 'To be a traitor you have to believe in something. I don't.'

'Not the King across the water?'

'No longer. That cause died on Culloden Moor. The corpse just refuses to lie down.'

'So your loyalty is only to yourself?'

'The only King left. The one you now threaten.'

He shifted the gun again and Jack's grip tightened on the knife, watching the man's eyes, not his finger. The eyes would give it away and Jack would have to take his chances and strike. He had the speed of youth. But the old drunk had gunpowder. Then, as he watched, something seemed to sag in Pounce's face.

'You spoke of a choice?'

Jack breathed out. 'I can prevent the letter being sent. And I will not reach London for months perhaps. You have time.'

'Time for what?'

'Time to disappear.'

The eyes narrowed, almost vanishing into the fleshy face. Then Pounce sighed. 'I have indeed grown to suspect that I am too old for all this. I have even begun some plans, a villa in the hills near . . .' He focused on Jack. 'What would I have to do in return for this temporary silence?'

Jack's fingers relaxed slightly on the knife's hilt. 'Get me out of Rome.'

This silence was shorter. 'And if I did this? I could not expect you to conceal anything from Colonel Turnville. You are still young enough to believe in your duty. But will you swear, on something you truly believe in, that if you do meet him again, you will say nothing of my aid to the Irishman? He would be displeased, to say the least. He would find me, or have others do so, however well I hid. And *I* have not saved his life.'

Jack took a step forward, his empty hand outstretched. 'I will swear it on my honour. And that, as the Irishman will discover, is something I never compromise.' He still saw the hesitation in Pounce's eyes, even if the pistol point was tipping away, coming to rest on the table. 'You need not fear him, Watkin. For I will be after him, and when I next see Red Hugh McClune, he will be dead. For I am going to kill him.'

'That would indeed be a feat.' Pounce studied him for a long moment. 'Your honour demands it?' On Jack's nod, he continued. 'Well, I hazard I know the cause. Laetitia, the Countess di Cavalieri. Née Fitzpatrick?' Jack stayed silent. 'She married in great splendour, did you know? King James was there, risen from his sick bed. His cardinal son Henry officiated.'

'I did not know.'

'And it is said she is now carrying an heir to the house.'

'Indeed.' Jack had almost reached the table now. 'Are we agreed?'

There was a final moment of hesitation, a last search of Jack's eyes. Then the pistol was laid down. Jack placed his knife beside it.

'Agreed,' said Watkin Pounce, eyeing the blade with a shudder. Heaving his bulk from the chair, he said, 'Arrangements must be made, certain people suborned. Do you have any gold?'

'I gave you fifty *scudi* to hire horses. Where is it?'

'Here,' said Pounce, rubbing his belly.

Jack reached for his fallen satchel. 'Then I will divide what I have left with you.' He counted. 'There's near twenty apiece.'

'Twenty?' The disappointment was pronounced. 'Not much, is it?'

'Twenty and my silence, Watkin. Remember that.'

'True.' With the coins in his hand, Pounce's excitement seemed to banish his drunkenness and he started for the door. 'I'll get to it. The fellows who will help us do not keep regular hours.' Looking back, he said, 'And one will know if there is a ship at Civitavecchia bound for Lisbon.'

'Lisbon?' said Jack, surprised.

'Well, did you not say you would be after McClune?'

'I did.'

'Then you will find him in Portugal. All communications are to be forwarded to a certain house in Lisbon. Perhaps I should not have told you that.' He smiled faintly. 'Though *he* will not be there himself, of course. Besides, do you not read the newspapers?'

Jack grunted. 'The Inquisition is lax in providing them.'

Pounce gestured to the foot of the bed. 'There's one from London. Quite recent, only took five weeks to get here. I always believe a young man should attend to the affairs of the world.' Then he was gone.

The paper referred to, the *London Advertiser*, was dated 15 June 1762. Pounce had circled a section in pencil.

*With regard to the late compact between the Bourbon
tyrannies of France and Spain and the King's declaration
of war against the latter, a strong force is being dispatched
to aid our doughty ally the King of Portugal and his
noble people. Under the command of the illustrious Earl
of Loudoun will be the 3rd, 67th, Boscawen's and Crawford's regiments of Foot together with those Hibernian
hammers of the French, the regiments Armstrong's and
Traherne's . . .*

Jack paused. Irish regiments could be trouble. One was never
sure where their loyalties lay. The French had several
battalions in their own army ever delighted to fight the
British. And there was always something a-stir in their
homeland. He read on.

*In addition, and fresh from winning laurel wreathes in
the late action upon Belleisle, two troops of the 16th Light
Dragoons have joined the other four direct from
Portsmouth to present, under their noble Colonel, John
Burgoyne, the most fearsome aspect of cavalry the
Spaniard has ever had to face.*

Startled, Jack read the same sentences again and again. The
whole of the 16th – the comrades he'd left training in
London when he'd been sent as King's Messenger to
Quebec three years before – were engaged in this campaign.
And somewhere nearby – concealed, no doubt, by a new
name and uniform – was an Irish Grenadier Jack particularly wanted to meet again. What had he said at their last
encounter in the prison? That he was always looking to
do something 'spectacular'? Something even greater than
the killing of a King? Scanning the column again, Jack
could have no doubts: McClune would be seeking that
opportunity in Portugal.

'So,' Jack said aloud, reaching for his glass of wine, raising it before him, 'it appears it is time for me to rejoin the regiment.'

— FIVE —

Dead Man's Shoes

'You are dead, Cornet Absolute.'

Jack made no reply. It didn't do to contradict one's superior, especially on one's first day back with the regiment. Besides even Captain Onslow – who Jack now remembered was referred to by all the junior officers during training as, simply, 'Slow' – would eventually figure it out.

He had some way to go yet. 'Says so here, d'ye see?' The man spun a sheaf of papers around. ' "Missing, presumed dead. September seventeen fifty-nine." One is only presumed dead for so long, Absolute, until one *is* dead, hmm?'

Jack sighed, less at the man's blockheadedness than at the conspiracy that had written his epitaph. In September 1759 he'd been captured by the Abenaki at the end of the first battle before Quebec. He *had* been thought dead then. But General Murray had used him as a spy in the subsequent campaign and then Turnville had also sent him to Rome in the same role.

'Did Colonel Turnville not inform you, sir, that I had been transferred, temporarily, to his command?'

'Turnville? Never heard of him. Sounds like a Frog to me.' Onslow puffed out his cheeks, perhaps in imitation. 'What regiment?'

'I am not sure. He was in charge of some intelligence matters for which he—'

'Intelligence?' The Captain had thrown himself back in his chair as if the word were a pile of ordure Jack had just dumped upon his desk. 'Don't much like "intelligence", man.'

'That's obvious,' Jack muttered.

'What's that?'

It had long ceased to surprise Jack how many officers considered intelligence to be like a sneaky ball in a game of cricket. 'Sir,' he said, 'Colonel Turnville said that he would inform you of my return and my transfer to his operation. That he did not may suggest the delicacy of that mission?'

The words, their quiet delivery, had the desired effect. 'Ah, yes, quite, quite!' Onslow flapped his hands as if waving away flies, which he might well have been as the room was so full of them. 'Less said, eh?'

'Yes, sir. But, as you see, I am not, in fact, dead. Indeed I am quite fit and ready for active service.'

The captain took out a handkerchief and wiped sweat from his brow. Portugal was held in a terrible heatwave and the Dragoon uniform, despite the earliness of the hour, only magnified its effects. Jack, in a linen sailor's shirt and trousers of brown Osnaburg canvas, was a cool contrast.

His superior was now eyeing these distastefully. 'Active service, eh? Well, I suppose we *do* have a uniform for you, since poor old Peers got his brains blown out on Belleisle. And his death did cause a vacancy at captain of the third troop. Lieutenant Crawford is moving up to that. But Cornet Stokey was to occupy the lieutenancy, with young Worsley made up from the ranks. We were only waiting for Colonel Burgoyne to arrive for his final approval.' He started flicking through some other rolls. 'What date was your commission, d'ye happen to remember?'

'Fourteenth of June seventeen fifty-nine,' Jack said.

'And Stokey's was . . . the nineteenth of June.' He grunted in disappointment. 'So you are senior.'

'And a lieutenant already, sir. General Murray was so good as to appoint me—'

'A brevet promotion, unconnected to the procedures of the regiment!' Onslow glared. 'Still, you are senior, so,' he sighed, 'I suppose you must have the lieutenancy. I can tell you now, though, it will not be popular. These men have all served together on Belleisle. They wanted one of their own.'

Jack shrugged. That was their problem, not his. He'd earned his lieutenancy and the perks that went with it.

Onslow still looked dubious. 'Speaking of serving – are you up with the latest drills?'

The man had obviously not taken in what Jack had just told him. 'I have been unable to keep up, sir, being with—'

The hand flapped again. 'Yes, yes! Well, you will have to be taught, sirrah. Can't have someone who doesn't know how to dress his ranks, hmm? And have you ever been in a charge?'

'Actually, sir,' Jack thought back to Quebec, his seizing of the Frenchman's horse, his pursuit of the enemy that day, 'I did—'

'Never mind. You will just have to learn. Since the vacancy is in the third troop, you will report to Sergeant Puxley. He'll put you through it, never fear.' He wiped his brow again. 'You may go.'

'Yes, sir. Uh, where, sir?'

'See my clerk out there,' the man almost shouted. 'We officers mess at the Praho Taberna. Be there at eight tonight. Don't be late! And shave, for God's sake, man. You look like a Dago wagon driver!'

A shaken handkerchief dismissed him. As Jack shut the door, he scratched his chin beneath the full growth. He supposed he'd have to trim his hair also, now halfway down his back. He'd let both grow to aid his escape from Rome, as he'd remained in the city for two weeks while the hue and cry abated and the Inquisition thought him already gone. He'd kept the look in case of pursuit and because it suited his guise as a Languedocian cod trader, returning to his base in Portugal. But now that he was at his destination, the regimental base in the town of Abrantes, he supposed the look would no longer do. Not in the Queen's Light Dragoons.

Jack stared at the stains. When Captain Onslow had told him that the officer he was to replace had had his brains blown out, he'd neglected to mention that so many of them still remained on the man's uniform. While the rest of the wardrobe was acceptable – the late Sir William Peers being of a similar height and chest to Jack, though the jockey boots were a snug fit – this short coat clearly was not. He could not appear with such an obvious reminder of recent tragedy. It would spook the men. Ecod, it would spook him! The brains must be removed. And since the troop was out watering the horses, there was no one to hire as a batman. He would have to do the cleaning himself.

A Portuguese groom fetched buckets of water and a bar of lye soap to an empty stable stall. The terrible mid-morning heat and the vigour with which he was forced to scrub the coat made him sweat in profusion. Taking his shirt off, he set to again, gratified to see progress. He began to hum an Iroquois battle chant.

So intent was he at his task that the sound of many horses barely impinged. It was the voice that roused him, rich in rolling Welsh vowels and profanity. 'Oi, you Dago turd, where's your fucking master?'

Jack – crouched over the bucket, coat in hand – looked up. Standing in the doorway was a man he vaguely remembered from his scant weeks of training with the Dragoons before he shipped out to Canada. 'Right here, Sergeant Puxley. Master and man. Lieutenant Absolute. How very good to see you again.'

He could see shock working its way over the man's face in the sagging jaw, widened eyes and bushy eyebrows rising to the cavalry helm on his head. He knew what the man was seeing – thick beard, shaggy long hair, skin darkened from his weeks at sea – the wagon driver Onslow had labelled him. What distinguished him was obviously the voice, an officer's undoubtedly, though the tattoos Até had so painfully embroidered on his body threw everything back into confusion.

'Who?' was all the man could manage for the moment.

Jack laid the coat down, wiped his hands on his trousers, stepped forward. 'Cornet Absolute that was, Sergeant. Promoted to the vacancy in the third. You may remember me?'

'Can't say I do.' Puxley had taken the proffered hand in reflex and was shaking it mechanically, though his eyes were fixed on the blue-inked wolf's head on Jack's shoulder.

'I was sent to North America, bearing dispatches at the King's command?'

Puxley's eyes rose to meet his. 'Absolute? You're dead.'

'Apparently not,' said Jack, detaching his hand. 'And eager to resume my duties. Though, as the Captain pointed out, I may be a little rusty on the finer points of drill. He said you may be able to refresh me?'

Puxley was obviously not a man to remain perplexed for long. 'Absolute! Got you, now. Cocky little sh . . .' He paused. 'You could ride a bit though . . . sir. Am I right?'

'Again, it's been a while but I am confident I'll recall the mechanics.'

'Well, we can only hope the rest will come back as well.' Puxley had straightened, all his discountenance gone. 'No time like the present, eh? I was just about to take the troop through some drills. Would you?'

He gestured through the door. 'Delighted,' said Jack, 'but I think . . .' He stroked his beard with the back of his hand. 'Not regulation, is it?'

'Hardly, sir. We have a trooper who's not bad with shears and blade. Shall I send him in?'

'Do. And could you hang this in the sun to dry?'

Puxley took the jacket. 'Captain Peers's, ain't it? But you've stripped off the lace.'

Jack nodded. 'Learned to do that in Canada. Makes too inviting a target.'

'So Captain Peers discovered.' Puxley's eyes were appraising. 'Seen some action, have you?'

'Some.'

'Good. Many of our officers haven't. I'll send Wallace in.'

Puxley left and Jack inspected the rest of his inherited equipment. Aside from the standard lawn shirts, black stocks, white cloth breeches, boots, gloves and saddlery, the regiment had its distinguishing designations: the japanned, black copper cap with its ridge plume of reddened horse hair, the King's cipher and crown enamelled on it; the scarlet cloak with red half-cape lined with the regimental facings of black. Together with the now-drying short coat, this uniform was nearly as good as the one he'd had made for himself in Newport. It signified that his days as privateer, prisoner, fugitive and even spy had come, at least temporarily, to an end. And looking at the scarlet and the black facings of his regiment, Jack found that he was not at all unhappy at the exchange.

He was not so sure three hours later. Puxley had indeed 'put him through it'. There did not seem to be a part of him that was not sore, chafed, aching – and they hadn't even started riding yet. His right-hand knuckles were skinned because there were only so many times you could draw and return swords before flesh struck hilt or pommel. His thighs throbbed from the innumerable times they'd dismounted,

271

which required at least nine different movements that Jack could count. And his brain ached as he tried to remember the drill of linking, in which horses could be joined at their collar rings so that one man would take care of up to ten horses alone. But since the movement to link required one man to step one way and the man next to them to step the other, and since Puxley kept changing his position, it took Jack some time to remember that when he was right he went left about and when left, the opposite. Only after numerous errors on his part, each one causing an increase of muttering in the ranks – his clumsiness was forcing the men to work longer – was Sergeant Puxley satisfied and allowed the troop some water.

'And now we'll train for the parade,' he announced. 'For Colonel Burgoyne is to rejoin us shortly and will want to review the regiment. And you wouldn't want to shame me, would you, boys?'

The sun had the sky to itself the entire day; it was like exercising in a bread oven. The air was oppressive and sweat soaked their clothes. Jack realized he might have spared himself his washerwoman exertions, for his scarlet short coat was sopping.

Jack took his place – as Lieutenant his position was the first file of the third rank. The gelding he stood beside was large, upwards of seventeen hands and biddable, though Jack would not know that truly until he had put him through his paces. But he was obviously a replacement as his coat was distinctly grey and stood out in the troop of almost uniform brown. Jack wondered if it was just the lace that had drawn the sniper's fire to its former owner. Grey horses were usually avoided for precisely that reason.

'Make ready to mount!'

He placed his left foot in the stirrup, left hand on the pommel, right on the centre of the cantle, fingers turned toward the crop in the approved manner and waited.

'Mount!'

The horse shifted slightly under him as he tied up the collar. He chk-chk'd quietly and it settled.

'Now, boys, let me remind you . . .'

Laughter interrupted the lesson. It came from the house adjoining the stableyard. Though Jack was meant to face front, he couldn't help but look. Three officers strode down the steps, still laughing. As they reached the gate, the eldest of them, a fellow probably in his mid-twenties, called out, 'Sergeant Puxley, we'll practise the parade, if you please.'

'Yes, sir,' replied the Welshman, not commenting that they were just about to do that.

The three officers waited as grooms brought their mounts, then each wheeled his horse around the rear of the troop. The Captain – Crawford, Onslow had named him, new since Jack's time – took up his position in the first rank, two before Jack. The Cornet, also unknown, wheeled his horse till its arse was the required one horse length just before him.

'What the devil?' The voice came from beside him. 'Trooper, you are in my place.'

Jack turned. Beside him was a very angry-looking cavalryman. Under the black, jappaned hat he saw a face he vaguely remembered.

'Hullo, Stokey,' he said.

The usual mix of confusion and searching went on. This man got it quicker than most. 'Absolute?'

'Yes.'

'But you're dead.'

Give me strength, Jack thought, but said, 'No, I am not. Look, I am awfully sorry about this, Stokey. I know how disappointing my resurrection will be. You see—'

The man's colour had gone a deeper red, but before he could let loose his temper, the two files before Jack wheeled their horses. 'What's this? What's this?' said Crawford, the newly promoted Captain. 'Who, pray, are you?'

Jack saluted. 'Lieutenant Jack Absolute, sir. Sixteenth Light Dragoons . . .' He paused. Of course, they knew his regiment.

Stokey spoke. 'Fellow's a damned interloper. Swans off, comes back, wants my damned commission.'

'Is that true?' Crawford was turning as red as his subordinate. 'Are you trying to usurp Bob's promotion?'

'I'd rather not, of course, sir. But I believe you'll find that I was the senior cor—'

'And I believe *you'll* find, Lieutenant whatever-your-blasted-name-is that I make the decisions in my own troop, damn your eyes!'

'Yes, sir.' Jack looked right. The whole of the third troop, the men he'd forced to work for so long under a blazing sun, looked back. He turned again. 'I was hoping Captain Onslow would have informed you—'

'As Senior Captain, Onslow is attending upon Major Somerville. So you'd better do the informing and swiftly.'

'Yes, sir. Might I suggest . . .' Jack waved toward the house.

At last, his brother officers became aware of their audience. 'Well, indeed,' murmured Crawford. 'Puxley, you're in command.'

'Sir!'

'You – all three of you – come with me.'

Leaving the third troop temporarily officer-less, the four men dismounted, gave the reins to grooms and entered the house.

The explanation he'd given to Onslow, and partly to Puxley, was given again. It failed to satisfy, and the repeated jeers and interruptions only confirmed the first impression Jack had made of Bob Stokey. He was the type of officer his father complained was taking over the cavalry, especially the more prestigious regiments. Too much blue blood, too little reaching the brain. Jack had schooled with many of that ilk at Westminster.

'Look here, Chancer Jack, or whatever you call yourself—'

'Jack will do, though "sir" will be better before the men.'

'I'll be damn'd if I'll "sir" you, sir!' The repetition reddened the face still further. 'You suddenly appear from nowhere, having failed to take part in the regiment's recent actions, having skulked some place away from the fighting—'

'I have fought,' Jack said quietly. 'Rather more than you, I suspect.'

'You dare to . . .' Stokey stepped forward, meaty hands reaching before him. He was a large man and Jack took a step back. Not from fear; but if it came to a dance he'd want a little room for the steps.

'Bob! Desist!' Crawford's command brought the younger man to heel like a beagle. He turned back to Jack and though he was obviously still as angry as his subordinate – and favourite, that was clear – he must have decided that this was an argument that could not be settled here. 'I will certainly be hearing all this again from Captain Onslow. I shall complain to the Major. Indeed, since Colonel Burgoyne is due to take command himself any day, he shall also hear my protest.'

Jack nodded. 'I shall, of course, be ruled by the Colonel, sir.'

'I should think you shall, you puppy.'

With that, Crawford, his beagle close behind him – now the image was present in his head, Jack could not shake it – turned and left the house.

A long silence was finally interrupted. 'Where I am from, they do say that the more you mess with an old turd the worse 'ee do stink.'

Jack turned in some amazement to the hitherto silent

275

member of the triumvirate. His accent was undoubtedly from the West Country. 'Cornet . . . Worsley is it?'

'Aye.' The man – boy, really, he could have been no more than sixteen, with a sprouting of ginger hair emerging from beneath his cap, and a rosy glow to match – smiled at him. He was the first soldier to do so since Jack arrived and it gladdened him.

'Well, I am sorry that you too will suffer from my return, Worsley. You've come up from ranks, have you not?'

'I have. And will be happy to return to them, if I'm honest.' He grinned. 'I never wanted the commission, no more than a toad wants side pockets, if you understand my meaning.'

Jack smiled. 'We have the same expression where I was born. You're a Devonian, are you not?'

'Barnstaple born and . . . was going to say bred, but my father was a tinker so who knows?' He winked. 'And you?'

'Cornish.'

'Well,' the lad sighed, 'I'll not hold it against ye.' He moved to the door, nodded out of it in the direction of the disappearing officers. '*They* might, though.'

With that he was gone. Jack looked out. Puxley was organizing the troop as if for a review. Of the officers there was no sign; gone, no doubt, to protest. The red ranks shimmered in heat haze and, for a moment, Jack was tempted to remain in the relative cool of the porch. But ignorance would only give his new enemies something else to hold against him. He had been many things already in his short life but only briefly a cavalryman.

He went out, strode to his horse, mounted, rode up to Puxley. 'May I rejoin you, Sergeant?'

'You may. If you'll first redress your saddle cloth. Exactly and only one six-inch showing beneath the leather. We are on parade now, sir! Parade!'

Parade was followed by a trot to a piece of scrub land where wheeling, column to ranks, the reverse and finally a charge were practised. Jack returned exhausted to the stables and was told he was billeted in a nearby house. The dead officer's trunk had been brought and Jack pillaged it for the plain, unlaced frock suits that officers inevitably wore in the mess. A glance in the mirror told him that the rush had not aided his appearance. He was glowing with the exertions of a hot day, and what had been concealed beneath the beard was now a livid red, contrasting with the sea-brown above. His hair was a little shorter but still a black tangle. However, for the moment there was nothing to be done.

He had to be in the mess by eight and he pushed open the door of the Praho Taberna as the last toll from a local church sounded. He entered to a silence, as the men already at the table turned to stare. Stokey was just sitting down, his face as scarlet as his coat, the heat no doubt conjured by the words he'd just spoken.

Wonder what he's been saying? thought Jack, though he believed he knew. 'Lieutenant Jack Absolute, reporting to the mess,' he said. 'Good evening, gentlemen.' He gave a small bow and closed the door behind him.

– SIX –

The Wager

It was difficult to decide which hurt more – his stomach or his head. The one felt as if washerwomen were trying to squeeze his innards dry by twisting them into coils, while the other seemed to have been occupied by a marching band consisting mainly of timpani. It was impossible to tell now which had done the most damage: the filthy, overly-spiced food; or the vast mix and quantity of liquor. A combination, no doubt, if the contents of the reeking bucket that lay beside his head on the floor were testament. He'd failed to make it onto the bed; just one of the many things of which he had absolutely no recollection. Indeed, virtually nothing after his entrance into the tavern was clear to him. There were toasts, he knew, a huge variety of them. He may even have proposed a few himself. Indeed there was the vaguest memory of . . . overcompensation, as if, by showing himself to be a stout fellow, he could overcome the obvious antipathy for the interloper he'd seen on every face.

'Great Christ!' Jack groaned aloud, one hand over his eyes, feebly trying to block out the vicious sunlight invading the room through the half-open shutters. He shifted slightly and other aches came to his attention. His thighs, unused lately to sitting a horse, throbbed; his knuckles were raw from scraping the sword hilt; his toes had a blister apiece from being crammed into a dead man's too-small boots, while the skin that had been protected by a full beard was burnt and raw from exposure to the sun. Yet these were minor inconveniences compared to the agony of gut and head. In prison in Rome, with only his own company to keep, he had never drunk to excess. One could be as out of training with liquor as with any other exercise.

Someone knocked. Snatching up the sheet, he crawled onto the bed and whispered, 'Enter!'

A face thrust around the door, framed in ginger curls. 'Good morning, sir. And a fine one, is it not?'

'It will be better one if you desist from shouting,' Jack snapped, the effort of raising his head causing it to pulse violently, a tremor that spread to his stomach, which jiggled and tried to eject something. Swallowing hard, Jack fell back and muttered, 'Who the hell are you and what do you want?'

'Worsley, sir. Do you not remember? Your fellow from the West?'

Jack opened one eye. He did seem familiar. 'Worsley,' he croaked. It came back. 'Cornet Worsley.'

'Cornet no more.' The man came in, putting a bucket of water down beside the bed, dipping a wooden cup into it and handing that to Jack, who sat up too quickly, drank too fast, retched, steadied, drank more. 'Back to the ranks, me, and happier than a pig in shit about it.'

Jack stared at him, at the orange hair, the face reddened by sun and youthful spots. Memory stirred. 'But you were there last night, weren't you? In the mess?'

'I was. My last act as an officer, for the present.' He refilled Jack's cup. 'But now it's been settled that one of you will be Lieutenant and one Cornet, there's no need for me, is there?'

'I will be Lieutenant,' Jack muttered. 'I *am* the Lieutenant, damn it.'

'That's what I like, sir. Confidence.' Worsley got up, began to collect the various pieces of clothing Jack had managed to discard before he collapsed.

Jack continued to regard him with just one eye. 'What are you about, fellow?'

Worsley straightened. 'Thought I might be your batman, sir, if you've need of one.'

'From cornet to servant in a night? Don't you mind it?'

'I don't if you don't.' He grinned. 'Rather serve a West Countryman – even if you are from the wrong county – than one of them society officers, if you get my meaning.'

'Why serve at all?'

Worsley sighed. 'Do you remember how much they pays us? Lucky if we get three pence a day and doubly so if we ever sees it. Haven't for weeks now, anyhow.' He grinned. 'And it's well known how liberal Cornishmen are with their money, ain't that the truth of it, sir?'

'It's well known that Devonians are a soft-brained bunch of knucklydowns.' Jack smiled, the first time he'd felt like doing so that morning. It hurt. 'Why do you assume I've got any coin?'

'You will have, now the regiment's on the march. Always issue the officers something to settle up with when we move bivouacs.'

Jack swung his legs onto the floor. 'Move? Does that mean I should be,' he shuddered, 'on parade now?'

'You may rest easy, sir, for the moment. Parade's not till evening on account of us riding out tonight. Time for those who can do to settle their liquor bills, those who can't to stay hidden and those who have them to kiss their sweet'arts goodbye.'

Jack lifted his hand from his face. 'Do you have one, Worsley?'

'Oh, aye. Lass by the name of . . . Jacinta? Jocasta?' He leaned forward, his voice quieter. 'I could send her to see you, if you like. Lovely girl if you don't look too closely in her mouth. Arse like an Exmoor heifer.' He whistled, spreading his arms wide.

Jack shook his head. 'I think I'll leave it, thank 'ee all the same.'

The man shrugged. 'Just part of a servant's duty to his officer, like.' He cocked his head. 'If I am your servant, that is?'

Jack thought for just a moment. He had few enough allies as it was. None, in fact. And a servant was a source of information also. 'Why not,' he said, extending a hand.

'Whoo-hoo!' Worsley shook the hand once then did a little jig. Stopping, he said, 'Then I'll be about your business, sir. If you let me have that shirt and them britches . . .'

Jack struggled out of them, then sat back naked on the bed. Worsley stopped his scurrying to look down with some concern. 'I do hope, sir, that I have backed the right horse here. I'd far rather be the batman of a lieutenant than the man what got my cornetcy.'

'And you are.'

Jack rubbed his head then looked up. Worsley was staring at him hard. 'You do remember last night, don't you, sir?'

'Of course.' Jack nodded. 'Um, what specifically?'

'The wager?'

'Ah yes. The wager. What wager?'

Worsley looked heavenwards then down again. 'You was complaining about the stew. Stokey, who had volunteered the meal on account of his promotion, asked you to provide something better. You declared you'd be hard pressed to find worse.' He sighed. 'And on it all went from there.'

Jack searched his mind. He did have the vaguest recollection of such a conversation, but not its conclusion 'And where did it all end?'

'With him challenging you to obtain decent meat for the Queen's birthday feast in two days' time. And you not only agreein' but also wagering your lieutenancy against a cask of brandy that you would do it.'

Jack looked at the man in the alarm of sudden recollection. 'But no one took me seriously, surely? I mean, it can't be binding, can it? I am still Lieutenant by virtue of seniority and . . .' He became aware that his voice was rapidly rising to a whine and stopped. While what he had just said was true, he also knew that if he had agreed to step down in Stokey's favour before all their brother officers he must do so. It was his word, his honour pledged to it.

He reached over to his satchel, took out his purse. He had four gold scudi left from what he had split with Pounce in Rome. Though he was sure he would get an appalling rate, there would be someone who would give him Portuguese coin for the gold at least. 'How much will we need to buy, say, a cow?'

'A cow?' Worsley laughed. 'Sir, this land's in a drought and has armies criss-crossing it. I'll warrant Stokey paid more than what's in your hand for the dog you ate last night.'

Jack felt his gorge rise, quelled it. 'So what do I do?'

'Well, you was boasting of your time in Canada . . .'

'Boasting? I recall a few small anecdotes . . .'

'. . . and told of some painted savage what could track game 'cross forest, marsh, mountain, lake, through the very air, you said! And how he taught you everything he knew.'

Até had also taught Jack not to make promises with his mouth that his arse could not keep. 'Is there game here?' he asked tentatively.

'I don't know. I'm from Barnstaple. Only thing we hunt is crabs. Both kinds!' He grinned. 'But,' he went behind the door, pulled out a long, slim leather satchel, 'I was batman to the late Sir William afore 'ee, and his everything you have inherited. He was very proud of this.'

He handed the case over. Jack undid the buckles and

gasped. For out slid a simply beautiful gun, with a stock of polished walnut, its silver mounts and thumb plate engraved with scenes from the chase. The lock was signed 'Tanner à Gotha', a renowned Saxon gunsmith. It was not the very latest of designs, but a quick glimpse down the barrel showed it was rifled, and it was certainly a better weapon than any he'd hunted with in the Colonies. 'Is there flint and ball for it?'

'Yes, sir.' Worsley waved at the chest.

'How d'you manage to preserve this booty from the other officers?'

'First thing I hid.'

Jack laid the stock to his shoulder. 'Clever lad.'

'A bit of Sir William's brains must 'ave rubbed off.' He grinned. 'If you'll forgive the expression.'

Jack laughed, lowered the gun. 'What time do we ride tonight?'

'Not till midnight. Out of the sun and to keep the movements secret, 'tis said.'

'Where are we bound?'

'Secret, too. But forward, not back. Seems we're going to war at last, 'Bout time, I says. Soldier can only have so much rum and women afore 'ee fights, don't ye agree, sir?'

He left. Jack raised the weapon again, sighted on a crow atop a neighbouring roof. His vision was still a trifle impaired but it would clear. A smile came on a realization. He had, perhaps too swiftly, tried to integrate back into army life in ways that befitted his rank and station. He had gotten horribly drunk. He had made a reckless wager. And he was headed for war. There was just one thing left for an English gentleman to do.

Hunt.

When the regiment reached its destination, the town of Castelo de Vide – near the Spanish border – in the early evening of the next day, Jack set out immediately. There'd been no occasion to hunt on the forced march, so relentlessly did they travel. But tiredness, compounded with the lateness of the hour, turned up no deer, though skulls and antlers displayed on the walls of taverns indicated that deer were to be found. Or had been, at least, though God only knew where the drought might have driven them.

The rising sun had not yet crested the hills above the town when he climbed into them the next day. As Até had taught him, he travelled light: a rope-wrapped bottle of water mixed with wine; the half-loaf of bread Worsley had miraculously scrounged; a length of rope, all carried in his satchel; a large knife on his belt that he'd taken off the Maltese sailor in Valetta to prevent the man sticking it into him; the rifle and the pouch, which contained just six cartridges of paper, gunpowder and ball. He'd only need one, though. If he missed he'd not get a second shot.

The cork trees soon merged into aspen, and there were signs here of deer, some pellets, crumbled to disgorge the tree's small black seeds, that could not have been upon the ground for very long. There was also the thinnest of creeks still running, concealed under brush. It was barely deep enough to wet his feet. But deer in Portugal would, he felt sure, be little different from their American equivalent. They would seek shelter, food and water. In this arid land, this tiny creek was perhaps one of their few sources.

As he traced the trickle higher up, he thought about how the day might end – a Queen's birthday feast consisting of beans and a few pieces of stringy chicken. The only man who would be pleased with the fare would be Stokey, for he would have the lieutenancy and, as he had not failed to remind Jack, command over him.

'We'll see if we cannot make you into a soldier again, Absolute. You are slack, sir. Devilishly slack. Can't have the

Cornet of *my* troop let me down,' he'd said, when Jack had returned empty-handed the previous night.

A rabbit ran across his path but there was no point even reaching for the gun. The wager had been clarified by a quorum of officers as requiring enough meat to feed the entire mess with flesh, not the flavouring for a soup! Still, the sign of even so much life was better than none at all. With that little hope he pressed on, to an area he'd scouted the day before that contained other features a deer might like.

He took the last few hundred yards most carefully, rifle loaded and at port, eyes seeking between the trunks. But nothing moved as he came up to a thicker stand that concealed what he'd noticed the day before – a slight flattening of the land, the barest pooling of water. Before the drought this was undoubtedly a pond some four foot across. Jack bent to look. Yesterday there had been a congregation of hoof prints on the pool's western edge. He had used a branch to obliterate all trace, creating a smooth surface to the dust. And, today, right in the middle of the swept area was the unmistakeable sight of a new hoofprint.

Jack rose, scanned the area. The slope rose up steeply from this point, increasingly tree-less, climbing toward the high bluffs above. It was the sort of land deer loved – a north-facing slope to shelter from the worst of the sun's heat; pockets of brush for concealment; good views over all approaches; and, above all, good escape routes. Even through the trees Jack could see trails through the shrub, disappearing up over the granite cliffs.

He stepped over the puddle and climbed a little way up the slope. A crag of rock gave him a natural wall to shelter behind and slashed branches, from the pines that now predominated, provided a roof. For the moment he was downwind of the pool. Jack took a sip of water, checked that powder was still in the pan and lay down.

The scent of pine sap from the cut branches, the steady

drone of flying insects, the call of cicadas and the heat all conspired to take Jack back to his time in Canada, in 1760, when he and Até had acted as scouts for Murray's army, as it chased the French from Quebec back to Montreal. They had supplemented their meagre allowance with money paid for game supplied for the camp cook's pot, competing as they always did in everything, to bring in the most. Até had had a clear advantage in the beginning, his forest skills honed by virtue of hunting from the moment he could stand. He had taken three to Jack's one in the first month. However, Jack was – disputedly, of course – the better shot, and his own tracking skills developed in observation of his companion; Até gave no lessons but by the end of that campaign, Jack was level in kills.

'Até,' he whispered, missing him suddenly. He would have enjoyed this whole situation, hunting and war and wagers. He'd also have relished the chance to mock Jack for the choices that had brought him here, via Bath and Rome. Where was his Mohawk blood brother now? Probably at the school he'd told Jack he was hoping to be sent to, somewhere in Connecticut. It made Jack chuckle to think of Até in a shirt and collar, diligent over his grammar, passionate about his verse. If he was still there then they had shared another experience – a winter in prison. Yet Jack had no doubt that Até would stay the course. If he set his mind to something, he would see it through, his desire for knowledge outweighing his longing for freedom.

Jack smiled. Perhaps he had started that, when they'd spent that whole winter in a cave, covered in bear grease, using Jack's battered copy of *Hamlet* to teach Até English and Jack Iroquois; and it had turned Até into a fanatic! He quoted it ad nauseam and in any situation, much to Jack's annoyance. But the Dane had saved their lives, he supposed. Without the copy his mother had given him before he went on campaign, what would they have done the winter long, trapped by snow? Killed each other, he supposed. Instead they'd become brothers and quarrelled like any siblings. The debates they'd had! Até saw the play as a story of redemption while, for Jack, it was a tale of vengeance . . .

A rabbit scurried down to the water and Jack carefully raised the rifle, sighted on its head. He had fired several shots on the march, knew that the gun threw fractionally left. There was barely a wind so, at this range of some fifty paces, it would not need to be compensated for.

'Phew.' He blew his lips out in explosion. The rabbit hopped away, disappearing into shrub. Vengeance, Jack thought. What had Hamlet said? He stared up at the sheltering trees. Something about 'greatly finding quarrel with straws, when Honour's at the stake. How stand I then . . .' Jack lowered the rifle, draped the cloth he'd soaked over the barrel, a cool barrel shooting more truly, and sighed. He had no 'father slain' but Sir James *had* been compromised when he'd tried to match-make for Jack. And his own honour *was* at the stake, from the moment the Irishman cozened him, tried to link him to . . .

Jack shook his head. He had tried to hate Laetitia. But he'd had plenty of time to think on the affair, in Rome and since; its hectic, almost farcical beginning, its tragic end. The story belonged upon a stage, not in anyone's life! Yet finally, he had realized that she, as much as he, had been the pawn to another man's ambitions. It was not Letty Fitzpatrick who had dishonoured him but her cousin, Red Hugh McClune. The man had been his friend, they had caroused together, fought at each other's side, each saved the other's life. It was what made the betrayal all the greater and what must be avenged – if he could find him again, if he was indeed here somewhere, looking to do something 'spectacular'.

The animal came with barely a sound, a buck, young but near to full size, sporting its first antlers. It strode to the water hardly glancing around the little dell, fearing nothing, bending to lap. Jack raised the rifle. He had oiled the mechanism so that it gave barely a sound as he cocked it though even that click was enough to make the stag raise its head, glance towards him, open its magnificent tufted chest to him, expose its heart.

'My thoughts be bloody or be nothing worth,' thought Jack, breathing out on the line, squeezing gently.

The powder flashed, the gun jerked. The buck leapt straight up, snorted, turned its head and bolted the way it had come. Throwing back his pine covering, Jack followed but at a trot, not a run. He could hear the animal's flight, no attempt on its part at stealth. He could not see it but he could see its signs, the earth churned by hooves, the spots of blood.

He found it slumped beneath an aspen a hundred paces further on. As he approached, it raised its head, antlers levelled; but even as he walked up Jack could see life fading.

'Go well, brother,' he whispered softly in Iroquois as he knelt, holding a hand to the bloodied chest where a lead ball had entered the heart. 'I give you thanks for your sacrifice.'

The last light left the brown eyes. Jack stayed kneeling for a while, then reached into his satchel for his rope.

'Do you think you might be able to use this, Corporal?'

Jack slipped the knots over his head and tipped the deer from off his shoulders onto the wooden slab. The bliss of having that weight off him! He felt as though he might float to the ceiling of the wooden cookhouse, or collapse onto its floor, so sore were his knees after the stumbling descent from the forest.

The cook of the third troop, who'd leapt in some shock at the sudden appearance of the beast before him, now stepped back and whistled. 'You did 'er, then, sir,' he said, wiping his hands across his remarkably hairy and quite bare chest.

'Right 'appy I am, even though I put a shilling to five to say you wouldn't.'

Jack was barely surprised at the betting though a little at the shortness of the odds. It either meant that the cook was not an adept gambler or that someone had been talking him up. Worsley probably. 'I know it's customary to hang it for a while but—'

''Ang be bugger'd, beggin' yours, sir. A young buck by its looks, and there's ways of cookin' it that'll make 'un tender enough. But the lads are that 'ungry, they'd eat yon while it stood and pissed against a tree!' He looked up, a little doubt growing. 'That is, if you ain't reserving this only for officers, like?'

'What's the strength of the troop at present, Corporal?'

'Well, we lost a couple of lads on Belleisle but we suffered less than t'others. There's fifty-one, including non-commissioneds, aside from officers.'

'And how far will a buck like this go, less, let us say, the left haunch?'

'With the best of the guts and the blood for pudding and all,' the man pursed his lips, 'it'll feed sixty and give us stew for three days.'

'Good. A haunch for the mess tonight will suffice. Spread the rest as wide as you can. And tell the lads to give three cheers for Her Majesty.'

'I will, sir. And three for you as well.'

Jack shrugged with as much modesty as he could muster. 'I'd be grateful, though, if you could set aside just a few choice strips of belly flesh for me and dry them over the fire.'

'Jerky, is it?' Jack nodded. 'Know the way of it, sir. I've some sugar to spare and I'll pick wild sage for the coals to give it some savour.' He puffed out his huge bare chest. 'Served in Canada five year mesself.'

'Did you indeed?' A bugle sounded outside and Jack

looked through the door to see part of the regiment riding past. 'And if you could also set aside the antlers?'

'A fine trophy indeed, sir. I'll clean 'em personal.'

'Thank you.' As the cook started bellowing orders to his subordinates, Jack stepped out of the door and stood in the shade beneath the thatched, sloping roof. The cavalrymen looked as exhausted as he after a morning spent in the hot sun, eating dust. Most of the first two troops paid him no mind. Neither did Crawford, leading the third. But Worsley spotted him instantly, raising his eyebrows. When Jack nodded, he let out a whoop that drew the attention of Bob Stokey – now Cornet Stokey once again.

He glowered down at Jack who smiled back and, when the horse drew quite level, pulled at the shirt he was wearing. It gave from his chest with a slight sucking sound, so soaked was it in blood. Stokey stared, shock, anger and bitterness chasing each other across his bulbous features. The rest of the regiment had turned the corner but still he glared back so Jack stepped further into the street and gave him the traditional two-fingered salute.

Later, he was lying on his bed, convinced he'd never get up again, when Worsley burst in. 'You did it, sir. By God, I knew you would.'

'Is that why you bet against me with the cook?'

Worsley did not look abashed one jot. 'That was just covering myself, like, for the fool took five to one. I made plenty more from the ones who swore you could not do it and gave me eights.' He beamed down. 'Now, sir, in Devon, after a kill, there's many a lad, feeling so manly now, looks for a different kind of sport. So how's about I fetch up my friend, Jocasta, who just could not bear to see the regiment leave Abrantes without 'er. My shout, like, by way of thanks. She's just below 'ere.'

'Worsley, will you cease trying to pimp for me!' Jack

bellowed. 'I am perfectly capable of finding my own whores should the need arise.'

'Oh, I'm sure you are, sir,' the man replied, tongue wedged in his cheek.

'But if you wish to show your gratitude there is something you could get me.'

'Anything you like, sir.'

Jack regarded the blood and dust that covered him. 'I cannot appear at the Queen's feast looking like Banquo's ghost. Can you get me a bath?'

Though the taberna the officers had selected for their mess in Castelo de Vide was smaller than their former one in Abrantes, the door swung open on an almost identical scene. True, the two lines of men that turned as Jack entered, late as ever, were dressed better, for they were not clad in their casual frock coats but in their best uniforms, just as Jack was. But their expressions as they looked at him were about the same; most bland, one glowering – Stokey, of course, glaring at the rack of antlers Jack bore. The main difference of the table was that, at the president's end where Major Somerville stood, no pot of thin stew awaited. Instead the Major was poised, carving knife and fork in hand, over a steaming haunch of venison.

'Nearly gave up on you,' he snapped. Jack could almost see the drool gathering in his mouth. Indeed, the savour of roasted meat brought an immediate rush of saliva to his own. 'Take your place, man.'

Jack marched to the one empty chair but before he could sit, Somerville, laying down the cutlery, spoke again. 'Gentlemen, now we are all *finally* gathered,' he called, and the officers rose to a man, bumpers to hand, 'I give you the Queen's Birthday.'

'The Queen! God bless her.' Bumpers were drained, swiftly refilled by scurrying servants. The wine was good, better than at Abrantes, Jack thought. He was about to sit when he noticed no one else was. Somerville looked at him again and said, 'And I also give you three huzzahs for the man who provides the feast: *Lieutenant* Jack Absolute.'

'Huzzah! Huzzah! Huzzah!'

— SEVEN —

The Storming of
Valencia de Alcántara

It had been a fine evening, infinitely superior to that previous
one in food, drink and society. For the first, the deer haunch
was not as tough as Jack feared, the cook having stewed it
first in some of the region's sweet wine, then larded it
liberally with fat from some other source, which was not
worth dwelling upon. The drink, too, as Jack's first quaff had
told him, was better than before. And as for the company,
only Glowering Bob, as Jack had by now dubbed him,
remained frozen to him. The rest, even Captain Crawford,
thawed.

Jack was unable to avoid drinking when he was toasted –
he was not going to give up these fellows' estimation by not
holding his own – but he was moderate when unobserved,
drinking far less than he had before.

Others, indeed most of them, were not so restrained. By
midnight, those who had not rested their heads upon the
table for a doze were beginning to collect the stocks and
jackets they had discarded when the action got boisterous.
Jack, though tired, was content for the moment just to sit.
Many a night in Rome he had dreamed of such conviviality
and he was not desperate for it to end. Thus he was probably
the only one sober enough to note the door that led to the

rest of the inn opening again. He stood swiftly because it was a rule for the night that, just in case a lady should enter, the regiment's officers must be upstanding at all entrances. The last one on his feet would be forced to drink a bumper, which accounted for Glowering Bob's recumbent position under the table; he'd spent too much time staring malevolently and had paid the forfeit once too often.

No one else noticed the man who came in. He remained in the doorway, one hand upon the wood, taking in the scene. He was wearing a pale-blue hunting jacket, a ruffled shirt and a waistcoat of emerald-dyed silk. It was the quality and cut of the clothes that reminded Jack who the man was, rather than the face. John Burgoyne was probably the only regimental commander who actually took his tailor to war with him.

'Lieutenant-Colonel Commandant Burgoyne in the mess!' Jack bellowed.

Few stirred. Major Somerville only raised his head from the table to say, 'Bugger off, man. Enough of your japes,' before lowering it again.

'Actually, Hugh, the fellow's quite right.'

The voice was low-pitched, warm yet carried. It brought everyone to their feet, some swifter than others. Only Stokey lay still.

Somerville was desperately trying to put on his jacket. 'Sir! Colonel! I am most sorry, we—'

Burgoyne waved away his blusters. 'Nothing to apologize for, my good man. ''Tis the Queen's Birthday and I was hoping to be here to spend it with you. Portuguese roads, alas. But I trust you have all done the regiment credit with your celebrations?' He was peering down at the debris on the table, his gaze finally falling on the much-hacked haunch of meat. 'Great Christ, what's that?'

'Venison, sir.'

'Venison, be god? I suspect I've tasted nothing meatier

than rat in a week.' He was still wearing riding gauntlets, which he now jerked off and threw down. 'Any left?'

Somerville lifted his knife dubiously. 'I may be able, sir—'

Burgoyne sat at the middle of the table. 'Never mind that, just fling the carcass here,' he said. When it reached him, he twisted the end bone from its socket and threw the smaller piece to a hitherto unnoticed officer who had followed him in. 'You all remember my adjutant, Cornet Griffiths, do you not?'

The young man bobbed his head then set to upon meat and marrow. Meanwhile, Crawford had poured a bumper and handed it across. Burgoyne nodded his thanks, sipped and gnawed.

Somerville cleared his throat. 'May I assume, sir, that the fact that you are here means, uh—'

'That we are finally going into battle? Indeed you may.'

A muttering passed around the group of still-standing men.

Crawford leaned forward. 'Would you be good enough to tell us where, sir?'

Burgoyne, still savaging the bone, swallowed. 'Not now. There is much to discuss and we will all need clear heads to do so. I, for one, am exhausted. All I will tell you is that we are to ride tomorrow, under cover of night, and that we are to ride directly against the enemy the night after that.' He stood, raised his glass. 'Gentleman, I give you the Queen and her Sixteenth Light Dragoons. Huzzah!'

'Huzzah!' Bumpers were pledged and drained.

Burgoyne placed his before him, then said, 'Now, if one of you would be so good as to show me to my billet?'

Jack stepped forward. 'May I have that honour, sir?'

'Of course you may, young whatsyername?' Burgoyne passed a hand over his eyes. 'Sorry, my boy. Long road and memory fails. You are?'

'Lieutenant Absolute, sir.'

He was sure it was a sight not many saw – John Burgoyne's composure wavering. 'Ab-Absolute? Well, kiss my arse!'

Jack smiled. 'I know, sir. I am dead.'

'No, you're not. I encountered your parents before I left London. They said you'd been in Bath then vanished. Thought you'd run off with some woman.' He smiled. 'Which made sense. Seem to remember that women were your problem, hmm?'

Talk about pot and kettle, Jack thought. Burgoyne's *affaires d'amour* were legendary. But all he said was, 'There's a little more to it than that, sir.'

'Well, you can tell me as we walk,' said Burgoyne, snagging a bottle.

As Jack led the way to the villa commandeered for the Colonel, their route took them down a street of low taverns and brothels. Naturally, many men from the regiment were there and, in front of one particularly large *bordel*, Jack found himself in the novel situation of acknowledging salutes and cheers from both the soldiers of the third troop and their whores.

Burgoyne raised an eyebrow. 'How long have you been back with your troop, Absolute?'

'Three days, sir.'

'Really? You seem inordinately popular.'

Jack flushed. 'Ah, well, you see, that deer, sir,' he pointed to the haunch which the Colonel still carried and was nibbling on periodically, 'I killed it this morning.'

'Did you? And you saw that the men under your command shared your bounty?'

'Yes, sir.'

'Good man.' Burgoyne smiled. 'There's officers who rule by fear and others who make themselves loved. I prefer the latter – just so long as the proper authority is also maintained, hmm?'

'I agree, sir.'

'Excellent.' Burgoyne tossed the bone to a scabrous dog that had followed them since they'd set out. 'Now, Absolute. Tell me where the hell you've been since we sent you off to Canada and how the hell you've found your way back again.'

Even the simplest version took some time. Burgoyne had not only gained admittance to his billet, but had washed, changed into the nightgown his valet had laid out and was stretched upon the bed before Jack had concluded the Roman part of his tale. He showed no signs, however, of wanting to sleep.

'I know Colonel Turnville. He does a fine job against England's enemies.' He sighed. 'There are those who decry espionage as almost unsporting. I am not one of them. We will win this war – any war – with intelligence, intelligently used. The opposite is also true.' He sat up. 'This McClune? I don't recall the name. You are certain he is in Portugal?'

'It was where I heard he was headed, sir. Somewhere he could do maximum damage to England's cause. And he has numerous aliases.'

Burgoyne scissored his legs off the bed, went and fetched a cylindrical map case, opened it, fished out a map and then spread it on the bed. 'I suppose he may have sought sanctuary with one of our Irish regiments – Armstrong's or Traherne's. When last I heard of them, they were both somewhere here in the north, stiffening the resolve of the chaotically organized Portuguese.' He waved his hand over the country. 'But, with the Spaniards' vast superiority in numbers, we will not be able to hold the whole of Portugal. We will contract to defend the heartland – here.' He traced a line behind the River Tagus, to Lisbon. 'Meantime, we can delay their advance, indeed sting them quite badly, by our own actions in the next few days. For the Spanish are collecting vast stores for their invasion . . . here. He jabbed at a point just across the border into Spain. 'Valencia de Alcántara. That is where we are headed tomorrow.' The older man straightened, rubbed at the small of his back. 'So, for the moment, though I expect you, nay *require* you, to keep one eye open for this Irishman, t'other must be pointed towards Spain. Think you can manage that without going cock-eyed?'

'Yes, sir.' Jack stared down at the map, trying to see, amidst the brown-inked hills and the blue rivers, a shock of red hair.

Something must have shown in his eyes. 'This McClune? I fancy there's something more than just employment in Turnville's service about this, isn't there?'

Jack had left out any reference to Letty, implying an entirely professional reason for his hunt. But Burgoyne's shrewd glance would not be gainsaid. 'There is something else involved,' he admitted. 'Someone. I would rather not say any more. Other than it touches upon my honour.' Jack looked straight into those appraising eyes. 'I hope that will suffice.'

'*Cherchez la femme?*' murmured Burgoyne. 'I was right what I said about you before, eh?'

'Perhaps, sir. But I can assure you that I will always put my duty first and my personal ambitions second.'

'Don't doubt it for a moment, lad. As sure as your name is Absolute. Or Truman. Or Dag . . . what was your Iroquois name again?'

'Daganoweda. It means, "Inexhaustible".'

'Wish I was!' Burgoyne's smile became a yawn.

'I'll leave you, sir.'

Jack was at the door when he remembered. 'Pardon, General, but a last question?'

'Hmm?'

'You mentioned you saw my parents?'

'Indeed. Saw them at Drury Lane the week before I sailed.'

'Their exile is over, then?'

'Aye. Certain representations, mine own as well as others, were made to the King and his ministers. Seems Lord

298

Melbury's death was not as, um, universally mourned as we first feared. Your father is pardoned and is once more in residence in Mayfair.'

'I am delighted to hear it.'

'Your mother was all concerned about you when I saw her at Drury Lane. But Sir James was,' he chuckled, 'angry. Claims you cozened him in Bath and then disappeared. It was hard to comprehend entirely because of the volume. But the gist, I think, was that he believes you tried to gull him into letting you marry some penniless girl.'

Jack sighed. 'My father tends to interpret events in a rather unique way.'

'Indeed he does. Perhaps you should write to them and tell them something of your adventures.'

'I will, sir.'

Jack was nearly out the door when Burgoyne spoke again, his voice very drowsy: 'Do not your Mohawk brothers take scalps as the prize of war, Absolute? Well, it seems your father, in service in Germany, took a few of his own. Metaphorically, I am sure. Well, almost sure.' Another yawn came. 'We could do with Mad Jamie Absolute the day after tomorrow when we storm Valencia de Alcántara.'

In the dried-up creek bed a vow of silence held, as binding as in any monastery. From his elevated position at the valley's end, the moonlight showed Jack the shadowy forms of the entire force: four hundred cavalrymen of the 16th Light Dragoons and two hundred Grenadiers, all stretched upon the ground, recovering from the two nights of hard riding that had brought them within a mile of Valencia de Alcántara.

Linked horses fed from nosebags, their riders sharing field provisions. Jack had already chewed upon a string of his newly acquired jerky. He had no desire to sit or lie down. Not when he was about to go into battle with his regiment for the first time since he'd joined them three years before. All the officers were standing on or near this knoll, staring to a point beneath the crest of the concealing ridge where Burgoyne, Somerville and Fanshawe, the Grenadier Captain, were conversing with the Portuguese scouts and their extravagantly moustachioed, wildly gesticulating translator.

'Man looks like an Italian knife-thrower,' whispered Worsley, breaking the silence. 'What's he saying, d'ye think?'

'Oops!' Jack murmured, and both men laughed quietly.

Stokey turned to glare at them but, as he did, all saw Burgoyne's shadow, Cornet Griffiths, detach himself from the group.

'Senior officers' council beneath the bluff,' he said softly as he came near. Immediately, the captains and lieutenants rose and made their way up. Only one cornet went with them – Glowering Bob, helping Captain Crawford whose horse had stumbled in the darkness, throwing him and breaking his arm. They gathered in a crescent, just below Burgoyne.

'Stroke of luck, lads,' he said, rubbing his hands before him, 'for it seems the Dagoes are so unconcerned about attack they've left the main gate of the town ajar. I say "seems" because it is possible they may have had wind of our coming and are trying to lure us into a trap. I believe not, as does our friend, Major Gonzalo here.'

The Portuguese Major, his uniform as gaudy as his facial hair was extensive, bowed and nodded vigorously. 'Spanish stupid men,' he growled. 'Drunk and stupid and asleep.'

'That we shall see,' said Burgoyne, dryly, 'and soon enough, for if they are, we shall ride in and take the town. Saves storming the walls which I feared we would have to do.' He leaned down. 'May I remind you of our mission, gentlemen: we do not know the extent of the force opposing us. One regiment of foot, certainly, maybe two. More than us, anyway. So we do not want a pitched battle. We want to capture the stores they have amassed for their invasion of

Portugal if we have the time, destroy them if we have not.' He smiled. 'But if they are indeed soused and napping, we may be able to take the town and accomplish the rest at leisure. Any thoughts so far?'

No one spoke. He went on. 'So I have it in mind to send one troop to seize and hold that open gate, the rest to follow fast. If it's a trap we'll know soon enough and wheel away sharpish.'

Crawford raised a hand, the unbroken one, and at Burgoyne's nod, asked, 'Which troop, sir?'

'Well, it was going to be you and yours, Crawford, since it was your third as well as the fourth that saw recent action on Belleisle.' He sighed. 'But as you are now wingless . . .'

'I wouldn't let that worry you, sir, I . . .' Crawford, in gesticulating, grimaced in pain.

Jack had raised his hand. At a nod, he spoke. 'Might I volunteer, sir?'

The Captain of the First, Onslow, now stepped forward. 'Now look here, sir, my men and I are more than fit—'

Burgoyne raised his hand, and silence returned. 'I have no doubt as to your lads' merits, Geoffrey. But I mentioned the fear of a trap. If there is one, I think I'd rather sacrifice a knight than a bishop, eh?' He smiled. 'Besides, Absolute here's been swanning around, 'personating savages and playing at pirates. 'Bout time he won his spurs, don'tcha think?'

The faintest of dawn's light was touching the sky when Jack led the third troop over the ridge. It seemed to make the town below them even darker, a silent, black presence sprawled over at least two hills, a castle's tower on one, walls girdling the whole. A track ran to their left, the main egress from the valley behind them, and swept down to a narrow stone bridge. From there, it was no more than a three-hundred-yard dash to the gate.

Jack halted the troop fifty paces down the slope and went twenty further on himself. He was not concerned about being spotted. If it was a trap, they would have noted him anyway; if not, a dozing guard was unlikely to notice a deeper darkness against the escarpment. 'Puxley,' he called back softly, and was immediately joined by the Sergeant. He had no hesitation in asking the man's opinion out of earshot of the men. 'What do you think?'

The Welshman gazed down. 'The highway's little better than a ploughed field to my mind. But we'd not want to stray off it in this light; too many rocks and holes in the fields beside. So no line, I'd say.'

Jack nodded. 'Just my thought. Careful to the track, walk to the bridge, form column the other side then – straight to the gallop and damn the furrows?'

'Reckon that's right, sir.'

He wheeled his horse about, and Jack called after, 'Oh, and Sergeant?'

'Sir?'

'Other side of the bridge? Draw swords, I think. Give the command.'

'Sir.'

Jack led the way, stopping just beyond the bridge. He heard his men trot over it, the noise suddenly harsh in the dawn quiet, then halt.

'Sir?' came the soft call.

'If you please, Puxley.'

The voice was low but clear. 'Draw *swords*.'

Jack, with all the others, threw his right hand across his body, seized the handle of his sword, grazing no knuckle this time, withdrew the blade two inches. Counted silently.

'One. *Two*.'

He drew it out, taking his hand to opposite his right breast, his fingernails turned in, sword side flat to his body.

'*One*.'

Dropping his hand smoothly down, he swivelled his knuckles front, turning the straight blade of the sword forward and sloping it across his chest, its tip before the point of his left shoulder.

'Forward,' Jack said then, though he had to say it twice, his throat catching the first time. As he moved the first few paces at a walk, he was aware of the regard of the fifty men behind him, many more undoubtedly beginning to emerge from the canyon above. He swallowed, called, 'Trot.'

His horse, as biddable in the field as it had been at drill, needed just the word, not a touch of heel. He reacted as well to the next two words: 'Canter. Gallop!'

The advance guard of the 16th Light Dragoons began their race toward the gates of Valencia de Alcántara.

After about a hundred yards, Jack was suddenly unaware of how far he was ahead of his men. He was riding solus, after all, they were in a body. Yet he didn't think it would do his reputation any good to look back, or rein in. Alarmingly, all he could hear were his own hoofbeats and he suddenly recalled how someone had told him that his mount was probably the swiftest in the whole regiment. 'Lucky' was its name, a new one bestowed when its previous owner and his brains became separated. Army humour!

Dead Man's Horse, he thought, as the town gates drew nearer. Dead Man's Sword. Dead Man's Damn Pinching Boots.

He could make out the gate now. And the bloody thing *was* open. Whether that was good or bad he was yet to discover.

At fifty yards, no more, he heard a shout, saw a man jerking up from where he'd been slumped against one of the open gate doors. As Jack watched, he turned, hands scrabbling at the wood. At twenty yards Jack swung his sword down, leaned forward, his weight behind the weapon.

The 16th, unlike most Dragoons, favoured the straight blade, thrust home with the weight of the charge.

The man must have felt it approaching. With a shriek he gave up his futile shoving and threw himself to the ground. Jack's point passed over him. He was through the gate. He reined in, his horse coming to an immediate halt under the gate tower. To his left the guard cowered in the dust. To his right was a door. Two men came out of it. One had a musket.

'Yee-ah!' cried Jack, spurring his mount forward, pulling back almost instantly on the reins. Lucky came up on his rear legs, front hooves striking out, forcing both men back. When the hooves came down, Jack lunged, the sword point striking the gun near its lock, knocking it from the soldier's arms. Its charge exploded, the noise thunderous in the stillness.

It had taken seconds. With the shrieking man falling backwards, Jack was suddenly aware of another noise, a rumble from the ground. Jerking the reins yet again, he forced Lucky to the side, just before the third troop charged in.

His orders had been clear and thoroughly explained to the men. So though three Spaniards had begun to run, screaming into the town, no trooper gave chase. Instead they rallied in the open space behind the gates.

'Dismount! Handle your carbines!' Jack's commands, reinforced by Puxley's, had the whole troop off in moments, horses linked and led to the side, the three ranks of the troop acting as divisions. The first two ran to the corner of the nearest house, where the main street into the town began. The third rank rallied to Jack at the gate.

'Stokey!' Jack called, and the fellow ran over fast, enmity swallowed by exhilaration. Jack grabbed his shoulder, turned him to the gate. 'Out there, man. Sound the advance.'

As the bugle coughed out its staccato call, Jack led his own rank forward. There was one other entrance to the gate square, a narrower road, and, as he advanced, Jack could see some Spaniards about a hundred yards away, moving cautiously along it.

'Poise your firelocks! Cock your firelocks! Present your firelocks! Hold now, men. Hold!'

The enemy had begun to advance quicker now, a good twenty of them, bearing muskets, officers driving them on with the flats of their swords. Suddenly they halted, there was a shouted command and a ragged volley made some of his men duck.

'Steady,' he called, then, 'Fire!'

It was a pretty good volley, for cavalrymen, in the near dark. The Spaniards certainly thought so, taking to their heels, two white-clad bodies kicking on the cobbles behind them.

Jack turned to see the main wave of cavalry, Burgoyne at their head, begin to sweep through the gate.

The Colonel reined in beside him. 'All to order, Absolute?'

'Yes, sir. The men are holding the streets here. The Dagoes *were* asleep.' He grinned. 'But they're awake now.'

Burgoyne smiled back. 'Well, let's see how they like our lullabies.' He turned to Hugh Somerville at his side. 'Major, sixth troop to secure the gate. And send all spare horses back to Onslow, so he can bring the Grenadiers up smartly.' He faced forward. 'According to our hirsute Portuguese friend, the town square is dead ahead and where the main barracks lie. Coming, Absolute?'

Lucky was being held nearby. Swiftly unlinking, Jack mounted in a moment. 'Gladly, sir.'

He was not quite so glad a few moments later when, on the street they cantered down, shutters were thrown back and ball began to thrum around them. It seemed that, as in the British Army, men were billeted all over the town. Men who had their muskets with them.

'Fourth and fifth troop to dismount by divisions when

fired upon and engage the enemy,' Burgoyne bellowed. 'The rest with me.'

There were no niceties of drill, just a harum-scarum half-gallop down the narrow, curving streets, men spilling from horses when guns were discharged at them, carbines aimed up at shutters, wooden gates in arched doorways battered in to root out the sniping enemy. Jack pushed on with all the others, now ahead of Burgoyne, now behind him. Occasionally there would be figures standing beyond a sweeping corner. Powder would flash, bullets pass near or ricochet off walls, and then Jack, like all the others, would crouch behind his horse's neck, sword thrust ahead, using the weight of speeding beast and the sharpness of metal to scatter the enemy. More than once he felt his blade clash with metal, wood, or bone. But there was no time to note wound or death, the impetus was forward, the nearness of the square indicated by an increasing resistance. And then they were in it, the open space acting like air sucked in after too long spent under water. The three troops, one hundred and fifty men, spread out fast, driving those who opposed them into doorways and back down the streets and alleys that radiated outwards.

Jack had become separated from Burgoyne, but Puxley was still to his left and Worsley, whom Jack had not seen since before the charge, had suddenly appeared on his right. 'Westward ho!' yelled the Devonian, sweeping his sword over the Cornishman and the Welshman, causing Jack to duck. He was about to curse the fool when he noticed something else. Before the biggest house on the square – three storeys high, with huge oak doors, a red-tiled archway and elegant iron balconies – stood a man wearing a nightgown, which was not that unusual, and a huge tricorn hat, which was. It was of a similar kind to their Major Gonzalo's but had twice the quantity of gold emblems and silver lace. Jack had no doubt that he was looking at a colonel at the least, a guess confirmed by the man's apoplectic yelling at all around him.

'With me, lads,' Jack cried, kicking Lucky into his stride. The three horses scattered the knot of men around the officer, bumping some to the ground, the others fleeing to the house's porch. The General – for that's what Jack thought him now – had somehow stood his ground, a younger officer guarding him with a heavy sabre. In a moment, Jack was off his horse; in another, he'd attacked. The young man's curved weapon was cumbersome in comparison to Jack's straight English blade and was dislodged at the third pass, the officer staggering back. He looked as if he would reach for it again but his commander said something sharp, something Jack caught but did not understand. On these words, the young Spaniard turned and sprinted into the house.

The General had a sword, too, but he did not level it. Instead he reversed it, held it out to Jack, said something that, to Jack's ears, sounded vaguely Italian but he presumed was Spanish.

'I am not the one to give your sword to, sir,' Jack said slowly.

The man, his tight-cropped beard as grey as his hair, considered then said, 'To whom, please?' The English phrasing was slow and precise.

'Him,' Jack replied. His own commander had suddenly appeared from the throng, leading a party that had subdued the last resistance upon the porch. 'Colonel,' Jack yelled and, in a moment, Burgoyne was there.

'Absolute. What have we here?'

'Someone who has something for you, I believe.'

'General Ignacio de Irunibeni.' The man bowed stiffly. 'And your captive, sir.'

The sword was offered again, and this time taken.

307

'Lieutenant-Colonel John Burgoyne.' He bowed, returned the sword. 'I assume the obligation, General.' He smiled. 'Do you think we could persuade your men to be so obliging?'

'I can try. But I must warn you, sir, the regiment of Seville has never surrendered,' the General replied, his accent full of lisps.

'Well, I wonder if we can persuade them to this day? For the town is ours, and further sacrifice needless.'

Jack looked beyond this vacuum of politeness to the mayhem beyond. The square had largely been taken but, judging by the explosions and shouts in the neighbouring streets, Burgoyne's declaration was premature. He was just about to call Puxley to help him rally the rest of their troop, when he noticed the officer's sabre, the one who'd dashed off, upon the ground. As he bent slowly to it, he realized the General was staring at him, concern in his eyes, calculation, as if he were attempting to gauge Jack's mind and precede him to a conclusion. When their gazes held, the Spaniard stepped forward, spoke. 'I wonder, sir, if this gallant officer would be my escort.'

'Absolute? I'm sure he would. Why?'

And suddenly Jack knew. The General was trying to remove him from the board. If war was chess, as Burgoyne had said earlier, then the Spaniard was still playing a game.

'Excuse me, sir, I think I know why. Puxley, Worsley, with me.'

The General actually tried to grab his sleeve as he passed but neither that, nor Burgoyne's shouted question, halted him. The porch of the house was cleared, men in scarlet coats had already begun to venture cautiously into the hall. But if Jack was right, this was not time for caution. He took the stairs two at a time, ran onto the first floor landing. The house was designed around a courtyard, four corridors thus in a square. Running left, Jack realized he had been fortunate in his guess when he saw two men standing outside a door, both with muskets at port.

He could not hesitate. 'Charge,' he cried, as the startled soldiers fired and missed. 'Take them,' he yelled, and ran between the two men – defending themselves with bayonet and gun stock against his companions' sword thrusts – into the room.

It was as he suspected it would be. The young officer was crouched before the fireplace, desperately trying to fan a small flame onto a piece of paper in his hand. The pistol however, hastily snatched up by the Spaniard, was more unexpected.

'*Hijo de puta!*' hissed the man, but the room was small and Jack was already running. He was across it just before the barrel levelled. Then his hand was upon the gun, forcing it up as it flashed. He felt his palm and fingers burn, heard the smash of glass exploding. He still had his sword in his hand but he was too close to use its point so he used the guard instead, driving it into the man's jaw. The Spaniard flew back, lay still upon the floor. Jack bent, snatched the paper from his hand, snuffed the flame that had caught upon its side. Then, clutching it, he sank onto a chair.

'What was that all about, sir?'

Jack looked to the young man in the doorway, Puxley behind him, sword resting on the shoulder of one of the Spanish guards. Jack could see the soles of a pair of boots just poking round the doorframe. He shuddered. 'Spanish, Worsley.'

'Sir?'

'There's a distinct similarity to Italian.'

'Is there indeed?' Worsley gave the sort of humouring laugh one man gives to another who's succumbed to battle madness.

Jack sighed. He was suddenly too tired to explain. But, as something of a linguist, he was rather pleased to realize that the first Spanish phrase he had learned was because of time spent in a Roman prison. In Italy, the General would have ordered his officer to *'Distruggi il documento.'* In Valencia de Alcántara what he did say was: *'Destruye el documento.'* But in England his command would have been: 'Destroy the document.'

— EIGHT —

A Different Game

Jack threw down the pencil, closed his eyes. The dots, however, continued to crash around behind his lids like billiard balls on baize. The more he looked the more muddled he became.

He left the paper on the desk, crossed to the open window and looked down onto the town. It had grown quiet in the hour after midnight. Until then, the soldiers of the 16th had been out upon the streets, celebrating their return to their quarters at Castelo de Vide with the food they had seized from the defeated Spaniards, washed down with wine they could purchase now in abundance in exchange for what they'd looted. There was more than wine on offer, however, and that, Jack realized, accounted for the relative silence. There was a curfew, the troopers back in their billets to rest before the morning's planned departure. But they did not have to rest in their billets alone . . .

He would have liked to be down there, celebrating their victory. Drink a lot of wine and, depending on how much, find a pretty enough señora to bed down with for the night. It had been a long time since that garden in Bath. Jocasta, ever attached to Worsley's arm, would wink at him whenever

311

he looked; though, to be honest, he wasn't sure if that were not some condition of her eye.

Damn him! Did not other men manage perfectly well with whores? Were not many of his brother officers down there tonight? He just never seemed to have found the knack. Too romantic to be practical. Perhaps it was just as well that Burgoyne had ordered him to work on the only booty he'd taken in Valencia de Alcántara – the paper the young officer had been trying to burn.

'Why me, sir?' he'd asked.

Burgoyne had smiled. 'You are the only one with experience, Absolute. You are Turnville's man, after all.'

His protest that his talents lay in tracking, disguise and perhaps killing but not in codes had gone unheard. He was the spy among them, he must have the answers.

Not tonight, Jack thought as he sat, stared again at the dots, letters and numbers in three lines. They had to be words, but they did not form themselves into anything resembling a readable pattern:

H1 .. 14 .. 23 ... 21 .. 2 . H1 .. 12 .. 2 . R N
2 .. 1 . L1 .. L2 . 2 .
43 .. 2 . LH1.

Jack had only figured out two things and neither really helped. Firstly, that since there were two 'L's' in the second line, what he'd taken to be a small 'l' was actually the number 'one'. Secondly, he could only hope Spanish was like English in the order of its most common letters because then '2 dot' that appeared five times would be the letter 'E'.

Numbers one to four were repeated, as were the same four letters: H, L, R, N. He'd tried separating them out, remixing them in a different order, scattering them at random over a page. Nothing leapt out at him. He'd found three hand-kerchiefs in the room where he'd found the code, a different shape cut out of each of them – a wine bottle, a cross, an hourglass – but these masks, laid upon the charred paper, illuminated nothing.

He tried one again, just in case, then threw it aside. Temptation arose. The Spanish officer who he'd caught trying to burn *this* page first – thus testifying to its primary importance, Jack felt – was their prisoner. He could not speak because Jack's blow had broken his jaw, but some felt – Major Gonzalo prominent among them – that he could be 'coerced' into writing answers to questions. Burgoyne, supported by Jack, had disagreed. Leaving distaste aside, the man was obviously a proud Castilian and would probably be hard to break down. He was also clever enough, presumably, to give answers that would appear to elucidate but would, in fact, confuse.

No, it was down to him. He laid out a fresh sheet of paper. Four numbers. Four winds? Horsemen of the Apocalypse? Seasons? Four corners, as on a billiard table? He wrote them as corners of a square. Then he copied the four letters in a line in the middle and stared at the result. What was it about the letters that seemed odd? 'H' was number eight in the alphabet, 'L' number twelve, a gap of four. 'N' was just two away, 'R' four on again.

Did they have to be written on the same line?

He drew them in a cross instead . . .

H

L   N

R

He leaned in, his face flushing, another idea occurring. Swiftly, he drew a grid, filled in the letters of the alphabet beside the ones he had and suddenly the whole alphabet was there before him in five rows of five, only the 'Z' missing. Then he placed the numbers at each of the grid's corners.

He looked again at the coded message.

What did the dots mean?

It was luck, when he saw it; or perhaps the patterns were just clearer now in his head. But, having decided that 2 . must be 'E', he put one dot in the E box – corner 2 – then a single dot in each of the other corner boxes. Then he began a frantic dotting, counting down from the top numbers, up from the bottom ones, until all the boxes had both letters and one, two or three dots in them, all except the ones that could not be reached directly from a number, vertically, horizontally or diagonally – H, L, N, R:

```
1                           2

A . B . . C . . . D . . E .
J . . I . . H  G . . F . .
K . . . L M . . . N O . . .
T . . S . . R Q . . P . .
U . V . . W . . . X . . Y .

4                           3
```

He looked at the grid again, then took another single number and dot that occurred in the code – 1. – which had to be 'A', and, taking the 'l' diagonal he saw that 1.. would be 'I'. So if a single number led to a diagonal, a double digit would give the horizontal or vertical . . .

By God, he had it! Chuckling, he matched the code on the burnt paper to his grid and wrote out the words:

> Hijo de Hibern
> Galilee
> Velha

'Hijo' he knew meant 'son' because he had asked Major Gonzalo what he'd been called by the Spanish officer just before he'd hit him – 'Hijo de puta' or 'Son of a whore'. So this was 'Son of Hibern?' A place in Spain? Like Galilee was a place in the Holy Land and Velha sounded like a place in Portugal?

Then he saw it, at first in complete shock, then with a slowly widening smile. He picked up his almost untouched wine glass, drained it in one, then reached for his red coat.

Burgoyne was not asleep, but he had company. It took some minutes after his most reluctant adjutant went in before his door opened and a large, dark-haired lady of middling years scurried out, a dressing gown clutched at the neck and, without looking at Jack, went into a room opposite. It seemed that his commander had not merely commandeered the largest house in Castelo de Vide but its owner as well.

The Colonel sat at a small writing table. He wore a shirt and breeches though Jack noticed that the latter were not fully buttoned up. 'Is this vengeance, young man, for keeping you from the celebrations?' he said, an eyebrow raised.

'Not at all, sir.' Jack was careful not to smile. 'But your orders were to inform you the first moment I cracked the code.'

'I believe I said first thing in the morning,' came the muttered reply. 'Very well, show me.'

Jack took both the original, singed page and his reworking, and laid them on the table. 'I believe, sir,' he said eagerly, 'that this type of code is known as a "pigpen". I was able to deduce that it all fitted on a grid and that letters, numbers and dots combined to—'

'Absolute!' Burgoyne put a hand to his head. 'One of the reasons I bought my promotions so swiftly was precisely so I would not have to learn about such things but could instead assign to them bright young fellows like yourself.' He smiled. '*Précis*, sir. *Précis*.'

'Sir.' Jack pointed to his decoding. 'Perhaps you would just read it.'

'"*Hijo*", I know, means "son". Lady of the house has three, apparently, and she'd be so *grateful* if I'd take one on my staff.' He looked up. 'Gratitude's a marvellous thing. So's hope.' He looked down, mumbled the other words. 'Not much other sense. Biblical reference, you think? What the devil's "Hibern"?'

'Short for "Hibernia", perhaps?'

'Ireland. So, "son of Ireland".' But "Velha" and "Galilee"?'

'The first I can tell you, sir. I ran into Major Gonzalo,' "Ran into" was not quite right. Stumbled over his legs where he lay drunk in a doorway, 'and he said that Velha was probably Villa Velha, an area to the west.'

Burgoyne reached for a map of Portugal, spread it out. 'There,' he pointed, 'back towards Lisbon.' He pursed his lips. 'The plain of Villa Velha's on this side of the River Tagus. When the Spanish recover from our raid on Valencia de Alcántara and finally invade Portugal – they are massing here, here and here,' he jabbed his finger down three times, 'we shall retire to the opposite bank to hold them.' He looked again to Jack's scrawl. 'I am still at a loss as to the inland sea.'

'I, too, sir.' Jack allowed himself a smile. 'But I *do* know a son of Ireland.'

Burgoyne tipped his head. 'What? Your Jacobite fellow? Wouldn't that be too much of a coincidence?'

'Possibly. But why would a Spanish general, poised to invade Portugal, order his adjutant to destroy this document first? Unless it was of great import?'

'Hmm. We could ask him if he wasn't on his way to prison in England.' Burgoyne was staring at the map again. 'Well, all will become clearer reasonably soon. Within a month anyway. Because our line of retirement to the Tagus will take us very close to the plain of Villa Velha, if not directly across it. And since all British forces will be doing the same, we should finally be able to contact those two Irish regiments – Armstrong's and Traherne's.' He looked up. 'Perhaps then, young Absolute, you truly *will* have to keep your eyes swivelled in both directions.'

There had been many times on this campaign when he'd dreamed of plunging into water, but those torrid August days were long gone. Besides, the river before him presented no cool green waves rushing to a Cornish beach, but an expanse of dullest brown, swirling with uprooted bushes and the other detritus of autumn. Jack was sure he'd spent colder Octobers in Canada. But he'd never been this wet for this long. The fighting retreat before the Spanish Army had admitted only the briefest of pauses, occupied with the feeding of horses and of men. They'd had the meagrest of shelters for nearly a week now. And it had been raining, without let-up, for three.

Jack ignored the rain that dripped from his nose, counter-pointing the flow off Lucky's. Man and horse stared down to another man and horse. The brown water had reached the rider's boot soles; the horse's legs were submerged. Then, in a sudden movement, the beast's footing was lost and it was swimming, the flow pushing it downstream. Pulling on the reins, the man managed to guide the horse around, back to the shore. He didn't pause on the little stretch of flat riverbank but tapped his heels and rode up to where Jack waited above.

'It's like we thought, sir,' Puxley said as he reined in. 'Most of it will be a swim.'

Jack shivered. 'Can we do that?'

The Welshman nodded. 'Oh, aye. The horses will have no problem, so long as we keep coaxing them. But the men might because I doubt if there's many of them that can swim.'

'Well, they better hang on tight, then, hadn't they?'

'There's no chance of?' Puxley nodded to the north.

'No.' While his sergeant had been testing the water, one of Jack's outriders had come in. There was a ford a few miles upstream but a regiment of Spanish cavalry now stood between them and it. They'd taken on some odds in snarling little skirmishes during the six-week retreat across the Alentejo to the projected defensive line at the Tagus; but a regiment was too strong even for his third troop. There'd be no going south because there were even greater concentrations of the enemy there, no going back for the same reason. 'It's across here and that's the end of it. Do you have a suggestion, Puxley?' Jack had learned much in the time since he'd rejoined the regiment, but deferring to his experienced sergeant had been the first lesson.

The Welshman ran his hand over his forehead, flicking water away. 'I'd link by subdivision, sir, give each man a bit of support from his mate.'

'Not quarter ranks?'

'Four men would be too awkward and if one was in trouble they all would be.' Puxley shook his head. 'Two's grand.'

'Then make it so, if you please. We'll cross in three separate ranks to prevent bunching. You lead the first across, Stokey will take the second. I'll come last.'

'Sure, sir? I'd be happy—'

'I want to make certain everyone makes it over. And I need to bring the last outrider in.'

'Aye, sir.' Puxley saluted, wheeled his horse and rode over the rise to the slight hollow where the rest of the third waited, most of them lying on the sodden grass.

Well, thought Jack, turning to look at the swirling brown water, they can't get much wetter. He squinted. The Tagus was less than a hundred yards wide at this point, but the downpour and the dusk rendered the far bank insubstantial. Still, he could see the two lights Burgoyne had promised would always be lit for him, if he was forced into the option of swimming not fording. Jack had managed to bring his troop to the exact point on the bank opposite the regiment's camp. Now he just had to make sure they all got across. He hadn't lost a single man in the retreat across Portugal and he was damned if he was going to begin now.

He rode to the edge of the rise and looked down. Puxley's orders were being swiftly obeyed. His men were linking, one collar extended back to meet the one behind. Each two-man subdivision was used to working as a pair. He could only hope they would not let each other drown.

It was rapidly done, collars linked, carbines, packs and blankets strapped to shoulders. Every man there knew that the Spanish were coming fast and, while Jack was sure that all of them shared his distaste for the plunge that lay ahead, they would also prefer it to a Spanish gaol, though there had been times on this march when he'd missed his dry Roman one.

'Ready, sir.'

'If you please, Sergeant,' Jack replied, and moved Lucky off the slight path. The first rank came up, Puxley in the lead. Down the slope he went, did not hesitate, driving his horse straight into the flood, the first of the men following. All, at the same point, began swimming.

With the first rank afloat, Jack called down, 'Now, Cornet Stokey.' Glowering Bob led the second rank up. The fellow was still sullen, his face set in lines of discontent.

'Where's Worsley?' Jack asked as the man drew level.

'Still out.' Stokey jerked his head behind him, down the canyon they'd ridden to the water. Jack looked, but rain blurred all vision.

Worsley had volunteered to be the last outrider. But he'd

been told to report back long before this. 'How long since you last blew?' he asked, pointing at Stokey's bugle.

'Not long,' the man muttered, and Jack knew he was lying. With everything else going on, he'd ignored the fact that he hadn't heard the recall blown this half-hour. Still, there was not time for reprimands. 'Give that to me,' he said, reaching and taking the instrument, 'and get your men over.'

The second rank did not pass as smoothly. Just over half the troop had gone when three of the horses baulked, spooking others. They were led back, blinkers applied. The animals re-entered the water reluctantly but were coaxed forward to swim behind the rest, although the delay had caused a bottleneck of cavalry upon the bank.

Frustrated, Jack turned back again, to the third rank below him and the canyon beyond. He'd have to let Stokey sort it out. He had his own rank to get over and a last man to find.

He rode down to his corporal. 'When the Cornet has them in the water,' he instructed, 'you follow.'

'Sir.' The man hesitated. 'Where will you be, sir?'

'Looking for my damned batman.' Spurring his mount, Jack rode up the other side of the rise, stopped at its crest. He looked down at the instrument. In his brief time of training with the regiment before Canada, one of the things he was meant to have learnt was the use of, and signals for, the bugle. He had managed neither especially well.

He pursed his lips, applied them to the mouthpiece, blew. A sound like a wet fart dribbled out. Cursing, he adjusted his lips, blew again. This time he sounded a note, strained, cracking. Sure he could get at least an approximation now, he took a deep lungful of air and then realized he wouldn't need it. Worsley was galloping toward him. But he wasn't alone. About twenty lengths behind him were five other cavalrymen.

'Spaniards!' screamed Worsley, unnecessarily.

Jack's carbine was loaded, but it was wrapped in cloth in

an attempt to keep it dry. However he had a pistol tucked under his greatcoat. By the time he'd fumbled his buttons open and jerked the weapon out, his man was about twenty yards away and the enemy had closed the gap.

Jack levered the hammer back, levelled, pulled the trigger. There was little aiming involved but the bullet must have passed at least close enough to the leading pursuer for the Spaniard to feel its wind, for he twitched his reins right, his horse moving almost at right angles to its previous course, the other horses following. They swept up the side of the canyon, turned completely about and rode out of it again.

Worsley came to an excited halt just by him. 'Bloody hell,' Jack said, lowering the pistol. 'Why have we been running from these bastards when a single pistol will scare five of 'em off?'

'Uh, sir?' Worsley was gesturing behind him. Jack turned – and there was the whole of the third rank drawn up in a rough line, carbines levelled.

'Ah,' said Jack. Swiftly reholstering, he said, 'Now, Corporal, take 'em across. Smartly now.' The troopers, remounted, began to move fast toward the river, Jack and his batman bringing up the rear. 'So, many of them out there?'

'About a squadron.' The younger man grinned. 'Was going to charge 'em but then thought: Don't you be greedy now, Thomas Worsley. You leave some Dagoes for the Colonel to kill.'

'Very considerate of you. Now, if you'll kindly link horses with me, let's see if we can join him.'

'The Colonel's compliments, sir. Was wondering if you could see him in his tent?' It was Griffiths, Burgoyne's adjutant.

When someone had coughed outside his canvas, Jack had been hoping that it was Worsley bearing the results of his scrounging. It was his major skill and Jack had rarely been disappointed. He'd been promised rum in hot tea at the least, which he hoped would begin to dissipate the shivers. Ever since his semi-immersion in the River Tagus two hours before, it was as if he'd been cursed with an ague.

'I, uh, haven't got a uniform,' he said to Griffiths, gesturing at the sodden scarlet and grey-white breeches thrown over his trunk.

'Oh, that's all right, sir. All the other officers will be in their red clothes as well.'

Jack sighed, threw back the blanket. If the man was surprised to see that beneath it he was already wearing the unlaced frock coat in which all officers slouched about in camp, he didn't reveal it. Though he might have raised an eyebrow if he'd known that, beneath it, Jack was wearing all three of his dry shirts.

His batman met him as he emerged from the tent. 'Here, sir, best I could do.'

He ate as he walked, Worsley alternately holding the mug of tea – at least half of which was rum – and the platter of thin, brown stew. By the time they reached the command tent, Jack was feeling better. At least the worst of the shakes had stopped.

'Ah, young Absolute.' Burgoyne was bent over one end of a table and straightened when Jack entered what was more a pavilion than a tent. 'Glad you're safe. Your men?'

'All accounted for, thank you, sir.'

The Colonel was eyeing the bulkiness of his clothing. 'And you seem to have put on weight. Must be the only soldier in this campaign who's managed that. Sit, lad. Take a mug.'

Jack sat at the lower end of the table with the six other lieutenants. The six captains rose in two rows above them in order of seniority up to Major Somerville standing at Burgoyne's right hand. There was a pot of tea before Jack and he poured himself a mugful, nodding as he did to his fellow subalterns. He immediately smelled the rum in it and took care just to sip; the other one had done its job so well he was beginning, within his four layers, to feel hot.

The senior officers were discussing matters in quiet tones. Some of his fellow lieutenants were straining to hear but Jack felt he had made quite enough decisions in the last month and was thus content to await orders.

'Gentlemen,' said Burgoyne at last, straightening again, 'now that the third troop has been brought back safe by Lieutenant Absolute,' he tipped his head toward Jack, 'the Sixteenth is at last all in one place and, blessedly, pretty near to full strength. We have lost barely a dozen men in the campaign to date, which I put down to both providence and our unique *esprit de corps*.'

'Here, here,' called a voice, and rummy tea was lifted, pledged, drunk.

'This damned rain,' Burgoyne continued, gesturing to the pounding on the canvas roof, 'may be a nuisance to us but it has been a disaster for the enemy. His large forces have been hard to move up and his heavy guns nigh-on impossible. I doubt he's fully in position yet, while we are comfortably established at all the crossing points on a river that is just getting deeper. Bridges and fords are manned largely by British forces, if you understand me, though, of course, I mean no disrespect to the gallantry of our esteemed Portuguese allies.'

This was said with a slight nod to Major Gonzalo, whose moustaches had suffered from the excessive water in the air and now drooped where once they had soared. He bowed, though he was perhaps the only one there not to detect the subtlety in Burgoyne's remark. No-one could doubt Portuguese courage, their passionate defence of their homeland against their oldest foe. But it was professionalism that won wars and that quality was variable in their army.

The Colonel now gestured at his adjutant, who lifted the

map from the table and held it open toward the officers; each leaned forward for a better view. Burgoyne picked up a baton and pointed at a spot on the map. 'This is where we are, opposite Villa Velha whose hills the Spaniards are now finally occupying. We are between two crossing points, ready to ride to the aid of either – the bridge at Perriales guarded by the sixty-seventh and the ford at . . .' He squinted. 'Well, it doesn't appear to have a name but it is held by Traherne's regiment of Foot. They've been there over two months and have built quite the little fort, apparently, to house themselves and two batteries of Portuguese artillery. Anyway, if the rain continues to fall in this manner, they will not be needed there much longer for even the ford will be too deep for guns. And then, the Dagoes will pack up and go home for the winter. The lull will allow our politicians the time to make some dreadful accommodation and give up everything we soldiers have won.'

A murmur of disgust at politicians of all nations ran around the room. Smiling, Burgoyne added, 'Still, with fortune ever with us, next spring could see us returned to England to the kisses of our loved ones and the wreaths of a grateful nation for our triumph at Valencia de Alcántara.'

'Huzzah!' The officers stood and cheered.

'Gentlemen, that is all we need discuss for the present. I am sure you are as desirous of sleep as I. Goodnight, and may tomorrow bring us more rain and a quiet life.'

To a further cheer, the officers dispersed. The mere mention of sleep had caused Jack's eyes to droop; that and the rum tea. He got up a little slower than his fellows, was one of the last at the entrance. A conversation there blocked his progress and he turned, saw Burgoyne still staring down at the map. A word from his last speech came to him. A name. He turned back.

'Sir?'

'Absolute?'

'May I have a word?'

'Have to be quick, lad.' Burgoyne yawned.

'Traherne's, sir.'

'What about them?'

'One of the Irish regiments, is it not?'

'It is.' Realization came. 'Oh, I see. Your concerns about Hibernians.'

Major Somerville, busy folding maps, looked up. 'Hibernians, sir?'

'The message the lad decoded. He is suspicious of the loyalty of our Irish brethren.'

'Not of all of them, sir. I am half-Irish myself,' Jack said, hastily. He knew Somerville had been born in Londonderry.

The Major was thinking too hard to take offence. 'You know, that's queer, sir,' he said, 'because an officer I know in the third Foot served alongside Traherne's in the north. He mentioned that they were not . . .'

'Not?'

'Not entirely steady.'

'Really?' Burgoyne sat down again and beckoned the other two to do the same. 'In what way? I understand they were hastily recruited. Perhaps their training was not of the fullest?'

'It was only a remark, *en passant*, sir. And it had been a . . . long evening, so I struggle to remember it accurately. But the intimation was that – unlike Armstrong's, also Irish, but loyal and fierce – Traherne's was not a regiment you'd want to come to your aid in a hot situation.'

'Shirkers?'

'Malcontents was the term used, as I recall.'

Burgoyne sucked in his lower lip. 'Do you have the officer's roll anywhere?'

'I believe I do, sir.' The Major went to a collection of papers, rooted among it. 'Here.'

The Colonel spread out the tube of paper, flicked through

the pages. 'Crawford's, Armstrong's . . . ah, Traherne's.' He spun the roll around. 'Anything you see there, Absolute?'

Jack scanned the list of ranks and surnames. He knew McClune would not be there and he struggled to remember the aliases he'd read on the papers Turnville had shown him. 'O'Malley. Riordan. Lawson. Treach. Burnett . . .' He looked up into the concerned faces. 'I am afraid, sir, I . . .' He glanced back, saw it. 'Well, well.'

'Lieutenant?'

Jack tapped the page. 'I think one of McClune's aliases was Lawson. There's a Lieutenant Lawson here.'

'Not an uncommon name.'

'No, sir,' Jack replied, 'except this is him. This is McClune.'

'How can you be so sure?'

'Because I've just realized what the middle part of the coded message meant.'

'Galilee?'

'Yes, sir.' Jack stood in his excitement, looked down at the other two men. 'I am not the greatest of believers, sir, but I did, of course, study scripture at Westminster.'

'Should hope so, too,' huffed Somerville, who insisted on a full turnout for services when Burgoyne wasn't around. 'So?'

'So,' Jack turned to the Major, 'wasn't it at the Sea of Galilee that Jesus performed a miracle?'

'He did. Matthew seventeen to twenty-one.'

'And what did he do there?'

'The miracle? Why, he fed the five thousand.'

Jack shook his head. 'But there was something else also.'

'Well, afterwards – verse twenty-five – he walked on water, of course. Surely—'

The Major was interrupted by his Colonel rising. 'Great Christ, Absolute,' said Burgoyne.

'Indeed, sir. The Son of God.' Jack nodded. 'He walked on water.'

They both said it.

'The ford.'

— NINE —

Mutiny

The rain had ceased but its effects had not. It was only five miles to the fort at the ford but every inch of what passed for a track was thick with mud, sucking at the horses' hooves when it wasn't causing them to slide. Their progress was also restricted to the speed of the slowest mount and the adeptness of each rider. As the whole of the third troop made up the vanguard, so fifty men dictated the pace, much to Jack's frustration, who would have charged ahead alone. But Burgoyne had insisted on numbers.

'We do not know how advanced their plot is,' he'd said. 'We may have to fight to suppress a mutiny, and for that we'll want horses and swords. So your troop will go first and the rest of the regiment will follow as swiftly as they are able.' He'd smiled. 'But Somerville and I will ride with you.'

Though each was most concerned with keeping their mounts upon the slick track, there were some minutes within a stretch of woodland when they could ride stirrup to stirrup. 'Is this ford so vital, Colonel?' Jack asked.

'Absolutely. Allowing the Spaniards to cross the Tagus in force at the ford would split the Allied army in half and they'd be able to deal with each part piecemeal. They could be in Lisbon in a week. We'd have no choice but to submit.'

What desire had Red Hugh confessed to in Rome? To do something 'spectacular'? Jack grimaced. Losing England a war would certainly be that!

They emerged from the wood to the rain's sudden cessation, and the subsequent shredding of clouds let a bulbous full moon poke through. Yet it was a good hour after their mounting before the troop reined in atop a slight rise and all could gaze down upon the fort three hundred paces away.

'Not bad,' said Burgoyne. 'Someone's been reading their Müller.'

'Sir?' queried Jack.

'*Elements of Fortification.*' Burgoyne pointed. 'Starpoint earthworks, probably faced with logs. A ravelin above a front trench. Detached bastions behind. They've even erected roofs to keep the gunners' powder dry.' He sighed. 'Quite good. Be a shame to hand it over to the enemy.' He dismounted, began to lead his horse back over the rise, out of sight of the fort. 'Conference, gentlemen.'

It was quickly decided. Somerville to wait with the troop, watch for a waved torch at the rear bastion's brazier and then come fast. Jack and two men to go in first.

'A troop galloping up will spook any aspiring mutineers and I wish to take them alive. We must learn how advanced this plot is because the two Irish regiments make up one-third of British infantry strength and it would not do to lose them. Cut out the cancer and the whole may be saved.' He smiled. 'Shall we?'

'We, sir?' asked Jack. 'You are coming?'

'Oh yes,' replied Burgoyne. 'I outrank Colonel Traherne and may need to remind him so.'

Jack selected his two volunteers, the inevitable Puxley and Worsley, and the four men spurred over the rise and down to the fort's rear gate. No challenge came, even though the party was perfectly visible in the moonlight. This caused Burgoyne to tsk several times and, when they reined in before the wooden doors, to call quite angrily, 'You there! Traherne's! Where are you, begod?'

A face suddenly appeared over the wooden posts above, clearly fresh from sleep. 'Whas'sat?' came the Irish voice. 'Who the divil's down dere?'

'The devil indeed! What do you mean by not challenging us as we approached? Get down here at once and open these gates.'

'And who would I be opening to, may I ask?' came the grumpy reply.

'Brigadier John Burgoyne. Swiftly, ye dog, or you'll receive a lick of the cat's tail before dawn.'

The grumbling continued, another voice joining in and a second face briefly appearing. But the bolt was soon shot and the gates flung open. 'Brigadier who?' said the man, stepping hastily aside as the four horses were ridden in.

'Burgoyne. And you are to take me to Colonel Traherne immediately, if you wish to keep skin on your back.'

The second Irishman to be awoken that night was as grumbly as the first.

'What do you mean, sir, by barging into my command at this hour?' Traherne said, tucking his shirt into his breeches. He was short and stout, with curly black hair. His face was flushed with anger.

'And what do you mean, sir, by allowing your sentinels to sleep? It's deuced slovenly, let me tell you. What if we had been Spaniards, sir?'

'The Spaniards will be coming from the water,' the man grumbled, 'not the landward side.'

'Not when they hear you don't keep watch.' Traherne went to reply but Burgoyne over-rode him. 'You ask what we are about? I'll tell you. We are here, sir, to prevent a mutiny.'

The man's mouth opened and closed. The angry red deepened. 'That is a damn calumny. I am exhausted by the insults you English officers heap upon my regiment. By god, if we were not at war, I'd—' His hand went to where his sword would be if he were dressed.

Burgoyne prevented any further discussion. 'Do you have a Lieutenant Lawson here?'

'Lawson? Of course. Recruited personally last year by my father, when he established the regiment. A fine, experienced man.' He thrust his chest out belligerently. 'We were lucky to get him.'

'Oh, I am sure.' Burgoyne nodded. 'And where would he be now?'

'Where all of us should be, sir.' The man glared. 'In bed.'

'Then I wonder if you would be so good as to help us wake him.'

There was more harrumphing as the man dressed, and a steady muttering as he led the party out of his room and onto the parade square. 'There.' He pointed to the last in a row of doors. 'That is Lawson's room, in the corner. He shares it with Lieutenant Treach.'

'May I scout first, sir?'

'Certainly, Absolute.'

Drawing his pistol, pointing at the carbines in Worsley and Puxley's hands, he put a finger to his lips then beckoned them forward. The barracks was built flush to the wooden ramparts so there was no egress from the rear but there was a small, paper-filled window to the side. Signalling that Puxley should remain beneath it, he returned to the front door, pressed his ear to it. A faint sound of snoring came. He turned, raised his eyebrows to Burgoyne who stood back five paces, also with a drawn pistol. At his Colonel's nod, he gestured to Worsley that he should take the left, then he reached for the handle and shoved in the door.

He moved straight to the right bed, to the figure he perceived, in faint moonlight, to be slumbering there. He lay the muzzle of the barrel against the flesh above the ear. 'Right, you bastard,' he said softly. 'Wake up!'

It took a moment. A hand rose to brush at the metal on his scalp. Then a voice came. 'Eh? What . . .'

Jack jerked back the covers, reached down, grabbed a shank of hair, twisted the head around. The voice came again, panicked, in pain. 'Jesu! What are you—'

Jack grabbed the back of the neck, dragged the man out, threw him down against the wall, into the patch of moonlight coming through the open door. Before the hands rose up to protect him from the gun that was thrust at him, Jack was able to see clearly.

The man was not Red Hugh McClune.

He spun, to the other bed. But Worsley had already checked. There was no one there.

'Got him, Lieutenant?'

Jack turned to Burgoyne in the doorway. 'He's not here, sir.'

'What the hell is happening?' The other officer, Treach, had lowered his hands, his voice loud in fear and a growing anger.

'Quiet!' said Jack, waving the pistol at him. He turned to the door, where Traherne had now arrived. 'Any idea where Lawson might be, sir?'

'Taking a piss?'

It was possible. Swift glances revealed no chamber pots under the camp beds. 'Perhaps we should all step inside.' He went over, pushed the paper of the window out. 'Puxley, come here.'

With all of them in the room and the door closed, Jack turned again to the still recumbent officer. 'Where's Lawson?'

'I have no idea. Fellow was snoring there when I finally managed to fall asleep.'

Jack felt the sheets Worsley had disrupted. There was a hint of warmth to them. Then he heard something.

'Absolute?'

'Shh!'

'That's "Shh, *sir*",' muttered Burgoyne.

All were quiet. Then he heard the sound again, maybe by some play of the wind. He recognized it. Not only the fiddle, but the song being played, because he'd heard it sung in the forecastle hold of the *Sweet Eliza*.

' "Lochaber, no more, boys," ' he murmured, standing up.

'What's that?'

'A Jacobite air, sir,' he said as he passed Burgoyne on his way to the door.

They all stood before the hut, even Treach in his shirt and nothing else. The wind blew and they listened.

'There,' Worsley said. 'It's coming from over there, ain't it?'

They followed his finger, which pointed to a low, long building.

'What's there, Traherne?' asked Burgoyne.

'Barracks,' came the reply.

'And you allow your men to sport at night?'

'Don't see any harm in it. Once in a while.' The Irishman swallowed. 'Shall I turn out the guard?'

'Not yet.' Burgoyne turned to Puxley. 'Sergeant, would you go and signal down the rest of the troop. Tell them to dismount and wait out of sight in the lee of the gatehouse.'

'Sir!'

'Shall I scout again, Colonel?'

'A moment, Absolute. I know how keen you are. But let's have a little force to back your hunch, eh?'

They watched the flare waved, and it was not even a minute before they heard the faint jingle of harness, a few equine snorts. Then Major Somerville appeared. 'Sir?'

'Our man would appear to be in yon barrack house. Is there another way out, Traherne?'

'No. There's loopholes in the walls, too narrow for a man. The front door's the only way in or out.'

'Have your men ready to rush it on my command.'

'Sir.' Somerville snapped a salute, returned to the shadows.

The fiddle had increased in volume, or the wind had funnelled it their way. It seemed to reach a crescendo. Then it died.

'Now, sir?' Jack felt like a dog leashed in, the scent of his quarry making him shuffle and twist.

'Not yet.' Burgoyne took Jack's arm, led him a few paces apart. 'Listen, man,' he said softly, 'I do not know why you have such enmity for this fellow. It goes beyond the natural revulsion for a traitor, of that I am certain. I do not pry. But you did tell me once that it was to do with honour. Now that's fine upon the duelling ground – but not here. Here we are dealing with a traitor who threatens our entire campaign, perhaps even the outcome of this war. So, though I would prefer it if he were taken alive, if it comes to it, you must not hesitate. You must kill him. That is my command.' He leaned in till he could look straight into Jack's eyes. 'Is it clear?'

Jack swallowed. He'd prefer McClune at his sword's point. But preference gave way to his country's need and his Colonel's command. He nodded his assent.

'Good,' said Burgoyne, slapping his back. 'Now go.'

Jack strode forward, into the light rain that had begun again. There seemed little point in concealment now. If whoever was inside had a sentinel, the movement on the parade ground would already have drawn attention. If they didn't . . .

They did. He *was* at one of the loopholes, though he wasn't facing out but in, too interested in the scene in the centre of the room. Jack shifted to another slot, a better view, and saw what so captivated the man.

Red Hugh McClune, in the scarlet of King George, was crouched in the centre of a ring of perhaps two dozen men. A lamp was on the ground before him and lit his face in a way that reminded Jack of some of the paintings he'd seen in Rome; a moment caught and rendered into art, the surrounding darkness emphasizing the action of the foreground. And Jack knew that Red Hugh had arranged it exactly so, understood the effect he was having on his audience, just as he'd held the Forecastle Club of the *Sweet Eliza*, with Jack as captured as any. Except there, his reason for the beguiling was good fellowship, the passing of the tedious hour. Here, his reason was mutiny and Jack could almost smell it in the air. He leaned in, listened.

The man spoke softly but even his quietness had a strength that carried. 'Enough, Cavan? We few? More than enough, I say, and so we are. For are not the men ripe to be led by those they trust, their sergeants and corporals here assembled? Has not every son of Ireland dreamed of striking a blow for the Cause back on our blessed isle, where cruel oppression rages? There, though, it would be in vain, glorious, futile. Here, we have the chance to do something great. Something that could shake the very throne the Hanoverian has usurped.'

A murmur came at the rhetoric, the men looking around at each other, nodding. Red Hugh spoke even more softly, drawing them in. 'Now . . .'

Jack didn't hear what followed. Someone had stumbled out of the front door, wobbled a few paces into the parade ground. There followed a fumbling, then the sound of the man relieving himself, a hiccough accompanying the cascade. A punctuated humming began.

Jack had flattened himself against the wall. He looked now at the man pissing and wondered what to do – for when he turned he would be bound to see Jack. He could fire his pistol and Burgoyne would bring the 16th at a clip. But there was more to be learned about the conspiracy, how many were involved and if Traherne's was the only regiment tainted. For Jack knew that, once captured, Red Hugh would reveal nothing.

Then it came to him and he acted at once on the impulse. He stepped out of the shadows and stood beside the man. 'Evenin',' he said, in a soft Irish accent as he undid his buttons, 'a wet one, to be sure.'

'And wetter now for the pair of us,' came the reply.

Jack laughed. This close, he could smell the rum. The man barely looked at him, glimpsing, no doubt, similar red clothes to those he wore himself. Though Jack had started later, he finished well before but he did not button himself up until he saw the other man doing so, then turned with him and followed him back to the door, his heart thumping. He let his companion go in first and, over the man's shoulder, saw Red Hugh glance briefly up. When the eyes returned to his audience, Jack slipped into the shadows beyond the lamplight.

'The night after's the one. A near full moon to guide our Spanish friends over the water, if the rain lets up. If it does not, then it will dampen the powder of our Portuguese artillery, and we'll take the fort by bayonet.'

There were grunts, queries raised. Someone was asking something in the Gaelic and Red Hugh answered in the same. Jack moved slightly closer.

'Has anyone anything more to say?' Red Hugh asked, again in English.

'I do, McClune,' came a voice, 'and that's, as certain as my name is Michael O'Flaherty, I reserve to mesself the right to slit the bastard throat of that bastard Traherne for the lashes he laid upon me this Michaelmas past.'

This would have been all right if the man speaking hadn't

stood directly before Jack. And if he hadn't chosen to kneel at the same time.

McClune's gaze went down as the man descended, a smile forming. Then it froze halfway. The eyes rose up and looked directly into Jack's.

'Shite,' the Irishman said.

There was a moment's pause, just a small one, as the two men regarded each other. Then they both moved simultaneously, Jack stepping back and jerking the pistol out, Red Hugh throwing himself, still in his crouch, between the camp beds behind him.

Jack cocked and levelled the gun. As soon as he'd seen him again he'd realized the only way this man would stop was when he was dead. And Jack had his orders. Aiming at the barest curl of red hair visible above the straw-filled bed, he fired.

The blast broke the silence that had held them all. Men started like untrained horses, shying from the shot, making for the door. At the same time, there was shouting from outside, the sound of running. The entranceway was narrow, admitting only two troopers at a time, so four men met in the doorway, smashing into each other, the force from without stronger, as well as armed. The leading Irishmen tumbled back in, the rest scattering to the far sides of the long room.

'Hold the door,' Jack screamed at Puxley and Worsley, the first two in, though the instant clamour drowned all hope of hearing. He himself ducked through the throng, against the tide, towards the entrance, drawing his sword as he ran. Traherne had said there was only one way out. Red Hugh must come to him.

Three more cavalrymen had rushed in but these bunched in the doorway, heads ducked as if anticipating blow or shot. They blocked the entrance of those beyond for a moment.

And above their shouts and the yells of the trapped men, a voice came. Loud. Commanding. Familiar.

'Sons of Ireland,' Red Hugh shouted, 'we are all hanged men. But rather than dancing on a noose, let us dance our way across the water to our friends from Spain. For Eire!'

Jack could not tell where the voice came from. But he saw the joint stool that accompanied the defiant shout flying from a crowd of bodies, striking one of the troopers at the door. He fell with a yelp and, on the instant, stools, buckets, a bed frame, all were being hurled. Puxley ducked, crouched, fired; an Irishman cried out. Worsley, who had dived to avoid the avalanche, rose, shot. Two more troopers came through, one immediately down, one firing. The barracks filled with smoke and shrieking.

Jack had not got very far before the Irishmen's volley of wood halted him, and he had thrown himself behind a trunk. Now he raised his head, just in time to see Puxley felled, scarlet-clad men hesitating at the entranceway and the emboldened mutineers rushing towards it en masse.

'Eire!' screamed the charging men, two in the lead using a bed frame like a battering ram, their force driving the troopers back. Men poured out to meet men trying to burst in, the waves smashing together, the sounds of furious combat instant, carbine shots, wood on bone, screams choked off in blood. Still Jack searched in the crowd, which was not short of red-haired men, for one particular one. He did not see him.

And then he did. Not there in the struggle near the door but back, towards the rear of the barracks. McClune was hoisting himself up onto a roof joist from the shoulders of another man. Then he began driving a bayonet between the beams to make a hole in the roof.

Jack advanced, the last of the Irishmen passing ahead of him as they surged to the door. A quick glance told him that most had got through it, were struggling, killing and dying outside. Before him, splinters of wood were falling onto the man who'd lifted McClune. He had a sabre in his hands and stepped forward now to Jack.

There could be no hesitation. Not when the man he'd chased twice across a continent was trying to escape. Jack came at a run, ducked under the swung blade, thrust at the gut. The man stepped back fast, his weapon arcing down, smashing into Jack's and nearly dislodging it. Forced to the left, Jack stayed low, sliced his own weapon back across the man's front, causing another step back, this time into a camp bed. He wobbled – just slightly, just enough – and Jack drove his sword straight into the man's stomach. He collapsed, fell away with a scream. Something hit Jack, stinging where it struck his head. A plank fell past his eyes and he looked up. Red Hugh McClune had started wriggling through the hole he'd gouged in the roof.

Jack leapt and grabbed his dangling legs. Red Hugh slipped, frantically jerking, then the boot Jack held came off. He fell, landed with a thump that hurt, and watched as the two feet found their purchase again on the beam. Strangely, Jack noticed that the stockinged one had a huge hole, recalling in a flash the Irishman's always scrupulous attire. He'd sheathed his sword to jump, leapt again, but the man was gone.

'No,' screamed Jack. He looked about him and saw Worsley, his face blood-smeared, moving towards him.

'Hands!' he yelled.

In a moment, Jack had a foot in Worsley's palms, two hands on his shoulders, then on his head. The Devonian was strong, raised him swiftly high enough to grab the beam. In a moment he was atop it, in another he'd thrust his head through.

It took several seconds to spot him through the now fast-falling rain. McClune was leaning against the slope of the roof, one hand steadying himself against the earthen wall. He was making his way towards stairs at the barracks' end which rose to the ramparts above.

Jack pulled himself through, his feet immediately slipping on the slick wooden slats. Then he noticed the Irishman's second boot near the hole and he jerked his off. It gave him grip and he crabbed his way up to the wall. Once there, he again copied the man he pursued, leaned against the earthen surface with one hand, his feet gaining traction on the wood. He didn't glance down. A slip, he knew, would have him rolling down the slope to crash onto the combat below, one that continued fiercely, he could hear. Water had soaked powder, so no more shots were fired. The troopers of the 16th were fighting Traherne's mutineers with musket stock, foot and fist.

He had gained. McClune was now just ten feet ahead, swinging himself onto the stairs, running fast up them. Jack risked looking straight up, though his feet slipped when he did. A head poked out from the roofed bastion above.

'Stop him!' Jack shouted up.

The sentry heard an officer yell but saw one of his own running at him. 'What's the fuss, Lieutenant?' Jack heard him say, just as McClune made the ramparts.

'None at all, lad,' came the easy reply.

Jack was scrambling again so he did not see the blow but he heard it and the accompanying clatter as the sentry fell. He gained the stairs, ran up, reached the elevation only in time to see knuckles white on the rampart planks and fingers releasing. He stepped to the edge.

The drop was not huge, fifteen feet perhaps, but the earthworks that had been thrown up against the log frontage of the fort were a slope and McClune had tumbled on landing, rolled down. He lay at its base for a moment as if dazed, then, rising, began to stumble towards the river.

There was no time to consider. Jack took the same route: up, over, a moment's dangling, a release. He landed hard, unable to stop the roll that followed down the slope. Then he staggered in pursuit.

Someone shouted from behind him. A musket cracked, a second, fire directed from the bastion where the powder would be dry. There was no time to turn and tell them to aim at the traitor, not his pursuer. Hunching his shoulders against both rain and ball, he ran on. He passed a red coat in the mud, stripped his own off, aware that McClune was leading him in a strange dance of divestment. But the Irishman was moving away from the ford where a British picket was posted. And if he was going to swim, Jack must be ready to follow.

He crested a last slope and looked down to the figure standing on the edge of the water, peering at it like a heron about to strike. The man must have heard hard breathing, because he turned before Jack could start down the hill.

'Absolute!' he said. 'The sight of you back there was enough to stop my poor auld heart. You're never going to force me to tax it further with a cold plunge?'

Jack took a step towards him. 'There's warmth back at the fort, Hugh.'

A slight smile. 'I think the warmth you have in mind would be too dearly bought. And not at all guaranteed.' He sighed. 'No, I think the water calls – for both of us perhaps. Are you a strong swimmer, lad?'

'Strong enough.' Jack was now just ten paces away. 'Do you wish to wager?'

Something changed in the face, a hardness came. 'I should have killed you when I had the chance,' he said. Then he turned, plunged in.

Jack ran and dived. When he broke the surface he saw the other head straight before him and he struck out after it. And as he swam he remembered the first time he'd seen Red Hugh McClune, in the even more frigid waters off Rhode Island, a lifetime before.

Something fizzed into the water in front of him, the crack of gunfire coming almost simultaneously. Cursing, he glanced back, but no red coats appeared on that shore. He looked forward and saw a flash, just before a second ball plunged closer and he understood why the Irishman had avoided the ford and made instead to this spot where he had friends concealed. Spanish friends.

Jack took a deep breath, drove himself beneath the surface and angled back towards the bank he'd come from. Another bullet came, passing close enough so that, despite the murk, he could see it. Kicking harder, he found footing on the sloping shelf of the river, cautiously thrust his head up. He was among the reeds and, as he looked back, he could just make out some movement on the far bank. He heard a jingle of harness, the snort of a horse. When his shivering became near uncontrollable, he began to clamber up through the reeds.

— TEN —

Honour, Part Two

The pain was unbearable. It radiated down from the hollows beneath his eyes to spread throughout his entire face. Since they'd taken up their position, silence had been ordered and a sneeze had become a suppressed snort. The quantity of mucus provoked was astonishing, yet no matter how many times Jack dismounted to void it, more swiftly reappeared to drown him. And though Portugal had returned to what Major Gonzalo assured him was its customary October warmth, the clearing of the rain clouds had happened too late to save him. He still felt continually damp, still shivered as he had since his dip in the Tagus two nights before. Burgoyne had even suggested that he should be replaced when the rest of the third troop rode out with the forces sent to surprise the enemy on the hills of Villa Velha. He had done enough, his Colonel reasoned, foiling the mutiny. But when a Spanish deserter had told them that '*el Irlandes*' was still in their encampment, Jack knew that he could not remain behind.

He watched Captain Crawford riding back just below the ridge line, felt the men stir around him. Their leader was returning from his conference with Colonel Lee, the operation's commander, and would have their orders.

'Absolute, Stokey, to me, please. And bring your sergeants,' the man called softly, descending his horse with the aid of his bat-soldier. His arm was out of its sling but still not quite healed.

They gathered so they could peer over the crest at two hills not more than three hundred yards across a small valley. The Spanish tents were clearly visible in the moonlight. 'We're the reserve,' Crawford said, to at least one audible sigh of relief. Glaring, he continued, 'The thousand men of the Portuguese Royal Volunteers are to go in first with the bayonet because it is their land that's been invaded and they'll stick the poor bloody Dagoes in their tents. They'll be backed by the two battalions of Grenadiers in a second wave and we're to follow them in at a walk, to be used as need arises. Questions?'

Cornet Stokey raised a hand. 'Will they not see us the moment we move over this crest, sir?'

'Colonel Lee doesn't think so. Thinks they are as dozy as the shambles we thrashed at Valencia.' He pointed. 'Remember, if they expect an attack it will be from their front, across the ford. They won't have reckoned on us marching for two days to take 'em in the rear.' He looked around. 'Anything else? Absolute?'

He supposed that his raised head and narrowed eyes indicated a question, rather than the sneeze that exploded. 'No, sir. Excuse me.'

Crawford shook his head in annoyance. 'Very well, then. Muster the men. Colonel Lee will order a flag waved when he is ready. That is all.'

Jack walked with Puxley back to the troop. 'Nosebags off,' he ordered quietly. He could see the same motions taking place all down the line. He took a couple of paces up the slope, till he could just see over the crest. 'You're still there, aren't you, McClune?' he muttered to himself, staring hard, as if sight could pierce canvas and reveal his quarry. Yet it was prayer as much as comment, for he knew the Irishman could already have slipped away, or might yet in the chaos of combat to come. 'Bloody reserve,' he said, sniffing hard. He'd wanted the 16th to charge in first. Not because he wished to stick any poor bloody Dago in his tent. Because he wanted to end this for ever. If he lost him here, who knew when or even if he'd ever come across him again?

A cough came from beside him. 'Lucky's ready, sir,' said Worsley. 'And the order's just been passed to stand to the horses.'

'Good.' Jack began to move down the slope, then grabbed the younger man's arm, halting them both. 'Listen. McClune's over there.'

'The traitor? Are you sure, sir?'

Jack nodded, though he wasn't. 'If we get a chance to ride for the camp, I might get . . . separated. For a time. Would you . . .' He stopped, seeking the man's eyes in the moonlight.

'Get separated, too? Reckon I might. Us West Country boys should be as tight as a Plymouth landlord's purse-strings, right?'

'Right.' Jack smiled, clapped Worsley's back and went to stand beside his horse. Reaching up to his saddle roll, he checked that the long package he'd wrapped in oilskin was still securely cinched to his saddle.

'Make ready to mount,' came the soft call. 'Mount!'

The first rank was immediately led by Crawford over the ridge. Stokey, as Cornet, brought over the second, with Jack bringing up the rear and last. They assembled in their three ranks, halted and waited. To their right, a narrow defile emerged from the ravine and from this, almost immediately, a column of infantry issued forth. These were the Royal Volunteers, some of the best of the Portuguese infantry. The terrain did not allow much in the way of marching order and it was not their special skill anyway, but they went bravely, eagerly forward, the cheers they would normally have given restrained by the need for surprise. Officers attempted to order the ranks but the column started to spread as the defile opened out onto the slopes of Villa Velha, and soon the most eager of the men were rushing past their futilely gesturing leaders.

'Here we go,' muttered Worsley to his right and, almost on his words, there came a cry of warning from up the far hill. A shot followed and, with a universal yell, the fast walk of the infantry became a charge as they rushed upon their foe. The outlying tents were quickly reached and all could see men rushing into them, hear the screams that ensued.

The more ordered formation of the British Grenadiers now emerged from the defile and marched towards the enemy. At the same time, Crawford moved to a position a horse's length before the centre file of the front rank, raised his unbroken arm and called, 'Sixteenth will advance one hundred paces. March!'

They had not covered even half the ground when the tumult that had been building ahead soared to a higher pitch. On the southerly hill, as yet unattacked, Jack suddenly noticed a large number of horses and men. Though they were in some disorder yet, several troops of cavalry were being rallied. If they achieved it, the Grenadiers, caught on broken ground between the two hills, would be vulnerable.

Crawford had seen it, too. 'Halt!' The Third Troop of the 16th stopped almost as one, slight adjustments being made to dress the ranks. 'Draw swords . . .' Jack did, then looked to check the dressing, could just see the nose of the man next but one. All was well.

'March!' came the call, and the troop moved forward. Jack had been schooled in what to do as rank and file leader but doing it was different! He looked at two objects in the distance in line with each other – a flag pole furthest, a bush closer to. He made himself the third point, covered the farther with the nearer and advanced toward it, always keeping that man-once-removed's nose in the edge of his vision.

This was easy enough in the march. Even the trot he did not find too difficult. But the gallop? It was hard to maintain, required all his concentration. So much so that he had no time to be frightened, barely any to realize that he was in his first true cavalry charge.

To the piercing notes of the bugle and the cry of 'Charge!', the 16th swept down the slope and up into the Spanish camp, the hooves as synchronous as the lines were straight, so that it seemed as though only one set of hoofbeats sounded. Their standard of the King's Cipher streamed before them and suddenly Jack forgot everything: his cold, his dampness, his dreams of vengeance. All were lost in the soft thunder of their approach.

Some of the rallying Spaniards had pistols and several were fired. The horse to Jack's right slewed toward him, slipped, and he needed to pull Lucky's head sharp away to avoid the tumble. But he had fifty paces to redress into his line, to lower his head down beside his mount's, to reach forward with his sword. Not at a standing man as at Valencia de Alcántara. Here their opponents were also mounted. His blade was extended as if Lucky were a unicorn and the sword was its horn.

The Spanish cavalry were stationary and the 16th smashed into them, sweeping the first milling groups aside, scattering those behind them. Jack felt his blade connect, saw a body tumble. Then he was passed, no one before him, riderless horses skittering by, kicking their heels as if free at last of all toil and restraint. Such fight as there was had broken up into separate encounters – a group here, two couples there, individuals flailing at each other with swords. Up here, the two hilltops almost merged into one, a slight dip dividing them. Some of the Spaniards had fled along the crests, towards the thickest cluster of tents, as if shelter could be found behind canvas. Immediately, Jack spurred Lucky after them, using the fleeing as an excuse to pursue, ignoring the command of the bugle urging the rally. Challenged later, he knew he could use the excuse of battle madness. If he had just killed someone in the charge, that was an act of war. But there was no glory in the guttings that were taking place around him now and there was only one other man whose death he sought this day.

He found him exactly where he'd thought he would be. Two Spanish officers, who were standing at the entrance of a tent so large it had to be the Commandant's, ran as soon as the two Englishmen – Worsley had indeed followed – reined in. Not so the man inside. He sat at the end of a long table with a glass of wine before him.

'You know, as soon as I heard that bugle,' Red Hugh said, 'I thought to myself: That's young Absolute on his way.' He nodded. 'And was I not right?'

Jack drew a pistol out of his coat and turned to Worsley. 'My carbine's on Lucky and you'll find another pistol in the roll. Shoot whomever would disturb us and hold the entrance.'

Worsley took the gun and looked at the Irishman. 'Why don't I just shoot him?'

'Keep everyone out,' Jack said, 'and I will owe you a debt which will be well rewarded.'

'I likes the sound of that,' said Worsley. He stepped outside and, as he did, Jack jerked the stays of the tent flaps. They fell, and Jack turned at last to face the enemy who had once been his friend.

The silence held for a while – until Jack broke it with a sneeze. 'Your health!' declared Red Hugh. 'That sounds like an evil cold you have there. Or is it a reoccurrence of the grippe? If so,' he smiled, 'there's mistletoe in my hat brim still, and I'm certain there'd be a spider about somewhere.'

'My head's fine, thank you. And we have no time for your cures.'

'Now there's a pity.' The Irishman cocked his head to one side, listened. 'Is that because of the furore your lads are causing? Or because you have come to kill me?' Jack did not answer. 'Ah, the latter. Why, lad?'

'You know why.'

'Would it be honour?' He sighed. 'Of course. A young man's obsession. I killed my first man because of it and I've regretted it ever since. I would not fight for honour now.'

'What would you fight for?'

Red Hugh looked to the canvas roof, shrugged. 'For my life. My family and my Cause.'

'And I fight for the same.' Jack had not moved from the entrance and now he did, came forward from the shadows into the light thrown by the three lamps, laid down the oilskin he was bearing upon the table that ran nearly the length of one wall. He began to untie it as he spoke. 'My life in the hazard. My cause, which is opposed to yours and is represented by this uniform I wear. And my family, whose name you have dishonoured by linking it to your treason.'

'Ah, honour! What does the poet, Cato, call it? "A fine, imaginary notion." Its pursuit? "Hunting a shadow."' A sad smile came. 'A shadow, Jack. Yet I suspect you fight for something with more substance, do you not? Admit it, man. Isn't this really about the girl?'

Jack was silent a long moment. When he spoke, it was with the bitterness of certainty. 'It used to be. I had only been infatuated before, never truly cared. When you betrayed me with her, when you used my love for your ends, when you broke my heart . . .' He faltered slightly, then went on, 'I thought then that *there* was reason enough to kill you.' He shook his head. 'But I had time to think on it, when you left me in that prison. It *is* about my honour. And there is nothing imaginary about it.'

The rain had doubled in force, smashing onto the roof of the pavilion with a noise that reduced the conflict to distant rolls of thunder. He flicked back the oilskin.

Red Hugh craned to look. 'Ah, small swords, is it? My, you have taken some care.' He sighed. 'And I am sad to see you so resolved, for 'tis a sorry thing to kill a friend.'

'I'm sure you would know.'

'I would, God forgive me. I did not think I would ever commit that particular sin again.'

Jack licked at his cracked lips. 'Are you so certain that you will kill me?'

Red Hugh drained his glass then rose slowly. Jack took a step back. Though both swords were in their scabbards, he had seen how fast this man could strike. 'My friend, we both know that, if we fight, I will triumph. We've crossed swords twice and both times I have taken you.' A harder edge came to the lilting voice. 'And you must know that this time I will not – cannot – spare you. The moment I saw you in that barracks back there, I realized that you will never rest until I am dead. And I have things yet to do. Spectacular things.' He stretched out a hand. 'So, lad, a last appeal. Shall we forswear honour this once and save ourselves the unpleasantness?'

Jack swallowed, eyeing the man, his easy confidence. But there was nothing he could say. Here, at last, there was nothing. He shook his head.

Red Hugh sighed, the hand dropped. 'Then let us to it.'

They stepped away from each other, hands reaching for the sheathed weapons, then moved till they each stood at either end of the table. The tent was long, about the same length as Jack's prison room in Rome had been, but shallower. And from the moment he had entered and gone to the right side of the tent, Jack had begun the fight. For the first rule of fighting a left-hander, Ubaldi had taught him, was keeping to the man's left side, so blade was level with blade. The table prevented the Irishman from gaining the right.

Both men cleared their scabbards, came *en garde*. Neither moved. There were perhaps five feet between the tips of their weapons.

Jack felt the tickle in his nose, raised his sword point to the roof. 'A moment?' he said, stepping back, then sneezed.

'Your health.'

'And yours.'

Both men saluted, came *en garde* again. The rain drummed even louder. Out of the corner of his eye, Jack could see their shadows stretched along one wall. The gap between their blades was distorted, huge, but it reminded him of the differences between the French school the Irishman had trained in, and Jack's Italian teacher. Red Hugh had always waited at a distance, luring Jack forward, then covering the gap with speed. It was something Jack could not allow again. Like the Roman he'd been taught by, he closed with his opponent in a pace and a lunge.

He looked to the eyes for his enemy's moves, not his sword point. And he could see the smile in them, the older man reassured that the youth had lost none of his impetuosity. Twice before Jack had attacked just so, twice he'd been beaten. It suited Jack for the man to think him yet rash and he strove hard to confirm it, relying on his speed to counter the ripostes his 'rashness' drew upon him.

Three times he thrust, at the man's chest, belly and groin; three times the man parried, circling Jack's blade outwards, opening him to the riposte that Red Hugh finally drove home with a lunge of his own. It would have gone through Jack's whole body if he had not anticipated it, already lightening the weight on his front foot, and thrown himself backwards. It looked as awkward as it was.

'Oh, lad,' sighed Red Hugh, coming on.

The thrusts came the other way now, and Jack

remembered and used Ubaldi's second rule for left-handers: no fancy parries, no circles, just straight across the body in *quarte*, retiring a step with each one. Five came and he did nothing but parry, step back, parry, step back, till his trailing hand reached canvas as his one in Rome had reached wallpaper. There was a bare half-second of hesitation then, and Jack only saw it because he was staring so closely into the Irishman's eyes. For the first time in their three encounters, McClune had paused to consider an alternative thrust. For the first time he had made a mistake.

Dropping back and low till his shoulder was against the tent wall, Jack sprang forward, sword point aimed diagonally up at the eye. Red Hugh jerked his head to the side, his own blade coming up, encountering air, for Jack had withdrawn his weapon, lunged again straight to the chest. The ground lost was regained. In a jumble of thrusts and missed parries, he ran back the length of the tent and suddenly it was the Irishman whose back was flat to the wall, the Englishman who was pinning him there. Red Hugh tried to pull his sword back, put something into a counter thrust, but his elbow pressed into canvas didn't give him the force required, the point went high and Jack ducked fast, his own blade pushed up almost square, guiding his enemy's steel just over his head. And as he did he realized that it was time for the maestro's secret move.

Still crouched, he twisted his weapon sharply across and down, elbow and left leg both shooting back. Then, as the Irishman recovered, brought his blade hard back, Jack rose from his crouch, switching hands as he did, dropping the sword into his left. Lunging with his left leg forward, he thrust diagonally up with the whole force of his rising body behind it. The lunge slipped well under the parry that was warding against the right-sided attack. It entered flesh somewhere just below the ribs and did not stop.

Red Hugh's weapon came across again, the blunt edge of

the blade aimed at Jack's ear. But the blow was weak and Jack ducked it easily, backing away fast, forced to release the sword that would not come.

The Irishman had not moved. He stood there now, weapon lowering to the floor, Jack's sword lodged in his chest. The pale skin had gone white, making his hair seem even more vibrantly red, as if suddenly shot through with flame. 'By Christ, man,' he said, his eyes wide, startled. 'By . . .'

He took a pace forward, shuddering, as the sword, which had pierced the tent wall, came out of it. Blood ran from his nose and appeared at his lips, bubbles forming as he tried to speak. Jack moved further away, reaching the opposite wall in rapid steps. Red Hugh fell. His body crumpled straight down until he was sitting on the floor, his arms resting on his thighs, his head lolled over.

Cautiously, Jack approached. The Irishman made an attempt to lift the sword still clutched in his hand, but it slipped from his fingers. Jack stepped in, moved the weapon aside, knelt.

The head came up. Eyes opened. 'You've killed me, Jack.'

'No.' Now he was looking at what he'd done, he could not remember why he had done it. 'I'll call a surgeon—'

'I'm past their skills. Not even a McClune could have the curing of this one.' He coughed and blood surged again through the whitening lips. In a moment Jack had his handkerchief out and was dabbing at the flow, as if cloth could hold in life. ' 'Twas well done, lad. I was certain you had not the skill.'

'I did not. Until Rome.'

'Rome?' Another cough, more blood. 'Please tell me I didn't spare your life so you could learn to take mine?' Jack stayed silent, and a little smile came to the reddened mouth. 'Now isn't that a thing?'

His voice was fainter now. Jack moved around, so the man

could lean back against his knees. 'Wine?' he muttered, and Jack reached up, grabbed the bottle, brought it to the Irishman's lips. When it touched, the eyes opened again.

'My last pledge,' he whispered. 'What shall it be to, Jack? The King across the water?'

Jack watched the liquor flow out of the man's mouth, then took the bottle and raised it to his own. He shook his head. 'No, Hugh. To you.'

He drank as a breath came, just one more, an exhalation. Then there were no other sounds save for the rain upon the canvas roof, the fall of blood upon the earth. Jack listened to both and, for the longest time, did not move.

— ELEVEN —

Home

Jack lay on his bed in Absolute House, listening to the roar of London. Four years before that noise would have thrilled him, had him seeking in his wardrobe for suitably fashionable attire to wear upon the town. There would have been friends at a rendezvous, some hostelry in Covent Garden or Soho, turtle soup to be eaten there, ale or arrack punch to be drunk, the playhouse to be visited followed by the bagnio, the billiard hall, the brothel; perhaps all these in a night and more.

But that was four years before and his wardrobe contained clothes measured for the boy he'd been then. Even if they'd still been fashionable – which they were decidedly not, that much he had seen in the week he'd been back! – none now fitted him, and he had so far avoided his mother's offer to accompany him to Jermyn Street for a new set.

He sighed. Perhaps he should go out? Yet none of his Westminster friends were around. Marks and Ede were on the Grand Tour – Jack shuddered to think what would have happened if they'd brayed his name across the Piazza di Spagna when he was spying there – and Fenby was up at Trinity. And what would they have made of their old Westminster school fellow now anyway? He had accompanied his mother the previous night to Drury Lane, in uniform. He could again. But the theatre, he had discovered, held little delight. Artifice just seemed so . . . artificial after the reality of war.

He sighed again. He was in a funk, no question about it. He had spent the whole day upon this bed, trying to discover why. Sometimes he thought it was the contrast between the last time he'd lain there, who he'd been then and who was lying there now. The same person, despite the broadening, the tattoos, the scars, yet not the same person at all. Nothing old delighted him. Nothing new had replaced it.

He heard the sound of cannon fire and turned instinctively toward it. It came from Hyde Park where the regiments that had returned from European operations were drilling for the victory parades that would take place the next day. Since the Peace of Paris had been signed in February 1763 just two months before, he knew that his comrades in Canada might only now be hearing the news. It was his good fortune, he supposed, that the 16th were the *Queen's* Dragoons and thus had been hurried home from Spain to take part. Just in time, he felt. Fighting had not resumed after Villa Velha due to the winter and then the negotiations, but idleness, port wine and prostitutes had the potential to wreak more damage on the regiment than the Spanish had ever done.

A third sigh galvanized him. This was absurd! He couldn't lie about like this any longer. He would have to go out. He did have an errand to run. Bibb's were making him a new sword for the parade, since he'd managed to lose his own one in the aftermath of battle and had survived on a borrowed one since. The sword-makers were in Newport Street, right between the Garden and Soho. He could check on the weapon's progress and retire to a tavern thereafter for a pint of porter. Or six. It was the one aspect of London of which he could never tire.

His footfall on the stairs drew a shout from the parlour. 'Who's there?' He went across, pushed the door. Sir James sat in a large armchair, newspaper across his knees, a pipe and a bowl of chocolate on a table at his side. Lady Jane perched before a stitching frame pushing thread through cloth.

'Jack,' they both declared as one before his mother went on, 'We didn't know you were about. Where have you been?'

'In my room.'

'You were never wont to be so quiet,' Sir James grunted. 'What have you been doing up there?'

'Nothing, sir. Thinking.'

'Thinking?' His father looked at him with suspicion.

Lady Jane gestured to a chair. 'Sit, Jack. I'll have Nancy fetch up some chocolate.'

Jack hesitated. 'I was on my way to Bibb's, mother. Collect my sword.'

'Bibb's, eh? You treat yourself well.' His father's eyes gleamed. 'I'll come with you, then. Could use a new sabre myself.'

He was half-way out of his chair when Lady Jane spoke again. 'Jack, the regiment only released you fully to us yesterday and we've hardly talked about your adventures. Can you not spare your parents a moment?'

Jack sat reluctantly. It was the lesser of two evils. He and his father had not been alone together and so had never had a chance to discuss Letty. He knew that Sir James had learnt of the dismal outcome and that he'd been horribly gulled in Bath when he'd thought the match was with a noble, influential house. Burgoyne had told Jack so in Portugal. But how much more did his father know?

He sat. A bell was rung, Nancy was summoned then dispatched to fetch another bowl. Fortunately Sir James had become distracted again by the newspaper and went on a prolonged rant about the wickedness of the peace and the concessions made, yet again, to craven Frog and perfidious Dago. It was thus a while, and Jack halfway through his bowl, before the talk returned to him.

'And so, Jack,' his mother stuck the needle into the design, crossed her hands in her lap, 'since you succeeded in writing us only two letters in the four years you have been away, and since you told your father in Bath things he has largely failed to remember,' she smiled at her husband indulgently, 'might you not vouchsafe us a tale or two?'

A tale? Which one could he tell his mother? His life as a slave with the Abenaki? His stupidity in love? His slaying of a friend? Did parents truly want to hear all that? Then he suddenly thought of one. 'I killed a bear in Canada, Mama.'

'A bear, eh?' Sir James put down the paper and leaned forward. 'Brown or black?'

'Black.'

'Shotgun or rifle?'

'Fire and rope.'

'Pardon?'

It was a fortunate choice of story. Time had removed the horror of it, though not the scars the bear's claws had made upon his calf. These were exposed and the story told with suitable movements and sounds. More bowls of chocolate were ordered and Nancy invited to remain for the recitation, which Jack then had to recommence. By the end, all were laughing hard, with Jack not quite sure how the story had turned into a comedy, yet happy that it was so.

However, he knew that one tale would not suffice. His father especially would want to hear of the recent campaign in Portugal. Indeed, when Nancy went to start supper, his father poured sherry and said, 'Your mother and I have had a letter from Lieutenant-Colonel Burgoyne. Full of praise for your conduct both in combat and in matters of intelligence.' He glanced at his wife, smiled. 'Seems you have inherited from *both* sides of the family, then. He also says he will have you carry the Sixteenth's standard in the parade tomorrow.'

Burgoyne had told him the same the day before. It was news that had filled him both with pride and, at the same time, some unaccountable dread. This feeling dominated now, under his father's beaming smile. He swallowed. 'Do you, sir, parade tomorrow as well?'

'Indeed. The Hanoverians I served with in the recent war are not present, of course. But a friend in the Eighth Dragoons, my old unit, has offered me a place with them.' The smile widened. 'So even if the Absolutes, *pater et filius*, did not go to war together, they will celebrate the victory so. Perhaps a vacancy will come up with the Sixteenth, eh? For I have no doubt that there will be many other occasions in the future when we shall have the opportunity of killing Frenchmen side by side. Ecod! Our ancestors have been doing it for seven hundred years now and this latest peace will be merely another interlude in the dispute, mark my words.'

His father raised his glass in salute and drank half of it. Jack automatically raised his, yet it did not quite reach his lips. His mother was frowning, with a darkness in her eyes he now recognized, staring at the men she'd sent off to war, seeing herself doing it again and again. And in her eyes he saw the pair of them reflected back, and beyond them an endless parade of Absolutes, all killing Frenchmen, Spaniards, Scots . . . Irishmen. Immediately, his mind went to another parade, the one that had come to him in his dream in the tavern in Bristol. His victims. How many had he added since? Just turned twenty and he'd killed – twelve men? Fifteen? He could not remember. Surely it was not a good thing that he could not remember.

It came to him then, in her look, in that memory, that if he was as yet uncertain what he wanted from his life, he suddenly and clearly knew what he did not.

'Actually, I do have something to tell you. I am going to resign my commission.'

The relief when he said it aloud! But he had not a moment to dwell on his good feeling.

'What's that?' The smile still lingered, as if Sir James thought this merely another part of the bear story. 'Resign? You mean, of course, to go on half-pay.'

It was an option Jack had considered. Many regiments were fully disbanded at war's end. The 16th were luckier, only losing two troops. Though Burgoyne would object, Jack could volunteer to be one of the officers to go onto the half-pay establishment, collect the paltry money on offer and retain his rank. But there was a catch, as his father now pointed out.

'That way, when we do fight Frenchie again, you'll be straight back to your regiment.'

'But that's it, sir. I do not believe I wish to live under an obligation to serve.'

'Obligation?' Sir James's brow wrinkled. 'There is virtually no obligation on half-pay. Not planning on serving with a foreign army, are you?'

'No, sir.'

'Or entering Holy Orders?'

'Hardly.'

'Then I do not see the problem.'

'I may wish to travel abroad.'

'Hmm! Thought you would have had enough of that for a while. Still, even that's possible. You'll just have to return from your travels when the killing starts.'

And there's the rub, thought Jack. 'I do not wish to kill again, sir.'

'But for your King? Your country?'

'No, sir. Not for anyone.'

'What?' So far his father had kept his temper. This word exploded, threatening others.

But his mother, hitherto silent, now spoke softly. 'Let us hear what he has to say, James.'

The explosion was temporarily halted. Jack turned to her. 'I am not sure I *have* anything more to say, Mother. I just know,' he closed his eyes, 'that I have already killed my fair share.' He opened them again, so he would not have to see the shadows, dancing there upon a canvas wall. 'One more than my fair share, actually. I have killed enough.'

The Llandoger Trow on the Bristol Docks had not changed much in the two years since his stay, but his reception there had. He'd been slightly disappointed to discover that he no longer had his former allure for Clary the maid and the landlady, Mrs Hardcastle. There was no fighting over his blanket now. Partly because there wasn't one, partly because he was not alone in the bed but shared it by day with a Maltese sailor called Cunha and half the night with a Scot who had vouchsafed no name because he was always too drunk to recall it. The ladies remembered him well enough, to tell by their greetings; but they remembered his purse even better, it appeared, and when they were made aware that it now contained only the sparse five guineas his mother had managed to slip him when his father cut him off, they were quickly about other business.

Still, the tavern was the place to be, for all the news of the docks came to it with the clientele. If he were to find a ship, the name would be mentioned there first. But Cunha and the insensible Scot were just two of many who also lingered. The war's ending had thrown sailors out of service along with soldiers. The privateers had disbanded, the Navy reduced its establishment and the merchant fleet could take its pick of experienced seamen, thus severely reducing a landsman like Jack's hopes of working his passage. What was left of his guineas – most of it, he lived cheap – might buy him a fourth-rate berth in a fifth-rate tub. But he would have nothing left when he reached his destination.

Perhaps I should have stayed on half-pay, he thought, staring down into the dregs of ale that had lasted an hour. Or waited until our wages arrears were issued. But once his decision had been made, Absolute House was no longer welcoming. Burgoyne had offered him room with the regiment, obviously hoping that he would eventually persuade Jack to change his mind. But he was determined to be off.

He had got as far as Bristol and here he was stuck. Laying down his pint pot – the barman was encouraged to move lingerers on and had been eyeing Jack for a good quarter-hour – Jack decided to take another stroll around the docks. Ships came in all the time. Perhaps he could make himself useful to an owner during unloading, ingratiate himself into a berth.

He turned up the collar of his coat against the wind that blew in from the harbour mouth. It had been a chill May and, in the two weeks he'd been there, did not appear to be getting any warmer.

His walk took him to the Customs House. Captains would report there first and notices would often be placed in its windows regarding the hiring of crews. But the ones that greeted Jack were those he had already read, all vacancies filled. Disconsolate, he was about to turn away when he suddenly saw, in the left corner of a window, an announcement in newsprint that had not been there before. It was torn from the *London Gazette* and read:

This is to give notice to the officers, seamen and others belonging to the Sweet Eliza *that all disputes concerning the recent action against the French privateer,* Robuste, *have been settled at last and that the prize money for the capture of said privateer, together with the sale of all its goods, will be paid on Tuesday 17 May at nine o'clock in the morning, at the sign of the Llandoger Trow on the docks.*

Jack turned and ran back to the inn, straight to the rear of it where he forced a grumbling landlady to open the strong room. The woman stood over him as he threw up the lid of his trunk and riffled through the three books he had there. It was in the last one, a copy of Pope's *Rape of the Lock*, that he found it, marking his place.

Clutching the prize ticket, he turned and smiled up at the landlady. 'Mrs Hardcastle,' he said, 'is that charming room over the front still available?'

Both the landlady and her maid were suddenly as friendly as they had been during his previous stay, though Jack declined any offers beyond the best of food and ale. The prize agents were less so because they'd hoped that few of the *Sweet Eliza*'s crew would still be in Bristol after such a long delay and they would be able to hold the money in their banks on interest. But more than half showed up at the tavern the next morning with Jack first in the line. His fears that somehow Red Hugh had made it to Bristol before Portugal with the paper signing over Jack's share to him proved groundless.

'A lieutenant's six, is it?' The agent, an ill-shaved fellow with greasy black ringlets, looked up at him suspiciously. 'You don't look much like a seaman to me.'

'He's not. But he's a bonny fighter and you'll pay him straightway, Peters.'

Jack turned. 'Lieutenant Engledue,' he said, 'or is it Captain now?' The man looked vastly different from the old drinker Jack had known aboard. The capture of the *Robuste* had obviously been the beginning of his revival.

'Captain, aye.' The man nodded. 'And when we are done our business here, I'd be delighted to buy you a drink.'

'And I shall drink it with pleasure,' said Jack.

Because the *Sweet Eliza* was a merchantman with a small crew, and since many had died in the fight or of the subsequent sickness, there were fewer to share the bounty.

The owners having taken their half and money having been already set aside for legitimate relics of the fallen, each share was worth thirty pounds, Jack's six thus netting him thirty in coin and a promissory note on Coutts bank for one hundred and ten more, the advance being deducted. Handsome enough, even if the promise of fifty to each boarder had gone into the barrel along with Captain Link.

Much later, over many ales and not a few rums, with the fight refought from a dozen different angles, new heroes made, new villains damned and, at last, most of the crew asleep where they sat at the long tables of the tavern's back room, the two most sober – or least drunk – conversed.

'And now, Mr Absolute,' Engledue, on Jack's urging, had at last dropped the appellation Lieutenant, 'What will you be doing with your share of the prize?'

Jack swirled rum in the mug before him. 'The paper I'll trade for one in a colonial bank. The coin I'll use to buy a passage thither.'

'A most comfortable one, with change to spare.' Engledue nodded. 'Yet if you would forsake a little of that comfort for some pleasant company . . .'

'Sir?'

'I am just become master of a sweet little poleacre, the *Dublin Castle*. Part owner, too, for I bought a share on the promise of this payout. I have taken on most of the old crew from the *Sweet Eliza*.' He nodded at the snoring forms around them, then leaned forward to rest his arms upon the table. 'We are bound first for Jamaicy to take on sugar and then we proceed directly to New England. So if you would care to travel again with your old shipmates . . . ?'

'I would – so long as you do not traffic in slaves.'

'Ah, I remember now. How you incited poor dead Captain Link!' He smiled. 'And that Irish fellow. Quite the trickster. I was hoping to encounter him here today. Are you sure you never did hear of him again?'

Jack had enjoyed the tales of Red Hugh in the fight as much as the rest. But he'd said nothing further. 'Never,' he said.

'And you such shipmates?' Engledue sighed. 'Well, anyway, I can assure you there'll be no slaves aboard the *Dublin Castle*. Save Link's former one, Barabbas.' He pointed to a slumped black figure.

'Then I accept the invitation with delight.' Jack reached for a jug, poured two more tots of rum. 'And here's to a friend well met.'

They sipped, lowered. 'And with the French beaten we will not have to fight, thank God.' Engledue raised his glass, stood and shouted, 'Up, you drunken dogs! On your feet. Let's have a standing toast while still on land.' The company, such as could sway up, now did. 'To calm seas, kind winds and no pirates!'

'Huzzah!'

'And to his Majesty the King!'

'Huzzah!'

He happened to be glancing down, so he saw it, the one man there who did it: McRae, Jack remembered his name to be, a member of the Forecastle Club of the *Sweet Eliza*, passing his glass over the water jug before he drank.

Jack would not toast the King across the water. But there were two Irish cousins he could remember now. 'Aye,' he said softly to himself, raising his mug, 'to absent friends and old lovers.'

Indian Summer

Moors Charity School, Connecticut, September 1763

As soon as Dr Andrews turned to the board, the young man's gaze went to the window. It was a question of timing it just right, to be aware – even as he stared and yearned and imagined – of the black gown beginning to turn back. It would not do to be caught again, for it would be the third time in a week, and the punishments grew with each offence. The next one would be physical correction, made to bend before the class while a switch was liberally applied to his arse. The pain was nothing, an insect bite. But the indignity! Beyond these walls, he was still a member of the Wolf clan, a warrior of the Mohawk tribe of the Iroquois nation, and five scalps hung from his mother's lodge post. Here he was a schoolboy not even known by his tribal name but by his baptismal one, James.

The cloak swung back as did his face. Eleazar Andrews looked at him suspiciously, as if he'd detected movement, then gestured to the board. '*Ut* plus the subjunctive. It is called a conditional clause,' he said. 'You will turn to your Cicero and find me examples.'

Like the rest of them, he scrambled quickly for the text. The quickest, as always, was Joseph Brant, his hand shooting up, citing page and verse to the teacher's approving nods.

Joseph was the bright star in Andrews's little firmament, which galled since they both came from the same village, Canajoharie, and Joseph's triumphs had been told over the lodge fires again and again the previous summer. It had nearly made him refuse to return, especially after a season of freedom spent hunting again in his forests. It was only the thought of Brant jeering at his failure to William Johnson, who sponsored them both, that drove the young man back.

The gown turned; chalk scraped out the quote upon the black. He looked outside, to the higher ground and its scant remnants of forest. He'd sometimes see riders cresting the ridge road there – as one did even now.

The clause written, Andrews turned again, the young man's face swinging to meet him.

Why did it have to be Cicero? The lawyer was so dull. In Caesar's Gallic wars he'd have found a conditional clause as fast as his rival. In Shakespeare he knew a dozen, more. But he was not supposed to read Shakespeare, even though that was truly what he'd come to school to do. Once the rules of English grammar were safely driven into them, Dr Andrews did not believe further in living languages, except what came in King James's Bible. So solo study was reserved for the very few hours they were free, when he could retrieve his book from its hiding place in the barn. It contained all the plays and it had cost him most of the proceeds from his summer trapping. It was worth every fur.

'Anyone else?' For once Andrews was ignoring Joseph's thrust-up arm, staring over the dozen lowered heads, each one sporting the black hair of the Iroquois, cropped short above the stiff white collars of their shirts. Someone answered, a Seneca baptised Jeremiah. The cloak turned, he turned.

The rider was halfway to the school. Closer to, he thought there was something familiar about him. The man rode one horse, led another, both laden with wrapped bundles. He had probably seen him before, one of the many traders who passed through Lebanon, a trapper perhaps taking furs to New Haven or even Boston. Their numbers would grow as the winter drew closer, though this September was the kind that made him believe the snows would never return. Sweat still pooled under his collar each day, its stain to be scrubbed away each night.

'James!' The harsh cry jerked his head back. Andrews had turned, unnoted. 'I have warned you, boy—'

'Rider, sir,' he answered, wondering still how that voice could induce fear in him when, in another world, under another name, he'd killed five men. 'You asked to be warned of any approach.'

'Outside the classroom, and after class, I said.' Dr Andrews glared but did not reach for his stick. Instead, he peered over his spectacles through the window. 'And I told you that we were expecting the Reverend Wilson, from Mount Sinai. A true man of God to instill some respect into you Indians!' He glowered at them all. 'That is obviously some filthy tinker and you,' he pointed at him, 'had better pay closer attention.'

He faced the board and the young man immediately looked out again. The rider was only about a hundred yards off now and, if he did not look entirely clean, he could not be described as filthy. True, he had a thick beard that almost rode up to meet the uncocked hat, but both head covering and dark coat were clean of all but road dust, and the boots had spurs that sparkled in the late-afternoon sun. As he watched, he kept an ear on the scraping of chalk. As soon as the squeal stopped he would turn back. Till then, he could watch the traveller and remember what travelling was like.

The school was an outlying building of the town and the road went past the gate of their compound with its single whitewashed house, its brown stable and dormitory. Instead of riding out of view, however, the man reined in. One of Andrews's indentured servants was hoeing the cabbage patch nearby and the man called to him, perhaps asking him for directions to the nearest inn. There was only one in Lebanon, a place of notorious sin, the Doctor always said. So now he had even more envy for this traveller who had goods to trade. He would ride past the gate. He would go and sin.

Not yet. The man dismounted, tied both animals to a fence. Then he did a most unusual thing. He reached up and pulled one rifle from its leather sheath, then reached back and slipped another rifle from a bedroll. Then, shouldering both of them, he walked up the stairs and entered the house.

'You!' The shout came loud, startling. Andrews was facing him now, fury on his face, stick in hand. 'I have warned you. I have been lenient. Too lenient, it seems. Come up here.'

'Sir! Someone—'

'Now, boy. No more excuses!'

He had just risen, when the door opened. The traveller stood there, guns on shoulders, looking slowly around the room. And it was only then that he realized that the rider did not look familiar because he was of a type that rode past often; he looked familiar because the young man knew him. Different than he remembered; older, wider, taller. That beard. Also – and he could see this immediately – there was something in the eyes, some darkness that had not been there before.

Those eyes, searching, found him, despite the cropped hair, the white shirt, the stiff collar. A light came into them, banishing the darkness, changing the face.

'So, Até,' Jack Absolute said, holding out one gun, 'do you want to go hunting?'

AUTHOR'S NOTE

As many may remember, I played the role of Jack Absolute in 1987. This has led to an occasional weirdness in the writing process, with my old stage incarnation regularly appearing at my shoulder to demand better lines! Well, it got even weirder with this book – for in it I decided to tell the 'true' story of *The Rivals*.

In the first novel in the series, *Jack Absolute*, my hero witnessed a production of the play. During it he mused on how Sheridan, to whom he had told the story one drunken night, 'had usurped his youthful folly for a romantic comedy, when the original was more of a farce and, in the end, almost a tragedy.' The one word I regret now is 'almost'. But I only had the vaguest notions then of how this new novel would develop. It was one of the main reasons I had to return to the very beginning of Jack's life and tell his whole story – including the episode that became *The Rivals*.

An audience at the play (and I have seen it twice in the last two years, in London and New York) would spot the similarities – the baronet's son assuming the role of an impoverished Ensign to woo a young lady addicted to romantic novels; the pugnacious Irishman; the domineering father trying to force his son to marry whom he chooses . . . and choosing the very woman Jack wants to marry! I have had great fun blending, and distinguishing, play and novel. Jack does take the *nom de coeur* of Beverley, Fagg is his servant, Sir James is undoubtedly modelled on Sir Anthony Absolute in all his bellowing tyranny. And close readers may even spot the odd line – 'Thirsty work on the roads!'; 'Their regular hours stupefy!' and, especially, 'This is what comes . . . of reading!' I hope all this is considered homage and not plagiarism!

The episode Sheridan steals for his comedy (and I've stolen back – did I mention how weird it gets?) turns into the tragedy within these pages. I always hope that Jack grows with every outing, his experiences shaping the man. I want each book to be *about* something and this one, as the title suggests, is about honour. If men of the age were obsessed by it, living by it and very often dying for it, they still debated it fiercely – this 'fine, imaginary notion', this 'shadow', as Addison had it in his play, *Cato*. Jack is part of that debate; he assumes one thing, learns something else – perhaps that honour has a price that it is often very high indeed.

Research for this book, as ever, was partly on my feet. I did get to Bath, spending several days with one of my editors, the tremendous Rachel Leyshon. She not only lives there, but lives in Gay Street where, at this very period, one of my main sources, Tobias Smollett, began the great *Humphrey Clinker* whose pages I have pillaged for details of the town and its ways. It was not the only coincidence – while there I was browsing a theatre history in the library only to discover that an actor in the Theatre Royal company of 1760/1761 was one Mr Harper – this is *after* I knew that Fanny Harper (his wife) would have to be in the company there!

I didn't, annoyingly, get back to Rome. But Smollett was again very useful with his *Travels through France and Italy*, about manners, food and, especially, odours – Johnson didn't satirize him as Dr Smellfungus for nothing. And the collection *The Stuart Court in Rome* edited by Edward Corp was excellent. For all things Jacobite, Robert Louis Stevenson was my benchmark; and I was thrilled when, on my way back from Bath, I stopped at the Llandoger Trow pub on the old Bristol Docks, where they used to pay out the prize money (and where I used to drink when I was at the Old Vic Theatre), to discover that it was considered the model for the Admiral Benbow tavern in *Treasure Island*.

As readers of my other novels will know, I love to get to the battlefields, walking Saratoga for *Jack Absolute*, climbing the cliffs at Quebec for *The Blooding of Jack Absolute*. Alas, I couldn't get to Spain and Portugal for this one (I plead a baby boy at home!) but that was only part of my problem. The war fought there is little written about, at least in English, warranting a mere page and half in Fortescue's *History of the British Army*. But this campaign was where Jack's regiment, the Sixteenth Dragoons, fought and where John Burgoyne made his reputation for the dawn assault on Valencia de Alcántara. The Sixteenth's regimental history gave a little more detail – and I apologise to any descendents of Lieutenant Maitland for stealing his heroics for my man, both there and at Villa Velha. After that, it was down to maps and imagination – and the Internet, of course, that wonderful resource with its myriad photographs of the various scenes. Speaking of names, I have also changed the name of the Irish regiment involved in the attempted mutiny to Traherne's. I'm sure the stalwarts of the real Blayney's would have got up to no such shenanigans.

As with Sheridan, I was very excited to be able to do another tribute in this book – to C. S. Forester's *Hornblower*. Though I admire Patrick O'Brian, I do find some of the jargon impenetrable – and decided to therefore attempt a slight pastiche, making Jack find it impenetrable too. *Naval Warfare in the Age of Sail* by Bernard Ireland, and N.A.M Rodger's *The Wooden World* were priceless resources, as was the hefty dictionary *The Sailor's Word Book*. For privateers, the contemporary *Voyages and Cruises of Commodore Walker* was astonishing in its detail. I think/hope it's all accurate but this is such a well-known field I'm sure one of you will write to let me know that I've braced the mizzen sail to larboard when I should have shorten'd afore!

Other aspects: for grenades, I found a marvellous period manual *Royal Engineers Field Instructions*. And my cavalry manoeuvres and drill were superbly set out in a *Field Exercise for Gentleman and Yeoman Cavalry by An Officer of the Light Dragoons*. Red Hugh's cures are genuine folk remedies for fevers from the period – those spiders must have been much employed! As for his rendering of men unconscious – pressing the wrist at a certain point – this is a technique from Akido which I have studied (but never perfected). Japanese, I know. But I tend to believe that warriors the world over know the same tricks. For his language, I have returned to plays and discovered an original copy in the British Library of a work by Sheridan's father, Thomas, entitled *The Brave Irishman*. As to the name itself – my editor was informed that McClune would have been a surname of an Ulster Protestant and thus an unlikely candidate for a Jacobite assassin. Fortunately, I did not have to shed his mellifluous moniker – I simply re-checked my *Family Names in Ireland* to confirm that McClune is 'to be distinguished from MacCloon which is an Ulster variant' while McClune is an ancient ('Dalcassian') and thus Catholic – name from Ballymaclune, County Clare.

Once again, I have many people to thank. Since much of the plot hinged on triumphing over a left-handed swords-man, the time I spent at the Haverstock Fencing Club, invited by their secretary Jackie Harvey and talking to countless fencers, was priceless. I am always indebted to my wife, Aletha, for good advice and help, and to my son, Reith Frederic, for starting to sleep through the night, as well as

Piers Johnson for giving me shelter during the day to write. My agents at ICM were their usual calm and thorough selves, especially Kate Jones and, in America, Liz Farrell, who has broken me through there at last.

Rachel Leyshon was, as always, a great copy-editor and, this time, a great guide to Bath as well. I should also again mention my Canadian publisher, the ever enthusiastic Kim McArthur and her wonderful team of Ann Ledden, Janet Harron and Taryn Manias. While, in the UK, Susan Lamb, Juliet Ewers, Genevieve Pegg and Angela McMahon are equally brilliant and tireless.

But a special thanks must go to the man to whom this book is dedicated. Jon Wood is not only a terrific editor of the words, he is also a tireless advocate of my work whose support and friendship is one of the main reasons I can now write for a living.

Perhaps though, at the end of this novel especially, I should again acknowledge a man who has given me so much pleasure and inspiration – Richard Brinsley Sheridan. Your health, sir, wherever you are, and . . . oh yes, thanks for the plot!

C.C. Humphreys
London, December 2005